A VORKOSIGAN ADVENTURE

CETAGANDA

A VORKOSIGAN ADVENTURE
CETAGANDA

LOIS McMASTER BUJOLD

BAEN

CETAGANDA

This is a work of fiction. All the characters and events portrayed in this book are fictional, and any resemblance to real people or incidents is purely coincidental.

Copyright © 1996 by Lois McMaster Bujold

All rights reserved, including the right to reproduce this book or portions thereof in any form.

A Baen Books Original

Baen Publishing Enterprises
P.O. Box 1403
Riverdale, NY 10471

ISBN: 0-671-87701-1

Cover art by Gary Ruddell

First printing, January 1996

Distributed by Simon & Schuster
1230 Avenue of the Americas
New York, NY 10020

Library of Congress Cataloging-in-Publication Data

Bujold, Lois McMaster.
    Cetaganda / by Lois McMaster Bujold.
        p.   cm.
    "A Baen books original"—CIP info.
    ISBN 0-671-87701-1 (hard)
    I. Title.
    PS3552.U397.C48   1995
    813'.54—dc20   95-33243
                                                    CIP

Typeset by Windhaven Press, Auburn, NH
Printed in the United States of America

To

Jim and Toni

CHAPTER ONE

"Now is it, 'Diplomacy is the art of war pursued by other men,'" asked Ivan, "or was it the other way around? 'War is diplo—'"

"All diplomacy is a continuation of war by other means," Miles intoned. "Chou En Lai, twentieth century, Earth."

"What are you, a walking reference library?"

"No, but Commodore Tung is. He collects Wise Old Chinese Sayings, and makes me memorize 'em."

"So was old Chou a diplomat, or a warrior?"

Lieutenant Miles Vorkosigan thought it over. "I think he must have been a diplomat."

Miles's seat straps pressed against him as the attitude jets fired, banking the personnel pod in which he and Ivan sat across from each other in lonely splendor. Their two benches lined a short fuselage. Miles craned his neck for a glimpse past the pod pilot's shoulder at the planet turning below them.

Eta Ceta IV, the heart and homeworld of the sprawling Cetagandan empire. Miles supposed eight developed planets and an equal fringe of allied and puppet dependencies qualified as a sprawl in any sane person's lexicon. Not that the Cetagandan ghem-lords wouldn't

1

like to sprawl a little farther, at their neighbors' expense, if they could.

Well, it didn't matter how huge they were, they could only put military force through a wormhole jump one ship at a time, just like everybody else.

It was just that some people had some damned *big* ships.

The colored fringe of night slid around the rim of the planet as the personnel pod continued to match orbits from the Barrayaran Imperial courier vessel they had just left, to the Cetagandan transfer station they were approaching. The nightside glittered appallingly. The continents were awash in a fairy dust of lights. Miles swore he might read by the glow of the civilization, as if from a full moon. His homeworld of Barrayar seemed suddenly a dull vast swatch of rural darkness, with only a few sparks of cities here and there. Eta Ceta's high-tech embroidery was downright . . . gaudy. Yes, overdressed, like a woman weighted down with too much jewelry. Tasteless, he tried to convince himself. *I am not some backcountry hick. I can handle this. I am Lord Vorkosigan, an officer and a nobleman.*

Of course, so was Lieutenant Lord Ivan Vorpatril, but the fact did not fill Miles with confidence. Miles regarded his big cousin, who was also craning his neck, eyes avid and lips parted, drinking in their destination below. At least Ivan looked the part of a diplomatic officer, tall, dark-haired, neat, an easy smile permanently plastered on his handsome face. His fit form filled his officer's undress greens to perfection. Miles's mind slid, with the greased ease of old bad habit, to invidious comparison.

Miles's own uniforms had to be hand-tailored to fit, and insofar as possible disguise, the massive congenital defects that years of medical treatments had done so much to correct. He was supposed to be grateful, that the medicos had done so much with so little. After

a lifetime of it he stood four-foot-nine, hunchbacked
and brittle-boned, but it beat being carried around in
a bucket. Sure.

But he *could* stand, and walk, and run if need be,
leg braces and all. And Barrayaran Imperial Security
didn't pay him to be pretty, thank God, they paid him
to be smart. Still, the morbid thought did creep in that
he had been sent along on this upcoming circus to
stand next to Ivan and make him look good. ImpSec
certainly hadn't given him any more interesting missions, unless you could call Security Chief Illyan's last
curt ". . . and stay out of trouble!" a secret assignment.

On the other hand, maybe Ivan had been sent along
to stand next to Miles and make him *sound* good. Miles
brightened slightly at the thought.

And there was the orbital transfer station, coming
up right on schedule. Not even diplomatic personnel
dropped directly into Eta Ceta's atmosphere. It was
considered bad etiquette, likely to draw an admonition
administered by plasma fire. Most civilized worlds had
similar regulations, Miles conceded, if only for purposes
of preventing biological contaminations.

"I wonder if the Dowager Empress's death was really
natural?" Miles asked idly. Ivan, after all, could hardly
be expected to supply the answer. "It was sudden
enough."

Ivan shrugged. "She was a generation older than
Great Uncle Piotr, and he was old since forever. He
used to unnerve the hell out of me when I was a kid.
It's a nice paranoid theory, but I don't think so."

"Illyan agrees with you, I'm afraid. Or he wouldn't
have let *us* come. This could have been a lot less dull
if it had been the Cetagandan emperor who'd dropped,
instead of some tottering little old haut-lady."

"But then we would not be here," Ivan pointed out
logically. "We'd both be on duty hunkering down in

some defensive outpost right now, while the prince-candidates' factions fought it out. This is better. Travel, wine, women, song—"

"It's a State *funeral*, Ivan."

"I can hope, can't I?"

"Anyway, we're just supposed to observe. And report. What or why, I don't know. Illyan emphasized he expects the reports in writing."

Ivan groaned. "How I spent my holiday, by little Ivan Vorpatril, age twenty-two. It's like being back in school."

Miles's own twenty-third birthday would be following Ivan's soon. If this tedious duty ran to schedule, he should actually be back home in time for a celebration, for a change. A pleasant thought. Miles's eyes glinted. "Still, it could be fun, embroidering events for Illyan's entertainment. Why should official reports always have to be in that dead dry style?"

"Because they're generated by dead dry brains. My cousin, the frustrated dramatist. Don't get too carried away. Illyan has no sense of humor, it would disqualify him for his job."

"I'm not so sure. . . ." Miles watched as the pod wove through its assigned flight path. The transfer station flowed past, vast as a mountain, complex as a circuit diagram. "It would have been interesting to meet the old lady when she was still alive. She witnessed a lot of history, in a century and a half. If from an odd angle, inside the haut-lords' seraglio."

"Low-life outer barbarians like us would never have been let near her."

"Mm, I suppose not." The pod paused, and a major Cetagandan ship with the markings of one of the out-planet governments ghosted past, on and on, maneuvering its monstrous bulk to dock with exquisite care. "All the haut-lord satrap governors—and their retinues—are supposed to be converging for this. I'll bet Cetagandan imperial security is having fun right now."

"If any two governors come, I suppose the rest have to show up, just to keep an eye on each other." Ivan's brows rose. "Should be quite a show. Ceremony as Art. Hell, the Cetagandans make blowing your nose an art. Just so they can sneer at you if you get the moves wrong. One-upmanship to the nth power."

"It's the one thing that convinces me that the Cetagandan haut-lords are still human, after all that genetic tinkering."

Ivan grimaced. "Mutants on purpose are mutants still." He glanced down at his cousin's suddenly stiff form, cleared his throat, and tried to find something interesting to look at out the canopy.

"You're so diplomatic, Ivan," said Miles through a tight smile. "Try not to start a war single . . . mouthed, eh?" *Civil or otherwise.*

Ivan shrugged off his brief embarrassment. The pod pilot, a Barrayaran tech-sergeant in black fatigues, slid his little ship neatly into its assigned docking pocket. The view outside shrank to blank dimness. Control lights blinked cheery greetings, and servos whined as the flex-tube portals matched and locked. Miles snapped off his seat straps just a shade more slowly than Ivan, pretending disinterest, or savoir faire, or something. No Cetagandan was going to catch him with his nose pressed to the glass like some eager puppy. He was a Vorkosigan. His heart beat faster anyway.

The Barrayaran ambassador would be waiting, to take his two high-ranking guests in hand, and show them, Miles hoped, how to go on. Miles mentally reviewed the correct greetings and salutations, and the carefully memorized personal message from his father. The pod lock cycled, and the hatch on the side of the fuselage to the right of Ivan's seat dilated.

A man hurtled through, swung himself to a sudden halt on the hatch's handlebar, and stared at them with wide eyes, breathing heavily. His lips moved, but whether in curses, prayers, or rehearsals Miles wasn't sure.

He was elderly but not frail, broad-shouldered and at least as tall as Ivan. He wore what Miles guessed was the uniform of a station employee, cool gray and mauve. Fine white hair wisped over his scalp, but he had no facial hair at all on his shiny skin, neither beard nor eyebrows nor even down. His hand flew to his left vest, over his heart.

"Weapon!" Miles yelled in warning. The startled pod pilot was still snaking his way clear of his seat straps, and Miles was physically ill-equipped to jump anyone, but Ivan's reflexes had been honed by plenty of training, if not actual combat. He was already moving, rotating around his own hand-hold point-of-contact and into the intruder's path.

Hand-to-hand combat in free fall was always incredibly awkward, due in part to the necessity of having to hang on tightly to anybody one wanted to seriously hit. The two men quickly ended up wrestling. The intruder clutched wildly, not at his vest but at his right trouser pocket, but Ivan managed to knock the glittering nerve disruptor from his hand.

The nerve disruptor tumbled away and whanged off the other side of the cabin, now a random threat to everyone aboard.

Miles had always been terrified of nerve disruptors, but never before as a projectile weapon. It took two more cross-cabin ricochets for him to snatch it out of the air without accidentally shooting himself or Ivan. The weapon was undersized but charged and deadly.

Ivan had meanwhile worked around behind the old man, attempting to pinion his arms. Miles seized the moment to try to nail down the second weapon, dragging open the mauve vest and going for that lump in the inner pocket. His hand came away clutching a short rod that he first took for a shock-stick.

The man screamed and wrenched violently. Greatly startled and not at all sure what he'd just done, Miles launched himself away from the struggling pair and ducked prudently behind the pod pilot. Judging from that mortal yell Miles was afraid he'd just ripped out the power pack to the man's artificial heart or something, but he continued to fight on, so it couldn't have been as fatal as it sounded.

The intruder shook off Ivan's grip and recoiled to the hatchway. There came one of those odd pauses that sometimes occur in close combat, everyone gulping for breath in the rush of adrenaline. The old man stared at Miles with the rod in his fist; his expression altered from fright to—was that grimace a flash of triumph? Surely not. Demented inspiration?

Outnumbered now as the pilot joined the fray, the intruder retreated, tumbling back out the flex tube and thumping to whatever docking bay deck lay beyond. Miles scrambled after Ivan's hot pursuit just in time to see the intruder, now firmly on his feet in the station's artificial gravity field, land Ivan a blow to his chest with a booted foot that knocked the younger man backward into the portal again. By the time Miles and Ivan had disentangled themselves, and Ivan's gasping became less alarmingly disrupted, the old man had vanished at a run. His footsteps echoed confusingly in the bay. Which exit—? The pod pilot, after a quick look to ensure that his passengers were temporarily safe, hurried back inside to answer his comm alarm.

Ivan regained his feet, dusted himself off, and stared around. Miles did too. They were in a small, dingy, dimly lit freight bay.

"Y'know," said Ivan, "if that was the customs inspector, we're in trouble."

"I thought he was about to draw on us," said Miles. "It looked like it."

"You didn't see a weapon before you yelled."

"It wasn't the weapon. It was his eyes. He looked like someone about to try something that scared him to death. And he did draw."

"*After* we jumped him. Who knows what he was about to do?"

Miles turned slowly on his heel, taking in their surroundings in more detail. There wasn't a human being in sight, Cetagandan, Barrayaran, or other. "There's something very wrong here. Either he wasn't in the right place, or we weren't. This musty dump can't be our docking port, can it? I mean, where's the Barrayaran ambassador? The honor guard?"

"The red carpet, the dancing girls?" Ivan sighed. "You know, if he'd been trying to assassinate you, or hijack the pod, he should have come charging in with that nerve disruptor already in his hand."

"That was no customs inspector. Look at the monitors." Miles pointed. Two vid-pickups mounted strategically on nearby walls were ripped from their moorings, dangling sadly down. "He disabled them before he tried to board. I don't understand. Station security should be swarming in here right now. . . . D'you think he wanted the pod, and not us?"

"You, boy. No one would be after me."

"He seemed more scared of us than we were of him." Miles concealed a deep breath, hoping his heart rate would slow.

"Speak for yourself," said Ivan. "He sure scared *me*."

"Are you all right?" asked Miles belatedly. "I mean, no broken ribs or anything?"

"Oh, yeah, I'll survive . . . you?"

"I'm all right."

Ivan glanced down at the nerve disruptor in Miles's right hand, and the rod in his left, and wrinkled his nose. "How'd you end up with all the weapons?"

"I . . . don't quite know." Miles slipped the little nerve disruptor into his own trouser pocket, and held the mysterious rod up to the light. "I thought at first this was some kind of shock-stick, but it's not. It's something electronic, but I sure don't recognize the design."

"A grenade," Ivan suggested. "A time-bomb. They can make them look like anything, y'know."

"I don't think so—"

"My lords," the pod pilot stuck his head through the hatch. "Station flight control is ordering us not to dock here. They're telling us to stand off and wait clearance. Immediately."

"I *thought* we must be in the wrong place," said Ivan.

"It's the coordinates they gave me, my lord," said the pod pilot a little stiffly.

"Not your error, Sergeant, I'm sure," Miles soothed.

"Flight control sounds very forceful." The sergeant's face was tense. "Please, my lords."

Obediently, Miles and Ivan shuffled back aboard the pod. Miles refastened his seat straps automatically, his mind running on overdrive, trying to construct an explanation for their bizarre welcome to Cetaganda.

"This section of the station must have been deliberately cleared of personnel," he decided aloud. "I'll bet you Betan dollars Cetagandan security is in process of conducting a sweep-search for that fellow. A fugitive, by God." Thief, murderer, spy? The possibilities enticed.

"He was disguised, anyway," said Ivan.

"How do you know?"

Ivan picked a few fine white strands from his green sleeve. "This isn't real hair."

"Really?" said Miles, charmed. He examined the clump of threads Ivan extended across the aisle to him. One end was sticky with adhesive. "Huh."

The pod pilot finished taking up his new assigned coordinates; the pod now floated in space a few hundred meters from the row of docking pockets. There were no other pods locked onto the station for a dozen pockets in either direction. "I'll report this incident to the station authorities, shall I, my lords?" The sergeant reached for his comm controls.

"Wait," said Miles.

"My lord?" The pod pilot regarded him dubiously, over his shoulder. "I think we should—"

"Wait till they ask us. After all, we're not in the business of cleaning up Cetagandan security's lapses after them, are we? It's their problem."

A small grin, immediately suppressed, told Miles the pilot was amenable to this argument. "Yes, sir," he said, making it an order-received, and therefore Miles's lordly officer's responsibility, and not that of a lowly tech-sergeant. "Whatever you say, sir."

"Miles," muttered Ivan, "what do you think you're doing?"

"Observing," said Miles primly. "I'm going to observe and see how good Cetagandan station security is at their job. I think Illyan would want to know, don't you? Oh, they'll be around to question us, and take these goodies back, but this way I can get more information in return. Relax, Ivan."

Ivan settled back, his disturbed air gradually dissipating as the minutes ticked on with no further interruptions to the boredom in the little pod. Miles examined his prizes. The nerve disruptor was of some exceptionally fine Cetagandan civilian make, not military issue, in itself odd; the Cetagandans did not encourage the dispersal of deadly anti-personnel weapons among their general populace. But it did not bear the fancy decorations that would mark it as some ghem-lord's toy. It was plain and functional, of a size meant to be carried concealed.

The short rod was odder still. Embedded in its transparent casing was a violent glitter, looking decorative; Miles was sure microscopic examination would reveal fine dense circuitry. One end of the device was plain, the other covered with a seal which was itself locked in place.

"This looks like it's meant to be inserted in something," he said to Ivan, turning the rod in the light.

"Maybe it's a dildo," Ivan smirked.

Miles snorted. "With the ghem-lords, who can say? But no, I don't think so." The indented seal on the end-cap was in the shape of some clawed and dangerous-looking bird. Deep within the incised figure gleamed metallic lines, the circuit-connections. Somewhere somebody owned the mate, a raised screaming bird-pattern full of complex encodes which would release the cover, revealing . . . what? Another pattern of encodes? A key for a key . . . It was all extraordinarily elegant. Miles smiled in sheer fascination.

Ivan regarded him uneasily. "You are going to give it back, aren't you?"

"Of course. If they ask for it."

"And if they don't?"

"Keep it for a souvenir, I suppose. It's too pretty to throw away. Maybe I'll take it home as a present to Illyan, let his cipher-laboratory elves play with it as an exercise. For about a year. It's not an amateur's bauble, even I can tell that."

Before Ivan could come up with more objections, Miles undid his green tunic and slipped the device into his own inner breast pocket. Out of sight, out of mind. "Ah—you want to keep this?" He handed the nerve disruptor across to his cousin.

Ivan plainly did. Placated by this division of the spoils, Ivan, a partner in crime now, made the little weapon disappear into his own tunic. The weapon's secret and sinister presence would do nicely, Miles calculated, to keep Ivan distracted and polite all through the upcoming disembarkation.

At last the station traffic control directed them to dock again. They locked onto a pod pocket two up from the one they had been assigned before. This time the door opened without incident. After a slight hesitation, Ivan exited through the flex tube. Miles followed him.

Six men awaited them in a gray chamber almost identical to the first one, if cleaner and better lit. Miles recognized the Barrayaran ambassador immediately. Lord Vorob'yev was a stout solid man of about sixty-standard, sharp-eyed, smiling, and contained. He wore a Vorob'yev House uniform, rather formal for the occasion Miles thought, wine-red with black trim. He was flanked by four guards in Barrayaran undress greens. Two Cetagandan station officials, in mauve and gray garb of similar style but more complex cut than the intruder's, stood slightly apart from the Barrayarans.

Only two stationers? Where were the civil police, Cetagandan military intelligence, or at least some ghem-faction's private agents? Where were the questions, and the questioners Miles had been anticipating dissecting?

Instead, he found himself greeting Ambassador Vorob'yev as if nothing had happened, just as he'd first rehearsed. Vorob'yev was a man of Miles's father's generation, and in fact had been his appointee, back when Count Vorkosigan had still been Regent. Vorob'yev had been holding down this critical post for six years, having retired from his military career to take up Imperial service on the civil side. Miles resisted an urge to salute, and gave the ambassador a formal nod instead.

"Good afternoon, Lord Vorob'yev. My father sends you his personal regards, and these messages."

Miles handed across the sealed diplomatic disk, an act duly noted by a Cetagandan official on his report panel. "Six items of luggage?" the Cetagandan inquired with a nod, as the pod pilot finished stacking them on the waiting float pallet, saluted Miles, and returned to his ship.

"Yes, that's all," said Ivan. To Miles's eye, Ivan looked stuffed and shifty, intensely conscious of the contraband in his pocket, but apparently the Cetagandan official could not read his cousin's expression as well as Miles could.

The Cetagandan waved a hand, and the ambassador nodded to his guards; two of them split off to accompany the luggage on its trip through Cetagandan inspection. The Cetagandan re-sealed the docking port, and bore off the float-pallet.

Ivan anxiously watched it go. "Will we get it all back?"

"Eventually. After some delays, if things run true to form," said Vorob'yev easily. "Did you gentlemen have a good trip?"

"Entirely uneventful," said Miles, before Ivan could speak. "Until we got here. Is this a usual docking port for Barrayaran visitors, or were we redirected for some other reason?" He kept one eye on the remaining Cetagandan official, watching for a reaction.

Vorob'yev smiled sourly. "Sending us through the service entrance is just a little game the Cetagandans play with us, to re-affirm our status. You are correct, it is a studied insult, designed to distract our minds. I stopped allowing it to distract me some years ago, and I recommend you do the same."

The Cetagandan displayed no reaction at all. Vorob'yev was treating him with no more regard than a piece of furniture, a compliment he apparently returned by acting like one. It seemed to be a ritual.

"Thank you, sir, I'll take your advice. Uh . . . were you delayed too? We were. They cleared us to dock once and then sent us back out to cool."

"The runaround today seems particularly ornate.

Consider yourselves honored, my lords. Come this way, please."

Ivan gave Miles a pleading look as Vorob'yev turned away; Miles shook his head fractionally, *Wait. . . .*

Led by the expressionless Cetagandan station official and flanked by the embassy guards, the two young men accompanied Vorob'yev up several station levels. The Barrayaran embassy's own planetary shuttle was docked to a genuine passenger lock. It had a proper VIP lounge with its own grav system in the flex tube so nobody had to float. There they shed their Cetagandan escort. Once on board the ambassador seemed to relax a little. He settled Miles and Ivan in luxuriously padded seats arranged around a bolted-down comconsole table. At Vorob'yev's nod a guard offered them drinks of choice while they waited for their luggage and departure clearances. Following Vorob'yev's lead they accepted a Barrayaran wine of a particularly mellow vintage. Miles barely sipped, hoping to keep his head clear, while Ivan and the ambassador made small talk about their trip, and mutual Vorish friends back home. Vorob'yev seemed to be personally acquainted with Ivan's mother. Miles ignored Ivan's occasional raised-brow silent invitation to join the chat, and maybe tell Lord Vorob'yev all about their little adventure with the intruder, yes?

Why hadn't the Cetagandan authorities been all over them just now, asking questions? Miles ran scenarios through his heated brain.

It was a setup, and I've just taken the bait, and they're letting the line play out. Considering what he knew of Cetagandans, Miles placed this possibility at the head of his list.

Or maybe it's just a time lag, and they'll be here momentarily. Or . . . eventually. The fugitive must first be captured, and then made to disgorge his version of the encounter. This could take time, particularly if the man had been, say, stunned unconscious during arrest. If he was a fugitive. If the station authorities had indeed been sweeping the docking area for him. If . . . Miles studied his crystal cup, and swallowed a mouthful of the smoky ruby liquid, and smiled affably at Ivan.

Their luggage and its guards arrived just as they finished their drinks, experienced timing on Vorob'yev's part, Miles judged. When the ambassador rose to oversee its stowage and their departure, Ivan leaned across the table to whisper urgently to Miles, "Aren't you going to tell him about it?"

"Not yet."

"Why not?"

"Are you in such a hurry to lose that nerve disruptor? The embassy'd take it away from you as fast as the Cetagandans, I bet."

"Screw that. What are you up to?"

"I'm . . . not sure. Yet." This was not the scenario he'd expected to unfold. He'd anticipated bandying sharp exchanges with assorted Cetagandan authorities while they made him disgorge his prizes, and trading for information, consciously or unconsciously revealed. It wasn't his fault the Cetagandans weren't doing their job.

"We've got to at least report this to the embassy's military attaché."

"Report it, yes. But not to the attaché. Illyan told me that if I had any problems—meaning, of the sort *our* department concerns itself with—I was to go to Lord Vorreedi. He's listed as a protocol officer, but he's really an ImpSec colonel and chief of ImpSec here."

"The Cetagandans don't know?"

"Of course they know. Just like we know who's really who at the Cetagandan embassy in Vorbarr Sultana. It's a polite legal fiction. Don't worry, I'll see to it." Miles sighed inwardly. He supposed the first thing the colonel would do was cut him out of the information-flow. And he dared not explain why Vorreedi shouldn't.

Ivan sat back, temporarily silenced. Only temporarily, Miles was sure.

Vorob'yev joined them again, settling down and hunting his seat straps. "And that's that, my lords. Nothing taken from your possessions, nothing added. Welcome to Eta Ceta Four. There are no official ceremonies requiring your presence today, but if you're not too tired from your journey, the Marilacan Embassy is hosting an informal reception tonight for the legation community, and all its august visitors. I recommend it to your attention."

"Recommend?" said Miles. When someone with a career as long and distinguished as Vorob'yev's recommended, Miles felt, one attended.

"You'll be seeing a lot of these people over the next two weeks," Vorob'yev said. "It should provide a useful orientation."

"What should we wear?" asked Ivan. Four of the six cases they'd brought were his.

"Undress greens, please," said Vorob'yev. "Clothing is a cultural language everywhere, to be sure, but here it's practically a secret code. It is difficult enough to move among the ghem-lords without committing some defined error, and among the haut-lords it's nearly impossible. Uniforms are always correct, or, if not exactly correct, clearly not the wearer's fault, since he has no choice. I'll have my protocol office give you a list of which uniforms you are to wear at each event."

Miles felt relieved; Ivan looked faintly disappointed.

With the usual muted clinks and clanks and hisses, the flex tubes withdrew and the shuttle unlocked and undocked from the side of the station. No arresting authorities had poured through the hatch, no urgent communications had sent the ambassador hurrying forward. Miles considered his third scenario.

Our intruder got clean away. The Station authorities know nothing of our little encounter. In fact, no one knows.

Except, of course, the intruder. Miles kept his hand down, and did not touch the concealed lump in his tunic. Whatever the device was, that fellow knew Miles had it. And he could surely find out who Miles was. *I have a string on you, now. If I let it play out, something must surely climb back up it to my hand, right?* This could shape up into a nice little exercise in intelligence/counter-intelligence, better than maneuvers because it was real. No proctor with a list of answers lurked on the fringes recording all his mistakes for later analysis in excruciating detail. A practice-piece. At some stage of development an officer had to stop following orders and start generating them. And Miles wanted that promotion to ImpSec captain, oh yes. Might he somehow persuade Vorreedi to let him play with the puzzle despite his diplomatic duties?

Miles's eyes narrowed with new anticipation as they began their descent into the murky atmosphere of Eta Ceta.

CHAPTER TWO

Half-dressed, Miles wandered across the spacious bedchamber–sitting room the Barrayaran embassy had assigned to him, turning the glittering rod in his hand. "So if I'm meant to have this, am I meant to stash it here, or am I meant to carry it on my person?"

Ivan, neat and complete in the high-collared tunic, side-piped trousers, and half-boots of fresh undress greens, rolled his eyes ceilingward. "Will you quit fooling with that thing and get dressed, before you make us late? Maybe it's a fancy curtain-weight, and it's *meant* to drive you crazy trying to assign it some deep and sinister significance. Or drive me crazy, listening to you. Some ghem-lord's practical joke."

"A particularly subtle practical joke, if so."

"Doesn't rule it out," Ivan shrugged.

"No." Miles frowned, and limped to the comconsole desk. He opened the top drawer, and found a stylus and a pad of plastic flimsies embossed with the embassy seal. He tore off a flimsy and pressed it against the bird-figure on the rod's cap-lock, then traced the indentations with the stylus, a quick, accurate, and to-scale sketch. After a moment's hesitation, he left the rod in the drawer with the pad of flimsies, and closed it again.

"Not much of a hiding place," Ivan commented. "If it's a bomb, maybe you ought to hang it out the window. For the rest of our sakes, if not your own."

"It's not a bomb, dammit. And I've thought of a hundred hiding places, but none of them are scanner-proof, so there's no point. This should be in a lead-lined blackbox, which I don't happen to have."

"I bet they have one downstairs," Ivan said. "Weren't you going to confess?"

"Yes, but unfortunately Lord Vorreedi is out of the city. Don't look at me like that, I had nothing to do with it. Vorob'yev told me the haut-lord in charge of one of the Eta Cetan Jumppoint stations has impounded a Barrayaran-registered merchant ship, and its captain. For importation infractions."

"Smuggling?" said Ivan, growing interested.

"No, some complicated cockeyed Cetagandan regulations. With fees. And taxes. And fines. And a level of acrimony that's going asymptotic. Since normalizing trade relations is a current goal of our government, and since Vorreedi is apparently good at sorting out haut-lords and ghem-lords, Vorob'yev detailed him to take care of it while he's stuck here with the ceremonial duties. Vorreedi will be back tomorrow. Or the next day. Meanwhile, it won't hurt to see how far I can get on my own. If nothing interesting turns up, I'll bounce it over to the ImpSec office here anyway."

Ivan's eyes narrowed, as he processed this. "Yeah? So what if something interesting does turn up?"

"Well, then too, of course."

"So did you tell Vorob'yev?"

"Not exactly. No. Look, Illyan said Vorreedi, so Vorreedi it is. I'll take care of it as soon as the man gets back."

"In any case, it's *time*," Ivan reiterated.

"Yeah, yeah . . ." Miles shuffled over to his bed, sat, and frowned at his leg braces, laid out waiting. "I have to take the time to get my leg bones replaced. I've given up on the organics, it's time to go with plastic. Maybe I could persuade them to add a few centimeters of length while they're at it. If only I'd known I had all this dead time coming up, I could have scheduled surgery and been recovering while we traveled and stood around being decorative."

"Inconsiderate of the dowager empress, not to send you a note and warn you she was dropping dead," Ivan agreed. "Wear the damn things, or Aunt Cordelia will hold me responsible if you trip over the embassy cat and break your legs. Again."

Miles growled, not very loudly. Ivan could read him entirely too well, too. He closed the cool steel protection around his lumpy, discolored, too-many-times smashed legs. At least the uniform trousers concealed his weakness. He fastened his tunic, sealed the polished short-boots, checked his hair in the mirror over his dresser, and followed the impatient Ivan, already at the door. In passing he slipped the folded flimsy into his trouser pocket, and paused in the corridor to re-key the door lock to his own palm. A somewhat futile gesture; as a trained ImpSec agent Lieutenant Vorkosigan knew exactly how insecure palm locks could be.

Despite, or perhaps because of, Ivan's prodding, they arrived in the foyer at almost the same moment as Ambassador Vorob'yev. Vorob'yev was wearing his red and black House uniform again. Not a man who liked making a lot of decisions about clothing, Miles sensed. He shepherded the two younger men into the embassy's waiting groundcar, where they sank into soft upholstery. Vorob'yev politely took the rear-facing seat across from his official guests. A driver and a guard occupied the front compartment. The car ran on the city net's computer control, but the alert driver sat ready to hit the manual override in case of some non-natural emergency. The silvered canopies closed, and they oozed out into the street.

"You may regard the Marilacan embassy as neutral but non-secured territory tonight, gentlemen," Vorob'yev advised them. "Enjoy yourselves, but not *too* much."

"Will there be many Cetagandans present," Miles asked, "or is this party strictly for us off-worlders?"

"No haut-lords, of course," said Vorob'yev. "They're all at one of the late empress's more private obsequies tonight, along with some of the highest-ranking ghem-clan heads. The lower-ranking ghem-lords are at loose ends, and may be out in force, as the month of official mourning has reduced their usual social opportunities. The Marilacans have been accepting a great deal of Cetagandan 'aid' in the past few years, a greediness I predict they will come to regret. They think Cetaganda won't attack an ally."

The groundcar climbed a ramp, and swung around a corner offering a brief vista down a glittering canyon of high buildings, strung together with tubeways and transparent walks glowing in the dusk. The city seemed to go on forever, and this wasn't even the main center.

"The Marilacans aren't paying sufficient attention to their own wormhole nexus maps," Vorob'yev went on. "They imagine they are at a natural border. But if Marilac were directly held by Cetaganda, the next jump would bring them to Zoave Twilight, with all its cross-routes, and a whole new region for Cetagandan expansion. Marilac is in exactly the same relationship to the Zoave Twilight crossings as Vervain is to the Hegen Hub, and we all know what happened *there*." Vorob'yev's lips twisted in irony. "But Marilac has no interested neighbor to mount a rescue as your father did for Vervain, Lord Vorkosigan. And provocative incidents can be manufactured so easily."

The alert rush in Miles's chest faded. There was no personal, secret meaning in Vorob'yev's remarks. Everyone knew of Admiral Count Aral Vorkosigan's political and military role in creating the swift alliance and counter-attack that had driven off the attempted Cetagandan capture of its neighbor Vervain's wormhole jumps to the Hegen Hub. No one knew of the role ImpSec agent Miles Vorkosigan had played in bringing the Admiral to the Hegen Hub in so timely a fashion. And what no one knew, no one got credit for. *Hi, I'm a hero, but I can't tell you why. It's classified.* From Vorob'yev's and practically everybody else's point of view, Lieutenant Miles Vorkosigan was a low-ranking ImpSec courier officer, a nepotistic sinecure that shuffled him off into routine duties that took him out of the way. *Mutant.*

"I thought the Hegen Alliance gave the ghem-lords a bloody enough nose at Vervain to keep them subdued for a while," said Miles. "All the expansionist party ghem-officers in deep eclipse, ghem-General Estanis committing suicide—it was suicide, wasn't it?"

"In an involuntary sort of way," said Vorob'yev. "These Cetagandan political suicides can get awfully messy, when the principal won't cooperate."

"Thirty-two stab wounds in the back, worst case of suicide they ever saw?" murmured Ivan, clearly fascinated by the gossip.

"Exactly, my lord." Vorob'yev's eyes narrowed in dry amusement. "But the ghem-commanders' loose and shifting relationship to the assorted secret haut-lord factions lends an unusual degree of deniability to their operations. The Vervain invasion is now officially described as an unauthorized misadventure. The erring officers have been corrected, thank you."

"What do they call the Cetagandan invasion of Barrayar in my grandfather's time?" Miles asked. "A reconnaissance in force?"

"When they mention it at all, yes."

"All twenty *years* of it?" asked Ivan, half-laughing.

"They tend not to go into the embarrassing details."

"Have you shared your views on Cetagandan ambitions toward Marilac with Illyan?" Miles asked.

"Yes, we keep your chief fully informed. But there are no material movements at present to support my theory. I'm just reasoning on principle, so far. ImpSec is watching some key indicators for us."

"I'm . . . not in that loop," said Miles. "Need-to-know and all that."

"But I trust you grasp the larger strategic picture."

"Oh, yes."

"And—upper-class gossip is not always as guarded as it should be. You two will be in a position to encounter some. Plan to report it all to my chief of protocol, Colonel Vorreedi. He will be giving you daily briefings, as soon as he returns. Let him sort out which tidbits are important."

Check. Miles nodded to Ivan, who shrugged acquiescence.

"And, ah . . . try not to give away more than you gain?"

"Well, *I'm* safe," said Ivan. "I don't know anything." He smiled cheerily. Miles tried not to wince, nor mutter *We know, Ivan,* under his breath loud enough to be heard.

Since the off-planet legations were concentrated in one section of Eta Ceta's capital city, the drive was short. The groundcar descended a street-level, and slowed. It entered the Marilacan embassy building's garage and pulled into a brightly lit entry foyer made less subterranean by marble surfaces and decorative plants trailing from tiers of tubs. The car's canopy rose. Marilacan embassy guards bowed the Barrayaran party into the lift tubes. Doubtless they also discreetly scanned their guests—it seemed Ivan had mustered the good sense to leave that nerve disruptor in his desk drawer, too.

They exited the lift tube into a wide lobby, opening in turn onto several levels of connected public areas, already well populated with guests, the volume of their babble invitingly high. The center of the lobby was occupied by a large multi-media sculpture, real, not a projection. Trickling water cascaded down a fountain reminiscent of a little mountain, complete with impressionistic mountain-paths one could actually walk upon. Colored flakes swirled in the air around the mini-maze, making delicate tunnels. From their green color Miles guessed they were meant to represent Earth tree leaves even before he drew close enough to make out the realistic details of their shapes. The colors slowly began to change, from twenty different greens to brilliant yellows, golds, reds and black-reds. As they swirled they almost seemed to form fleeting patterns, like human faces and bodies, to a background of tinkling like wind chimes. So was it meant to be faces and music, or was it just tricking his brain into projecting meaningful patterns onto randomness? The subtle uncertainty attracted him.

"*That's* new," commented Vorob'yev, his eye also caught. "Pretty . . . ah, good evening, Ambassador Bernaux."

"Good evening, Lord Vorob'yev." Their silver-haired Marilacan host exchanged a familiar nod with his Barrayaran counterpart. "Yes, we think it's rather fine. It's a gift from a local ghem-lord. Quite an honor. It's titled 'Autumn Leaves.' My cipher staff puzzled over the name for half a day, and finally decided it meant 'Autumn Leaves.'"

The two men laughed. Ivan smiled uncertainly, not quite following the in-joke. Vorob'yev formally introduced them to Ambassador Bernaux, who responded to their rank with elaborate courtesy, and to their age by telling them where to find the food and pointedly turning them loose. It was the Ivan-effect, Miles decided glumly. They mounted stairs toward a buffet, cut off from getting to hear whatever private comments the two older men went on to exchange. Probably just social pleasantries, but still . . .

Miles and Ivan sampled the hors d'oeuvres, which were dainty but abundant, and selected drinks. Ivan chose a famous Marilacan wine. Miles, conscious of the flimsy in his pocket, chose black coffee. They abandoned each other with a silent wave, each to circulate after his own fashion. Miles leaned on the railing overlooking the lift-tube lobby. He sipped from the fragile cup and wondered where its stay-warm circuit was concealed—ah, there on the bottom, woven into the metallic glitter of the Marilacan embassy seal. "Autumn Leaves" was chilling down to the end of its cycle. The water in the trickling fountains froze, or appeared to, stilled to silent black ice. The swirling colors faded to the sere yellow and silver-gray of a winter sunset, the figures, if figures they were, now suggesting skeletal despair. The chime/music faded to discordant, broken whispers. It was not a winter of snow and celebration. It was a winter of death. Miles shivered involuntarily. *Damned effective.*

So, how to begin asking questions without revealing anything in return? He pictured himself buttonholing some ghem-lord, *Say, did one of your minions lose a code-key with a seal like this . . . ?* No. By far the best approach was to let his . . . adversaries, find him, but they were being tediously slow about it. Miles's eye swept the throng for men without eyebrows, without success.

But Ivan had found a beautiful woman already. Miles blinked, as he registered just how beautiful. She was tall and slim, the skin of her face and hands as delicately smooth as porcelain. Jeweled bands bound her blond-white hair loosely at the nape of her neck, and again at her waist. The hair did not trail to its silky end until halfway to her knees. Her dress concealed rather than revealed, with layers of underslips, split sleeves, and vests sweeping to her ankles. The dark hues of the over-garments set off the pallor of her complexion, and a flash of cerulean silk underneath echoed her blue eyes. She was a Cetagandan ghem-lady, without question—she had that attenuated-elf look that suggested more than a tinge of haut-lord genes in her family tree. True, the look could be mimicked with surgeries and other therapies, but the arrogant arch to her brow had to be genuine.

Miles sensed the pheromones in her perfume while still spiraling in from three meters away. It seemed redundant; Ivan was already on overdrive, his dark eyes sparkling as he decanted some story featuring himself as hero, or at least protagonist. Something about training exercises, ah, of course, emphasizing his Barrayaran martial style. Venus and Mars, right. But she was actually smiling at something Ivan had said.

It wasn't that Miles enviously sought to deny Ivan his luck with women; it would simply be nice if some of the overflow would trickle down his way. Though Ivan claimed you had to make your own luck. Ivan's resilient ego could absorb a dozen rejections tonight for some smiling thirteenth payoff. Miles thought he would be dead of mortification by Attempt Three. Maybe he was naturally monogamous.

Hell, you had to at least achieve monogamy before you could go on to larger ambitions. So far he had failed to attach even one woman to his sawed-off person. Of course, nearly three years in covert ops, and the period before that in the all-male environs of the military academy, had limited his opportunities.

Nice theory. So why hadn't similar conditions stopped Ivan?

Elena . . . Was he still holding out for the impossible, on some level? Miles swore he wasn't nearly as choosy as Ivan—he could hardly afford to be—yet even this lovely ghem-blonde lacked . . . what? The intelligence, the reserve, the pilgrim soul . . . ? But Elena had chosen another, and probably wisely. Time and past time for Miles to move on too, and carve out some luck of his own. He just wished the prospect didn't feel so bleak.

Spiraling in from the other side a moment or two after Miles came a Cetagandan ghem-lord, tall and lean. The face rising up out of his dark and flowing robes was young; the fellow was not much older than Ivan and himself, Miles guessed. He was square-skulled, with prominent round cheekbones. One cheekbone was decorated with a circular patch, a decal, Miles realized, a stylized swirl of color identifying the man's rank and clan. It was a shrunken version of the full face paint a few other Cetagandans present wore, an avant-garde youth fashion currently being disapproved of by the older generation. Was he come to rescue his lady from Ivan's attentions?

"Lady Gelle," he bowed slightly, and "Lord Yenaro," she responded with a precisely graded inclination of her head, by which Miles gathered that 1) she had a higher status in the ghem-community than the man, and 2) he was not her husband or brother—Ivan was probably safe.

"I see you have found some of the galactic exotics you were longing for," said Lord Yenaro to her.

She smiled back at him. The effect was downright blinding, and Miles found himself wishing she'd smile at him even though he knew better. Lord Yenaro, doubtless inoculated by a lifetime of exposure to ghem-ladies, seemed immune. "Lord Yenaro, this is Lieutenant Lord Ivan Vorpatril of Barrayar, and, ah—?" Her lashes swept down over her eyes, indicating Ivan should introduce Miles, a gesture as sharp and evocative as if she'd tapped Ivan's wrist with a fan.

"My cousin, Lieutenant Lord Miles Vorkosigan," Ivan supplied smoothly, on cue.

"Ah, the Barrayaran envoys!" Lord Yenaro bowed more deeply. "What luck to meet you."

Miles and Ivan both returned decent nods; Miles made sure the inclination of his head was slightly shallower than his cousin's, a fine gradation alas probably spoiled by the angle of view.

"We have an historical connection, Lord Vorkosigan," Yenaro went on. "Famous ancestors."

Miles's adrenaline level shot up. *Oh, damn, this is some relative of the late ghem-General Estanis, and he's out to get the son of Aral Vorkosigan. . . .*

"You *are* the grandson of General Count Piotr Vorkosigan, are you not?"

Ah. *Ancient* history, not recent. Miles relaxed slightly. "Indeed."

"I am in a sense your opposite number, then. My grandfather was ghem-General Yenaro."

"Oh, the unfortunate commander of the, uh, what do you folks call it? The Barrayaran Expedition? The Barrayaran Reconnaissance?" Ivan put in.

"The ghem-general who lost the Barrayaran War," Yenaro said bluntly.

"Really, Yenaro, must you bring him up?" said Lady Gelle. Did she actually want to hear the end of Ivan's story? Miles could have told her a much funnier one, about the time on training maneuvers when Ivan had led his patrol into gluey waist-deep mud, and they'd all had to be winched out by hovercar. . . .

"I am not a proponent of the hero-theory of disaster," Miles said diplomatically. "General Yenaro had the misfortune to be the last of five successive ghem-generals who lost the Barrayaran War, and thus the sole inheritor of a, as it were, tontine of blame."

"Oh, well put," murmured Ivan. Yenaro too smiled.

"Do I understand that thing in the lobby is yours, Yenaro?" the girl inquired, clearly hoping to steer the conversation away from a fast downslide into military history. "A trifle banal for your crowd, isn't it? My mother liked it."

"It is but a practice piece." A slightly ironic bow acknowledged this mixed review. "The Marilacans were delighted with it. True courtesy considers the tastes of the recipient. It has some levels of subtlety only apparent when you walk through it."

"I thought you were specializing in the incense contests."

"I'm branching out into other media. Though I still maintain scent is a subtler sense than sight. You must let me mix for you sometime. That civet-jasmine blend you're wearing tonight absolutely clashes with the third-level formal style of your dress, you know."

Her smile went thin. "Does it."

Miles's imagination supplied background music, a scrape of rapiers, and a *Take that, varlet!* He tamped down a grin.

"Beautiful dress," Ivan put in earnestly. "You smell great."

"Mm, yes, speaking of your craving for the exotic," Lord Yenaro said to Lady Gelle, "did you know that Lord Vorpatril here is a biological birth?"

The girl's feather-faint brows drew in, making a tiny crease in her flawless forehead. "All births are biological, Yenaro."

"Ah, but no. The original sort of biology. From his mother's body."

"*Eeeuu.*" Her nose wrinkled in horror. "*Really*, Yenaro. You are so obnoxious tonight. Mother is right, you and your *retro-avant* crowd are going to go too far one of these days. You are in danger of becoming someone not to know, instead of someone famous." Her distaste was directed at Yenaro, but she shifted farther from Ivan, Miles noticed.

"When fame eludes, notoriety may serve," said Yenaro, shrugging.

I was a replicator birth, Miles thought of putting in brightly, but didn't. *Just goes to show, you can never tell. Except for the brain damage, Ivan had better luck than I. . . .*

"Good *evening,* Lord Yenaro." She tossed her head and moved off. Ivan looked dismayed.

"Pretty girl, but her mind is so unformed," murmured Yenaro, as if to explain why they were better off without her company. But he looked uncomfortable.

"So, uh . . . you chose an artistic career over a military one, did you, Lord Yenaro?" Miles tried to fill the breach.

"Career?" Lord Yenaro's mouth quirked. "No, I am an amateur, of course. Commercial considerations are the death of true taste. But I hope to achieve some small stature, in my own way."

Miles trusted that last wasn't a double entendre of some sort. They followed Lord Yenaro's gaze over the rail and down into the lobby, at his fountain-thing gurgling there. "You absolutely should come see it from the inside, you know. The view is entirely altered."

Yenaro was really a rather awkward man, Miles decided, his prickly exterior barely shielding a quiveringly vulnerable *artiste's* ego. "Sure," he found himself saying. Yenaro needed no further encouragement, and, smiling anxiously, led them toward the stairs, beginning to explain some thematic theory the sculpture was supposed to be displaying. Miles sighted Ambassador Vorob'yev, beckoning to him from the far side of the balcony. "Excuse me, Lord Yenaro. Ivan, you go on, I'll catch up with you."

"Oh . . ." Yenaro looked momentarily crushed. Ivan

watched Miles escape with a light of ire in his eye that promised later retribution.

Vorob'yev was standing with a woman, her hand familiarly upon his arm. She was about forty-standard, Miles guessed, with naturally attractive features free of artificial sculptural enhancement. Her long dress and robes were styled after the Cetagandan fashion, though much simpler in detail than Lady Gelle's. She was no Cetagandan, but the dark red and cream colors and green accents of her garments worked as cleverly with her olive skin and dark curls.

"There you are, Lord Vorkosigan," said Vorob'yev. "I've promised to introduce you. This is Mia Maz, who works for our good friends at the Vervani Embassy, and who has helped us out from time to time. I recommend her to you."

Miles snapped to attention at the key phrase, smiled, and bowed to the Vervani woman. "Pleased to meet you. And what do you do at the Vervani Embassy, ma'am?"

"I'm assistant chief of protocol. I specialize in women's etiquette."

"That's a separate specialty?"

"It is here, or should be. I've been telling Ambassador Vorob'yev for years that he ought to add a woman to his staff for that purpose."

"But we haven't any with the necessary experience," sighed Vorob'yev, "and you won't let me hire you away. Though I have tried."

"So start one without experience, and let her gain it," Miles suggested. "Would Milady Maz consider taking on an apprentice?"

"Now there's an idea. . . ." Vorob'yev looked much struck. Maz's brows rose approvingly. "Maz, we should discuss this, but I must speak to Wilstar, whom I see just hitting the buffet over there. If I'm lucky, I can catch him with his mouth full. Excuse me. . . ." His mission of introduction accomplished, Vorob'yev faded—how else?—diplomatically away.

Maz turned her whole attention gratefully upon Miles. "Anyway, Lord Vorkosigan, I wanted to let you know that if there's anything we at the Vervani Embassy can do for the son or the nephew of Admiral Aral Vorkosigan during your visit to Eta Ceta, well . . . all that we have is at your disposal."

Miles smiled. "Don't make that offer to Ivan; he might take you up on it personally."

The woman followed his glance down over the railing, to where his tall cousin was now being guided through the sculpture by Lord Yenaro. She grinned impishly, making a dimple wink in her cheek. "Not a problem."

"So, are, uh . . . ghem-ladies really so different from ghem-lords as to make a full-time study? I admit, most Barrayarans' views of the ghem-lords have been through range-finders."

"Two years ago, I would have scorned that militaristic view. Since the Cetagandan invasion attempt we've come to appreciate it. Actually, the ghem-lords are so much like the Vor, I'd think you'd find them more comprehensible than we Vervani do. The haut-lords are . . . something else. And the haut-ladies are even more something else, I've begun to realize."

"The haut-lords' women are so thoroughly sequestered . . . do they ever do anything? I mean, nobody ever sees them, do they? They have no power."

"They have their own sort of power. Their own areas of control. Parallel, not competing with their men. It all makes sense, they just never bother explaining it to outsiders."

"To inferiors."

"That, too." Her dimple flashed again.

"So . . . are you well up on ghem- and haut-lord seals, crests, marks, that sort of thing? I can recognize about fifty clan-marks by sight, and all the military insignia and corps crests, of course, but I know that just scratches the surface."

"I'm fairly well up. They have layers within layers; I can't claim to know them all by any means."

Miles frowned thoughtfully, then decided to seize the moment. There was nothing else going on here tonight, that was certain. He drew the flimsy from his pocket and flattened it out against the railing. "Do you know this icon? I ran across it . . . well, in an odd place. But it smelled ghemish, or hautish, if you know what I mean."

She gazed with interest at the screaming-bird outline. "I don't recognize it right off. But you're correct, it's definitely in the Cetagandan style. It's old, though."

"How can you tell?"

"Well, it's clearly a personal seal, not a clan-mark, but it doesn't have an outline around it. For the last three generations people have been putting their personal marks in cartouches, with more and more elaborate borders. You can practically tell the decade by the border design."

"Huh."

"If you like, I can try to look it up in my resource materials."

"Would you? I'd like that very much." He folded the flimsy back up and handed it to her. "Uh . . . I'd appreciate it if you wouldn't show it to anyone else, though."

"Oh?" She let the syllable hang there, *Oh . . . ?*

"Excuse me. Professional paranoia. I, uh . . ." He was getting in deeper and deeper. "It's a habit."

He was rescued from tripping further over his tongue by the return of Ivan. Ivan's practiced eye summed up the attractions of the Vervani woman instantly, and he smiled attentively at her, as sincerely delighted as he had been with the last girl, and would be with the next. And the next. The ghem-lord artiste was still glued to his elbow; Miles perforce introduced them both. Maz seemed not to have met Lord Yenaro before. In front of the Cetagandan, Maz did not repeat to Ivan her message of boundless Vervani gratitude to the Vorkosigan clan, but she was definitely friendly.

"You really ought to let Lord Yenaro take you on the tour of his sculpture, Miles," Ivan said ruthlessly. "It's quite a thing. An opportunity not to be missed and all that."

I found her first, dammit. "Yes, it's very fine."

"Would you be interested, Lord Vorkosigan?" Yenaro looked earnest and hopeful.

Ivan bent to Miles's ear to whisper, "It was Lord Yenaro's gift to the Marilacan embassy. Don't be a lout, Miles, you know how sensitive the Cetagandans are about their artsy, uh, things."

Miles sighed, and mustered an interested smile for Yenaro. "Certainly. Now?"

Miles excused himself with unfeigned regrets to Maz the Vervani. The ghem-lordling led him down the stairs to the lobby, and had him pause at the entrance of the walk-through sculpture to wait for the show-cycle to begin anew.

"I'm not really qualified to judge aesthetics," Miles mentioned, hoping to head off any conversation in that direction.

"So very few are," smiled Yenaro, "but that doesn't stop them."

"It does seem to me to be a very considerable technical achievement. Do you drive the motion with antigrav, then?"

"No, there's no antigrav in it at all. The generators would be bulky and wasteful of power. The same force drives the leaves' motion as drives their color changes— or so my technicians explained it to me."

"Technicians? I somehow pictured you putting all this together with your own hands."

Yenaro spread his hands—pale, long-fingered, and thin—and stared at them as if surprised to find them on the ends of his wrists. "Of course not. Hands are to be hired. Design is the test of the intellect."

"I must disagree. In my experience, hands are integral with brains, almost another lobe for intelligence. What one does not know through one's hands, one does not truly know."

"You are a man capable of true conversation, I perceive. You must meet my friends, if your schedule here permits. I'm hosting a reception at my home in two evenings' time—do you suppose—?"

"Um, maybe . . ." That evening was a blank as far as the funeral formalities went. It could be quite interesting, a chance to observe how the ghem-lordlings of his own generation operated without the inhibitions of their elders; a glimpse into the future of Cetaganda. "Yes, why not?"

"I'll send you directions. Oh." Yenaro nodded toward the fountain, which was starting up with its high-canopied summer greens again. "Now we can go in."

Miles did not find the view from inside the fountain-maze all that much different from the outside. In fact, it seemed less interesting, as at close range the illusion of forms in the flitting leaves was reduced. The music was clearer, though. It rose to a crescendo, as the colors began to change.

"Now you'll see something," said Yenaro, with evident satisfaction.

It was all sufficiently distracting that it took another moment for Miles to realize that he was *feeling* something—tingling and heat, coming from his leg braces lying against his skin. He schooled himself not to react, till the heat began to rise.

Yenaro was babbling on with artistic enthusiasm,

pointing out effects, *Now, watch this*— Brilliant colors swirled before Miles's eyes. A distinct sensation of scalding flesh crept up his legs.

Miles muffled his scream to a less-edged yell, and managed not to jump for the water. God knew, he might be electrocuted. The few seconds it took him to pelt out of the maze brought the steel of his braces to a temperature sufficient to boil water. He gave up dignity, dove for the floor, and yanked up his trouser legs. His first snatch at the clamps burned his hands, too. He swore, eyes watering, and tried again. He tore off his boots, snapped loose the braces, and flung them aside with a clatter, and curled up momentarily in overwhelming pain. The braces had left a pattern of rising white welts surrounded by an angry red border of flesh on shin, knees, and ankles.

Yenaro was flapping about in distress, calling loudly for help. Miles looked up to find himself the center of an audience of about fifty or so shocked and bewildered people, witnessing his display. He stopped writhing and swearing, and sat panting, his breath hissing through clenched teeth.

Ivan and Vorob'yev shouldered through the mob from different directions. "Lord Vorkosigan! What has happened?" asked Vorob'yev urgently.

"I'm all right," said Miles. He was not all right, but this was not the time or place to go into details. He pulled his trouser legs quickly back down, concealing the burns.

Yenaro was yammering on in dismay, "What happened? I had no idea—are you all right, Lord Vorkosigan? Oh *dear* . . ."

Ivan bent and prodded at a cooling brace. "Yes, what the hell . . . ?"

Miles considered the sequence of sensations, and their possible causes. Not antigrav, not noticeable to anyone else, and it had slid right past Marilacan

embassy security. Hidden in plain sight? Right. "I think
it was some sort of electro-hysteresis effect. The color-
changes in the display are apparently driven by a
reversing magnetic field at low level. No problem for
most people. For me, well, it wasn't quite as bad as
shoving my leg braces into a microwave, but—you get
the idea." Grinning, he got to his feet. Ivan, looking
very worried, had already collected his flung boots and
the offending braces. Miles let him keep them. He
didn't want to touch them just now. He blundered
rather blindly closer to Ivan, and muttered under his
breath, "Get me out of here. . . ." He was shivering
and shocky, as Ivan's hand on his shoulder could sense.
Ivan gave him a short, understanding nod, and swiftly
withdrew through the crowd of finely dressed men and
women, some of whom were already turning away.

Ambassador Bernaux hurried up, and added his worried apologies to Yenaro's one-man chorus. "Do you
wish to stop in to the embassy infirmary, Lord
Vorkosigan?" Bernaux offered.

"No. Thank you. I'll wait till we get home, thanks."
Soon, please.

Bernaux bit his lip, and regarded the still-apologiz-
ing Lord Yenaro. "Lord Yenaro, I'm afraid—"

"Yes, yes, turn it off at *once*," said Yenaro. "I will
send my servants to remove it immediately. I had no
idea—everyone else seemed to be enjoying—it must
be re-designed. Or destroyed, yes, destroyed at once.
I am so sorry—this is so embarrassing—"

Yes, isn't it? thought Miles. A show of his physical
weakness, displayed to a maximum audience at the
earliest possible moment . . .

"No, no, don't destroy it," said Ambassador Bernaux,
horrified. "But we certainly must have it examined by
a safety engineer, and modified, or perhaps a warning
posted. . . ."

Ivan reappeared at the edge of the dispersing crowd,

and gave Miles a thumbs-up signal. After a few more minutes of excruciating social niceties, Vorob'yev and Ivan managed to get him escorted back down the lift tube to the waiting Barrayaran embassy groundcar. Miles flung himself into the upholstery and sat, grinning in pain, breath shallow. Ivan eyed his shivering form, skinned out of his tunic, and tucked it around Miles's shoulders. Miles let him.

"All right, let's see the damages," demanded Ivan. He propped one of Miles's heels on his knee and rolled back the trouser leg. "Damn, that's got to hurt."

"Quite," agreed Miles thinly.

"It could hardly have been an assassination attempt, though," said Vorob'yev, his lips compressed with calculation.

"No," agreed Miles.

"Bernaux told me he had his own security people examine the sculpture before they installed it. Looking for bombs and bugs, of course, but they cleared it."

"I'm sure they did. This could not have hurt anyone . . . but me."

Vorob'yev followed his reasoning without effort. "A trap?"

"Awfully elaborate, if so," noted Ivan.

"I'm . . . not sure," said Miles. *I'm meant to be notsure. That's the beauty of it.* "It had to have taken days, maybe weeks, of preparation. We didn't even know we were coming here till two weeks ago. When did it arrive at the Marilacan embassy?"

"Last night, according to Bernaux," Vorob'yev said.

"Before we even arrived." *Before our little encounter with the man with no eyebrows. It can't possibly be connected—can it?* "How long have we been scheduled for that party?"

"The embassies arranged the invitations about three days ago," said Vorob'yev.

"The timing is awfully tight, for a conspiracy," Ivan observed.

Vorob'yev thought it over. "I think I must agree with you, Lord Vorpatril. Shall we put it down as an unfortunate accident, then?"

"Provisionally," said Miles. *That was no accident. I was set up. Me, personally. You know there's a war on when the opening salvo arrives.*

Except that, usually, one knew *why* a war had been declared. It was all very well to swear not to be blindsided again, but who was the enemy here?

Lord Yenaro, I bet you throw a fascinating party. I wouldn't miss it for worlds.

CHAPTER THREE

"The proper name for the Cetagandan imperial residence is the Celestial Garden," said Vorob'yev, "but all the galactics just call it Xanadu. You'll see why in a moment. Duvi, take the scenic approach."

"Yes, my lord," returned the young sergeant who was driving. He altered the control program. The Barrayaran embassy aircar banked, and shot through a shining stalagmite array of city towers.

"*Gently*, if you please, Duvi. My stomach, at this hour of the morning . . ."

"Yes, my lord." Regretfully, the driver slowed them to a saner pace. They dipped, wove around a building that Miles estimated must have been a kilometer high, and rose again. The horizon dropped away.

"Whoa," said Ivan. "That's the biggest force dome I've ever seen. I didn't know they could expand them to that size."

"It absorbs the output of an entire generating plant," said Vorob'yev, "for the dome alone. Another for the interior."

A flattened opalescent bubble six kilometers across reflected the late morning sun of Eta Ceta. It lay in the midst of the city like a vast egg in a bowl, a pearl

41

beyond price. It was ringed first by a kilometer-wide park with trees, then by a street reflecting silver, then by another park, then by an ordinary street, thick with traffic. From this, eight wide boulevards fanned out like the spokes of a wheel, centering the city. Centering the universe, Miles gained the impression. The effect was doubtless intended.

"The ceremony today is in some measure a dress rehearsal for the final one in a week and a half," Vorob'yev went on, "since absolutely everyone will be there, ghem-lords, haut-lords, galactics and all. There will likely be organizational delays. As long as they're not on our part. I spent a week of hard negotiating to get you your official rankings and place in this."

"Which is?" said Miles.

"You two will be placed equivalently to second-order ghem-lords." Vorob'yev shrugged. "It was the best I could do."

In the mob, though toward the front of it. The better to watch without being much noticed himself, Miles supposed. Today, that seemed like a good idea. All three of them, Vorob'yev, Ivan, and himself, were wearing their respective House mourning uniforms, logos and decorations of rank stitched in black silk on black cloth. Maximum formal, since they were to be in the Imperial presence itself. Miles ordinarily liked his Vorkosigan House uniform, whether the original brown and silver or this somber and elegant version, because the tall boots not only allowed but required him to dispense with the leg braces. But getting the boots on over his swollen burns this morning had been . . . painful. He was going to be limping more noticeably than usual, even tanked as he was on painkillers. *I'll remember this, Yenaro.*

They spiraled down to a landing by the southern-most dome entrance, fronted by a landing lot already crowded with other vehicles. Vorob'yev dismissed the driver and aircar.

"We keep no escort, my lord?" Miles said doubtfully, watching it go, and awkwardly shifting the long polished maplewood box he carried.

Vorob'yev shook his head. "Not for security purposes. No one but the Cetagandan emperor himself could arrange an assassination inside the Celestial Garden, and if he wished to have you eliminated here, a regiment of bodyguards would do you no good."

Some very tall men in the dress uniforms of the Cetagandan Imperial Guard vetted them through the dome locks. The guardsmen shunted them toward a collection of float-pallets set up as open cars, with white silky upholstered seats, the color of Cetagandan Imperial mourning. Each ambassadorial party was bowed on board by what looked to be senior servants in white and gray. The robotically-routed float-cars set off at a sedate pace a hand-span above the white-jade-paved walkways winding through a vast arboretum and botanical garden. Here and there Miles saw the rooftops of scattered and hidden pavilions peeking through the trees. All the buildings were low and private, except for some elaborate towers poking up in the center of the magic circle, almost three kilometers away. Though the sun shone outside in an Eta Ceta spring day, the weather inside the dome was set to a gray, cloudy, and appropriately mournful dampness, promising, but doubtless not delivering, rain.

At length they wafted to a sprawling pavilion just to the west of the central towers, where another servant bowed them out of the car and directed them inside, along with a dozen other delegations. Miles stared around, trying to identify them all.

The Marilacans, yes, there was the silver-haired Bernaux, some green-clad people who might be Jacksonians, a delegation from Aslund which included their chief of state—even they had only two guards, disarmed—the Betan ambassadoress in a black-on-purple brocade jacket and matching sarong, all streaming in to honor this one dead woman who would never have met them face-to-face when alive. *Surreal* seemed an understatement. Miles felt like he'd crossed the border into Faerie, and when they emerged this afternoon, a hundred years would have passed outside. The galactics had to pause at the doorway to make way for the party of a haut-lord satrap governor. *He* had an escort of a dozen ghem-guards, Miles noted, in full formal face paint, orange, green, and white swirls.

The decor inside was surprisingly simple—tasteful, Miles supposed—tending heavily to the organic, arrangements of live flowers and plants and little fountains, as if bringing the garden indoors. The connecting halls were hushed, not echoing, yet one's voice carried clearly. They'd done something extraordinary with acoustics. More palace servants circulated offering food and drinks to the guests.

A pair of pearl-colored spheres drifted at a walking pace across the far end of one hall, and Miles blinked at his first glimpse of haut-ladies. Sort of.

Outside their very private quarters haut-women all hid themselves behind personal force-shields, usually generated, Miles had been told, from a float-chair. The shields could be made any color, according to the mood or whim of the wearer, but today would all be white for the occasion. The haut-lady could see out with perfect clarity, but no one could see in. Or reach in, or penetrate the barrier with stunner, plasma, or nerve disruptor fire, or small projectile weapons or minor explosions. True, the force-screen also eliminated the opportunity to fire out, but that seemed not to be a haut-lady concern. The shield could be cut in half with a gravitic imploder lance, Miles supposed, but the imploders' bulky power packs, massing several hundred kilos, made them strictly field ordnance, not hand weapons.

Inside their bubbles, the haut-women could be wearing anything. Did they ever cheat? Slop around in old clothes and comfy slippers when they were supposed to be dressed up? Go nude to garden parties? Who could tell?

A tall elderly man in the pure white robes reserved for the haut- and ghem-lords approached the Barrayaran party. His features were austere, his skin finely wrinkled and almost transparent. He was the Cetagandan equivalent of an Imperial majordomo, apparently, though with a much more flowery title, for after collecting their credentials from Vorob'yev he provided them with exact instructions as to their place and timing in the upcoming procession. His attitude conveyed that outlanders might be hopelessly gauche, but if one repeated the directions in a firm tone and made them simple enough, there was a chance of getting through this ceremony without disgrace.

He looked down his hawk-beak nose at the polished box. "And this is your gift, Lord Vorkosigan?"

Miles managed to unlatch the box and open it for display without dropping it. Within, nestled on a black velvet bed, lay an old, nicked sword. "This is the gift selected from his collection by my Emperor, Gregor Vorbarra, in honor of your late Empress. It is the sword his Imperial ancestor Dorca Vorbarra the Just carried in the First Cetagandan War." One of several, but no need to go into that. "A priceless and irreplaceable historical artifact. Here is its documentation of provenance."

"Oh," the majordomo's feathery white brows lifted almost despite themselves. He took the packet, sealed with Gregor's personal mark, with more respect. "Please convey my Imperial master's thanks to yours." He half-bowed, and withdrew.

"*That* worked well," said Vorob'yev with satisfaction.

"I should bloody think so," growled Miles. "Breaks my heart." He handed off the box to Ivan to juggle for a while.

Nothing seemed to be happening just yet—organizational delays, Miles supposed. He drifted away from Ivan and Vorob'yev in search of a hot drink. He was on the point of capturing something steaming and, he hoped, non-sedating, from a passing tray when a quiet voice at his elbow intoned, "Lord Vorkosigan?"

He turned, and stifled an indrawn breath. A short and rather androgynous elderly . . . woman?—stood by his side, dressed in the gray and white of Xanadu's service staff. Her head was bald as an egg, her face devoid of hair. Not even eyebrows. "Yes . . . ma'am?"

"Ba," she said in the tone of one offering a polite correction. "A lady wishes to speak with you. Would you accompany me, please?"

"Uh . . . sure." She turned and paced soundlessly away, and he followed in alert anticipation. A lady? With luck, it might be Mia Maz of the Vervani delegation, who ought to be around somewhere in this mob of a thousand people. He was developing some urgent questions for her. *No eyebrows? I was expecting a contact sometime, but . . . here?*

They exited the hall. Passing out of sight of Vorob'yev and Ivan stretched Miles's nerves still further. He followed the gliding servant down a couple of corridors, and across a little open garden thick with moss and tiny flowers misted with dew. The noises from the reception hall still carried faintly through the damp air. They entered a small building, open to the garden on two sides and floored with dark wood that made his black boots echo unevenly in time with his limping stride. In a dim recess of the pavilion, a woman-sized pearlescent sphere floated a few centimeters above the polished floor, which reflected an inverted halo from its light.

"Leave us," a voice from the sphere directed the servant, who bowed and withdrew, eyes downcast. The transmission through the force screen gave the voice a low, flat timbre.

The silence lengthened. Maybe she'd never seen a physically imperfect man before. Miles bowed, and waited, trying to look cool and suave, and not stunned and wildly curious.

"So, Lord Vorkosigan," came the voice again at last. "Here I am."

"Er . . . quite." Miles hesitated. "And just who are you, milady, besides a very pretty soap-bubble?"

There was a longer pause, then, "I am the haut Rian Degtiar. Servant of the Celestial Lady, and Handmaiden of the Star Crèche."

Another flowery haut-title that gave no clue to its function. He could name every ghem-lord on the Cetagandan General Staff, all the satrap governors and their ghem-officers, but this female haut-babble was new to him. But the Celestial Lady was the polite name for the late Empress haut Lisbet Degtiar, and that name at least he knew—

"You are a relative of the late Dowager Empress, milady?"

"I am of her genomic constellation, yes. Three generations removed. I have served her half my life."

A lady-in-waiting, all right. One of the old Empress's personal retinue, then, the most inward of insiders. *Very* high rank, probably very aged as well. "Uh . . . you're not related to a ghem-lord named Yenaro, by chance, are you?"

"Who?" Even through the force-screen the voice conveyed utter bafflement.

"Never mind. Clearly not important." His legs were beginning to throb. Getting the damn boots back off when he returned to the embassy was going to be an even better trick than getting them on had been. "I could not help noticing your serving woman. Are there many folk around here with no hair?"

"It is not a woman. It is Ba."

"Ba?"

"The neuter ones, the Emperor's high-slaves. In his Celestial Father's time it was the fashion to make them smooth like that."

Ah. Genetically engineered, genderless servants. He'd heard rumors about them, mostly connected, illogically enough, with sexual scenarios that had more to do with the teller's hopeful fantasies than with any likely reality. But they were reputed to be a race utterly loyal to the lord who had, after all, literally created them. "So . . . not all ba are hairless, but all the hairless ones are ba?" he worked it out.

"Yes . . ." More silence, then, "Why have you come to the Celestial Garden, Lord Vorkosigan?"

His brow wrinkled. "To hold up Barrayar's honor in this circu—um, solemn procession, and to present your late Empress's bier-gift. I'm an envoy. By appointment of Emperor Gregor Vorbarra, whom *I* serve. In my own small way."

Another, longer pause. "You mock me in my misery."

"*What?*"

"What do you *want*, Lord Vorkosigan?"

"What do *I* want? You called me here, Lady, isn't it the other way around?" He rubbed his neck, tried again. "Er . . . can I help you, by chance?"

"*You?!*"

Her astonished tone stung him. "Yeah, me! I'm not as . . ." *incompetent as I look.* "I've been known to accomplish a thing or two, in my time. But if you won't give me a clue as to what this is all about, I can't. I will if I do know but I can't if I don't. Don't you see?" Now he had confused himself, tongue-tangled. "Look,

can we start this conversation over?" He bowed low.
"Good day, I am Lord Miles Vorkosigan of Barrayar.
How may I assist you, milady?"

"Thief—!"

The light dawned at last. "*Oh*. Oh, no. I am a
Vorkosigan, and no thief, milady. Though as possibly
a recipient of stolen property, I may be a fence," he
allowed judiciously.

More baffled silence; perhaps she was not familiar
with criminal jargon. Miles went on a little desperately,
"Have you, uh, by chance lost an object? Rod-shaped
electronic device with a bird-crest seal on the cap?"

"You have it!" Her voice was a wail of dismay.

"Well, not *on* me."

Her voice went low, throaty, desperate. "You still have
it. You must return it to me."

"Gladly, if you can prove it belongs to you. I certainly
don't pretend it belongs to me," he added pointedly.

"You would do this . . . for nothing?"

"For the honor of my name, and, er . . . I *am*
ImpSec. I'd do almost anything for information. Sat-
isfy my curiosity, and the deed is done."

Her voice came back in a shocked whisper, "You
mean you don't even know what it *is*?"

The silence stretched for so long after that, he was
beginning to be afraid the old lady had fainted dead
away in there. Processional music wafted faintly through
the air from the great pavilion.

"Oh, shi—er, oh. That damn parade is starting, and
I'm supposed to be near the front. Milady, how can I
reach you?"

"You can't." Her voice was suddenly breathless. "I
have to go too. I'll send for you." The white bubble
rose, and began to float away.

"Where? When—?" The music was building toward
the start-cue.

"Say nothing of this!"

He managed a sketchy bow at her retreating maybe-
back, and began hobbling hastily across the garden. He
had a horrible feeling he was about to be very publicly late.

When he'd wended his way back into the reception
area, he found the scene was every bit as bad as he'd
feared. A line of people was advancing to the main exit,
toward the tower buildings, and Vorob'yev in the
Barrayaran delegation's place was dragging his feet,
creating an obvious gap, and staring around urgently.
He spotted Miles and mouthed silently, *Hurry up,
dammit!* Miles hobbled faster, feeling as if every eye
in the room was on him.

Ivan, with an exasperated look on his face, handed
over the box to him as he arrived. "Where the hell were
you all this time, in the lav? I looked there—"

"Sh. Tell you later. I've just had the most bizarre
. . ." Miles struggled with the heavy maplewood box,
and straightened it around into an appropriate pre-
sentational position. He marched forward across a
courtyard paved with more carved jade, catching up
at last with the delegation in front of them just as
they reached the door to one of the high-towered
buildings. They all filed into an echoing rotunda.
Miles spied a few white bubbles in the line ahead,
but there was no telling if one was his old haut-lady.
The game plan called for everyone to slowly circle
the bier, genuflect, and lay their gifts in a spiral pattern in order of seniority/status/clout, and file out the
opposite doors to the Northern Pavilion (for the haut-
lords and ghem-lords), or the Eastern Pavilion (for
the galactic ambassadors) where a funereal luncheon
would be served.

But the steady procession stopped, and began to pile
up in the wide arched doorways. From the rotunda
ahead, instead of quiet music and hushed, shuffling
footsteps, a startled babble poured. Voices were raised

in sharp astonishment, then other voices in even sharper command.

"What's gone wrong?" Ivan wondered, craning his neck. "Did somebody faint or something?"

Since Miles's eye-level view was of the shoulders of the man ahead of him, he could scarcely answer this. With a lurch, the line began to proceed again. It reached the rotunda, but then was shunted out a door immediately to the left. A ghem-commander stood at the intersection, directing traffic with low-voiced instructions, repeated over and over, "Please retain your gifts and proceed directly around the outside walkway to the Eastern Pavilion, please retain your gifts and proceed directly to the Eastern Pavilion, all will be re-ordered presently, please retain—"

At the center of the rotunda, above everyone's heads on a great catafalque, lay the Dowager Empress in state. Even in death outlander eyes were not invited to look upon her. Her bier was surrounded by a force-bubble, made translucent; only a shadow of her form was visible through it, as if through gauze, a white-clad, slight, sleeping ghost. A line of mixed ghem-guards apparently just drafted from the passing satrap governors stood in a row from catafalque to wall on either side of the bier, shielding something else from the passing eyes.

Miles couldn't stand it. *After all, they can't massacre me here in front of everybody, can they?* He jammed the maplewood box at Ivan, and ducked under the elbow of the ghem-officer trying to shoo everyone out the other door. Smiling pleasantly, his hands held open and empty, he slipped between two startled ghem-guards, who were clearly not expecting such a rude and impudent move.

On the other side of the catafalque, in the position reserved for the first gift of the haut-lord of highest status, lay a dead body. Its throat was cut, and

quantities of fresh red blood pooled on the shimmering green malachite floor all around, soaking into its
gray and white palace servitor's uniform. A thin jeweled knife was clutched rigorously in its outflung right
hand. *It* was exactly the term for the corpse, too. A
bald, eyebrowless, man-shaped creature, elderly but not
frail . . . Miles recognized their intruder from the personnel pod even without the false hair. His own heart
seemed to stop in astonishment.

Somebody's just raised the stakes in this little game.

The highest-ranking ghem-officer in the room
swooped down upon him. Even through the swirl of
face paint his smile was fixed, the look of a man con-
strained to be polite to someone he would more naturally have preferred to bludgeon to the pavement.
"Lord Vorkosigan, would you rejoin your delegation,
please?"

"Of course. Who was that poor fellow?"

The ghem-commander made little herding motions
at him—the Cetagandan was not fool enough to actually touch him, of course—and Miles allowed himself
to be moved off. Grateful, irate, and flustered, the man
was actually surprised into an unguarded reply. "It is
Ba Lura, the Celestial Lady's most senior servitor. The
Ba has served her for sixty years and more—it seems
to have wished to follow on and serve her in death as
well. A most tasteless gesture, to do it *here* . . ." The
ghem-commander buffeted Miles near enough to the
again-stopped line of delegates for Ivan's long arm to
reach out, grab him, and pull him in, and march him
doorward with a firm fist in the middle of his back.

"What the hell is going *on?*" Ivan bent his head to
hiss in Miles's ear from behind.

*And where were you when the murder took place,
Lord Vorkosigan?* Except that it didn't look like a murder, it really did look like a suicide. Done in a most
archaic manner. Less than thirty minutes ago. While

he had been off talking with the mysterious white bubble, who might or might not have been haut Rian Degtiar, how the hell was he to tell? The corridor seemed to be spinning, but Miles supposed it was only his brain.

"You should not have gotten out of line, my lord," said Vorob'yev severely. "Ah . . . what was it you saw?"

Miles's lip curled, but he tamped it back down. "One of the late Dowager Empress's oldest ba servants has just cut its throat at the foot of her bier. I didn't know the Cetagandans made a fashion of human sacrifice. Not officially, anyway."

Vorob'yev's lips pursed in a soundless whistle, then flashed a brief, instantly stifled grin. "How *awkward* for them," he purred. "They are going to have an interesting scramble, trying to retrieve *this* ceremony."

Yes. So if the creature was so loyal, why did it arrange what it must have known would be a major embarrassment for its masters? Posthumous revenge? Admittedly, with Cetagandans that's the safest kind . . . .

By the time they completed an interminable hike around the outside of the central towers to the pavilion on the eastern side, Miles's legs were killing him. In a huge hall, the several hundred galactic delegates were being seated at tables by an army of servitors, all moving just a little faster than strict dignity would have preferred. Since some of the bier-gifts the other delegates carried were even bulkier than the Barrayarans' maplewood box, the seating was going slowly and more awkwardly than planned, with a lot of people jumping up and down and re-arranging themselves, to the servitors' evident dismay. Somewhere deep in the bowels of the building Miles pictured a squadron of harried Cetagandan cooks swearing many colorful and obscene Cetagandan oaths.

Miles spotted the Vervani delegation being seated about a third of the way across the room. He took advantage of the confusion to slip out of his assigned chair, weave around several tables, and try to seize a word with Mia Maz.

He stood by her elbow, and smiled tensely. "Good afternoon, m'lady Maz. I have to talk—"

"Lord Vorkosigan! I tried to talk with you—" they cut across each other's greetings.

"You first," he ducked his head at her.

"I tried to call you at your embassy earlier, but you'd already left. What in the world happened in the rotunda, do you have any idea? For the Cetagandans to alter a ceremony of this magnitude in the middle— it's unheard of."

"They didn't exactly have a choice. Well, I suppose they could have ignored the body and just carried on around it—*I* think that would have been much more impressive, personally—but evidently they decided to clean it up first." Again Miles repeated what he was beginning to think of as "the official version" of Ba Lura's suicide. He had the total attention of everyone within earshot. To hell with it, the rumors would be flying soon enough no matter what he said or didn't say.

"Did you have any luck with that little research question I posed to you last night?" Miles continued. "I, uh . . . don't think this is the time or place to discuss it, but . . ."

"Yes, and yes," Maz said.

And not over any holovid transmission channel on this planet, either, Miles thought, *supposedly secured or not.* "Can you stop by the Barrayaran Embassy, directly after this? We'll . . . take tea, or something."

"I think that would be very appropriate," Maz said. She watched him with newly intensified curiosity in her dark eyes.

"I need a lesson in etiquette," Miles added, for the benefit of their interested nearby listeners.

Maz's eyes twinkled in something that might have been suppressed amusement. "So I have heard it said, my lord," she murmured.

"By—" *whom?* he choked off. *Vorob'yev, I fear.* "'Bye," he finished instead, rapped the table cheerily, and retreated back to his proper place. Vorob'yev watched Miles seat himself with a slightly dangerous look in his eyes that suggested he was thinking of putting a leash on the peripatetic young envoy soon, but he made no comment aloud.

By the time they had eaten their way through about twenty courses of tiny delicacies, which more than made up in numbers what they lacked in volume, the Cetagandans had reorganized themselves. The haut-lord majordomo was apparently one of those commanders who was never more masterly than when in retreat, for he managed to get everyone marshaled in the correct order of seniority again even though the line was now being cycled through the rotunda in reverse. One sensed the majordomo would be cutting *his* throat later, in the proper place and with the proper ceremony, and not in this dreadful harum-scarum fashion.

Miles laid down the maplewood box on the malachite floor in the second turning of the growing spiral of gifts, about a meter from where Ba Lura had poured out its life. The unmarked, perfectly polished floor wasn't even damp. And had the Cetagandan security people had time to do a forensics scan before the cleanup? Or had someone been counting on the hasty destruction of the subtler evidence? *Damn, I wish I could have been in charge of this, just now.*

The white float-cars were waiting on the other side of the Eastern Pavilion, to carry the emissaries back to the gates of the Celestial Garden. The entire ceremony had run only about an hour late, but Miles's sense of time was inverted from his first whimsical vision of Xanadu as Faerie. He felt as if a hundred years had gone by inside the dome, while only a morning had passed in the outside world. He winced painfully in the bright afternoon light, as Vorob'yev's sergeant-driver brought the embassy aircar to their pickup point. Miles fell gratefully into his seat.

I think they're going to have to cut these bloody boots off, when we get back home.

CHAPTER FOUR

"Pull," Miles said, and set his teeth.

Ivan grasped his boot by the ankle and heel, braced his knee against the end of the couch upon which Miles lay, and yanked dutifully.

"Yeow!"

Ivan stopped. "Does that hurt?"

"Yes, keep going, dammit."

Ivan glanced around Miles's personal suite. "Maybe you ought to go downstairs to the embassy infirmary again."

"Later. I am not going to let that butcher of a physician dissect my best boots. Pull."

Ivan put his back into it, and the boot at last came free. He studied it in his hand a moment, and smiled slowly. "You know, you're not going to be able to get the other one off without me," he observed.

"So?"

"So . . . give."

"Give what?"

"Knowing your usual humor, I'd have thought you'd be as amused by the idea of an extra corpse in the funeral chamber as Vorob'yev was, but you came back looking like you'd just seen your grandfather's ghost."

57

"The Ba had cut its throat. It was a messy scene."

"I think you've seen messier corpses."

Oh, yes. Miles eyed his remaining booted leg, which was throbbing, and pictured himself limping through the corridors of the embassy seeking a less demanding valet. No. He sighed. "Messier, but no stranger. You'd have twitched too. We met the Ba yesterday, you and I. You wrestled with it in the personnel pod."

Ivan glanced toward the comconsole desk drawer where the mysterious rod remained concealed, and swore. "That does it. We've got to report this to Vorob'yev."

"If it *was* the same Ba," Miles put in hastily. "For all I know, the Cetagandans clone their servants in batches, and the one we saw yesterday was this one's twin or something."

Ivan hesitated. "You think so?"

"I don't know, but I know where I can find out. Just let me have one more pass at this, before we send up the flag, please? I've asked Mia Maz from the Vervani embassy to stop in and see me. If you wait . . . I'll let you sit in."

Ivan contemplated this bribe. "Boot!" Miles demanded, while he was thinking. Somewhat absently, Ivan helped pull it off.

"All right," he said at last, "but after we talk to her, we report to ImpSec."

"Ivan, I *am* ImpSec," snapped Miles. "Three years of training and field experience, remember? Do me the honor of grasping that I may just possibly know what I'm doing!" *I wish to hell I knew what I was doing.* Intuition was nothing but the subconscious processing of subliminal clues, he was fairly sure, but *I feel it in my bones* made too uncomfortably thin a public defense for his actions. *How can you know something before you know it?* "Give me a chance."

Ivan departed for his own room to change clothes

without making any promises. Freed of the boots, Miles staggered to his washroom to gulp down some more painkillers, and skin out of his formal House mourning and into loose black fatigues. Judging by the embassy's protocol list, Miles's private chamber was going to be the only place he could wear the fatigues.

Ivan returned all too soon, breezily trim in undress greens, but before he could continue asking questions Miles couldn't answer or demanding justifications Miles couldn't offer, the comconsole chimed. It was the staffer from the embassy's lobby, downstairs.

"Mia Maz is here to see you, Lord Vorkosigan," the man reported. "She says she has an appointment."

"That's correct. Uh . . . can you bring her up here, please?" Was his suite monitored by embassy security? He wasn't about to draw attention by inquiring. But no. If ImpSec were eavesdropping, he'd certainly have had to deal with some stiff interrogation from their offices below-stairs by now, either via Vorob'yev or directly. They were extending him the courtesy of privacy, as yet, in his personal space— though probably not on his comconsole. Every public forum in the building was guaranteed to be bugged, though.

The staffer ushered Maz to Miles's door in a few moments, and Miles and Ivan hastened to get her comfortably seated. She too had stopped to change clothes, and was now wearing a formfitting jump suit and knee-length vest suitable for street wear. Even at forty-odd her form supported the style very nicely. Miles got rid of the staffer by sending him off with an order for tea and, at Ivan's request, wine.

Miles settled down on the other end of the couch and smiled hopefully at the Vervani woman. Ivan was forced offsides to a nearby chair. "Milady Maz. Thank you for coming."

"Just Maz, please," she smiled in return. "We Vervani don't use such titles. I'm afraid we have trouble taking them seriously."

"You must be good at keeping a straight face, or you could not function so well here."

Her dimple winked at him. "Yes, my lord."

Ah yes, Vervain was one of those so-called democracies; not quite as insanely egalitarian as the Betans, but they had a definite cultural drift in that direction. "My mother would agree with you," Miles conceded. "She would have seen no inherent difference between the two corpses in the rotunda. Except their method of arriving there, of course. I take it this suicide was an unusual and unexpected event?"

"Unprecedented," said Maz, "and if you know Cetagandans, you know just how strong a term that is."

"So Cetagandan servants do not routinely accompany their masters in death like a pagan sacrifice."

"I suppose the Ba Lura was unusually close to the Empress, it had served her for so long," said the Vervani woman. "Since before any of us were born."

"Ivan was wondering if the haut-lords cloned their servants."

Ivan cast Miles a slightly dirty look, for being made the stalking horse, but did not voice an objection.

"The ghem-lords sometimes do," said Maz, "but not the haut-lords, and most certainly never the Imperial Household. They consider each servitor as much a work of art as any of the other objects with which they surround themselves. Everything in the Celestial Garden must be unique, if possible handmade, and perfect. That applies to their biological constructs as well. They leave mass production to the masses. I'm not sure if it's a virtue or a vice, the way the haut do it, but in a world flooded with virtual realities and infinite duplication, it's strangely refreshing. If only they weren't such awful snobs about it."

"Speaking of things artistic," said Miles, "you said you had some luck identifying that icon?"

"Yes." Her gaze flicked up to fix on his face. "Where did you say you saw it, Lord Vorkosigan?"

"I didn't."

"Hm." She half-smiled, but apparently decided not to fence with him over the point just now. "It is the seal of the Star Crèche, and not something I'd expect an outlander to run across every day. In fact, it's not something I'd expect an outlander to run across *any* day. It's most private."

Check. "And hautish?"

"Supremely."

"And, um . . . just what is the Star Crèche?"

"You don't know?" Maz seemed a little surprised. "Well, I suppose you fellows have spent all your time studying Cetagandan military matters."

"A great deal of time, yes," Ivan sighed.

"The Star Crèche is the private name of the haut-race's gene bank."

"Oh, that. I was dimly aware of—do they keep backup copies of themselves, then?" Miles asked.

"The Star Crèche is far more than that. Among the haut, they don't deal directly with each other to have egg and sperm united and the resulting embryo deposited in a uterine replicator, the way normal people do. Every genetic cross is negotiated and a contract drawn between the heads of the two genetic lines—the Cetagandans call them constellations, though I suppose you Barrayarans would call them clans. That contract in turn must be approved by the Emperor, or rather, by the senior female in the Emperor's line, and marked by the seal of the Star Crèche. For the last half-century, since the present regime began, that senior female has been haut Lisbet Degtiar, the Emperor's mother. It's not just a formality, either. Any genetic alterations—and the haut do a lot of them—have to be examined and cleared by the Empress's board of geneticists, before they are allowed into the haut genome. You asked me if the haut-women had any power. The Dowager Empress had final approval or veto over every haut birth."

"Can the Emperor override her?"

Maz pursed her lips. "I truly don't know. The haut are incredibly reserved about all this. If there are any behind-the-scenes power struggles, the news certainly doesn't leak out past the Celestial Garden's gates. I do know I've never heard of such a conflict."

"So . . . who is the new senior female? Who inherits the seal?"

"Ah! Now you've touched on something interesting." Maz was warming to her subject. "Nobody knows, or at least, the Emperor hasn't made the public announcement. The seal is supposed to be held by the Emperor's mother if she lives, or by the mother of the heir-apparent if the dowager is deceased. But the Cetagandan emperor has not yet selected his heir. The seal of the Star Crèche and all the rest of the empress's regalia is supposed to be handed over to the new senior female as the last act of the funeral rites, so he has ten more days to make up his mind. I imagine that decision is the focus of a great deal of attention right now, among the haut-women. No new genomic contracts can be approved until the transfer is completed."

Miles puzzled this through. "He has three young sons, right? So he must select one of their mothers."

"Not necessarily," said Maz. "He could hand things over to an Imperial aunt, one of his mother's kin, as an interim move."

A diffident rap at Miles's door indicated the arrival of the tea. The Barrayaran embassy's kitchen had sent along a perfectly redundant three-tiered tray of little petit fours as well. Someone had been doing their homework, for Maz murmured, "Ooh, my favorite."

One feminine hand dove for some dainty chocolate confections despite the Imperial luncheon they'd recently consumed. The embassy steward poured tea, opened the wine, and withdrew as discreetly as he had entered.

Ivan took a gulp from his crystal cup, and asked in puzzlement, "Do the haut-lords marry, then? One of these genetic contracts must be the equivalent of a marriage, right?"

"Well . . . no." Maz swallowed her third chocolate morsel, and chased it with tea. "There are several kinds of contracts. The simplest is for a sort of onetime usage of one's genome. A single child is created, who becomes the . . . I hesitate to use the term *property* . . . who is registered with the constellation of the male parent, and is raised in his constellation's crèche. You understand, these decisions are not made by the principals—in fact, the two parents may never even meet each other. These contracts are chosen at the most senior level of the constellation, by the oldest and presumably wisest heads, with an eye to either capturing a favored genetic line, or setting up for a desirable cross in the ensuing generation.

"At the other extreme is a lifetime monopoly—or longer, in the case of Imperial crosses. When a haut-woman is chosen to be the mother of a potential heir, the contract is absolutely exclusive—she must never have contracted her genome previously, and can never do so again, unless the emperor chooses to have more than one child by her. She goes to live in the Celestial Garden, in her own pavilion, for the rest of her life."

Miles grimaced. "Is that a reward, or a punishment?"

"It's the best shot at power a haut-woman can ever get—a chance of becoming a dowager empress, if her son—and it's always and only a son—is ultimately chosen to succeed his father. Even being the mother of one of the losers, a prince-candidate or satrap governor, is no bad deal. It's also why, in an apparently patriarchal culture, the output of the haut-constellations is skewed to girls. A constellation head—clan chief, in Barrayaran terminology—can never become an emperor or the father of an emperor, no matter how brightly his sons may shine. But through his daughters, he has a chance to become the grandfather of one. Advantages, as you may imagine, then accrue to the dowager empress's constellation. The Degtiar were not particularly important until fifty years ago."

"So the emperor has sons," Miles worked this out, "but everyone else is mad for daughters. But only once or twice a century, when a new emperor succeeds, can anyone win the game."

"That's about right."

"So . . . where does sex fit into all this?" asked Ivan plaintively.

"Nowhere," said Maz.

"Nowhere!"

Maz laughed at his horrified expression. "Yes, the haut have sexual relations, but it's purely a social game. They even have long-lasting sexual friendships that could almost qualify as marriages, sometimes. I was about to say there's nothing formalized, except that the etiquette of all the shifting associations is so incredibly complex. I guess the word I want is *legalized*, rather than formalized, because the rituals are intense. And weird, really weird, sometimes, from what little I've been able to gather of it all. Fortunately, the haut are such racists, they almost never go slumming outside their genome, so you are not likely to encounter those pitfalls personally."

"Oh," said Ivan. He sounded a little disappointed. "But . . . if the haut don't marry and set up their own households, when and how do they leave home?"

"They never do."

"Ow! You mean they live with, like, their mothers, forever?"

"Well, not with their mothers, of course. Their grand-parents or great-grandparents. But the youth—that is, anyone under fifty or so—do live as pensioners of their constellation. I wonder if that is at the root of why so many older haut become reclusive. They live apart because they finally *can*."

"But—what about all those famous and successful ghem-generals and ghem-lords who've won haut-lady wives?" asked Miles.

Maz shrugged. "They can't all aspire to become Imperial mothers, can they? Actually, I would point out this aspect particularly to you, Lord Vorkosigan. Have you ever wondered how the haut, who are not noted for their military prowess, control the ghem, who are?"

"Oh, yes. I've been expecting this crazy Cetagandan double-decked aristocracy to fall apart ever since I learned about it. How can you control guns with, with, art contests? How can a bunch of perfumed poetasters like the haut-lords buffalo whole ghem-armies?"

Maz smiled. "The Cetagandan ghem-lords would call it the loyalty justly due to superior culture and civili-zation. The fact is that anyone who's competent enough or powerful enough to pose a threat gets genetically co-opted. There is no higher reward in the Cetagandan system than to be Imperially assigned a haut-lady wife. The ghem-lords are all panting for it. It's the ultimate social and political coup."

"You're suggesting the haut control the ghem through these wives?" said Miles. "I mean, I'm sure the haut-women are lovely and all, but the ghem-generals can be such hard-bitten cast-iron bastards—I can't imag-ine anyone who gets to the top in the Cetagandan Empire being that susceptible."

"If I knew how the haut-women do it," Maz sighed, "I'd bottle it and sell it. No, better—I think I'd keep it for myself. But it seems to have worked for the last several hundred years. It is not, of course, the *only* method of Imperial control, to be sure. Only the most overlooked one. I find that, in itself, significant. The haut are nothing if not subtle."

"Does the, uh, haut-bride come with a dowry?" Miles asked.

Maz smiled again, and polished off another chocolate confection. "You have hit upon an important point, Lord Vorkosigan. She does not."

"I'd think keeping a haut-wife in the style to which she is accustomed could get rather expensive."

"Very."

"So . . . if the Cetagandan emperor wished to depress an excessively successful subject, he could award him a few haut-wives and bankrupt him?"

"I . . . don't think it's done quite so obviously as all that. But the element is there. You are very acute, my lord."

Ivan asked, "But how does the haut-lady who gets handed out like a good-conduct medal feel about it all? I mean . . . if the highest haut-lady ambition is to become an Imperial monopoly, this has got to be the ultimate opposite. To be permanently dumped out of the haut-genome—their descendants never marry back into the haut, do they?"

"No," confirmed Maz. "I believe the psychology of it all is a bit peculiar. For one thing, the haut-bride immediately outranks any other wives the ghem-lord may have acquired, and her children automatically become his heirs. This can set up some interesting tensions in his household, particularly if it comes, as it usually does, in mid-life when his other marital associations may be of long standing."

"It must be a ghem-lady's nightmare, to have one of

these haut-women dropped on her husband," Ivan mused. "Don't they ever object? Make their husbands turn down the honor?"

"Apparently it's not an honor one can refuse."

"Mm." With difficulty, Miles pulled his imagination away from these side-fascinations, and back to his most immediate worry. "That seal of the Star Crèche thing— I don't suppose you have a picture of it?"

"I brought a number of vids with me, yes, my lord," said Maz. "With your permission, we can run them on your comconsole."

Ooh, I adore competent women. Do you have a younger sister, milady Maz? "Yes, please," said Miles.

They all trooped over to the chamber's comconsole desk, and Maz began a quick illustrated lecture on haut crests and the several dozen assorted Imperial seals. "Here it is, my lord—the seal of the Star Crèche."

It was a clear cubical block, measuring maybe fifteen centimeters on a side, with the bird-pattern incised in red lines upon its top. *Not* the mysterious rod. Miles exhaled with relief. The terror that had been riding him ever since Maz had mentioned the seal, that he and Ivan might have accidentally stolen a piece of the Imperial regalia, faded. The rod was some kind of Imperial gizmo, obviously, and would have to be returned—anonymously, by preference—but at least it wasn't—

Maz called up the next unit of data, "And *this* object is the Great Key of the Star Crèche, which is handed over along with the seal," she went on.

Ivan choked on his wine. Miles, faint, leaned on the desk and smiled fixedly at the image of the rod. The original lay some few centimeters under his hand, in the drawer.

"And, ah—just what *is* the Great Key of the Star Crèche, m'la—Maz?" Miles managed to murmur. "What does it do?"

"I'm not quite sure. At one time in the past, I believe it had something to do with data retrieval from the haut gene banks, but the actual device may only be ceremonial by now. I mean, it's a couple of hundred years old. It has to be obsolete."

We hope. Thank God he hadn't dropped it. Yet. "I see."

"*Miles . . .*" muttered Ivan.

"Later," Miles hissed to him out of the corner of his mouth. "I understand your concern."

Ivan mouthed something obscene at him, over the seated Maz's head.

Miles leaned against the comconsole desk, and screwed up his features in a realistic wince.

"Something wrong, my lord?" Maz glanced up, concerned.

"I'm afraid my legs are bothering me, a bit. I had probably better pay another visit to the embassy physician, after this."

"Would you prefer to continue this later?" Maz asked instantly.

"Well . . . to tell you the truth, I think I've had about all the etiquette lessons I can absorb for one afternoon."

"Oh, there's *lots* more." But apparently he was looking realistically pale, too, for she rose, adding, "Far too much for one session, to be sure. Are your injuries much troubling you? I didn't realize they were that severe."

Miles shrugged, as if in embarrassment. After a suitable exchange of parting amenities, and a promise to call on his Vervani tutor again very soon, Ivan took over the hostly duties, and escorted Maz back downstairs.

He returned immediately, to seal the door behind him and pounce on Miles. "Do you have any idea how much trouble we're in?" he cried.

Miles sat before the comconsole, re-reading the official, and entirely inadequate, description of the Great

Key, while its image floated hauntingly before his nose above the vid plate. "Yes. I also know how we're going to get out of it. Do you know as much?"

This gave Ivan pause. "What else do you know that I don't?"

"If you will just leave it to me, I believe I can get this thing back to its rightful owner with no one the wiser."

"Its rightful owner is the Cetagandan emperor, according to what Maz said."

"Well, ultimately, yes. I should say, back to its rightful keeper. Who, if I read the signs right, is as chagrined about losing it as we are in finding it. If I can get it back to her quietly, I don't think she's going to go around proclaiming how she lost it. Although . . . I do wonder how she *did* lose it." Something was not adding up, just below his level of conscious perception.

"We mugged an Imperial servitor, that's how!"

"Yes, but what was Ba Lura doing with the thing on an orbital transfer station in the first place? Why had it disabled the security monitors in the docking bay?"

"Lura was taking the Great Key somewhere, obviously. To the Great Lock, for all I know." Ivan paced around the comconsole. "So the poor sod cuts its throat the next morning 'cause it lost its charge, its trust, courtesy of us—hell, Miles. I feel like we just killed that old geezer. And it never did us any harm, it just blundered into the wrong place and had the bad luck to startle us."

"Is that what happened?" Miles murmured. "Really . . . ?" *Is that why I am so desperately determined for the story to be something, anything, else?* The scenario hung together. The old Ba, charged with transporting the precious object, loses the Great Key to some outlander barbarians, confesses its disgrace to its mistress, and kills itself in expiation. Wrap. Miles felt ill. "So . . . if the key was that important, why wasn't the Ba traveling with a squadron of Imperial ghem-guards?"

"*God* Miles, I wish it *had* been!"

A firm knock sounded on Miles's door. Miles hastily shut down the comconsole and unsealed the door lock. "Come in."

Ambassador Vorob'yev entered, and favored him with a semi-cordial nod. He held a sheaf of delicately colored, scented papers in his hand.

"Hello, my lords. Did you find your tutorial with Maz useful?"

"Yes, sir," said Miles.

"Good. I thought you would. She's excellent." Vorobyev held up the colored papers. "While you were in session, this invitation arrived for you both, from Lord Yenaro. Along with assorted profound apologies for last night's incident. Embassy security has opened, scanned, and chemically analyzed it. They report the organic esters harmless." With this safety pronouncement, he handed the papers across to Miles. "It is up to you, whether or not to accept. If you concur that the unfortunate side-effect of the sculpture's power field was an accident, your attendance might be a good thing. It would complete the apology, repairing face all around."

"Oh, we'll go, sure." The apology and invitation were hand-calligraphed in the best Cetagandan style. "But I'll keep my eyes open. Ah . . . wasn't Colonel Vorreedi due back today?"

Vorob'yev grimaced. "He's run into some tedious complications. But in view of that odd incident at the Marilacan embassy, I've sent a subordinate to replace him. He should be back tomorrow. Perhaps . . . do you wish a bodyguard? Not openly, of course, that would be another insult."

"Mm . . . we'll have a driver, right? Let him be one of your trained men, have backup on call, give us both comm links, and have him wait for us nearby."

"Very well, Lord Vorkosigan. I'll make arrangements,"
Vorob'yev nodded. "And . . . regarding the incident in
the rotunda earlier today—"

Miles's heart pounded. "Yes?"

"Please don't break ranks like that again."

"Did you receive a complaint?" *And from whom?*

"One learns to interpret certain pained looks. The
Cetagandans would consider it impolite to protest—
but should unpleasant incidents pile high enough, not
too impolite for them to take some sort of indirect and
arcane retaliation. You two will be gone in ten days,
but I will still be here. Please don't make my job any
more difficult than it already is, eh?"

"Understood, sir," said Miles brightly. Ivan was looking intensely worried—was he going to bolt, pour out
confessions to Vorob'yev? Not yet, evidently, for the
ambassador waved himself back out without Ivan
throwing himself at his feet.

"*Nearby* doesn't cut it, for a bodyguard," Ivan pointed
out, as soon as the door sealed again.

"Oh, you're beginning to see it my way now, are you?
But if we go to Yenaro's at all, I can't avoid risk. I have
to eat, drink, and breathe—all routes for attack an
armed guard can't do much about. Anyway, my greatest
defense is that it would be a grievous insult to the
Cetagandan emperor for anyone to seriously harm a
galactic delegate to his august mother's funeral. I predict, should another accident occur, it will be equally
subtle and non-fatal." *And equally infuriating.*

"Oh, yeah? When there's been one fatality already?"
Ivan stood silent for a long time. "Do you think . . .
all these incidents could possibly be related?" Ivan nodded toward the perfumed papers still in Miles's hand,
and toward the comconsole desk drawer. "I admit, I
don't see how."

"Do you think they could possibly all be unrelated
coincidences?"

"Hm." Ivan frowned, digesting this. "So tell me," he pointed again to the desk drawer, "how *are* you planning to get rid of the Empress's dildo?"

Miles's mouth twitched, stifling a grin at the Ivan-diplomatic turn of phrase. "I can't tell you." *Mostly because I don't know yet myself.* But the haut Rian Degtiar had to be scrambling, right now. He fingered, as if absently, the silver eye-of-Horus ImpSec insignia pinned to his black collar. "There's a lady's reputation involved."

Ivan's eyes narrowed in scorn of this obvious appeal to Ivan's own brand of personal affairs. "Horseshit. *Are* you running some kind of secret rig for Simon Illyan?"

"If I were, I couldn't tell you, now could I?"

"Damned if I know." Ivan stared at him in frustration for another moment, then shrugged. "Well, it's your funeral."

CHAPTER FIVE

"Stop here," Miles instructed the groundcar's driver. The car swung smoothly to the side of the street and with a sigh of its fans settled to the pavement. Miles peered at the layout of Lord Yenaro's suburban mansion in the gathering dusk, mentally pairing the visual reality with the map he had studied back at the Barrayaran embassy.

The barriers around the estate, serpentine garden walls and concealing landscaping, were visual and symbolic rather than effective. The place had never been designed as a fortress of anything but privilege. A few higher sections of the rambling house glimmered through the trees, but even they seemed to focus inward rather than outward.

"Comm link check, my lords?" the driver requested. Miles and Ivan both pulled the devices from their pockets and ran through the codes with him. "Very good, my lords."

"What's our backup?" Miles asked him.

"I have three units, arranged within call."

"I trust we've included a medic."

"In the lightflyer, fully equipped. I can put him down inside Lord Yenaro's courtyard in forty-five seconds."

"That should be sufficient. I don't expect a frontal assault. But I wouldn't be surprised if I encountered another little 'accident' of some sort. We'll walk from here, I think. I want to get the feel of the place."

"Yes, my lord." The driver popped the canopy for them, and Miles and Ivan exited.

"Is this what you call genteel poverty?" Ivan inquired, looking around as they strolled through open, unguarded gates and up Yenaro's curving drive.

Ah yes. The style might be different, but the scent of aristocratic decay was universal. Little signs of neglect were all around: unrepaired damage to the gates and walls, overgrown shrubbery, what appeared to be three-quarters of the mansion dark and closed-off.

"Vorob'yev had the embassy's ImpSec office make a background check of Lord Yenaro," Miles said. "Yenaro's grandfather, the failed ghem-general, left him the house but not the means to keep it up, having consumed his capital in his extended and presumably embittered old age. Yenaro's been in sole possession for about four years. He runs with an artsy crowd of young and unemployed ghem-lordlings, so his story holds up to that extent. But that thing in the Marilacan embassy's lobby was the first sculpture Yenaro's ever been known to produce. Curiously advanced, for a first try, don't you think?"

"If you're so convinced it was a trap, why are you sticking your hand in to try and trip another one?"

"No risk, no reward, Ivan."

"Just what reward are you envisioning?"

"Truth. Beauty. Who knows? Embassy security is also running a check on the workmen who actually built the sculpture. I expect it to be revealing."

At least he could make that much use of the machinery of ImpSec. Miles felt intensely conscious of the rod now riding concealed in his inner tunic pocket. He'd been carrying the Great Key in secret all day, through a tour of the city and an interminable afternoon performance of a Cetagandan classical dance company. This last treat had been arranged by Imperial decree especially for the off-planet envoys to the funeral. But the haut Rian Degtiar had not made her promised move to contact him yet. If he did not hear from his haut-lady by tomorrow . . . On one level, Miles was growing extremely sorry he had not taken the local ImpSec subordinates into his confidence on the very first day. But if he had, he would no longer be in charge of this little problem; the decisions would all have been hiked to higher levels, out of his control. *The ice is thin. I don't want anyone heavier than me walking on it just yet.*

A servant met them at the mansion's door as they approached, and escorted them into a softly lit entry foyer where they were greeted by their host. Yenaro was in dark robes similar to the ones he'd worn at the Marilacan embassy's reception; Ivan was clearly correct in his undress greens. Miles had chosen his ultra-formal House blacks. He wasn't sure how Yenaro would interpret the message, as honor, or reminder—*I'm the official envoy*—or warning—*don't mess with me.* But he was fairly certain it was not a nuance Yenaro would miss.

Yenaro glanced down at Miles's black boots. "And are your legs better now, Lord Vorkosigan?" he inquired anxiously.

"Much better, thank you," Miles smiled tightly in return. "I shall certainly live."

"I'm so glad." The tall ghem-lord led them around a few corners and down a short flight of steps to a large semicircular room wrapped around a peninsula of the garden, as if the house were undergoing some botanical invasion. The room was somewhat randomly furnished, apparently with items Yenaro had previously owned rather than to design; but the effect was pleasantly comfortable-bachelor. The lighting here, too, was soft, camouflaging shabbiness. A dozen ghem-types were already present, talking and drinking. The men outnumbered the women; two bore full face paint, most sported the cheek-decal of the younger set, and a few radical souls wore nothing above the neck but a little eye makeup. Yenaro introduced his Barrayaran exotics all around. None of the ghem were anyone Miles had heard of or studied, though one young man claimed a great-uncle on staff at Cetagandan headquarters.

An incense burner smoked on a cylindrical stand by the garden doors; one ghem-guest paused to inhale deeply. "Good one, Yenaro," he called to his host. "Your blend?"

"Thank you, yes," said Yenaro.

"More perfumes?" inquired Ivan.

"And a bit extra. That mixture also contains a mild relaxant suitable to the occasion. You would perhaps not care for it, Lord Vorkosigan."

Miles smiled stiffly. Just how much of an organic chemist was this man? Miles was reminded that the root word of *intoxication* was *toxic*. "Probably not. But I'd love to see your laboratory."

"Would you? I'll take you up, then. Most of my friends have no interest in the technical aspects, only in the results."

A young woman, listening nearby, drifted up at this and tapped Yenaro on the arm with one long fingernail glittering with patterned enamel. "Yes, dear Yenni, results. You promised me some, remember?" She was not the prettiest ghem-woman Miles had seen, but attractive enough in swirling jade-green robes, with thick pale hair clipped back and curling down to her shoulders in a pink-frosted froth.

"And I keep my promises," Lord Yenaro asserted. "Lord Vorkosigan, perhaps you would care to accompany us upstairs now?"

"Certainly."

"I'll stay and make new acquaintances, I think," Ivan bowed himself out of the party. The two tallest and most striking ghem-women present, a leggy blonde and a truly incredible redhead, were standing together across the room; Ivan somehow managed to make eye contact with both, and they favored him with inviting smiles. Miles sent up a short silent prayer to the guardian god of fools, lovers, and madmen, and turned to follow Yenaro and his female petitioner.

Yenaro's organic chemistry laboratory was sited in another building; lights came up as they approached across the garden. It proved to be a quite respectable installation, a long double room on the second floor— some of the money that wasn't going into home repairs was obviously ending up here. Miles walked around the benches, eyeing the molecular analyzers and computers while Yenaro rummaged among an array of little bottles for the promised perfume. All the raw materials were beautifully organized in correct chemical groupings, betraying a deep understanding and detailed love of the subject on the owner's part.

"Who assists you here?" Miles inquired.

"No one," said Yenaro. "I can't bear to have anyone else mucking about. They mess up my orderings, which I sometimes use to inspire my blends. It's not all science, you know."

Indeed. With a few questions, Miles led Yenaro on to talk about how he'd made the perfume for the woman. She listened for a while and then wandered off to sniff at experimental bottles, till Yenaro, with a pained smile, rescued them from her. Yenaro's expertise was less than professorial, but fully professional; any commercial cosmetics company would have hired him on the spot for their product development laboratory. So, and so. How did this square with the man who'd claimed *Hands are to be hired*?

Not at all, Miles decided with concealed satisfaction. Yenaro was unquestionably an artist, but an artist of esters. Not a sculptor. Someone else had supplied the undoubted technical expertise that had produced the fountain. And had that same somebody also supplied the technical information on Miles's personal weaknesses? *Let's call him . . . Lord X.* Fact One about Lord X: he had access to Cetagandan Security's most detailed reports on Barrayarans of military or political significance . . . and their sons. Fact Two: he had a subtle mind. Fact Three . . . there was no fact three. Yet.

They returned to the party to find Ivan ensconced on a couch between the two women, entertaining them—or at least, they were laughing encouragingly. The ghem-women fully matched Lady Gelle in beauty; the blonde might have been her sister. The redhead was even more arresting, with a cascade of amber curls falling past her shoulders, a perfect nose, lips that one might . . . Miles cut off the thought. No ghem-lady was going to invite *him* to dive into her dreams.

Yenaro departed briefly to oversee his servant—he seemed to have only one—and expedite the smooth arrival of fresh food and drinks. He returned with a small transparent pitcher of a pale ruby liquid. "Lord Vorpatril," he nodded at Ivan. "I believe you appreciate your beverages. Do try this one."

Miles went to alert-status, his heart thumping. Yenaro might not be a sculptor-assassin, but he would undoubtedly make a great poisoner. Yenaro poured from the pitcher into three little cups on a lacquered tray, and extended the tray to Ivan.

"Thanks," Ivan selected one at random.

"Oh, zlati ale," murmured one of the junior ghem-lords. Yenaro passed the tray to him, and took the last cup himself. Ivan sipped and raised his brows in surprised approval. Miles watched closely to be sure Yenaro actually swallowed. He did. Five different methods for presenting deadly drinks with just that maneuver and still being sure the victim received the right one, including the trick of the host consuming the antidote first, flashed through Miles's mind. But if he was going to be that paranoid, they ought not have come here in the first place. Yet he'd eaten and drunk nothing himself so far. *So what are you going to do, wait and see if Ivan falls over first, and then try it?*

Yenaro did not, this time, pause to confide to the two women bracketing Ivan the repulsive biological history of his birth. Hell. Maybe the incident with the fountain really had been an accident, and the man was sorry, and trying his very best to make it up to the Barrayarans. Nevertheless, Miles circled in, trying to get a closer look at Ivan's cup over his shoulder.

Ivan was in the process of the classic *I'm just resting my arm along the back of this couch* test of the redhead on his right, to see if she was going to flinch from or invite further physical contact. Ivan swiveled his head to repel his cousin with a toothy smile. "Go have a good time, Miles," he murmured. "Relax. Stop breathing up my neck."

Miles grimaced back in non-appreciation of the height-humor, and drifted off again. Some people just didn't want to be saved. He decided instead to try to talk with some of Yenaro's male friends, several of whom were clustered at the opposite end of the room.

It wasn't hard to get them to talk about themselves. It seemed that was all they had to talk about. Forty minutes of valiant effort in the art of conversation convinced Miles that most of Yenaro's friends had the minds of fleas. The only expertise they displayed was in witty commentary upon the personal lives of their equally idle compatriots: their clothes, various love affairs and the mismanagement thereof, sports—all spectator, none participatory, and mainly of interest due to wagers on the outcome—and the assorted latest commercial feelie dreams and other offerings, including erotic ones. This retreat from reality seemed to absorb by far the bulk of the ghem-lordlings' time and attention. Not one of them offered a word about anything of political or military interest. Hell, *Ivan* had more mental clout.

It was all a bit depressing. Yenaro's friends were excluded men, wasted wastrels. No one was excited about a career or service—they had none. Even the arts received only a ripple of interest. They were strictly feelie dream consumers, not producers. All in all, it was probably a good thing these youths had no political interests. They were just the sort of people who started revolutions but could not finish them, their idealism betrayed by their incompetence. Miles had met similar young men among the Vor, third or fourth sons who for whatever reason had not gained entry to a traditional military career, living as pensioners upon their families, but even they could look forward to some change in their status by mid-life. Given the average ghem life span, any chance of ascent up the social ladder by inheritance was still some eighty or ninety years off for most of Yenaro's set. They weren't inherently stupid—their genetics did not permit it—but their minds were damped down to some artificial horizon. Beneath the air of hectic sophistication, their lives were frozen in place. Miles almost shivered.

Miles decided to try out the women, if Ivan had left any for him. He excused himself from the group to pursue a drink—he might have left without explanation just as easily, for all anyone seemed to care about Lord Yenaro's most unusual, and shortest, guest. Miles helped himself at a bowl from which everyone else seemed to be ladling their drinks, and touched the cup to his lips, but did not swallow. He looked up to find himself under the gaze of a slightly older woman who had come late to the party with a couple of friends, and who had been lingering quietly on the fringes of the gathering. She smiled at him.

Miles smiled back, and slid around the table to her side, composing a suitable opening line. She took the initiative from him.

"Lord Vorkosigan. Would you care to take a walk in the garden with me?"

"Why . . . certainly. Is Lord Yenaro's garden a sight to see?" *In the dark?*

"I think it will interest you." The smile dropped from her face as if wiped away with a cloth the moment she turned her back to the room, to be replaced with a look of grim determination. Miles fingered the comm link in his trouser pocket, and followed in the perfumed wake of her robes. Once out of sight of the room's glass doors among the neglected shrubbery, her step quickened. She said nothing more. Miles limped after her. He was unsurprised when they came to a red-enameled, square-linteled gate and found a person waiting, a slight, androgynous shape with a dark hooded robe protecting its bald head from the night's gathering dew.

"The ba will escort you the rest of the way," said the woman.

"The rest of the way where?"

"A short walk," the ba spoke in a soft alto.

"Very well." Miles held up a restraining hand, and drew his comm link from his pocket, and said into it, "Base. I'm leaving Yenaro's premises for a while. Track me, but don't interrupt me unless I call for you."

The driver's voice came back in a dubious tone. "Yes, my lord . . . where are you going?"

"I'm . . . taking a walk with a lady. Wish me luck."

"Oh." The driver's tone grew more amused, less dubious. "Good luck, my lord."

"Thank you." Miles closed the channel. "All right."

The woman seated herself on a rickety bench and

drew her robes around herself with the air of one preparing for a lengthy wait. Miles followed the ba out the gate and past another residence, across a road-way, and into a shallow wooded ravine. The ba pro-duced a hand-light to prevent stumbles on rocks and roots, politely playing it before Miles's polished boots, which were going to be a lot less polished if this went on very far . . . they climbed up out of the ravine into what was obviously the back portion of another sub-urban estate in an even more neglected condition than Yenaro's.

A dark bulk looming through the trees was an appar-ently deserted house. But they turned right on an over-grown path, the ba pausing to sweep damp branches out of Miles's way, and then back down toward the stream. They emerged in a wide clearing where a wooden pavilion stood—some ghem-lord's former favorite picnic spot for *al fresco* brunches, no doubt. Duckweed choked a pond, crowding out a few sad water-irises. They crossed the pond on an arched foot-bridge, which creaked so alarmingly Miles was momen-tarily glad he was no bigger. A faint, familiar pearlescent glow emanated from the pavilion's vine-veiled openings. Miles touched the Great Key hidden in his tunic, for reassurance. *Right. This is it.*

The ba servitor pulled aside some greenery, gestured Miles inside, and went to stand guard by the footbridge. Cautiously, Miles stepped within the small, one-roomed building.

The haut Rian Degtiar or a close facsimile sat, or stood, or something, the usual few centimeters above the floor, a blank pale sphere. She had to be riding in a float-chair. Her light seemed dimmed, stopped down to a furtive feeble glow. *Wait. Let her make the first move.* The moment stretched. Miles began to be afraid this conversation was going to be as disjointed as their first one, but then she spoke, in the same breathless, transmission-flattened voice he had heard before. "Lord Vorkosigan. I have contacted you as I said I would, to make arrangements for the safe return of my . . . thing."

"The Great Key," said Miles.

"You know what it is now?"

"I've been doing a little research, since our first chat."

She moaned. "What do you want of me? Money? I have none. Military secrets? I know none."

"Don't go coy on me, and don't panic. I want very little." Miles unfastened his tunic, and drew out the Great Key.

"Oh, you have it *here!* Oh, give it to me!" The pearl bobbed forward.

Miles stepped back. "Not so fast. I've kept it safe, and I'll give it back. But I feel I should get something in return. I merely want to know exactly how it came to be delivered, or mis-delivered, into my hands, and why."

"It's no business of yours, Barrayaran!"

"Perhaps not. But every instinct I own is crying out that this is some kind of setup, of me, or of Barrayar through me, and as a Barrayaran ImpSec officer that makes it very explicitly my business. I'm willing to tell you everything I saw and heard, but you must return the favor. To start with, I want to know what Ba Lura was doing with a piece of the late Empress's major regalia on a space station."

Her voice went low and tart. "Stealing it. Now give it back."

"A key. A key is not of great worth without a lock. I grant it's a pretty elegant historical artifact, but if Ba Lura was planning on a privately funded retirement, surely there are more valuable things to steal from the Celestial Garden. And ones less certain to be missed. Was Lura planning to blackmail you? Is that why you murdered it?" A completely absurd charge—the haut-lady and Miles were each other's alibis—but he was curious to see what it would stir up in the way of response.

The reaction was instantaneous. "You vile little—! I did not drive Lura to its death. If anything, you are responsible!"

God, I hope not. "This may be so, and if it is, *I must know.* Lady—there is no Cetagandan security within ten kilometers of us right now, or you could have them strip this bauble off me and dump my carcass in the nearest alleyway right now. Why not? *Why* did Ba Lura steal the Great Key—for its pleasure? The Ba makes a hobby of collecting Cetagandan Imperial regalia, does it?"

"You are horrible!"

"Then to whom was Ba Lura taking the thing to sell?"

"*Not* sell!"

"Ha! Then you know who!"

"Not exactly . . ." she hesitated. "Some secrets are not mine to give. They belong to the Celestial Lady."

"Whom you serve."

"Yes."

"Even in death."

"Yes." A note of pride edged her voice.

"And whom the Ba betrayed. Even in death."

"No! Not betrayed . . . We had a disagreement."

"An honest disagreement?"

"Yes."

"Between a thief and a murderess?"

"No!"

Quite so, but the accusation definitely had her going. Some guilt, there. *Yeah, tell me about guilt.* "Look, I'll make it easy for you. I'll begin. Ivan and I were coming over from the Barrayaran courier jump-ship in a personnel pod. We docked into this dump of a freight bay. The Ba Lura, wearing a station employee uniform and some badly applied false hair, lumbered into our pod as soon as the lock cycled open, and reached, we thought, for a weapon. We jumped it, and took away a nerve disruptor and this." Miles held up the Great Key. "The Ba shook us off and escaped, and I stuck this in my pocket till I could find out more. The next time I saw the Ba it was dead in a pool of its own blood on the floor of the funeral rotunda. I found this unnerving, to say the least. Now it's your turn. You say Ba Lura stole the key from your charge. When did you discover the Great Key was missing?"

"I found it missing from its place . . . that day."

"How long could it have been gone? When had you last checked it?"

"It is not being used every day now, because of the period of mourning for the Celestial Lady. I had last seen it when I arranged her regalia . . . two days before that."

"So potentially, it could have been missing for three days before you discovered its absence. When did the Ba go missing?"

"I'm . . . not sure. I saw Ba Lura the evening before."

"That cuts it down a little. So the Ba could have been gone with the key as early as the previous night. Do the ba servitors pass pretty freely in and out of the Celestial Garden, or is it hard?"

"Freely. They run all our errands."

"So Ba Lura came back . . . when?"

"The night of your arrival. But the Ba would not see me. It claimed to be sick. I could have had it dragged into my presence, but . . . I did not want to inflict such an indignity."

They were in it together, right.

"I went to see the Ba in the morning. The whole sorry story came out then. The Ba was trying to take the Great Key to . . . someone, and entered into the wrong docking bay."

"Then *someone* was supposed to supply a personnel pod? Then *someone* was waiting on a ship in orbit?"

"I didn't say that!"

Keep pressing her. It's working. Though it did make him feel faintly guilty, to be badgering the distraught old lady so, even if possibly for her own good. *Don't let up.* "So the Ba blundered onto our pod, and—what was the rest of its story? Tell me exactly!"

"Ba Lura was attacked by Barrayaran soldiers, who stole the Great Key."

"How many soldiers?"

"Six."

Miles's eyes widened in delight. "And then what?"

"Ba Lura begged for its life, and head and honor, but they laughed and ejected the Ba, and flew away."

Lies, lies at last. And yet . . . the Ba was only human. Anyone who had screwed up so hugely might re-tell the story so as to make themselves look less at fault. "What exactly did it say we said?"

Her voice grated with anger. "You insulted the Celestial Lady."

"Then what?"

"The Ba came home in shame."

"So . . . why didn't the Ba call on Cetagandan security to shake us down and get the Great Key back on the spot?"

There was a longer silence. Then she said, "The Ba could not do that. But it confessed to me. And I came to you. To . . . humble myself. And beg for the return of my . . . charge and my honor."

"Why didn't the Ba confess to you the night before?"

"I don't know!"

"So while you set about your retrieval task, Ba Lura cut its throat."

"In great grief and shame," she said lowly.

"Yeah? Why not at least wait to see if you could coax the key back from me? So why not cut its throat privately, in its own quarters? Why advertise its shame to the entire galactic community? Isn't that a bit *unusual*? Was the Ba supposed to attend the bier-gifting ceremony?"

"Yes."

"And you were too?"

"Yes . . ."

"And you believed the Ba's story?"

"Yes!"

"Lady, I think you are lost in the woods. Let me tell you what happened in the personnel pod as *I* saw it. There were no six soldiers. Just me, my cousin, and the pod pilot. There was no conversation, no begging or pleading, no slurs on the Celestial Lady. Ba Lura just yelped, and ran off. It didn't even fight very hard. In fact, it scarcely fought us at all. Strange, don't you think, in a hand-to-hand struggle for something so important that the Ba slit its own throat over its loss the next day? We were left scratching our heads, holding the damned thing and wondering what the hell? Now you know that one of us, me or the Ba, is lying. I know which one."

"Give the Great Key to me," was all she could say. "It's not yours."

"But I think I was framed. By someone who apparently wants to drag Barrayar into a Cetagandan internal . . . disagreement. *Why?* What am I being set up *for*?"

Her silence might indicate that these were the first new thoughts to penetrate her panic in two days. Or . . . it might not. In any case, she only whispered, "Not yours!"

Miles sighed. "I couldn't agree with you more, milady, and I am glad to return your charge. But in light of the whole situation, I would like to be able to testify—under fast-penta, if need be—just *who* I gave the Great Key back to. You could be anyone, in that bubble. My Aunt Alys, for all I know. Or Cetagandan security, or . . . who knows. I will return it to you . . . face-to-face." He held out his hand half-open, the key resting invitingly across his palm.

"Is that . . . the last of your price?"

"Yes. I'll ask no more."

It was a small triumph. He was going to see a haut-woman, and Ivan wasn't. It would doubtless embarrass the old dragon, to reveal herself to outlander eyes, but dammit, given the runaround Miles had suffered, she owed him something. And he was deathly serious about being able to identify where the Great Key went. The haut Rian Degtiar, Handmaiden of the Star Crèche, was certainly not the only player in this game.

"Very well," she whispered. The white bubble faded to transparency, and was gone from between them.

"Oh," said Miles, in a very small voice.

She sat in a float-chair, clothed from slender neck to ankle in flowing robes of shining white, a dozen shimmering textures lying one atop another. Her hair glinted ebony, masses of it that poured down across her shoulders, past her lap, to coil around her feet. When she stood, it would trail on the floor like a banner. Her enormous eyes were an ice blue of such arctic purity as to make Lady Gelle's eyes look like mud-puddles. Skin . . . Miles felt he had never seen skin before, just blotched bags people wore around themselves to keep from leaking. This perfect ivory surface . . . his hands ached with the desire to touch it, just once, and die. Her lips were warm, as if roses pulsed with blood. . . .

How old was she? Twenty? Forty? This was a haut-woman. Who could tell? Who could care? Men of the old religion had worshipped on their knees icons far less glorious, in beaten silver and hammered gold. Miles was on his knees now, and could not remember how he'd come to be there.

He knew now why they called it "falling in love." There was the same nauseating vertigo of free fall, the same vast exhilaration, the same sick certainty of broken bones upon impact with a rapidly rising reality. He inched forward, and laid the Great Key in front of her perfectly shaped, white-slippered feet, and sank back, and waited.

I am Fortune's fool.

CHAPTER SIX

She bent forward, one graceful hand darting down to retrieve her solemn charge. She laid the Great Key in her lap, and pulled a long necklace from beneath her layered white garments. The chain held a ring, decorated with a thick raised bird-pattern, the gold lines of electronic contacts gleaming like filigree upon its surface. She inserted the ring into the seal atop the rod. Nothing happened.

Her breath drew in. She glared down at Miles. "What have you done to it!"

"Milady, I, I . . . nothing, I swear by my word as Vorkosigan! I didn't even drop it. What's . . . supposed to happen?"

"It should open."

"Um . . . um . . ." He would break into a desperate sweat, but he was too damned cold. He was dizzy with the scent of her, and the celestial music of her unfiltered voice. "There are only three possibilities, if there's something wrong with it. Someone broke it—not me, I swear!" Could that have been the secret of Ba Lura's peculiar intrusion? Maybe the Ba had broken it, and had been seeking a scapegoat upon whom to shuffle the blame? "—or someone's re-programmed it, or, least likely, there's been some kind of substitution pulled. A duplicate, or, or . . ."

Her eyes widened, and her lips parted, moving in some subvocalization.

"*Not* least likely?" Miles hazarded. "It would surely be the most difficult, but . . . it crosses my mind that maybe someone didn't think you would be getting it back from me. If it's a counterfeit, maybe it was meant to be on its way to Barrayar in a diplomatic pouch right now. Or . . . or something." No, that didn't quite make sense, but . . .

She sat utterly still, her face tense with panic, her hands clutching the rod.

"Milady, talk to me. If it's a duplicate, it's obviously a very good duplicate. You now have it, to turn over at the ceremony. So what if it doesn't work? Who's going to check the function of some obsolete piece of electronics?"

"The Great Key is not obsolete. We used it every day."

"It's some kind of data link, right? You have a time-window, here. Nine days. If you think it's been compromised, wipe it and re-program it from your backup files. If that thing in your hand is some kind of a non-working dummy, you've maybe got time to make a real duplicate, and re-program *it*." *But don't just sit there with death in your lovely eyes.* "Talk to me!"

"I must do as Ba Lura did," she whispered. "The Ba was right. This is the end."

"No, why?! It's just a, a *thing*, who cares? Not me!"

She held up the rod, her arctic-blue eyes fixing on his face at last. Her gaze made him want to scuttle into the shadows like a crab, to hide his merely human ugliness, but he held fast before her. "There is no backup," she said. "This is the sole key."

Miles felt faint, and it wasn't just from her perfume. "No backup?" he choked. "Are you people *crazy*?"

"It is a matter of . . . control."

"What does the damn thing really do, anyway?"

She hesitated, then said, "It is the data-key to the haut gene bank. All the frozen genetic samples are stored in a randomized order, for security. Without the key, no one knows what is where. To re-create the files, someone would have to physically examine and re-classify each and every sample. There are hundreds of thousands of samples—one for every haut who has ever lived. It would take an army of geneticists working for a generation to re-create the Great Key."

"This is a real disaster, then, huh?" he said brightly, blinking. His teeth gritted. "Now I *know* I was framed." He climbed to his feet, and threw back his head, defying the onslaught of her beauty. "Lady, what is *really* going on here? I'll ask you one more time, with feeling. What in God's green ninety hells was the Ba Lura *ever* doing with the Great Key on a *space station*?"

"No outlander may—"

"*Somebody made* it my business! Sucked me right into it. I don't think I could escape now if I tried. And I think . . . you need an ally. It took you a day and a half just to arrange this second meeting with me. Nine days left. You don't have *time* to go it alone. You need . . . a trained security man. And for some strange reason, you don't seem to want to get one from your own side."

She rocked, just slightly, in frozen misery, in a faint rustle of fabrics.

"If you don't think I'm worthy of being let in on your secrets," Miles went on wildly, "then explain to me how you think I could possibly make things any *worse* than they are right now!"

Her blue eyes searched him, for he knew not what. But he thought if she asked him to open his veins for her, right here and now, the only thing he'd say would be *How wide?*

"It was my Celestial Lady's desire," she began fearfully, and stopped.

Miles clutched at his shredded self-control. Everything she'd spilled so far was either obviously deducible, or common knowledge, at least in her milieu. Now she was getting to the good stuff, and knew it. He could tell by the way she'd stalled out.

"Milady." He chose his words with extreme care. "If the Ba did not commit suicide, it was certainly murdered." *And we both have good reason to prefer the second scenario.* "Ba Lura was your servitor, your colleague . . . dare I guess, friend? I saw its body in the rotunda. A very dangerous and daring person arranged that hideous tableau. There was . . . a deep mischief and mockery in it."

Was that pain, in those cool eyes? So hard to tell . . .

"I have old and very personal reasons to particularly dislike being made the unwitting target of persons of cruel humor. I don't know if you can understand this."

"Perhaps . . ." she said slowly.

Yes. Look past the surface. See me, not this joke of a body. . . . "And I am the one person on Eta Ceta *you know* didn't do it. It's the only certainty we share, so far. I claim a *right* to know who's doing this to us. And the only chance in hell I have to figure out who, is to know exactly *why*."

Still she sat silent.

"I already know enough to destroy you," Miles added earnestly. "Tell me enough to save you!"

Her sculpted chin rose in bleak decision. When she blessed him with her outward attention at last, it was total and terrifying. "It was a long-standing disagreement." He strained to hear, to keep his head clear, to concentrate on the words and not just on the enchanting melody of her voice. "Between the Celestial Lady and the Emperor. My Lady had long thought that the haut gene bank was too centralized, in the heart of the

Celestial Garden. She favored the dispersal of copies, for safety. My Lord favored keeping it all under his personal protection—for safety. They both sought the good of the haut, each in their own way."

"I see," Miles murmured, encouraging her with as much delicacy as he could muster. "All good guys here, right."

"The Emperor forbade her plan. But as she neared the end of her life . . . she came to feel that her loyalty to the haut must outweigh her loyalty to her son. Twenty years ago, she began to have copies made, in secret."

"A large project," Miles said.

"Huge, and slow. But she brought it to fruition."

"How many copies?"

"Eight. One for each of the planetary satraps."

"Exact copies?"

"Yes. I have reason to know. I have been the Celestial Lady's supervisor of geneticists for five years, now."

"Ah. So you are something of a trained scientist. You know about . . . extreme care. And scrupulous honesty."

"How else should I serve my Lady?" she shrugged.

But you don't know much, I'll bet, about covert ops chicanery. Hm. "If there are eight exact copies, there must be eight exact Great Keys, right?"

"No. Not yet. My Lady was saving the duplication of the key to the last moment. A matter of—"

"Control," Miles finished smoothly. "How did I guess?"

A faint flash of resentment at his humor sparked in her eyes, and Miles bit his tongue. It was no laughing matter to haut Rian Degtiar.

"The Celestial Lady knew her time was drawing near. She made me and the Ba Lura the executors of her will in this matter. We were to deliver the copies of the gene bank to each of the eight satrap governors upon the occasion of her funeral, which they would be certain to all attend together. But . . . she died more suddenly than she had expected. She had not yet made arrangements for the duplication of the Great Key. It was a problem of considerable technical and cipher skill, as all of the Empire's resources went into its original creation. Ba Lura and I had all her instructions for the banks, but nothing for how the key was to be duplicated and delivered, or even when she had planned this to happen. The Ba and I were not sure what to do."

"Ah," Miles said faintly. He dared not offer any comment at all, for fear of impeding the free flow, at last, of information. He hung on her words, barely breathing.

"Ba Lura thought . . . if we took the Great Key to one of the satrap governors, he might use his resources to duplicate it for us. I thought this was a very dangerous idea. Because of the temptation to take it exclusively for himself."

"Ah . . . excuse me. Let me see if I follow this. I know you consider the haut gene bank a most private matter, but what are the *political* side-effects of setting up new haut reproductive centers on each of Cetaganda's eight satrap planets?"

"The Celestial Lady thought the empire had ceased to grow at the time of the defeat of the Barrayar expedition. That we had become static, stagnant, enervated. She thought . . . if the empire could only undergo mitosis, like a cell, the haut might start to grow again, become re-energized. With the splitting of the gene bank, there would be eight new centers of authority for expansion."

"Eight new potential Imperial capitals?" Miles whispered.

"Yes, I suppose."

Eight new centers . . . civil war was only the beginning of the possibilities. Eight new Cetagandan Empires, each expanding like killer coral at their

neighbors' expense . . . a nightmare of cosmic propor-
tions. "I think I can see," said Miles carefully, "why perhaps the Emperor was less than enthused by his
mother's admittedly sound biological reasoning. Something to be said on both sides, don't you think?"

"I serve the Celestial Lady," said the haut Rian
Degtiar simply, "and the haut genome. The Empire's
short-term political adjustments are not my business."

"So all this, ah, genetic shuffling . . . would the
Cetagandan Emperor, by chance, regard this as treason on your part?"

"How?" said the haut Rian Degtiar. "It was my duty
to obey the Celestial Lady."

"Oh."

"The eight satrap governors have all committed treason in it, though," she added matter-of-factly.

"*Have* committed?"

"They all took delivery of their gene banks last week
at the welcoming banquet. Ba Lura and I succeeded
in that part of the Celestial Lady's plan, at least."

"Treasure chests for which none of them have keys."

"I . . . don't know. Each of them, you see . . . the
Celestial Lady felt it would be better if each of the
satrap governors thought that he alone was the recipient of the new copy of the haut gene bank. Each would
strive better to keep it secret, that way."

"Do you know—I have to ask this." *I'm just not sure
I want to hear the answer.* "Do you know to *which* of
the eight satrap governors Ba Lura was trying to take
the Great Key for duplication, when it ran into us?"

"No," she said.

"Ah," Miles exhaled in pure satisfaction. "Now, *now*
I know why I was set up. And why the Ba died."

Fine lines appeared on her ivory brow as she stared
at him.

"Don't you see it too? The Ba didn't hit us
Barrayarans on the way out. It hit us on the way *back*.

Your Ba was suborned. Ba Lura *did* take the key to
one of the satrap governors, and received in return not
a true copy, because there was no time for the extensive
decoding required, but a decoy. Which the Ba then was
sent to deliberately lose to us. Which it did, although
not, I suspect, in quite the manner it had originally
planned." *Almost certainly not as planned.*

He found himself pacing, keyed up and hectic. He
ought not to limp before her, it brought attention to
his deformities, but he could not keep still. "And while
everybody is off chasing Barrayarans, the satrap governor quietly goes home with the only real copy of
the Great Key, getting a large jump-start on the haut-
competition. After first arranging the Ba's reward for
its double-treason, and incidentally eliminating the only
witness to the truth. Oh. Yes. It works. Or it would
have worked, if only . . . the satrap governor had
remembered that no battle-plan survives first contact
with the enemy." *Not when the enemy is me.* He stared
into her eyes, willing her to believe in him, striving
not to melt. "How soon can you analyze this Great
Key, and support or explode these theories?"

"I will examine it immediately, tonight. But whatever
has been done to it, my examination will not tell me
who did it, Barrayaran." Her voice grew glacial with
this thought. "I doubt you could have created a true
duplicate, but a non-working forgery is certainly within
your capabilities. If this one is false—where is the real
one?"

"It seems that is just what I must discover, milady,
to, to clear my name. To redeem my honor in your
eyes." The intrinsic fascination of an intellectual puzzle
had brought him to this interview. He'd thought curiosity was his strongest driving force, till suddenly his
whole personality had become engaged. It was like
being under—no, like *becoming* an avalanche. "If I can
discover this, will you . . ." *what*? Look favorably upon

his suit? Despise him for an outlander barbarian all the same? " . . . let me see you again?"

"I don't . . . know." Reminded, her hand drifted to the control on her float-chair for the concealing force-screen.

No, no, don't go. . . . "We must have some way of communicating," he said hastily, before she could disappear again behind that faintly humming barrier.

Her head tilted, considering this. She drew a small comm link from her robes. It was undecorated, utilitarian, but like the nerve disruptor he'd taken from Ba Lura perfectly designed in what Miles was beginning to recognize as the haut style. She whispered a command into it. In a moment, the androgynous ba appeared from its guard post beside the pond. Did its eyes widen just slightly, to see its mistress without her shell?

"Give me your comm link, and wait outside," haut Rian Degtiar ordered.

The little ba nodded, and turned the device over to her without question, and withdrew silently.

She held the comm link out to Miles. "I use this to communicate with my senior servitors, when they run errands outside the Celestial Garden for me. Here."

He wanted to touch her, but scarcely dared. He instead extended his cupped hands toward her like a shy man offering flowers to a goddess. She dropped the comm link into them gingerly, as into the hands of a leper. Or an enemy.

"Is it secured?" he dared to ask.

"Temporarily."

In other words, it was the lady's private line only as long as no one in higher-level Cetagandan security troubled to break in. Right. He sighed. "It won't work. You can't send signals into my embassy without causing my superiors to ask a whole lot of questions I'd rather not answer just now. And I can't give you my comm link either. I'm supposed to turn it in, and I don't think I can get away with telling them I lost it." Reluctantly, he handed the link back to her. "But we have to meet again somehow." *Yes, oh yes.* "If I'm going to be risking my reputation and maybe my life on the validity of my reasoning, I'd like to prop it up with a few facts." One fact was almost certain. Someone with enough wit and nerve to murder one of the most senior Imperial servitors under the nose of Cetaganda's own emperor would hardly balk at threatening a decidedly un-senior female Degtiar. The thought was obscene, hideous. A Barrayaran scion's diplomatic immunity would be an even more useless shield, no doubt, but that was merely the price of the game. "I think you could be in grave danger. It might be better to play along for a bit—don't reveal to anyone you have obtained this key from me. I have a funny feeling I'm not following his script, y'see." He paced nervously back and forth before her. "If you can find out anything at all about Ba Lura's real activities in the few days before it died—don't run afoul of your own security, though. They have to be following up on the Ba's death."

"I will . . . contact you when and how I can, Barrayaran." Slowly, one pale hand caressed the control pad on the arm of the float-chair, and a dim gray mist coalesced around her like a fairy spell of seeming.

The ba servitor returned to the pavilion to escort not Miles but its mistress away. Miles was left to stumble back through the dark to Yenaro's estate alone.

It was raining.

Miles was not surprised to find that the ghem-woman was no longer waiting on the bench by the red-enameled gate. He let himself in quietly, and paused just outside the lighted garden doors to brush as many of the water droplets as possible off his formal blacks, and to wipe his face. He then sacrificed the handkerchief to the redemption of his boots, and quietly dropped the sodden object behind a bush. He slipped back inside.

No one noticed his entry. The party was continuing, a little louder, with a few new faces replacing some of the previous ones. The Cetagandans did not use alcohol for inebriation, but some of the guests had a late-party dissociated air about them similar to over-indulgers Miles had witnessed at home. If intelligent conversation had been difficult before, it was clearly hopeless now. He felt himself no better off than the ghemlings, drunk on information, dizzy with intrigue. *Everyone to their own secret addictions, I suppose.* He wanted to collect Ivan and escape, as swiftly as possible, before his head exploded.

"Ah, there you are, Lord Vorkosigan." Lord Yenaro appeared at Miles's elbow, looking faintly anxious. "I could not find you."

"I took a long walk with a lady," Miles said. Ivan was nowhere to be seen. "Where is my cousin?"

"Lord Vorpatril is taking a tour of the house with Lady Arvan and Lady Bennello," said Yenaro. He glanced through a wide archway at the room's opposite side, which framed a spiral staircase in a hall beyond. "They've been gone . . . an astonishingly long time." Yenaro's smile attempted to be knowing, but came out oddly puzzled. "Since before you . . . I don't quite . . . ah, well. Would you care for a drink?"

"Yes, please," said Miles distractedly. He took it from Yenaro's hand and gulped without hesitation. His eyes almost crossed, considering the possibilities of Ivan plus two beautiful ghem-women. Though to his haut-dazzled senses, all the ghem-women in the room looked as coarse and dull as backcountry slatterns just now. The effect would wear off with time, he hoped. He dreaded the thought of his own next encounter with a mirror. What had the haut Rian Degtiar seen, looking at him? A simian black-clad gnome, twitching and babbling? He pulled up a chair and sat rather abruptly, the spiral staircase bracketed in his sights. *Ivan, hurry up!*

Yenaro lingered by his side, and began a disjointed conversation about proportional theories of architecture through history, art and the senses, and the natural esters trade on Barrayar, but Miles swore the man was as focused on the staircase as he was. Miles finished his first drink and most of a second before Ivan appeared in the shadows at the top of the stairs.

Ivan hesitated in the dimness, his hand checking the fit of his green uniform, which appeared fully assembled. Or re-assembled. He was alone. He descended with one hand clutching the curving rail, which floated without apparent support in echo of the stair's arc. He jerked a stiff frown into a stiff smile before entering the main room and the light. His head swiveled till he spotted Miles, toward whom he made a straight line.

"Lord Vorpatril," Yenaro greeted him. "You had a long tour. Did you see everything?"

Ivan bared his teeth. "Everything. Even the light."

Yenaro's smile did not slip, but his eyes seemed to fill with questions. "I'm . . . so glad." A guest called to him from across the room, and Yenaro was momentarily distracted.

Ivan bent down to whisper behind his hand into Miles's ear, "Get us the hell out of here. I think I've been poisoned."

Miles looked up, startled. "D'you want to call down the lightflyer?"

"No. Just back to the embassy in the groundcar."

"But—"

"*No*, dammit," Ivan hissed. "Just quietly. Before that smirking bastard goes upstairs." He nodded toward

Yenaro, who was now standing at the foot of the staircase, gazing upward.

"I take it you don't think it is acute."

"Oh, it was cute all right," Ivan snarled.

"You didn't murder anybody up there, did you?"

"No. But I thought they'd *never* . . . Tell you in the
car."

"You'd better." Miles clambered to his feet. They
perforce had to pass Yenaro, who attached himself to
them like a good host, and saw them to his front door
with suitably polite farewells. Ivan's good-byes might
have been etched in acid.

As soon as the canopy sealed over their heads, Miles
commanded, "Give, Ivan!"

Ivan settled back, still seething. "I was set up."

This comes as a surprise to you, coz? "By Lady Arvan
and Lady Benello?"

"They *were* the setup. Yenaro was behind it, I'm sure
of it. You're right about that damned fountain being
a trap, Miles, I see it now. Beauty as bait, all over
again."

"What happened to you?"

"You know all those rumors about Cetagandan aph-
rodisiacs?"

"Yes . . ."

"Well, sometime this evening that son-of-a-bitch
Yenaro slipped me an *anti*-aphrodisiac."

"Um . . . are you sure? I mean, there are natural
causes for these moments, I'm told. . . ."

"It was a *setup*. I didn't seduce them, they seduced
me! Wafted me upstairs to this amazing room—it had
to have been all arranged in advance. God, it was, it
was . . ." His voice broke in a sigh, "it was *glorious*.
For a little while. And then I realized I couldn't, like,
perform."

"What did you do?"

"It was too late to get out gracefully. So I winged it. It was all I could do to keep 'em from noticing."

"*What?*"

"I made up a lot of instant barbarian folklore—I told 'em a Vor prides himself on self-control, that it's not considered polite on Barrayar for a man to, you know, before his lady has. Three times. It was considered insulting to her. I stroked, I rubbed, I scratched, I recited poetry, I nuzzled and nibbled and—cripes, my fingers are cramped." His speech was a bit slurred, too, Miles noticed. "I thought they'd *never* fall asleep." Ivan paused; a slow smirk displaced the snarl on his face. "But they were smiling, when they finally did." The smirk faded into a look of bleak dismay. "What do you want to bet those two are the biggest female ghem-gossips on Eta Ceta?"

"No takers here," said Miles, fascinated. *Let the punishment fit the crime.* Or, in this case, the trap fit the prey. Someone had studied his weaknesses. And someone just as clearly had studied Ivan's. "We could have the ImpSec office do a data sweep for the tale, over the next few days."

"If you breathe a *word* of this I'll wring your scrawny neck! If I can find it."

"You've got to confess to the embassy physician. Blood tests—"

"Oh, yes. I want a chemical scan the instant I hit the door. What if the effect's *permanent?*"

"Ba Vorpatril?" Miles intoned, eyes alight.

"Dammit, I didn't laugh at *you.*"

"No. That's true, you didn't," Miles sighed. "I expect the physician will find whatever it was metabolizes rapidly. Or Yenaro wouldn't have drunk the stuff himself."

"You think?"

"Remember the zlati ale? I'd bet my ImpSec silver eyes that was the vector."

Ivan relaxed slightly, obviously relieved at this

professional analysis. After a minute he added, "Yenaro's done you now, and he's done me. Third time's a charm. What's next, do you suppose? And can we do him first?"

Miles was silent for a long time. "That depends," he said at last, "on whether Yenaro's merely amusing himself, or whether he too is being . . . set up. And on whether there's any connection between Yenaro's backer and the death of Ba Lura."

"Connection? What possible connection?"

"We are the connection, Ivan. A couple of Barrayaran backcountry boys come to the big city, and ripe for the plucking. Somebody is using us. And I think somebody . . . has just made a major mistake in his choice of tools." *Or fools.*

Ivan stared at his venomous tone. "Have you got rid of that little toy you're packing yet?" he demanded suspiciously.

"Yes . . . and no."

"Oh, *shit.* I *knew* better than to trust—what the hell do you mean by *Yes and no*? Either you have or you haven't, right?"

"The object has been returned, yes."

"That's that, then."

"No. Not quite."

"*Miles* . . . You had better start talking to me."

"Yes, I think I better had," Miles sighed. They were approaching the legation district. "After you're done in the infirmary, I have a few confessions to make. But if—when—you talk to the ImpSec night-duty officer about Yenaro, don't mention the other. Yet."

"Oh?" drawled Ivan in a tone of deep suspicion.

"Things have gotten . . . complex."

"You think they were simple before?"

"I mean complex beyond the scope of mere security concerns, into genuine diplomatic ones. Of extreme delicacy. Maybe too delicate to submit to the sort of

booted paranoids who sometimes end up running local
ImpSec offices. That's a judgment call . . . that I'll have
to make myself. When I'm sure I'm ready. But this isn't
a game anymore, and it's no longer feasible for me to
run without backup." *I need help, God help me.*

"We knew *that* yesterday."

"Oh, yes. But it's even deeper than I first thought."

"Over our heads?"

Miles hesitated, and smiled sourly. "I don't know,
Ivan. How good are you at treading water?"

Alone in his suite's bathroom, Miles slowly peeled
off his black House uniform, now in desperate need
of attention from the embassy's laundry. He glanced
at himself sideways in the mirror, then resolutely looked
away. He considered the problem, as he stood in the
shower. To the haut, all normal humans doubtless
looked like some lower life-form. From the haut Rian
Degtiar's foreshortened perspective, perhaps there was
little to choose between him and, say, Ivan.

And ghem-lords did win haut wives, from time to
time, for great deeds. And the Vor and the ghem-lords
were very much alike. Even Maz had said so.

How great a deed? *Very great.* Well . . . he'd always
wanted to save the Empire. The Cetagandan just wasn't
the empire he'd pictured, was all. Life was like that,
always throwing you curveballs.

*You've gone mad, you know. To hope, to even think
it . . .*

If he defeated the late Dowager Empress's plot,
might the Cetagandan emperor be grateful enough
to . . . give him Rian's hand? If he advanced the
late Dowager Empress's plot, might the haut Rian
Degtiar be grateful enough to . . . give him her love?
To do both simultaneously would be a tactical feat
of supernatural scope.

Barrayar's interests lay, unusually, squarely with the

interests of the Cetagandan emperor. Obviously, it was his clear ImpSec duty to foil the girl and save the villain.

Right. My head hurts.

Reason was returning to him, slowly, the astonishing effect of the haut Rian Degtiar wearing off. Wasn't it? She hadn't exactly tried to suborn him, after all. Even if Rian was as ugly as the witch Baba Yaga, he'd still have to be following up on this. To a point. He needed to prove Barrayar had not filched the Great Key, and the only certain way of doing *that* was to find its real thief. He wondered if one could get a hangover from excess passion. If so, his was apparently starting while he was still drunk, which did not seem quite fair.

Eight Cetagandan satrap governors had been led into treason by the late empress. Optimistic, to think that only *one* could be a murderer. But only one possessed the real Great Key.

Lord X? Seven chances of guessing wrong, against one of guessing right. Not favorable odds.

I'll . . . figure something out.

CHAPTER SEVEN

Ivan was taking a long time, downstairs in the infirmary. Miles shucked on his black fatigues and, barefoot, fired up his comconsole for a quick review of the
eight haut-lord satrap governors.

The satrap governors were all chosen from a pool of
men who were close Imperial relations, half-brothers
and uncles and great-uncles, in both paternal and mater-
nal lines. Two current office-holders were of the Degtiar
constellation. Each ruled his satrapy for a set term of
only five years, then he was required to shift—sometimes to permanent retirement back at the capital on
Eta Ceta, sometimes to another satrapy. A couple of
the older and more experienced men had cycled this
way through the entire empire. The purpose of the term
limitation, of course, was to prevent the build-up of a
personal local power base to anyone who might harbor
secret Imperial pretensions. So far so sensible.

So . . . which among them had been tempted into
hubris by the dowager empress, and Ba Lura? For that
matter, how had she contacted them all? If she'd been
working on her plan for twenty years, she'd had lots
of time . . . still, that long ago, how could she have predicted which men would be satrap governors on the

unknown date of her death? The governors must have
all been brought into the plot quite recently.

Miles stared narrow-eyed at the list of his eight suspects. *I have to cut this down somehow. Several
somehows.* If he assumed Lord X had personally murdered the Ba Lura, he could eliminate the weakest and
most fragile elderly men . . . a premature assumption.
Any of the haut-lords might possess a ghem-guard both
loyal and capable enough to be delegated the task,
while the satrap governor lingered front and center in
the bier-gifting ceremonies, his alibi established before
dozens of witnesses.

No disloyalty to Barrayar intended, but Miles found
himself wishing he were a Cetagandan security man
right now—specifically, the one in charge of whatever
investigation was progressing on Ba Lura's supposed
suicide. But there was no way he could insert himself inconspicuously into that data flow. And he wasn't
sure Rian had the mind-set for it, not to mention the
urgent necessity of keeping Cetagandan security's attention as far from her as possible. Miles sighed in frustration.

It wasn't his task to solve the Ba's murder anyway.
It was his task to locate the real Great Key. Well, he
knew in general where it was—in orbit, aboard one of
the satrap governors' flagships. How else to finger the
right one?

A chime at his door interrupted his furious meditations. He hastily shut down the comconsole and called,
"Enter."

Ivan trod within, looking extremely dyspeptic.

"How did it go?" Miles asked, waving him to a chair.
Ivan dragged a heavy and comfortable armchair up to
the comconsole, and flung himself across it sideways,
scowling. He was still wearing his undress greens.

"You were right. It was taken by mouth, and it metabolizes rapidly. Not so rapidly that our medics couldn't

get a sample, though." Ivan rubbed his arm. "They said it would have been untraceable by morning."

"No permanent harm done, then."

"Except to my reputation. Your Colonel Vorreedi just blew in, I thought you might like to know. At least *he* took me seriously. We had a long talk just now about Lord Yenaro. Vorreedi didn't strike me as a booted paranoid, by the way." Ivan let the implication, *So hadn't you better go see him?*, hang in the air; Miles left it there.

"Good. I think. You didn't mention, ah—?"

"Not yet. But if you don't cough up some explanations, I'm going back to him for another pass."

"Fair enough." Miles sighed, and steeled himself. As briefly as the complications permitted, he summed up his conversation with the haut Rian Degtiar for Ivan, leaving out only a description of her incredible beauty, and his own stunned response to it. *That* was not Ivan's business. That *especially* was not Ivan's business.

" . . . so it seems to me," Miles ran down at last, "that the only way we can certainly prove that Barrayar had nothing to do with it is to find which satrap governor has the real Great Key." He pointed orbit-ward.

Ivan's eyes were round, his mouth screwed up in an expression of total dismay. "We? We? Miles, we've only been here for two and a half days, how did *we* get put in charge of the Cetagandan Empire? Isn't this *Cetagandan* security's job?"

"Would you trust them to clear us of blame?" Miles shrugged, and forged on into Ivan's hesitation. "We only have nine days left. I've thought of three strings that could maybe lead us back to the right man. Yenaro is one of them. A few more words in our protocol officer's ear could put the machinery of ImpSec here into tracing Yenaro's connections, without bringing up the matter of the Great Key. Yet. The next string is Ba Lura's murder, and I haven't figured out how I can pull that one. Yet. The other string lies in astro-political analysis, and that I *can* do. Look." On the comconsole, Miles called up a schematic three-dimensional map of the Cetagandan empire, its wormhole routes, and its immediate neighbors.

"The Ba Lura could have foisted that decoy key onto any number of outlander delegations. Instead, it picked Barrayarans, or rather, its satrap-governor master did. Why?"

"Maybe we were the only ones there at the right time," Ivan suggested.

"Mm. I'm trying to *reduce* the random factors, please. If Yenaro's backer is the same as our man, we were picked in advance to be framed. Now." He waved at the map. "Picture a scenario where the Cetagandan empire breaks apart and the pieces begin an attempt to expand. Which, if any, benefit from trouble with Barrayar?"

Ivan's brows went up, and he leaned forward, staring at the glowing array of spheres and lines above the vid plate.

"Well . . . Rho Ceta is positioned to expand toward Komarr, or would be, if we weren't sitting on two thirds of the wormhole jumps between. Mu Ceta just got a bloody nose, administered by us, when it attempted to expand past Vervain into the Hegen Hub. Those are the two most obvious. These other three," Ivan pointed, "and Eta Ceta itself are all interior, I don't see any benefit to them."

"Then there's the other side of the nexus," Miles waved at the display. "Sigma Ceta, bordering the Vega Station groups. And Xi Ceta, giving onto Marilac. If they were seeking to break out, it might be expedient for them to have the empire's military resources tied up far away against Barrayar."

"Four out of eight. It's a start," Ivan conceded.

Ivan's analysis matched his own, then. Well, they'd

both had the same strategic training, it stood to reason. Still Miles was obscurely comforted. It wasn't all the hallucination of his own over-driven imagination, if Ivan could see it too.

"It's a triangulation," said Miles. "If I can get any of the other lines of investigation to eliminate even part of the list, the final overlap ought to . . . well, it would be *nice* if it all came down to one."

"And then what?" Ivan demanded doggedly, his brows drawn down in suspicion. "What do you have in mind for *us* to do then?"

"I'm . . . not sure. But I do think you'd agree that a quiet conclusion to this mess would be preferable to a splashy one, eh?"

"Oh, yeah." Ivan chewed on his lower lip, eyeing the wormhole nexus map. "So when *do* we report?"

"Not . . . yet. But I think we'd better start documenting it all. Personal logs." So that anybody who came after them—Miles trusted not posthumously, but that was the unspoken thought—would at least have a chance of unraveling the events.

"I've been doing *that* since the first day," Ivan informed him grimly. "It's locked in my valise."

"Oh. Good." Miles hesitated. "When you talked to Colonel Vorreedi, did you plant the idea that Yenaro had a high-placed backer?"

"Not exactly."

"I'd like you to talk to him again, then. Try to direct his attention toward the satrap governors, somehow."

"Why don't you talk to him?"

"I'm . . . not ready. Not yet, not tonight. I'm still assimilating it all. And technically, he is my ImpSec superior here, or would be, if I were on active duty. I'd like to limit my, um . . ."

"Outright lies to him?" Ivan completed sweetly.

Miles grimaced, but did not deny it. "Look, I have an *access* in this matter that no other ImpSec officer

could, due to my social position. I don't want to see
the opportunity wasted. But it also limits me—I can't
get at the routine legwork, the down-and-dirty details
I need, I'm too conspicuous. I have to play to my own
strengths, and get others to play to my weaknesses."

Ivan sighed. "All right. I'll talk to him. Just this once."
With a tired grunt, he heaved himself out of his chair,
and wandered toward the door. He looked back over
his shoulder. "The trouble, coz, with your playing the
spider in the center of this web, pulling all the strings,
is that sooner or later all the interested parties are going
to converge back along those strings to you. You do
realize that, don't you? And what are you going to do
then, O Mastermind?" He bowed himself out with all-
too-effective irony.

Miles hunched down in his station chair, and
groaned, and keyed up his list again.

The next morning, Ambassador Vorob'yev was called
away from what was becoming his customary breakfast with Barrayar's young envoys in his private dining
room. By the time he returned, Miles and Ivan had
finished eating.

The ambassador did not sit down again, but instead
favored Miles with a bemused look. "Lord Vorkosigan.
You have an unusual visitor."

Miles's heart leapt. *Rian, here? Impossible . . .* His
mind did a quick involuntary review of his undress
greens, yes, his insignia were on straight, his fly was
fastened—"Who, sir?"

"Ghem-colonel Dag Benin, of Cetagandan Imperial
Security. He is an officer of middle rank assigned to
internal affairs at the Celestial Garden, and he wants
to speak privately with you."

Miles tried not to hyperventilate. *What's gone
wrong . . . ? Maybe nothing, yet. Calm down.* "Did
he say what about?"

"It seems he was ordered to investigate the suicide of that poor ba-slave the other day. And your, ah, erratic movements brought you to his negative attention. I thought you'd come to regret getting out of line."

"And . . . am I to talk to him, then?"

"We have decided to extend that courtesy, yes. We've shown him to one of the small parlors on the ground floor. It is, of course, monitored. You'll have an embassy bodyguard present. I don't suspect Benin of harboring any murderous intentions, it will merely be a reminder of your status."

We have decided. So Colonel Vorreedi, whom Miles still had not met, and probably Vorob'yev too, would be listening to every word. Oh, shit. "Very good, sir." Miles stood, and followed the ambassador. Ivan watched him go with the suffused expression of a man anticipating the imminent arrival of some unpleasant form of cosmic justice.

The small parlor was exactly that, a comfortably furnished room intended for private tête-à-têtes between two or three persons, with the embassy security staff as an invisible fourth. Ghem-Colonel Benin apparently had no objection to anything *he* had to say being recorded. A Barrayaran guard, standing outside the door, swung in behind Miles and the ambassador as they entered, and took up his post stolidly and silently. He was tall and husky even for a Barrayaran, with a remarkably blank face. He wore a senior sergeant's tabs, and insignia of commando corps, by which Miles deduced that the low-wattage expression was a put-on.

Ghem-Colonel Benin, waiting for them, rose politely as they entered. He was of no more than middle stature, so probably not over-stocked with haut-genes in his recent ancestry—the haut favored height. He had likely acquired his present post by merit rather than social rank, then, not necessarily a plus from Miles's point of view. Benin was very trim in the dark red Cetagandan dress uniform that was everyday garb for security staff in the Celestial Garden. He wore, of course, full formal face paint in the Imperial pattern rather than that of his clan, marking his primary allegiance; a white base with intricate black curves and red accents that Miles thought of as the bleeding-zebra look. But by association, it was a pattern that would command instant and profound respect and total, abject cooperation on eight planets. Barrayar, of course, was not one of them.

Miles tried to judge the face beneath the paint. Neither youthful and inexperienced nor aged and sly, Benin appeared to be a bit over forty-standard, young for his rank but not unusually so. The default expression of the face seemed to be one of attentive seriousness, though he managed a brief polite smile when Vorob'yev introduced him to Miles, and a brief relieved smile when Vorob'yev left them alone together.

"Good morning, Lord Vorkosigan," Benin began. Clearly well trained in the social arena, he managed to keep his glance at Miles's physique limited to one quick covert summation. "Did your ambassador explain to you why I am here?"

"Yes, Colonel Benin. I understand you were assigned to investigate the death of that poor fellow—if *fellow* is the right term—we saw so shockingly laid out on the floor of the rotunda the other day." *The best defense is a good offense.* "Did you finally decide it was a suicide?"

Benin's eyes narrowed. "Obviously." But an odd timbre in his voice undercut the statement.

"Well, yes, it was obvious from the exsanguination that the Ba died on the spot, rather than having its throat cut elsewhere and the body transported. But it has occurred to me that if the autopsy showed the Ba was stunned unconscious when it died, it would rather rule out suicide. It's a subtle test—the shock of death tends to cover the shock of stunning—but you can find the traces if you're looking. Was such a test done, do you know?"

"No."

Miles was not sure if he meant it wasn't done, or—no, Benin had to know. "Why not? If I were you, it's the first test I'd ask for. Can you get it done now? Though two days late is not ideal."

"The autopsy is over. The Ba has been cremated," Benin stated flatly.

"What, already? Before the case was closed? Who ordered that? Not you, surely."

"Not—Lord Vorkosigan, this is not your concern. This is not what I came to talk with you about," Benin said stiffly, then paused. "Why this morbid interest in the Celestial Lady's late servant?"

"I thought it was the most interesting thing I'd seen since I came to Eta Ceta. It's in my line, you see. I've done civil security cases at home. Murder investigations—" well, one, anyway, "successfully, I might add." Yes, what *was* this Cetagandan officer's experience in such things? The Celestial Garden was such a well-ordered place. "Does this sort of thing happen here often?"

"No." Benin stared at Miles with intensified interest.

So the man might be well read, but lacked hands-on experience, at least since he'd been promoted to this post. He was damned quick at catching nuances, though. "It seems awfully premature to me, to cremate the victim before the case is closed. There are always late-occurring questions."

"I assure you, Lord Vorkosigan, Ba Lura was not carried unconscious into the funeral rotunda, dead or alive. Even the ceremonial guards would have noticed *that*." Did the slight spin on his tone hint that perhaps the ceremonial guards were chosen for beauty rather than brains?

"Well, actually, I had a theory," Miles burbled on enthusiastically. "You're just the man to confirm or disprove it for me, too. *Has* anyone testified noticing the Ba enter the rotunda?"

"Not exactly."

"Ah? Yes, and the spot where it lay dead—I don't know what kind of vid coverage you have of the building, but that area *had* to have been occluded. Or it could not have been, what, fifteen, twenty minutes before the body was discovered, right?"

Another thoughtful stare. "You are correct, Lord Vorkosigan. Normally, the entire rotunda is within visual scan, but because of the height and width of the catafalque, two—well, there is some blockage."

"Ah, ha! So how did the Ba know exactly—no, let me rephrase that. Who all could have known about the blind spot at the late Empress's feet? Your own security, and who else? Just how high up did your orders come down from, Colonel Benin? Are you by chance under pressure from above to deliver a quick confirmation of suicide and close your case?"

Benin twitched. "A quick conclusion to this vile interruption of a most solemn occasion is certainly desirable. I desire it as ardently as anyone else. Which brings me to *my* questions for *you*, Lord Vorkosigan. If I may be permitted!"

"Oh. Certainly." Miles paused, then added, just as Benin opened his mouth, "Are you doing this on your own time, then? I admire your dedication."

"No." Benin took a breath, and composed himself again. "Lord Vorkosigan. Our records indicate you left the reception hall to speak privately with a haut-lady."

"Yes. She sent a ba servant with an invitation. I could hardly refuse. Besides . . . I was curious."

"I can believe that," muttered Benin. "What was the substance of your conversation with the haut Rian Degtiar?"

"Why—surely you monitored it." Surely they had not, or this interview would have taken place two days ago, before Miles had ever left the Celestial Garden—and been a lot less politely conducted, too. But Benin doubtless had a vid of Miles's exit from and entrance to the reception area, and testimony from the little ba escort as well.

"Nevertheless," said Benin neutrally.

"Well—I have to admit, I found the conversation extremely confusing. She's a geneticist, you know."

"Yes."

"I believe her interest in me—excuse me, I find this personally embarrassing. I believe her interest in me was genetic. I am widely rumored to be a mutant. But my physical disabilities are entirely teratogenic, damage done by a poison I encountered pre-natally. Not genetic. It's *very important* to me that be clearly understood." Miles thought briefly of his own ImpSec eavesdroppers. "The haut-women, apparently, collect unusual natural genetic variations for their research. The haut Rian Degtiar seemed quite disappointed to learn I held nothing of interest, genetically speaking. Or so I gathered. She talked all around the subject— I'm not sure but what she perceived her own interest as being rather, um, questionable. I'm afraid I don't find haut motivations entirely comprehensible." Miles smiled cheerfully. There. That was the vaguest convincing-sounding uncheckable bullshit he could come up with on the spur of the moment, and left a good deal of turning-room for whatever the Colonel had got out of Rian, if anything.

"What *did* interest me, though, was the haut-lady's force-bubble," Miles added. "It never touched the ground. She had to be riding in a float-chair in there, I figured."

"They often do," said Benin.

"That's why I asked you about who saw the Ba Lura

enter the chamber. Can anyone use a haut-bubble? Or are they keyed in some way to the wearer? And are they as anonymous as they look, or do you have some way of telling them apart?"

"They are keyed to the wearer. And each has its own unique electronic signature."

"Any security measure made by man can be unmade by man. If he has access to the resources."

"I am aware of this fact, Lord Vorkosigan."

"Hm. You see the scenario I'm driving at, of course. Suppose the Ba was stunned elsewhere—a theory that hurried cremation has rendered uncheckable, alas— carried unconscious inside a haut-bubble to the blind spot, and had its throat cut, silently and without a struggle. The bubble glides on. It wouldn't have taken more than fifteen seconds. It wouldn't have required great physical strength on the part of the murderer. But I don't know enough about the specs of the bubbles to judge the technical likelihood. And I don't know if any bubbles went in and out—how much traffic *was* there in the funeral rotunda during the time-window we're talking about? There can't have been *that* much. Did any haut-lady bubbles enter and exit?"

Benin sat back, pursing his lips, regarding Miles with keen interest. "You have an alert way of looking at the world, Lord Vorkosigan. Five ba servants, four guards, and six haut-women crossed the chamber during the time in question. The ba have duties there, tending to the botanical arrangements and keeping the chamber perfectly clean. The haut-women frequently come to meditate and pay respects to the Celestial Lady. I have interviewed them all. None report noticing the Ba Lura."

"Then . . . the last one must be lying."

Benin tented his fingers, and stared at them. "It is not quite that simple."

Miles paused. "I despise doing internal investigations,

myself," he said at last. "I trust you are documenting every breath you're taking, at this point."

Benin almost smiled. "That's entirely my problem, isn't it."

Miles was actually beginning to like the man. "You are, considering the venue, of rather low rank for an investigation of this sensitivity, aren't you?"

"That too . . . is my problem."

"Sacrificable."

Benin grimaced. Oh, yes. Nothing Miles had said yet was anything Benin hadn't thought of too—if he'd dared to speak it aloud. Miles decided to continue sprinkling the favors.

"You've won yourself quite a pretty problem, in this murder, I'd say, ghem-Colonel," Miles remarked. Neither of them were keeping up the pretense about the suicide anymore. "Still, if the method was as I guess, you can deduce quite a lot about the murderer. His rank must be high, his access to internal security great, and—excuse me—he has a *peculiar* sense of humor, for a Cetagandan. The insult to the Empress nearly borders on disloyalty."

"So says an examination of the method," said Benin, in a tone of complaint. "It's motive that troubles me. That harmless old ba has served in the Celestial Garden for decades. Revenge seems most unlikely."

"Mm, perhaps. So if Ba Lura is old news, maybe it's the murderer who's newly arrived. And consider— decades of standing around sopping up secrets—the ba was well placed to *know* things about persons of extraordinarily high rank. Suppose . . . the ba had been tempted, say, into a spot of blackmail. I would think that a close tracing of Ba Lura's movements these last few days might be revealing. For instance, did the Ba leave the Celestial Garden at any time?"

"That . . . investigation is in progress."

"If I were you, I'd jump on that aspect. The Ba

might have communicated with its murderer." *Aboard his ship, in orbit, yes.* "The timing is peculiar, you see. To my eye, this murder shows every sign of having been rushed. If the murderer had had months to plan, he could have done a much better and quieter job. I think he had to make a lot of decisions in a hurry, maybe in that very hour, and some of them were, frankly, bad."

"Not bad enough," sighed Benin. "But you interest me, Lord Vorkosigan."

Miles trusted that wasn't too much of a double entendre. "This sort of thing is meat and drink to me. It's the first chance I've had to talk shop with anyone since I came to Eta Ceta." He favored Benin with a happy smile. "If you have any more questions for me, please feel free to stop by again."

"I don't suppose you would be willing to answer them under fast-penta?" Benin said, without much hope.

"Ah . . ." Miles thought fast, "with Ambassador Vorob'yev's permission, perhaps." Which would not, of course, be forthcoming. Benin's slight smile fully comprehended the delicacy of a refusal-without-refusing.

"In any case, I should be pleased to continue our acquaintance, Lord Vorkosigan."

"Any time. I'll be here nine more days."

Benin gave Miles a penetrating, unreadable look. "Thank you, Lord Vorkosigan."

Miles had about a million more questions for his new victim, but that was all he dared cram into the opening session. He wanted to project an air of professional interest, not frantic obsession. It was tempting, but dangerous, to think of Benin as an ally. But he was certainly a window into the Celestial Garden. Yeah, a window with eyes that looked back at you. But there had to be some reasonably subtle way to induce Benin to slap himself on the forehead and cry, *Say, I'd better take a closer look at those satrap governors!* He was definitely looking in the correct direction, up. And over his shoulder. A most uncomfortable position in which to work.

How much influence could the satrap governors, all near Imperial relations, put on the Celestial Garden's security? Not too much—they were surely regarded as potential threats. But one might have been building up convenient contacts for a long time now. One might, indeed, have been perfectly loyal till this new temptation. It was a dangerous accusation; Benin had to be right the first time. He wouldn't get a second chance.

Did anyone care about the murder of a ba slave? How much interest did Benin have in abstract justice? If a Cetagandan couldn't be one-up in any other way, holier-than-thou might do. An almost aesthetic drive— the Art of Detection. How much risk was Benin willing to run, how much did he have to lose? Did he have a family, or was he some sort of pure warrior-monk, totally dedicated to his career? To the ghem-Colonel's credit, by the end of the interview Benin had been keeping his eyes on Miles's face because he was interested in what Miles was saying, not because he was not-looking at Miles's body.

Miles rose along with Benin, and paused. "Ghem-Colonel . . . may I make a personal suggestion?"

Benin tilted his head in curious permission.

"You have good reason to suspect you have a little problem somewhere overhead. But you don't know where yet. If I were you, I'd go straight to the top. Make personal contact with your Emperor. It's the only way you can be sure you've capped the murderer."

Did Benin turn pale, beneath his face paint? No way to tell. "*That* high over—Lord Vorkosigan, I can hardly claim casual acquaintance with my celestial master."

"This isn't friendship. It's business, and it's *his* business. If you truly mean to be useful to him, it's time you began. Emperors are only human." Well, Emperor

Gregor was. The Cetagandan emperor was haut-human. Miles hoped that still counted. "Ba Lura must have been more to him than a piece of the furniture, it served him for over fifty years. Make no accusations, merely request that he protect your investigation from being quashed. Strike first, today, before . . . someone . . . begins to fear your competence." *If you're going to cover your ass, Benin, by God do it right.*

"I will . . . consider your advice."

"Good hunting," Miles nodded cheerfully, as if it wasn't *his* problem. "Big game is the best. Think of the honor."

Benin bowed himself out with a small, wry smile, to be escorted from the building by the embassy guard.

"See you around," Miles called.

"You may be sure of it." Benin's parting wave was almost, but not quite, a salute.

Miles's desire to dissolve into an exhausted puddle on the corridor floor was delayed by the arrival of Vorob'yev, doubtless from his listening post below-stairs, and another man. Ivan hovered behind them with an expression of morose anxiety.

The other man was middle-aged, middle-sized, and wearing the loose bodysuit and well-cut robes of a Cetagandan ghem-lord, in middle colors. They hung comfortably upon him, but his face was free of colored paint, and the haircut he sported was that of a Barrayaran officer. His eyes were . . . interested.

"A very well conducted interview, Lord Vorkosigan," said Vorob'yev, relieving Miles's mind. Slightly. An even wager who had interviewed whom, just now.

"Ghem-Colonel Benin obviously has a lot on his mind," said Miles. "Ah . . ." He glanced at Vorob'yev's companion.

"Allow me to introduce Lord Vorreedi," said the ambassador. "Lord Vorkosigan, of course. Lord Vorreedi is our particular expert in understanding the

activities of the ghem-comrades, in all their multitude of arenas."

Which was diplomatic-talk for *Head Spy*. Miles nodded careful greetings. "Pleased to meet you at last, sir."

"And you," Vorreedi returned. "I regret not arriving
sooner. The late empress's obsequies were expected to
be rather more sedate than this. I didn't know of your
keen interest in civil security, Lord Vorkosigan. Would
you like us to arrange you a tour of the local police
organizations?"

"I'm afraid time will not permit. But yes, if I hadn't
been able to get into a military career, I think police
work might have been my next choice."

A uniformed corporal from the embassy's ImpSec
office approached, and motioned away his civilian-
clothed superior. They conferred in low tones, and
the corporal handed over a sheaf of colored papers
to the protocol officer, who in turn handed them to
the ambassador with a few words. Vorob'yev, his
brows climbing, turned to Ivan.

"Lord Vorpatril. Some invitations have arrived for you
this morning."

Ivan took the sheets, their colors and perfumes clashing, and leafed through them in puzzlement. "Invitations?"

"Lady Benello invites you to a private dinner, Lady
Arvin invites you to a fire-pattern-viewing party—both
tonight—and Lady Senden invites you to observe a
court-dance practice, this afternoon."

"Who?"

"Lady Senden," the protocol officer supplied, "is
Lady Benello's married sister, according to last night's
background checks." He gave Ivan an odd look. "Just
what did you do to merit this sudden popularity, Lord
Vorpatril?"

Ivan held the papers gingerly, smiling thinly, by which
Miles deduced he hadn't told the protocol officer quite

everything about last night's adventure. "I'm not sure, sir." Ivan caught Miles's suffused gaze, and reddened slightly.

Miles craned his neck. "Do any of these women have interesting connections at the Celestial Garden, do you suppose? Or friends who do?"

"*Your* name isn't on these, coz," Ivan pointed out ruthlessly, waving the invitations, all hand-calligraphed in assorted colored inks. A faintly cheerful look was starting in his eyes, displacing his earlier glum dread.

"Perhaps some more background checks would be in order, my lord?" murmured the protocol officer to the ambassador.

"If you please, Colonel."

The protocol officer left with his corporal. Miles, with a grateful parting wave to Vorob'yev, tagged along after Ivan, who clutched the colored papers firmly and eyed him with suspicion.

"Mine," Ivan asserted, as soon as they were out of earshot. "You have ghem-Colonel Benin, who is more to your taste anyway."

"There are a lot of ghem-women here in the capital who serve as ladies-in-waiting to the haut-women in the Celestial Garden, is all," Miles said. "I'd . . . like to meet that ghem-lady I went walking with last night, for instance, but she didn't give me her name."

"I doubt many of Yenaro's crowd have celestial connections."

"I think this one was an exception. Though the people I *really* want to meet are the satrap governors. Face-to-face."

"You'd have a better chance at that at one of the official functions."

"Oh, yes. I'm planning on it."

CHAPTER EIGHT

The Celestial Garden was not quite so intimidating on the second visit, Miles assured himself. This time they were not lost in a great stream of galactic envoys, but were only a little party of three. Miles, Ambassador Vorob'yev, and Mia Maz were admitted through a side gate, almost privately, and escorted by a single servitor to their destination.

The trio made a good picture. Miles and the ambassador wore their ultra-formal House blacks again. Maz wore black linings and pure white over-robes, combining the two mourning colors, acknowledging the Cetagandan hue without over-stepping the boundaries of haut-privilege. No accident that it also displayed her own dark hair and lively complexion to advantage, and set off her two companions as well. Her dimple flashed with her smile of anticipation and pleasure, directed over Miles's head to Ambassador Vorob'yev. Miles, between them, felt like an unruly kid being escorted firmly by his two parents. Vorob'yev was taking no chances of unauthorized violations of etiquette today.

The offering of the elegiac poetry to the dead empress was not a ceremony normally attended by galactic delegates, with the exception of a very few high-ranking Cetagandan allies. Miles did not qualify on either count, and Vorob'yev had been forced to pull every string he owned to get them this invitation. Ivan had ducked out, pleading weariness from the court-dance practice and the fire-viewing parties of yesterday, and the excuse of four more invitations for this afternoon and evening. It was a suspiciously smug weariness. Miles had let him escape, his sadistic urge to make Ivan sit along with him through what promised to be an interminable afternoon and evening blunted by the reflection that his cousin could do little to contribute to what was essentially an information-gathering expedition. And Ivan might—just might—pick up some useful new contacts among the ghem. Vorob'yev had substituted the Vervani woman, to her obvious delight, and Miles's benefit.

To Miles's relief the ceremony was not carried out in the rotunda, with all its alarming associations, where the empress's body still lay. Neither did the haut use anything so crass as an auditorium, with people packed in efficient rows. Instead the servitor took them to a—dell, Miles supposed he might call it, a bowl in the garden lined with flowers, plants, and hundreds of little box-seat arrangements overlooking a complex array of daises and platforms at the bottom. As befitted their rank, or lack of it, the servitor placed the Barrayaran party in the last and highest row, three quarters of the way around from the best frontal view. This suited Miles—he could watch nearly the whole audience without being over-looked himself. The low benches were flawless wood, hand-smoothed to a high polish. Mia Maz, bowed gallantly to her seat by Vorob'yev, patted her skirts and stared around, bright-eyed.

Miles stared too, much less bright-eyed—he'd spent a great deal of time the last day peering into his comconsole display, swotting up background in hopes of finding an end to this tangle. The haut were filtering in to their places, men in flowing snowy robes escorting white bubbles. The dell was beginning to resemble a great bank of white climbing roses in a frenzy of bloom. Miles finally saw the purpose of the box seats—it gave room for the bubbles. Was Rian among them?

"Will the women speak first, or how do they organize this?" Miles asked Maz.

"The women won't speak at all, today," said Maz. "They had their own ceremony yesterday. They'll start with the men of lowest rank and work up through the constellations."

Ending with the satrap governors. All of them. Miles settled himself with the patience of a panther in a tree. The men he had come to see were filing into the bottom of the bowl even now. If Miles had owned a tail, it would have twitched. As it was, he stilled a tapping boot.

The eight satrap governors, assisted by their highest-ranking ghem-officers, sank into seats around a raised reserved dais. Miles squinted, wishing for rangefinder binoculars—not that he could have carried them past the tight security. With a twinge of sympathy he wondered what ghem-Colonel Benin was doing right now, and if Cetagandan security went as frantic behind the scenes as Barrayaran security did at any ceremony involving Emperor Gregor. He could just picture them.

But he had what he'd come for—all eight of his suspects, artistically arranged on display. He studied his top four with particular care.

The governor of Mu Ceta was one of the Degtiar constellation, the present emperor's half-uncle, being half-brother to the late empress. Maz too watched closely as he settled his aged body creakily into his seat, and brushed away his attendants with jerky, irritated motions. The governor of Mu Ceta had been at his present post only two years, replacing the governor who had been recalled, and subsequently quietly exiled into retirement, after the Vervain invasion debacle. The man was very old, and very experienced, and had been chosen explicitly to calm Vervani fears of a re-match. Not, Miles thought, the treasonous type. Yet by haut Rian's testimony, every man in the circle had taken at least one step over the line, secretly receiving the unauthorized gene banks.

The governor of Rho Ceta, Barrayar's nearest neighbor, worried Miles a great deal more. The haut Este Rond was middle-aged and vigorous, haut-tall though unusually heavy. His ghem-officer stood well back from his governor's sweeping movements. Rond's general effect was bullish. And he was bullishly tenacious in his efforts, diplomatic and otherwise, to improve Cetaganda's trade access through the Barrayaran-controlled Komarr wormhole jumps. The Rond was one of the more junior haut-constellations, seeking growth. Este Rond was a hot prospect for sure.

The governor of Xi Ceta, Marilac's neighbor, wafted in, proud-nosed. The haut Slyke Giaja was what Miles thought of as a typical haut-lord, tall and lean and faintly effeminate. Arrogant, as befit a younger half-brother of the emperor. And dangerous. Young enough to be a possibility, though older than Este Rond.

The youngest suspect, the haut Ilsum Kety, governor of Sigma Ceta, was a mere stripling of forty-five or so. In body type he was much like Slyke Giaja, who was in fact a cousin of his through their mothers, who were half-sisters though of different constellations. Haut family trees were even more confusing than the Vors'. It would take a full-time geneticist to keep track of all the semi-siblings.

Eight white bubbles floated into the basin, and took up an arc to the left of the circle of satrap governors. The ghem-officers took up a similar arc to the right. They, Miles realized, were going to get to *stand* through the entire afternoon's ceremony. Being a ghem-general wasn't all blood and beer. But could any of those bubbles be . . . ?

"Who are those ladies?" Miles asked Maz, nodding toward the octet.

"They are the satrap governors' consorts."

"I . . . thought the haut did not marry."

"There's no personal relationship implied in the title. They are appointed centrally, just like the governors themselves."

"Not by the governors? What's their function? Social secretaries?"

"Not at all. They are chosen by the empress, to be her representatives in all dealings having to do with the Star Crèche's business. All the haut living on a satrap planet send their genetic contracts through the consorts to the central gene bank here at the Celestial Garden, where the fertilizations and any genetic alterations take place. The consorts also oversee the return of the uterine replicators with the growing fetuses to their parents on the outlying planets. That has to be the strangest cargo run in the Cetagandan empire—once a year for each planet."

"Do the consorts travel back to Eta Ceta once a year, in that case, to personally accompany their charges?"

"Yes."

"Ah." Miles settled back, smiling fixedly. *Now* he saw how the Empress Lisbet had set up her scheme, the living channels she had used to communicate with each satrap governor. If every one of those consorts wasn't in on this plot to her eyebrows, he'd eat his boots. *Sixteen. I have sixteen suspects, not eight. Oh, God.* And he'd come here to cut *down* his list. But it followed logically that Ba Lura's murderer might not have had to borrow or steal a haut-lady's bubble. She might have owned one already. "Do the consort-ladies work closely with their satrap governors?"

Maz shrugged. "I really don't know. Not necessarily, I suppose. Their areas of responsibility are highly segregated."

A majordomo took center stage, and made a silent motion. Every voice in the dell went still. Every haut-lord dropped to his knees on padded rests thoughtfully provided in front of the benches. All the white bubbles bobbled—Miles still wondered how many of the haut-women cheated and cut corners at these ceremonies. After an anticipatory hush, the emperor himself arrived, escorted by guards in white and bloodred uniforms, zebra-faced, of terrible aspect if you took them seriously. Miles did, not for the face paint, but in certain knowledge of just how nervous and twitchy in the trigger-finger such an awesome responsibility could make a man.

It was the first time in his life Miles had seen the Cetagandan emperor in the flesh, and he studied the man as avidly as he had studied the satrap governors. Emperor the haut Fletchir Giaja was tall, lean, hawk-faced like his demi-cousins, his hair still untouched by gray despite his seventy-odd years. A survivor—he had succeeded to his rank at a fantastically young age for a Cetagandan, less than thirty, and held on through a wobbly youth to an apparently iron-secure mid-life. He seated himself with great assurance and grace of movement, serene and confident. Ringed by bowing traitors. Miles's nostrils flared, and he took a breath, dizzy with the irony. At another signal from the majordomo, everyone regained their seats, still in that remarkable silence.

The presentation of the elegiac poems in honor of the late haut Lisbet Degtiar began with the heads of the lowest-ranking constellations present. Each poem had to fit into one of half a dozen correct formal types, all mercifully short. Miles was extremely impressed with the elegance, beauty, and apparent deep feeling of about the first ten offerings. The recitation had to be one of those great formal ordeals, like taking an oath or getting married, in which the preparations wildly outmassed the moment of actualization. Great care was taken with movement, voice, and imperceptible variations of what to Miles's eye were identical white dress robes. But gradually, Miles began to be aware of stock phrases, repeated ideas; by the thirtieth man, his eyes were starting to glaze over. More than ever Miles wished Ivan by his side, suffering along with him.

Maz whispered an occasional interpretation or gloss, which helped fend off creeping drowsiness—Miles had not slept well last night. The satrap governors were all doing good imitations of men stuffed and mounted, except for the ancient governor of Mu Ceta, who slumped in open boredom, and watched through sardonic slitted eyes as his juniors, i.e., everyone else there, performed with various degrees of flop-sweat. The older and more experienced men, as they came on, at least had better deliveries, if not necessarily better poems.

Miles meditated on the character of Lord X, trying to match it with one of the eight faces ranged before him. The murderer/traitor was something of a tactical genius. He had been presented with an unanticipated opportunity to gain power, had committed rapidly to an all-out effort, evolved a plan, and struck. How fast? The first satrap governor had arrived in person only ten days before Miles and Ivan had, the last only four days before. Yenaro, the embassy's ImpSec office had finally reported, had put his sculpture together in just two days from designs delivered from an unknown source, working his minions around the clock. Ba Lura could only have been suborned since its mistress's death, not quite three weeks ago.

The aged haut thought nothing of taking on plans that took decades to mature, with can't-lose security.

Witness the old empress herself. They experienced time differently than Miles did, he was fairly sure. This whole chain of events smelled . . . young. Or young at heart.

Miles's opponent must be in an interesting frame of mind just now. He was a man of action and decision. But now he had to lie quiet and do nothing to draw attention to himself, even as it began to look more and more like Ba Lura's death was not going to pass as planned as a suicide. He had to sit tight on his bank and the Great Key till the funeral was over, and glide softly back to his planetary base—because he couldn't start the revolt from here; he'd prepared nothing in advance before he'd left home.

So would he send the Great Key on, or keep it with him? If he'd sent it back to his satrapy already, Miles was in deep trouble. Well, deeper trouble. Would the governor take the risk of losing the powerful tokens in transit? Surely not.

The droning amateur poets were getting to Miles. He found his subconscious mind not working along with the rest of it as it should, but going off on its own tangent. A poem of his own in honor of the late empress formed, unbidden, in his brain.

> A Degtiar empress named Lisbet
> Trapped a satrap lord neatly in his net.
>   Enticed into treason
>   For all the wrong reasons,
> He'll soon have a crash with his kismet.

He choked down a genuinely horrible impulse to bounce down to the center of the dell and declaim his poetic offering to the assembled haut multitude, just to see what would happen.

Mia Maz glanced aside in concern at his muffled snort. "Are you all right?"

"Yes. Sorry," he whispered. "I'm just having an attack of limericks."

Her eyes widened, and she bit her lip; only her deepening dimple betrayed her. "*Shhh,*" she said, with feeling.

The ceremony went on uninterrupted. Alas, there was all too much time to evolve more verse, of equal artistic merit. He gazed out at the banks of white bubbles.

> *A beautiful lady named Rian*
> *Hypnotized a Vor scion.*
>   *The little defective*
>   *Thinks he's a detective,*
> *but instead will be fed to the lion. . . .*

How did the haut live through these things? Had they bioengineered their bladders to some inhuman capacity, along with all the other rumored changes?

Fortunately, before Miles could think of two rhymes for *Vorob'yev,* the first satrap governor arose to take his place on the speaker's dais. Miles came abruptly awake.

The satrap governors' poems were all excellent, all in the most difficult forms—and, Maz informed Miles in a whisper, mostly ghost-written by the best hautwomen poets in the Celestial Garden. Rank hath its privileges. But try as he might, Miles could not read any useful sinister double meanings into them—his suspect was not using this moment to publicly confess his crimes, put the wind up his enemies, or any of the other really interesting possibilities. Miles was almost surprised. The placement of Ba Lura's body suggested Lord X had a weakness for the baroque in his plotting, when the simple would have done better. Making an Art of it?

The emperor sat through it with unruffled solemn

calm. The satrap governors all received polite nods of thanks from the chief mourner for their elegant praises. Miles wondered if Benin had taken his advice, and spoken with his master yet. He hoped so.

And then, abruptly, the literary ordeal was over. Miles suppressed an impulse to applaud; that was apparently Not Done. The majordomo came out and made another cryptic gesture, at which everyone went to their knees again; the emperor and his guards decamped, followed by the consort bubbles, the satrap governors, and their ghem-officers. Then everyone else was freed—to find a bathroom, Miles trusted.

The haut race might have divested itself of the traditional meanings and functions of sexuality, but they were still human enough to make the sharing of food part of life's basic ceremonies. In their own way. Trays of meat were sculpted into flowers. Vegetables masqueraded as crustaceans, and fruit as tiny animals. Miles stared thoughtfully at the plate of simple boiled rice on the buffet table. Every grain had been individually hand-arranged in an elaborate spiral pattern. He almost tripped over his own boots, boggling at it. He controlled his bemusement and tried to refocus on the business at hand.

The informal—by Celestial Garden standards—refreshments were served in a long pavilion open as usual to the garden, presently lit in a warm afternoon glow that invited relaxation. The haut-ladies in their bubbles had evidently gone elsewhere—someplace where they could drop their bubbles to eat, presumably. This was the most exclusive of several post-poetry buffet sites scattered around the Celestial Garden. The emperor himself was somewhere at the other end of the graceful building. Miles wasn't quite sure how Vorob'yev had got them in, but the man deserved a commendation for extraordinary service. Maz, eyes alight, hand on Vorob'yev's arm, was clearly in some sort of sociologist's heaven.

"Here we go," murmured Vorob'yev, and Miles went heads-up. The haut Este Rond's party was entering the crowded pavilion. The other haut, not knowing what to do about these out-of-place outlanders, had been trying to pretend the Barrayarans were invisible ever since they'd arrived. Este Rond did not have that option. The beefy, white-robed satrap governor, his painted and uniformed ghem-general by his side, paused to greet his Barrayaran neighbors.

A white-robed woman, unusual in this heavily male gathering, trailed the Rond's ghem-general. Her silver-blond hair was gathered in a looping queue down her back to her ankles, and she stood with downcast eyes, not speaking. She was much older than Rian, but certainly a haut-woman—*God* they aged well. She must be the Rond's ghem-general's haut-wife—any officer destined to such high planetary rank would have been expected to win one long ago.

Maz was giving Miles some inexplicable but urgent signal—a tiny head shake, and a *No, no!* formed silently on her lips. What was she trying to say? The haut-wife, apparently, did not speak unless spoken to—Miles had never seen anyone's body-language express such extraordinary reserve and containment, not even the haut Rian's.

Governor Rond and Vorob'yev exchanged elaborate courtesies, by which Miles gathered that the Rond had been their ticket in. Vorob'yev culminated his diplomatic coup by introducing Miles. "The lieutenant takes a very gratifying interest in the finer points of Cetagandan culture," Vorob'yev recommended him to the governor's attention.

The haut Rond nodded cordially; when Vorob'yev recommended someone it seemed even Cetagandan haut-lords attended.

"I was sent to learn, as well as serve, sir. It is my duty and my pleasure." Miles favored the haut-governor with a precisely calculated bow. "And I must say, I have certainly been having learning experiences." Miles tried by his edged smile to put as much double-spin on his words as possible.

The Rond smiled back, cool-eyed. But then, if Este Rond was Lord X, he ought to be cool. They exchanged a few empty pleasantries about the diplomatic life, then Miles ventured boldly, "Would you be so kind, haut Rond, as to introduce me to Governor haut Ilsum Kety?"

A razor-thin smile twitched the Rond's lips, and he glanced across the room at his fellow-governor and genetic superior. "Why, certainly, Lord Vorkosigan." If the Rond was going to be stuck with these outlanders, Miles gathered, he'd be happy to share the embarrassment.

The Rond shepherded Miles over. Vorob'yev was left talking with the Rho Cetan ghem-general, who was taking a sincere professional interest in his potential enemies. Vorob'yev shot Miles a warning not-quite-glower, just a slight creasing of his eyebrows; Miles opened his hand, down at his side, in an *I'll-be-good* promise.

As soon as they were out of the ambassador's earshot, Miles murmured to the Rond, "We know about Yenaro, you know."

"I beg your pardon?" said the Rond, in realistic-sounding bafflement, and then they arrived at the haut Ilsum Kety's little group.

Close-up, Kety seemed even taller and leaner than he had at a distance at the poetry-readings. He had cool chiseled features very much in the haut mold— hawk-noses had been the style ever since Fletchir Giaja had ascended the throne. A bit of silver-gray at the temples set off his dark hair. Since the man was only

in his mid-forties, and haut to boot . . . by God, yes.
The touch of frost was quite perfect, but it had to have
been artificially produced, Miles realized with well-
concealed inner amusement. In a world where the old
men had it all, there was no social benefit to a youthful
appearance when one actually *was* young.

Kety too was attended by his ghem-general, who also
kept a haut-wife on standby. Miles tried not to let his
eyes bug out too obviously. She was extraordinary even
by haut-standards. Her hair was a rich dark chocolate
color, parted in the middle and gathered in a thick
braid that trailed down her back to actually coil upon
the floor. Her skin was vanilla cream. Her eyes,
widening slightly as she glanced down at Miles
approaching by the Rond's side, were an astonishing
light cinnamon color, large and liquid. A complete confection indeed, wholly edible and scarcely older than
Rian. Miles was quietly grateful for his previous
exposure to Rian, which helped a great deal toward
keeping him on his feet and not crawling on his knees
toward her right now.

Ilsum Kety clearly had no time for or interest in
outlanders, but for whatever reason did not care or dare
to offend the Rond; Miles managed a brief exchange
of formal greetings with him. The Rond took the opportunity to skim Miles off his hands and escape to the
buffet.

The irritated Kety was failing to perform his social
duties. Miles took matters into his own hands, and
directed a half-bow at Kety's ghem-general. The general, at least, was of the customary Cetagandan age for
his position, i.e., antique. "General Chilian, sir. I have
studied you in my history texts. It is an honor to meet
you. And your fine lady. I don't believe I know her
name." He smiled hopefully at her.

Chilian's brows, going up, drew back down in a slight
frown. "Lord Vorkosigan," he acknowledged shortly. But

he didn't take up the hint. After a tiny glint of distaste in Miles's direction, the haut-woman stood as if she weren't there, or at least wishing so. The two men seemed to treat her as if she were invisible.

So if Kety were Lord X, what must be going through his mind right now, as he found himself cornered by his intended victim? He'd planted the false rod on the Barrayaran party, set up the Ba Lura to tell Rian and convince her to make accusations of theft, killed the Ba, and waited for the results. Which had been—a resounding silence. Rian had apparently done nothing, not said a word to anyone. Did Kety wonder if he'd killed Lura too soon after all, before it had made a chance to confess its loss? It must be very puzzling for the man. But nothing, not a twitch, showed on his haut face. Which would, of course, also be the case if the governor were totally innocent.

Miles smiled affably at the haut Ilsum Kety. "I understand we have a mutual hobby, governor," he purred.

"Oh?" said Kety unencouragingly.

"An interest in the Cetagandan Imperial regalia. Such a fascinating set of artifacts, and so evocative of the history and culture of the haut race, don't you think? And its future."

Kety stared at him blankly. "I would not regard that as a pastime. Nor a suitable interest for an outlander."

"It's a military officer's duty to know his enemies."

"I would not know. Those tasks belong to the ghem."

"Such as your friend Lord Yenaro? A slender reed for you to lean on, governor, I'm afraid you are about to find."

Kety's pale brow wrinkled. "Who?"

Miles sighed inwardly, wishing he could flood the entire pavilion with fast-penta. The haut were all so damned controlled, they looked like they were lying even when they weren't. "I wonder, haut Kety, if you would introduce me to Governor haut Slyke Giaja. As an Imperial relation of sorts myself, I can't help feeling he is something of my opposite number."

The haut Kety blinked, surprised into honesty. "I doubt *Slyke* would think so. . . ." By the look on his face he was balancing the annoyance to Prince Slyke Giaja of inflicting the outlander on him, versus the relief of being rid of Miles himself. Self-interest won, up to a point; the haut Kety motioned ghem-General Chilian nearer, and dispatched him to gain permission for the transfer. With a polite farewell and thank-you to Kety, Miles trailed after the ghem-general, hoping to take advantage of any indecision to press his suit. Imperial princes were not likely to make themselves so readily accessible as ordinary haut-governors.

"General . . . if the haut Slyke cannot speak with me, would you deliver a short message to him?" Miles tried to keep his voice even, despite his limping stride; Chilian was not shortening his steps in favor to the Barrayaran guest. "Just three words."

Chilian shrugged. "I suppose I can."

"Tell him . . . Yenaro is ours. Just that."

The general's brows rose at this cryptic utterance. "Very well."

The message, of course, would be repeated later to Cetagandan Imperial Security. Miles didn't mind the idea of Cetagandan Imperial Security taking a closer look at Lord Yenaro.

The haut Slyke Giaja was sitting with a small group of men, both ghem and haut, on the far side of the pavilion. Unusually, the party also included a white bubble, hovering near the Prince. Attendant upon it was a ghem-lady Miles recognized, despite the voluminous formal white robes she wore today—the woman who'd been sent to fetch him at Yenaro's party. The ghem-woman glanced across at him approaching, stared briefly, then looked resolutely away. So who was in the bubble? Rian? Slyke's consort? Someone else entirely?

Kety's ghem-general bent to murmur in his ear. Slyke Giaja glanced across at Miles, frowned, and shook his head. Chilian shrugged, and bent to murmur again. Miles, watching his lips move, saw his message or something very like it being delivered— the word *Yenaro* was quite distinctive. Slyke's face betrayed no expression at all. He waved the ghem-general away.

General Chilian returned to Miles's side. "The haut Slyke is too busy to see you at this time," he reported blandly.

"Thank you anyway," Miles intoned, equally blandly. The general nodded acknowledgment, and went back to his master.

Miles stared around, wondering how to leverage access to his next prospect. The Mu Cetan governor was not present—he'd probably departed directly from the garden amphitheater to take a nap.

Mia Maz drifted up to Miles, smiling, curiosity in her eyes. "Finding any good conversations, Lord Vorkosigan?" she asked.

"Not so far," he admitted ruefully. "Yourself?"

"I would not presume. I've mostly been listening."

"One learns more that way."

"Yes. Listening is the invisible conversational coup. I feel quite smug."

"What have you learned?"

"The haut topic at this party is each other's poetry, which they are slicing up along strict lines of dominance. By some coincidence everyone is agreeing that the men of higher rank had the better offerings."

"I couldn't tell the difference, myself."

"Oh, but we are not haut."

"Why were you wagging your eyebrows at me a while ago?" Miles asked.

"I was trying to warn you about a rare point of Cetagandan etiquette. How you are supposed to behave when you encounter a haut-woman outside of her bubble."

"It was . . . the first time I'd ever seen one," he lied strategically. "Did I do all right?"

"Hm, barely. You see, the haut-women lose the privilege of the force-shields when they marry out of the genome into the ghem-rank. They become as ghem-women—sort of. But the loss of the shield is considered a great loss of face. So the polite thing to do is to behave as if the bubble were still there. You must never directly address a haut-wife, even if she's standing right in front of you. Put all inquiries through her ghem-husband, and wait for him to transmit the replies."

"I . . . didn't say anything to them."

"Oh, good. And you must never stare directly at them, either, I'm afraid."

"I thought the men were being rude, to close the women out of the conversation."

"Absolutely not. They were being most polite, Cetagandan style."

"Oh. But the way they carry themselves, the women might as well still be in the bubbles. Virtual bubbles."

"That's the idea, yes."

"Do the same rules go for . . . haut-women who still have the privilege of their bubbles?"

"I have no idea. I cannot imagine a haut-woman talking face-to-face with an outlander."

Miles became aware of a ghostly gray presence at his elbow, and tried not to jump. It was the haut Rian Degtiar's little ba servant. The ba had passed into the room without a ripple, ignored by its inhabitants. Miles's heart began to race, a response he muffled in a polite nod at the servitor.

"Lord Vorkosigan. My lady wishes to speak with you," said the ba. Maz's eyes widened.

"Thank you, I would be pleased," Miles responded.

"Ah . . ." He glanced around for Ambassador Vorob'yev, who was still being buttonholed by the Rho Cetan ghem-general. Good. Permissions not requested could not be denied. "Maz, would you be so kind as to tell the ambassador I've gone to speak with a lady. Mm . . . I may be some time at it. Go on without me. I'll catch up with you back at the embassy, if necessary."

"I don't think—" began Maz doubtfully, but Miles was already turning away. He shot her a smile over his shoulder and a cheerful little wave as he followed the ba out of the pavilion.

CHAPTER NINE

The little ba, its expression devoid as ever of any comment on its mistress's affairs, led Miles on a lengthy walk through the garden's winding paths, around ponds and along tiny, exquisite artificial streams. Miles almost stopped to gape at an emerald-green lawn populated by a flock of ruby-red peacocks the size of songbirds, slowly stalking about. A sunny spot on a ledge a little further on was occupied by something resembling a spherical cat, or perhaps a bouquet of cat-fur, soft, white . . . yes, there was an animal in there; a pair of turquoise-blue eyes blinked once at him from the fuzz, and closed again in perfect indolence.

Miles did not attempt conversation or questions. He might not have been personally monitored by Cetagandan Imperial Security on his last trip to the Celestial Garden, when he'd been mixed in with a thousand other galactic delegates; this was certainly not the case today. He prayed Rian would realize this. Lisbet would have. He could only hope Rian had inherited Lisbet's safe zones and procedures, along with the Great Key and her genetic mission.

A white bubble waited in a cloistered walkway. The ba bowed to it and departed.

Miles cleared his throat. "Good evening, milady. You asked to see me? How may I serve you?" He kept his greeting as general as possible. For all he knew it was ghem-Colonel Benin and a voice-filter inside that damned blank sphere.

Rian's voice or a good imitation murmured, "Lord Vorkosigan. You expressed an interest in genetic matters. I thought you would care for a short tour."

Good. They were monitored, and she knew it. He suppressed the tiny part of himself that had been hoping against all reason for a love-affair cover, and answered, "Indeed, milady. All medical procedures interest me. I feel the corrections to my own damage were extremely incomplete. I'm always looking for new hopes and chances, whenever I have an opportunity to visit more advanced galactic societies."

He paced along beside her floating sphere, trying, and failing, to keep track of the twists and turns of their route, through archways and other buildings. He managed a suitably admiring comment or two on the passing scenery, so their silence would not be too obvious. He'd walked about a kilometer from the Emperor's buffet, he gauged, though certainly not in a straight line, when they came to a long, low white building. Despite the usual charming landscaping, it had "biocontrol" written all over it, in the details of its window seals and door-locks. The air lock required complicated encodations from Rian, though once it had identified her, it admitted him under her aegis without a murmur of protest.

She led him through surprisingly un-labyrinthine corridors to a spacious office. It was the most utilitarian, least artistic chamber he'd yet seen in the Celestial Garden. One entire wall was glass, overlooking a long room that had a lot more in common with galactic-standard bio-labs than with the garden outside. Form follows function, and this place was bristling with function: purpose, not the languid ease of the pavilions. It was presently deserted, shut down, but for a lone ba servitor moving among the benches doing some sort of meticulous janitorial task. But of course. No haut genetic contracts were approved or, presumably, carried out during the period of mourning for the Celestial Lady, putative mistress of this domain. A screaming-bird pattern decorated the surface of a comconsole, and hovered above several cabinet-locks. He was standing in the center of the Star Crèche.

The bubble settled by one wall, and vanished without a pop. The haut Rian Degtiar rose from her float-chair.

Her ebony hair today was bound up in thick loops, tumbling no farther than her waist. Her pure white robes were only calf-length, two simple layers comfortably draped over a white bodysuit that covered her from neck to white-slippered toe. More woman, less icon, and yet . . . Miles had hoped repeated exposure to her beauty might build up an immunity in him to the mind-numbing effect of her. Obviously, he would need more exposure than this. Lots more. Lots and lots and—*stop it. Don't be more of a idiot than you have to be.*

"We can talk here," she said, gliding to a station chair beside the comconsole desk and settling herself in it. Her simplest movements were like dance. She nodded to another station chair across from hers, and Miles lurched into it with a strained smile, intensely conscious that his boots barely touched the floor. Rian seemed as direct as the ghem-generals' wives were closed. Was the Star Crèche itself a sort of psychological force-bubble for her? Or did she merely consider him so sub-human as to be completely non-threatening, as incapable as a pet animal of judging her?

"I . . . trust you are correct," Miles said, "but won't

there be repercussions from your Security for bringing me in here?"

She shrugged. "If they wish, they can request the Emperor to reprimand me."

"They cannot, er, reprimand you directly?"

"No."

The statement was flat, factual. Miles hoped she was not being overly optimistic. And yet . . . by the lift of her chin, the set of her shoulders, it was clear that the haut Rian Degtiar, Handmaiden of the Star Crèche, firmly believed that within these walls *she* was empress. For the next eight days, anyway.

"I trust this is important. And brief. Or I'm going to emerge to find ghem-Colonel Benin waiting for an exit-interview."

"It's important." Her blue eyes seemed to blaze. "I know which satrap governor is the traitor, now!"

"Excellent! That was fast. Uh . . . how?"

"The Key was, as you said, a decoy. False and empty. As you knew." Suspicion still glinted in her eye, lighting upon him.

"By reason alone, milady. Do you have evidence?"

"Of a sort." She leaned forward intently. "Yesterday, Prince Slyke Giaja had his consort bring him to the Star Crèche. For a tour, he pretended. He insisted I produce the Empress's regalia, for his inspection. His face said nothing, but he gazed upon the collection for a long time, before turning away, as if satisfied. He congratulated me upon my loyal work, and left immediately thereafter."

Slyke Giaja was certainly on Miles's short list. Two data points did not quite make a triangulation, but it was certainly better than nothing. "He didn't ask to see the Key demonstrated, to prove it worked?"

"No."

"He knew, then." *Maybe, maybe . . .* "I bet we gave him food for thought, seeing his decoy sitting there all demure. I wonder which way he's going to jump next? Does he realize *you* know it's a decoy, or does he think you've been fooled?"

"I could not tell."

It wasn't just him, Miles thought with glum relief, even the haut couldn't read other haut. "He must realize he has only to wait eight days, and the truth will come out the first time your successor tries to use the Great Key. Or if not the truth, certainly the accusation against Barrayar. But is that his plan?"

"I don't know what his plan is."

"He wants to involve Barrayar somehow, that I'm sure of. Perhaps even provoke armed conflict between our states."

"This . . ." Rian turned one hand, curled as if around the stolen Great Key, "would be an outrage, but surely . . . not cause enough for war."

"Mm. This may only be Part One. This pis—angers you at us, logically Part Two ought to be something that angers us at you." An uncomfortable new realization. Clearly, Lord X—Slyke Giaja?—was not done yet. "Even if I'd handed the key back in that first hour—which I don't think was in his script—we still could not have proved we didn't switch it. I wish we hadn't jumped the Ba Lura. I'd give anything to know what story it was *supposed* to have primed us with."

"I wish you hadn't either," said Rian rather tartly, settling back in her station chair and twitching her vest, the first un-purposive move Miles had ever seen her make.

Miles's lips twisted in brief embarrassment. "But—this is important—the consorts, the satrap governors' consorts. You never told me about them. They're in on this, aren't they? Why not on both sides?"

She nodded reluctant acknowledgment. "But I do not suspect any of them of being involved in this treason. That would be . . . unthinkable."

"But surely your Celestial Lady used them—why unthinkable? I mean, here a woman's got a chance to make herself an instant empress, right along with her governor. Or maybe even independently of her governor."

The haut Rian Degtiar shook her head. "No. The consorts do not belong to *them*. They belong to *us*."

Miles blinked, slightly dizzy. "Them. The men. Us. The women. Right?"

"The haut-women are the keepers. . . ." She broke off, evidently hopeless of explaining it to an outlander barbarian. "It cannot be Slyke Giaja's consort."

"I'm sorry. I don't understand."

"It's . . . a matter of the haut-genome. Slyke Giaja is attempting to take something to which he has no right. It is not that he attempts to usurp the emperor. That is his proper part. It's that he attempts to usurp the *empress*. A vileness beyond . . . The haut-genome is ours and ours alone. In this he betrays not the empire, which is nothing, but the haut, which is everything."

"But the consorts are in favor, presumably, of decentralizing the haut-genome."

"Of course. They are all my Celestial Lady's appointees."

"Do they . . . hm. Do they rotate every five years along with their governors? Or independently of them?"

"They are appointed for life, and removed only by the Celestial Lady's direct order."

The consorts seemed powerful allies in the heart of the enemy camp, if only Rian could activate them on her behalf. But she dared not do so, alas, if one of them was herself a traitor. Miles thought bad words to himself.

"The empire," he pointed out, "is the support of the haut. Hardly *nothing*, even from a genetic point of view. The, er, prey to predator ratio is quite high."

She did not smile at his weak zoological joke. He probably ought not to treat her to a recitation of his limericks, then, either. He tried again. "Surely the Empress Lisbet did not mean to instantly fragment the support of the haut."

"No. Not this fast. Maybe not even in this generation," admitted Rian.

Ah. That made more sense, a timing much more in an old haut-lady's style. "But now her plot has been hijacked to another's purpose. Someone with short-term, personal goals, someone she did not foresee." He moistened his lips, and forged on. "I believe your Celestial Lady's plans have fractured at their weak spot. The emperor protects the haut-women's control of the haut-genome; in turn you lend him legitimacy. A mutual support in both your interests. The satrap governors have no such motive. You can't give power away and keep it simultaneously."

Her exquisite lips thinned unhappily, but she did not deny the point.

Miles took a deep breath. "It's not in Barrayar's interests for Slyke Giaja to succeed in his power-grab. So far, I can serve you in this, milady. But it's not in Barrayar's interests for the Cetagandan Empire to be de-stabilized in the way your empress planned, either. I think I see how to foil Slyke. But in turn you must give up your attempt to carry out your mistress's post-humous vision." At her astonished look he added weakly, "At least for now."

"How . . . would you foil Prince Slyke?" she asked slowly.

"Penetrate his ship. Retrieve the real Great Key. Replace it again with the decoy, if possible. If we're lucky he might not even realize the substitution till he got home, and then what could he do about it? You hand over the real Great Key to your successor, and it all passes away as smoothly as if it had never happened. Neither party can accuse the other without incriminating himself." *Or herself.* "I think it is, in all, the best outcome that can be humanly achieved. Any other scenario leads to disaster, of one sort or another. If we do nothing, the plot comes out in eight days regardless, and Barrayar gets framed. If I try and fail . . . at least I can't make it any worse." *Are you sure of that?*

"How could you get aboard Slyke's ship?"

"I have an idea or two. The governors' consorts—and their ghem-ladies, and their servitors—can they go up and down from orbit freely?"

One porcelain hand touched her throat. "More or less, yes."

"So you get a lady with legitimate access, preferably someone relatively inconspicuous, to take me up. Not as myself, of course, I'd have to be disguised somehow. Once I'm aboard, I can take it from there. This gives us a problem of trust. Who could you trust? I don't suppose you yourself could . . . ?"

"I haven't left the capital for . . . several years."

"You would not qualify as inconspicuous, then. Besides, Slyke Giaja has to be keeping a close eye on you. What about that ghem-lady you sent to meet me at Yenaro's party?"

Rian was looking decidedly unhappy. "Someone in the consort's train would be a better choice," she said reluctantly.

"The alternative," he pointed out coolly, "would be to let *Cetagandan* security do the job. Nailing Slyke would automatically clear Barrayar, and *my* problem would be solved."

Well . . . not quite. Slyke Giaja, if Lord X, was the man who'd somehow jiggered the orbital station's traffic control, and who'd known *just* what security blind spot would hold Ba Lura's body. Slyke Giaja had more security access than he bloody ought to. Was it so certain that Cetagandan Security would be able to pull off a *surprise* raid on the Imperial prince's ship?

"How would *you* disguise yourself?" she asked.

He tried to convince himself her tone was merely taken aback, not scornful. "As a ba servitor, probably. Some of them are as short as I am. And you haut treat those people like they're invisible. Blind and deaf, too."

"No man would disguise himself as a ba!"

"So much the better, then." He grinned ironically at her reaction.

Her comconsole chimed. She stared at it in brief, astonished annoyance, then touched its code pad. The face of a fit-looking middle-aged man formed over the vid-plate. He wore a Cetagandan security officer's ordinary uniform, but he was no one Miles recognized. Gray eyes glinted like granite chips from freshly applied zebra-striped face paint. Miles quailed, and glanced around quickly—he was out of range of the vid-pickup, at least.

"Haut Rian," the man nodded deferentially.

"Ghem-Colonel Millisor," Rian acknowledged. "I ordered my comconsole blocked to incoming calls. This is not a convenient time to speak." She kept her eyes from darting to Miles.

"I used the emergency override. I've been trying to reach you for some time. My apologies, Haut, for intruding upon your mourning for the Celestial Lady, but she would have been the first to wish it. We have succeeded in tracking the lost L-X-10-Terran-C to Jackson's Whole. I need the authorization of the Star Crèche to pursue out of the Empire with all due force. I had understood that the recovery of the L-X-10-Terran-C was one of our late Lady's highest priorities. After the field tests she was considering it as an addition to the haut-genome itself."

"This *was* true, ghem-Colonel, but . . . well, yes, it still should be recovered. Just a moment." Rian rose, went to one of the cabinets, and unlocked it with the encode-ring, fished from its chain around her neck. She rummaged within, and removed a clear block about fifteen centimeters on a side with the scarlet bird pattern incised upon the top, returned to her desk, and placed it over the comconsole's read-pad. She tapped out some codes, and a light flashed briefly within the block. "Very well, ghem-Colonel. I leave it entirely to your judgment. You knew our late Lady's mind on this. You are fully authorized, and may draw your resources as needed from the Star Crèche's special fund."

"I thank you, Haut. I will report our progress." The ghem-colonel nodded, and keyed off.

"What was that all about?" Miles asked brightly, trying not to look too predatory.

Rian frowned at him. "Some old internal business of the haut-genome. It has nothing to do with you or Barrayar, or the present crisis, I assure you. Life does go on, you know."

"So it does." Miles smiled affably, as if fully satisfied. Mentally, he filed the conversation away verbatim. It might make a nice tidbit to distract Simon Illyan with later. He had a bad feeling he was going to need some major distractions for Illyan, when he got home.

Rian put the Great Seal of the Star Crèche carefully away again in its locked cabinet, and returned to her station-chair.

"So can you do it?" Miles pursued. "Have a lady you trust meet me, with a ba servitor's uniform and real ID's, the false rod, and some way to check the real one? And send her up to Prince Slyke's ship on some valid pretext, with me in her train? And *when*?"

"I'm . . . not sure when."

"We have to set the meeting in advance, this time. If I'm going to go wandering away from my embassy's supervision for several hours, you can't just call me away at random. I have to cover my own a— concoct a cover story for my own security, too. Do you have a copy of my official schedule? You must, or we could not have connected before. I think we should rendezvous outside the Celestial Garden, this time, for starters. I'm going to be going to something called the Bioestheties Exhibit tomorrow afternoon. I think I could make up an excuse to get away from there, maybe with Ivan's help."

"So soon . . ."

"Not soon enough, in my view. There's not much time left. And we have to allow for the possibility that the first attempt may have to be aborted for some reason. You . . . do realize, your evidence against Prince Slyke is suggestive only. Not conclusive."

"But it's all I have, so far."

"I understand. But we need all the margin we can get. In case we have to go back for a second pass."

"Yes . . . you're right . . ." She took a breath, frowning anxiously. "Very well, Lord Vorkosigan. I shall help you make this attempt."

"Do *you* have any guesses where on his ship Prince Slyke might be inclined to store the Great Key? It's a small object, and a big ship, after all. My first guess would be his personal quarters. Once aboard, is there any way of detecting the Great Key's location? I don't suppose we're so fortunate as to have a screamer circuit on it?"

"Not as such. Its internal power system is an old and very rare design, though. At short range, it might be possible to pick it up with an appropriate sensor. I will see that my lady brings you one, and anything else I can think of."

"Every little bit helps." There. They were in motion at last. He suppressed a wild impulse to beg her to throw it all over and flee away with him to Barrayar. Could he even smuggle her out of the Cetagandan Empire? Surely it was no more miraculous a task

than the one now before him. Yes, and what would
be the effect on his career, not to mention his
father's, of installing a refugee Cetagandan haut-
woman and close relative of Emperor Fletchir Giaja's
in Vorkosigan House? And how much trouble would
trail him? He thought fleetingly of the story of the
Trojan War.

Still, it would have been flattering, if she had indeed
been trying to suborn him, if she'd at least tried a little
harder. She had not lifted a finger to attract him; not
an eyebrow arched in false invitation. She seemed
straightforward to the point of naiveté, to his own
ImpSec-trained, naturally convoluted mind. When
someone fell deeply and hopelessly in love with somebody, that somebody ought at least to have the courtesy to notice. . . .

The key word, boy, is hopelessly. Keep it in mind.

They shared no love, he and Rian, nor the chance
of any. And no goals. But they did share an enemy. It
would have to do.

Rian rose in dismissal; Miles scrambled up too, saying, "Has ghem-Colonel Benin caught up with you yet?
He was assigned to investigate the death of Ba Lura,
you know."

"So I understood. He has twice requested an audience with me. I have not yet granted his request. He
seems . . . persistent."

"Thank God. We've still got a chance to get our sto-
ries straight." Miles quickly summed up his own interview with Benin, with special emphasis on his fictional
first conversation with Rian. "We need to make up a
consistent account of this visit, too. I think he'll be back.
I rather encouraged him, I'm afraid. I didn't guess
Prince Slyke would give himself away to you so
quickly."

Rian nodded, walked to the window-wall, and, pointing to various sites within the laboratory, gave Miles

a brief description of the tour she'd given Prince Slyke yesterday. "Will that do?"

"Nicely, thanks. You can tell him I asked a lot of medical questions about . . . correcting various physical disabilities, and that you couldn't help me much, that I'd come to the wrong store." He could not help adding, "There's nothing wrong with my DNA, you know. All my damage was teratogenic. Outside your purview and all that."

Her face, always mask-like in its beauty, seemed to grow a shade more expressionless. Rattled, he added, "You Cetagandans spend an inordinate amount of time on appearances. Surely you've encountered false appearances before." *Stop it, shut up now.*

She opened a hand, acknowledging without agreeing or disagreeing, and returned to her bubble. Worn out, and not trusting his tongue any further, Miles paced silently beside it back to the main entrance.

They exited into a cool and luminous artificial dusk. A few pale stars shone in the apparently boundless dark blue hemisphere above. Sitting in a row on a bench across the entry walk from the Star Crèche were Mia Maz, Ambassador Vorob'yev, and ghem-Colonel Benin, apparently chatting amiably. They all looked up at Miles's appearance, and Vorob'yev's and Benin's smiles, at least, seemed to grow a shade less amiable. Miles almost turned around to flee back inside.

Rian evidently felt some similar emotion, for the voice from her bubble murmured, "Ah, your people are awaiting you, Lord Vorkosigan. I hope you found this educational, even if not to your needs. Good evening, then," and slipped promptly back into the sanctuary of the Star Crèche.

Oh, this whole thing is a learning experience, milady. Miles fixed a friendly smile on his face, and trod forward across the walkway to the bench, where his waiting watchers rose to greet him. Mia Maz had her usual cheerful dimple. Was it his imagination, or had Vorob'yev's diplomatic affability acquired a strained edge? Benin's expression was less easy to read, through the swirls of face paint.

"Hello," said Miles brightly. "You, uh, waited, sir. Thanks, though I don't think you needed to." Vorob'yev's brows rose in faint, ironic disagreement.

"You have been granted an unusual honor, Lord Vorkosigan," said Benin, nodding toward the Star Crèche.

"Yes, the haut Rian is a very polite lady. I hope I didn't wear her out with all my questions."

"And were all your questions answered?" asked Benin. "You *are* privileged."

One could not mistake the bitter edge to *that* comment, though one could, of course, ignore it. "Oh, yes and no. It's a fascinating place, but I'm afraid its technologies hold no help for my medical needs. I think I'm going to have to consider more surgeries after all. I don't like surgeries, they're surprisingly painful." He blinked mournfully.

Maz looked highly sympathetic; Vorob'yev looked just a little saturnine. *He's beginning to suspect there's something screwy going on. Damn.*

In fact, both Benin and Vorob'yev looked like only the presence of the other was inhibiting him from pinning Miles to the nearest wall and twisting till some truth was emitted.

"If you are finished, then, I shall escort you to the gate," said Benin.

"Yes. The embassy car is waiting, Lord Vorkosigan," Vorob'yev added pointedly.

They all herded obediently after Benin down the path he indicated.

"The real privilege today was getting to hear all that poetry, though," Miles burbled on. "And how are you doing, ghem-Colonel? Are you making any progress on your case?"

Benin's lips twitched. "It does not simplify itself," he murmured.

I'll bet not. Alas, or perhaps fortunately, this was not the time or place for a couple of security men to let their hair down and talk shop frankly.

"Oh, my," said Maz, and they all paused to take in the show a curve in the path presented. A woodsy vista framed a small artificial ravine. Scattered in the dusk among the trees and along the streamlet were hundreds of tiny, luminous tree frogs, variously candy-colored, all singing. They sang in *chords*, pitch-perfect, one chord rising and dying away to be replaced by another; the creatures' luminosity rose and fell as they sang, so the progress of each pure note could be followed by the eye as well as the ear. The ravine's acoustics bounced the not-quite music around in a highly synergistic fashion. Miles's brain seemed to stop dead for a full three minutes at the sheer absurd beauty of it all, till some throat-clearing from Vorob'yev broke the spell, and the party moved on again.

Outside the dome, the capital city's night was warm, humid, and apricot-bright, rumbling with the vast subliminal noise of its life. Night and the city, stretching to the horizon and beyond.

"I am impressed by the luxury of the haut, but then I realize the size of the economic base that supports it," Miles remarked to Benin.

"Indeed," said Benin, with a small smirk. "I believe Cetaganda's per capita tax rate is only half that of Barrayar's. The Emperor cultivates his subjects' economic well-being as a garden, I have heard it said."

Benin was not immune to the Cetagandan taste for one-upmanship. Taxes were always a volatile civil issue at home. "I'm afraid so," Miles returned. "We have to match you militarily with less than a quarter of your resources." He bit his tongue to keep from adding, *Fortunately, that's not hard,* or something equally snide.

Benin was right, though, Miles reflected, as the embassy's aircar rose over the capital. One was awed by the great silver hemisphere, till one looked at the city extending for a hundred kilometers in all directions, not to mention the rest of the planet and the other seven worlds, and did a little math. The Celestial Garden was a flower, but its roots lay elsewhere, in the haut and ghem control of other aspects of the economy. The Great Key seemed suddenly a tiny lever, with which to try to move this world. *Prince Slyke, I think you are an optimist.*

CHAPTER TEN

"You've got to help me out on this one, Ivan," Miles whispered urgently.

"Oh?" murmured Ivan, in a tone of extreme neutrality.

"I didn't know Vorob'yev would be sending *him* along." Miles jerked his chin toward Lord Vorreedi, who had stepped away for some under-voiced conference of his own with their groundcar's driver, the uniformed embassy guard, and the plainclothes guard. The uniformed man wore undress greens like Miles and Ivan; the other two wore the bodysuits and calf-length robes of Cetagandan street wear, the protocol officer with more comfortable practiced ease.

Miles continued, "When I set up this rendezvous with my contact, I thought we'd get Mia Maz as our native guide again, what with this exhibition being the Ladies' Division or whatever they call it. You won't just need to cover my departure. You may need to distract them when I make my break."

The plainclothes guard nodded and strode off. Outer-perimeter man; Miles memorized his face and clothing. One more thing to keep track of. The guard headed toward the entrance to the exhibition . . . hall,

it was not. When today's outing had first been described
to Miles, he had pictured some cavernous quadrangular
structure like the one that housed the District Agricultural Fair at Hassadar. Instead, the Moon Garden
Hall, as it was styled, was another dome, a miniature
suburban imitation of the Celestial Garden at the center of the city. Not too miniature—it was over three
hundred meters in diameter, arcing over steeply sloping
ground. Flocks of well-dressed ghem-types, both men
and women, funneled toward its upper entrance.

"How the hell am I supposed to do that, coz?
Vorreedi's not the distractible sort."

"Tell him I left with a lady, for . . . immoral purposes.
You leave with immoral ladies all the time, why not
me?" Miles's lips twisted in a suppressed snarl at Ivan's
rolled eyes. "Introduce him to half a dozen of *your* girl-
friends, I can't believe we won't run across some here.
Tell them he's the man who taught you all you know
about the Barrayaran Art of Love."

"He's not my type," said Ivan through his teeth.

"So use your initiative!"

"I don't have initiative. *I* follow orders, thank you.
It's much safer."

"Fine. I *order* you to use your initiative."

Ivan breathed a bad word, by way of editorial. "I'm
going to regret this, I know I am."

"Just hold on a little while longer. This will all be
over in a few hours." *One way or another.*

"*That's* what you said day before yesterday. You lied."

"It wasn't my fault. Things were a little more complicated than I'd anticipated."

"You remember the time down at Vorkosigan Surleau
when we found that old guerrilla weapons cache, and
you talked me and Elena into helping you activate the
old hovertank? And we ran it into the barn? And the
barn collapsed? And my mother put me under house-
arrest for two months?"

"We were ten years *old*, Ivan!"

"I remember it like yesterday. I remember it like day-before-yesterday, too."

"That old shed was practically falling down anyway. Saved the price of a demolition crew. For God's sake Ivan, this is serious! You can't compare it to—" Miles broke off as the protocol officer dismissed his men and, smiling faintly, turned back to the two young envoys. He shepherded them into the Moon Garden Hall.

Miles was surprised to see something so crass as a sign, even if made entirely of flowers, decorating an entry arch to a labyrinth of descending walkways spilling down the natural slope. *The 149th Annual Bioestheties Exhibition, Class A. Dedicated to the Memory of the Celestial Lady*. Which dedication had made it a mandatory stop on all polite funeral envoys' social calendars. "Do the haut-women compete here?" Miles asked the protocol officer. "I'd think this would be in their style."

"So much so that no one else could win if they did," said Lord Vorreedi. "They have their own annual bash, very privately, inside the Celestial Garden, but it's on hold till this period of official mourning is completed."

"So . . . these ghem-women exhibitors are, um, imitating their haut half-sisters?"

"Trying to, anyway. That's the name of the game, here."

The ghem-ladies' exhibits were arranged not in rows, but each set individually in its own curve or corner. Miles wondered briefly what kind of jockeying went on behind the scenes for favorable sites and spaces, and what kind of status-points one could win for obtaining the best ones, and if the competition went as far as assassinations. Character-assassinations, anyway, he judged from a few snatches of conversation from groups of ghem-ladies strolling about, admiring and critiquing.

A large tank of fish caught his eye. They were filmy-
finned, their iridescent scales colored in the exact pattern of one of the ghem-clan's face paintings: bright
blue, yellow, black and white. The fish swirled in a
watery gavotte. It was not too remarkable, genetic-
engineering-wise, except that the proud and hopeful
exhibitor hovering nearby appeared to be a girl of about
twelve. She seemed to be a mascot for her clan's ladies'
more serious exhibits. *Give me six years, and watch
out!* her small smile seemed to say.

Blue roses and black orchids were so routine, they
were used merely as framing borders for the real
entries. A young girl passed by, in tow of her ghem-
parents, with a unicorn about half a meter high scam-
pering after her on a golden leash. It wasn't even an
exhibit . . . maybe a commercial product, for all Miles
knew. Unlike Hassadar's District Agricultural Fair, utility
did not seem to be a consideration. It might even count
as a defect. The competition was for art; life was merely
the medium, a bio-palette supplying effects.

They paused to lean on a balcony railing that gave
a partial over-view down the hanging garden's slopes.
A green flicker by his feet caught Miles's eye. An array
of glossy leaves and tendrils was spiraling up Ivan's leg.
Red blossoms slowly opened and closed, breathing a
deep and delicate perfume, albeit the total effect was
unfortunately mouth-like. He stared in fascination for
a full minute before murmuring, "Uh, Ivan . . . ? Don't
move. But look at your left boot."

As Miles watched, another tendril slowly wrapped
itself around Ivan's knee and began hoisting. Ivan
glanced down, lurched, and swore. "What the hell *is*
it? Get it off me!"

"I doubt it's poisonous," said the protocol officer
uncertainly. "But perhaps you had better hold still."

"I . . . think it's a climbing rose. Lively little thing,
isn't it?" Miles grinned, and bent nearer, cautiously

checking for thorns before extending his hands. They might be retractable or something. Colonel Vorreedi made a hesitant restraining motion.

But before he mustered the nerve to risk skin and flesh, a plump ghem-lady carrying a large basket hurried up the path. "Oh, there you are, you bad thing!" she cried. "Excuse me, sir," she addressed Ivan without looking up, kneeling by his boot and commencing to unwind her quarry. "Too much nitrogen this morning, I'm afraid . . ."

The rose let go its last tendril from around Ivan's boot with a regretful recoil, and was unceremoniously plunged into the basket with some other writhing escapees, pink and white and yellow. The woman, her eyes darting here and there at corners and under benches, hurried on.

"I think it liked you," said Miles to Ivan. "Pheromones?"

"Get stuffed," murmured Ivan back. "Or I'll dip *you* in nitrogen, and stake you out under the . . . good God, what is this?"

They'd rounded a corner to an open area displaying a graceful tree, with large fuzzy heart-shaped leaves filling two or three dozen branches that arced and drooped again, swaying slightly with the burden of the podded fruit tipping each branch. The fruit was mewing. Miles and Ivan stepped closer.

"Now . . . now *that* is just plain *wrong*," said Ivan indignantly.

Bundled upside down in each fruit pod was a small kitten, long and silky white fur fluffing out around each feline face, framing ears and whiskers and bright blue eyes. Ivan cradled one in his hand, and lifted it to his face for closer examination. With one blunt finger he carefully tried to pet the creature; it batted playfully at his hand with soft white front paws.

"Kittens like this should be out chasing string, not

glued into damned *trees* to score points for some ghem-bitch," Ivan opined hotly. He glanced around the area; they were temporarily alone and unobserved.

"Um . . . I'm not so sure they're glued in," said Miles. "Wait, I don't think you'd better—"

Trying to stop Ivan from rescuing a kitten from a tree was approximately as futile as trying to stop Ivan from making a pass at a pretty woman. It was some kind of spinal reflex. By the glint in his eye, he was bent on releasing all the tiny victims, to chase after the climbing roses perhaps.

Ivan snapped the pod from the end of its branch. The kitten emitted a squall, convulsed, and went still.

"Kitty, kitty . . . ?" Ivan whispered doubtfully into his cupped hand. An alarming trickle of red fluid coursed from the broken stem across his wrist.

Miles pulled back the pod-leaves around the kitten's . . . corpse, he feared. There was no back half to the beast. Pink naked legs fused together and disappeared into the stem part of the pod.

" . . . I don't think it was ripe, Ivan."

"That's *horrible!*" Ivan's breath rasped in his throat with his outrage, but the volume was pitched way down. By unspoken mutual consent, they sidled quickly away from the kitten-tree and around the nearest unpeopled corner. Ivan glanced around frantically for a place to dispose of the tiny corpse, and so distance himself from his sin and vandalism. "Grotesque!"

Miles said thoughtfully, "Oh, I don't know. It's not any more grotesque than the original method, when you think about it. I mean, have you ever watched a mother cat give birth to kittens?"

Ivan covered his full hand with the other, and glared at his cousin. The protocol officer studied Ivan's dismay with a mixture of exasperation and sympathy. Miles thought that if he had known Ivan longer, the proportion of the first emotion to the second would be much higher, but Vorreedi only said, "My lord . . . would you like me to dispose of that for you . . . discreetly?"

"Uh, yes, please," said Ivan, looking very relieved. "If you don't mind." He hastily palmed off the inert pod of fluff onto the protocol officer, who hid it in a pocket handkerchief.

"Stay here. I'll be back shortly," he said, and went off to get rid of the evidence.

"Good one, Ivan," growled Miles. "Want to keep your hands in your pockets after this?"

Ivan scrubbed at the sticky substance on his hand with his own handkerchief, spat into his palm, and scrubbed again. *Out, out, damned spot . . .* "Don't you start making noises like my mother. It wasn't my fault. . . . Things were a little more complicated than I'd anticipated." Ivan stuffed his handkerchief back in his pocket, and stared around, frowning. "This isn't fun anymore. I want to go back to the embassy."

"You have to hang on till I meet my contact, at least."

"And when will that be?"

"Soon, I suspect."

They strolled to the end of the aisle, where another little balcony gave an enticing view of the next lower section.

"Damn," said Ivan.

"What do you see?" asked Miles, tracking his gaze. He stretched to stand on tiptoe, but it wasn't enough to spot what had caught Ivan's negative attention.

"Our good buddy Lord Yenaro is here. Two levels down, talking to some women."

"It . . . could be a coincidence. This place is lousy with ghem-lords, with the award ceremony this afternoon. The winning women gain honor for their clan, naturally they want to cash in. And this is just the sort of artsy stuff that tickles his fancy, I think."

Ivan cocked an eyebrow at him. "You want to bet on that?"

"Nope."

Ivan sighed. "I don't suppose there's any way we can get him before he gets us."

"Don't know. Keep your eyes open, anyway."

"No lie."

They stared around some more. A ghem-lady of middle-age and dignified bearing approached them, and gave Miles an acknowledging, if not exactly friendly, nod. Her palm turned outward briefly, displaying to him a heavy ring, with a raised screaming-bird pattern fili-greed with complex encodes.

"Now?" Miles said quietly.

"No." Her cultured voice was a low-pitched alto. "Meet me by the west entrance in thirty minutes."

"I may not be able to achieve precision."

"I'll wait." She passed on.

"Crap," said Ivan, after a moment's silence. "You're really going to try to bring this off. You will be the hell careful, won't you?"

"Oh, yes."

The protocol officer was taking a long time to find the nearest waste-disposal unit, Miles thought. But just as his nerves were stretching to the point of going to look for the man, he reappeared, walking quickly toward them. His smile of greeting seemed a little strained.

"My lords," he nodded. "Something has come up. I'm going to have to leave you for a while. Stay together, and don't leave the building, please."

Perfect. Maybe. "What sort of something?" asked Miles. "We spotted Yenaro."

"Our practical joker? Yes. We know he's here. My analysts judge him a non-lethal annoyance. I must leave you to defend yourselves from him, temporarily. But my outer-perimeter man, who is one of my sharpest fellows, has spotted another individual, known to us. A professional."

The term *professional*, in this context, meant a professional killer, or something along those lines. Miles nodded alertly.

"We don't know why he's here," Vorreedi went on. "I have some heavier backup on the way. In the meanwhile, we propose to . . . drop in on him for a short chat."

"Fast-penta is illegal here for anyone but the police and the imperials, isn't it?"

"I doubt this one would go to the authorities to complain," murmured Vorreedi, with a slightly sinister smile.

"Have fun."

"Watch yourselves." The protocol officer nodded, and drifted away, as-if-casually.

Miles and Ivan walked on, pausing to examine a couple more rooted floral displays that seemed less unnervingly uncertain of their kingdom and phylum. Miles counted minutes in his head. He could break away shortly, and reach his rendezvous right on time. . . .

"Well, *hello*, sweet thing," a musical voice trilled from behind them. Ivan turned around a beat faster than Miles. Lady Arvin and Lady Benello stood with arms linked. They unlinked arms and . . . oozed, Miles decided was the term, up on either side of Ivan, capturing one side each.

"Sweet thing?" Miles murmured in delight. Ivan spared him a brief glower before turning to his greeters.

"We heard you were here, Lord Ivan," the blonde, Lady Arvin, continued. Tall Lady Benello concurred, her cascade of amber curls bouncing with her nod. "What are you doing afterwards?"

"Ah . . . no particular plans," said Ivan, his head swiveling in an attempt to divide his attention precisely in half.

"Ooh," said Lady Arvin. "Perhaps you would care to have dinner with me, at my penthouse."

Lady Benello interrupted, "Or, if you're not in an urban mood, I know this place not far from here, on a lake. Each patron is rowed out to their own little tiny island, and a picnic is served, *al fresco*. It's *very* private."

Each woman smiled repellingly at the other. Ivan looked faintly hunted. "What a tough decision," he temporized.

"Come along and see Lady Benello's sister's pretties, while you think about it then, Lord Ivan," said Lady Arvin equably. Her eye fell on Miles. "You too, Lord Vorkosigan. We've been neglecting our most senior guest quite shamefully, *I* think. Upon discussion, we think this might be a regrettable oversight." Her hand tightened on Ivan's arm, and she peeked around his torso to give her red-haired companion a bright, meaningful smile. "This could be the solution to Lord Ivan's dilemma."

"In the dark all cats are gray?" Miles murmured. "Or at any rate, all Barrayarans?"

Ivan winced at the mention of felines. Lady Arvin looked blank, but Miles had a bad feeling the redhead had caught the joke. In any case, she detached herself from Ivan—was that a flash of triumph, crossing Lady Arvin's face?—and turned to Miles.

"Indeed, Lord Vorkosigan. Do you have any particular plans?"

"I'm afraid so," said Miles with a regret that was not entirely feigned. "In fact, I have to be going now."

"Right now? Oh, do come . . . see my sister's exhibit, at least." Lady Benello stopped short of linking arms with him, but seemed willing to walk by his side, even if it left her rival in temporary possession of Ivan.

Time. It wouldn't hurt to give the protocol officer

a few more minutes to become fully engaged with his
quarry. Miles smiled thinly, and allowed himself to be
dragged along in the wake of the party, Lady Arvin in
the lead towing Ivan. That tall redhead lacked the
porcelain delicacy of the haut Rian. On the other hand,
she was not nearly so . . . *impossible. The difficult we
do at once. The impossible takes . . .*

Stop it. These women are users, you know that.

Oh, God, let me be used. . . .

Focus, boy, goddammit.

They walked down the switchback pathway, arriving
at the next lower level. Lady Arvin turned in at a small
circular open space screened by trees in tubs. Their
leaves were glossy and jewel-like, but they were merely
a frame for the display in the center. The display was
a little baffling, artistically. It seemed to consist of three
lengths of thick brocade, in subtle hues, spiraling loosely
around each other from the top of a man-high pole to
trail on the carpet below. The dense circular carpet
echoed the greens of the bordering trees, in a complex abstract pattern.

"Heads up," murmured Ivan.

"I see him," breathed Miles.

Lord Yenaro, dark-robed and smiling, was sitting on
one of the little curving benches that also helped frame
the space.

"Where's Veda?" asked Lady Benello.

"She just stepped out," said Yenaro, rising and nodding greetings to all.

"Lord Yenaro has been giving my sister Veda a little
help with her entry," Lady Benello confided to Miles
and Ivan.

"Oh?" said Miles, staring around and wondering
where the trap was this time. He didn't see it yet. "And,
uh . . . just what is her entry?"

"I know it doesn't look very impressive," said Lady
Benello defensively, "but that's not the point. The

subtlety is in the smell. It's the cloth. It emits a perfume that changes with the mood of the wearer. I *still* wonder if we ought to have had it made up into a dress," this last comment seemed aimed at Yenaro. "We could have had one of the servitors stand here and model it all day."

"It would have seemed too commercial," Yenaro said to her. "This will score better."

"And, um . . . it's alive?" asked Ivan doubtfully.

"The scent glands in the cloth are as alive as the sweat glands in your body," Yenaro assured him. "Nevertheless, you are right, the display is a bit static. Step closer, and we'll hand-demonstrate the effects."

Miles sniffed, his paranoia-heightened awareness trying to individually check every volatile molecule that entered his nostrils. The dome was clouded with scents of every kind, drifting down from the displays upslope, not to mention the perfumes of the ghem-ladies and Yenaro in their robes. But the brocade did seem to be emitting a pleasant mixture of odors. Ivan didn't respond to the invitation to come closer either, Miles noticed. In addition to the perfumes, though, there was something else, a faint, oily acridity. . . .

Yenaro picked up a pitcher from the bench and walked toward the pole. "More zlati ale?" Ivan murmured dryly.

Recognition and memory zinged through Miles, followed by a wave of adrenaline that nearly stopped his heart before it began racing. "Grab that pitcher, Ivan! Don't let him spill it!"

Ivan did. Yenaro gave up his hold with a surprised snort. "Really, Lord Ivan!"

Miles dropped prone to the thick carpet, sniffing frantically. *Yes.*

"What are you *doing?*" asked Lady Benello, half-laughing. "The rug isn't part of it!"

Oh, yes it is. "Ivan," said Miles urgently, scrambling

back to his feet. "Hand me that—*carefully*—and tell me what you smell down there."

Miles took the pitcher much more tenderly than he would have a basket of raw eggs. Ivan, with a look of some bewilderment, did as he was told. He sniffed, then ran his hand through the carpet, and touched his fingers to his lips. And turned white. Miles knew Ivan had reached the same conclusion he had even before he turned his head and hissed, "Asterzine!"

Miles tiptoed back well away from the carpet, lifted the pitcher's lid, and sniffed again. A faint odor resembling vanilla and oranges, gone slightly wrong, wafted up, which was exactly right.

And Yenaro had been going to dump it all, Miles was sure. At his own feet. With Lady Benello and Lady Arvin looking on. Miles thought of the fate of Lord X's, Prince Slyke's, last tool, the Ba Lura. *No. Yenaro doesn't know. He may hate Barrayarans, but he's not that frigging crazy. He was set up right along with us, this time. Third time's a charm, all right.*

When Ivan rose, his jaw set and his eyes burning, Miles motioned him over and handed him the pitcher again. Ivan took it gingerly, stepping back another pace. Miles knelt and tore off a few threads from the carpet's edge. The threads parted with a gum-like stretching, confirming his diagnosis. "Lord Vorkosigan!" Lady Arvin objected, her brows drawn down in amused puzzlement at the Barrayarans' bizarre barbarian behavior.

Miles traded the threads to Ivan for the pitcher again, and jerked his head toward Yenaro. "Bring *him.* Excuse us, please, ladies. Um . . . man-talk."

Rather to his surprise, this appeal actually worked; Lady Arvin only arched her brows, though Lady Benello pouted slightly. Ivan wrapped one hand around Yenaro's upper arm, and guided him out of the display area. Ivan's grip tightened in silent threat when Yenaro tried to shrug him off. Yenaro looked angry and tight-lipped and just a little embarrassed.

They found an empty nook a few spaces down. Ivan stood himself and his captive with their backs to the path, shielding Miles from view. Miles gently set the pitcher down, stood, jerked up his chin, and addressed Yenaro in a low-pitched growl. "I will demonstrate what you almost did in just a moment. What I want to know now is just what the hell you *thought* you were doing?"

"I don't know what you're talking about," snapped Yenaro. "Let *go*, you lout!"

Ivan kept his hold, frowning fiercely. "Demonstrate first, coz."

"Right." The paving-stones were some cool artificial marble, and did not look flammable. Miles shook the threads off his finger, and motioned Ivan and Yenaro closer. He waited till there were no passersby in sight and said, "Yenaro. Take two drops on your fingers of that harmless liquid you were waving around, and sprinkle them on this."

Ivan forced Yenaro to kneel alongside Miles. Yenaro, with a cold glance at his captors, dipped his hand and sprinkled as ordered. "If you think—"

He was interrupted by a bright flash and a wave of heat that scorched Miles's eyebrows. The soft report, fortunately, was mostly muffled by their shielding bodies. Yenaro froze, arrested.

"And that was only about a gram of material," Miles went on relentlessly. "That whole carpet-bomb massed, what, about five kilos? You should know, I'm certain you carried it in here personally. When the catalyst hit, it would have gone up taking out this whole section of the dome, you, me, the ladies . . . it would have been quite the high point of the show."

"This is some sort of trick," grated Yenaro.

"Oh, it's a trick all right. But this time the joke was on you. You've never had any military training at all, have you? Or with your nose, you'd have recognized it too. Sensitized asterzine. Lovely stuff. Formable, dyeable, you can make it look like practically anything. And totally inert and harmless, till the catalyst hits it. Then . . ." Miles nodded toward the small scorched patch on the white pavement. "Let me put the question to you another way, Yenaro. What effect did your good friend the haut-governor *tell* you this was going to have?"

"He—" Yenaro's breath caught. His hand swept down across the dark and oily residue, then rose to his nose. He inhaled, frowning, then sat back rather weakly on his heels. His wide eyes lifted to meet Miles's gaze. "Oh."

"Confession," said Ivan meaningfully, "is good for the soul. And body."

Miles took a breath. "Once more, from the top, Yenaro. What did you *think* you were doing?"

Yenaro swallowed. "It . . . was supposed to release an ester. That would simulate alcohol poisoning. You Barrayarans are famous for that perversion. Nothing that you don't already do to yourselves!"

"Allowing Ivan and me to publicly stagger through the rest of the afternoon blind drunk, or a close approximation."

"Something like that."

"And yourself? Did you just ingest the antidote, before we showed up?"

"No, it was harmless! . . . supposed to be. I had made arrangements to go and rest, till it passed off. I thought it might be . . . an interesting sensation."

"Pervert," murmured Ivan.

Yenaro glared at him.

Miles said slowly, "When I was burned, that first night. All that hand-wringing on your part wasn't totally feigned, was it? You weren't expecting it."

Yenaro paled. "I expected . . . I thought perhaps the

Marilacans had done something to the power adjustment. It was only supposed to shock, not injure."

"Or so you were told."

"Yes," Yenaro whispered.

"The zlati ale was your idea, though, wasn't it," growled Ivan.

"You knew?!"

"I'm not an idiot."

Some passing ghem glanced in puzzlement at the three men kneeling in a circle on the floor, though fortunately they passed on without comment. Miles nodded to the nearest bench, in the curve of the nook. "I have something to tell you, Lord Yenaro, and I think you had better be sitting down." Ivan guided Yenaro to it and firmly pushed him down. After a thoughtful moment, Ivan then poured the rest of the pitcher of liquid into the nearest tree-tub, before settling between Yenaro and the exit.

"This isn't just a series of gratifying tricks played on the doltish envoys of a despised enemy, for you to chuckle at," Miles went on lowly. "You are being used as a pawn in a treason plot against the Cetagandan Emperor. Used, discarded, and silenced. It's beginning to be a pattern. Your last fellow-pawn was the Ba Lura. I trust you've heard what happened to *it*."

Yenaro's pale lips parted, but he breathed no word. After a moment he licked his lips and tried again. "This can't be. It's too crude. It would have started a blood feud between his clan and those of . . . all the innocent bystanders."

"No. It would have started a blood feud between their clans and *yours*. You were set up to take the fall for this one. Not only as an assassin, but as one so incompetent that he blew himself up with his own bomb. Following in your grandfather's footsteps, so to speak. And who would be left alive to deny it? The confusion would multiply within the capital, as well as between your Empire and Barrayar, while his satrapy made its break for independence. No, not crude. Downright elegant."

"The Ba Lura committed suicide. It was said."

"No. Murdered. Cetagandan Imperial Security is on to that one, too. They will unravel it in time. No . . . they will unravel it eventually. I don't trust that it will be in time."

"It is impossible for a ba servitor to commit treason."

"Unless the ba servitor thinks that it is acting loyally, in a deliberately ambiguous situation. I don't think even the ba are so un-human that they cannot be *mistaken*."

" . . . No." Yenaro looked up at both the Barrayarans. "You must believe, I would have no regrets whatsoever if you two fell off a cliff. But I would not push you myself."

"I . . . so I judged," said Miles. "But for my curiosity—what were you to get out of the deal, besides a week's amusement in embarrassing a couple of loutish barbarians? Or was this art for art's sake on your part?"

"He promised me a post." Yenaro stared at the floor again. "You don't understand, what it is to be without a post in the capital. You have no position. You have no status. You are . . . no one. I was tired of being no one."

"What post?"

"Imperial Perfumer." Yenaro's dark eyes flashed. "I know it doesn't sound very mighty, but it would have gained me entrance to the Celestial Garden, maybe the Imperial Presence itself. Where I would have worked among . . . the best in the empire. The top people. And I would have been *good*."

Miles had no trouble understanding ambition, no matter how arcane its form. "I imagine so."

Yenaro's lips twitched in half a grateful smile.

Miles glanced at his chrono. "God, I'm late. Ivan—can you handle this from here?"

"I think so."

Miles rose. "Good day, Lord Yenaro, and a better one than you were destined to have, I think. I may have used up a year's supply this afternoon already, but wish me luck. I have a little date with Prince Slyke now."

"Good luck," Yenaro said doubtfully.

Miles paused. "It *was* Prince Slyke, was it not?"

"No! I was talking about Governor the haut Ilsum Kety!"

Miles pursed his lips, and blew out his breath in a slow trickle. *I have just been either screwed or saved. I wonder which?* "Kety set you up . . . with all this?"

"Yes . . ."

Could Kety have sent his fellow governor and cousin Prince Slyke to scout out the Imperial Regalia for him, a stalking horse? Certainly. Or not. For that matter, could Slyke have set up Kety to operate Yenaro for him? Not impossible. *Back to square one. Damn, damn, damn!*

While Miles hovered in new doubt, the protocol officer rounded the corner. His hurried stride slowed as he spotted Miles and Ivan, and a look of relief crossed his face. By the time he strolled into the nook he was projecting the air of a tourist again, but he raked Yenaro with a knife-keen glance.

"Hello, my lords." His nod took all three in equally.

"Hello, sir," said Miles. "Did you have an interesting conversation?"

"Extraordinarily."

"Ah . . . I don't believe you've formally met Lord Yenaro, sir. Lord Yenaro, this is my embassy's protocol officer, Lord Vorreedi."

The two men exchanged more studied nods, Yenaro's hand going to his chest in a sketch of a sitting bow.

"What a coincidence, Lord Yenaro," Vorreedi went on. "We were just talking about you."

"Oh?" said Yenaro warily.

"Ah . . ." Vorreedi sucked his lip thoughtfully, then seemed to come to some internal decision. "Are you aware that you seem to be in the middle of some sort of vendetta at present, Lord Yenaro?"

"I—no! What makes you think so?"

"Hm. Normally, ghem-lords' personal affairs are not my business, only the official ones. But the, ah, chance of a good deed has come up so squarely in my path, I shall not avoid it. This time. I just had a short talk with a, ah, gentleman who informed me he was here today with the mission of seeing that you, in his precise phrasing, did not leave the Moon Garden Hall alive. He was a little vague about what method he proposed to use to accomplish this. What made him peculiar in this venue was that he was no ghem. A purely commercial artist. He did not know who had hired him, that information being concealed behind several layers of screening. Do you have any guesses?"

Yenaro listened to this recital shocked, tight-lipped, and thoughtful. Miles wondered if Yenaro was going through the same set of deductions he was. He rather thought so. The haut-governor, it appeared, whichever one it was, had sent Yenaro's ploy some backup. Just to make sure nothing went wrong. Such as Yenaro surviving his own bombing to accuse his betrayer.

"I . . . have a guess, yes."

"Would you care to share it?"

Yenaro regarded him doubtfully. "Not at this time."

"Suit yourself," Vorreedi shrugged. "We left him sitting in a quiet corner. The fast-penta should wear off in about ten minutes. You have that much lead-time to do—whatever you decide."

"Thank you, Lord Vorreedi," said Yenaro quietly. He gathered his dark robes about himself, and rose. He was pale, but admirably controlled, not shaking. "I think I will leave you now."

"Probably a good choice," said Vorreedi.

"Keep in touch, huh?" said Miles.

Yenaro gave him a brief, formal nod. "Yes. We must talk again." He strode away, glancing left and right.

Ivan chewed on his fingers. It was better than his blurting out everything to Vorreedi right here and now, Miles's greatest fear.

"Was that all true, sir?" Miles asked Colonel Vorreedi.

"Yes." Vorreedi rubbed his nose. "Except that I'm not so certain that it isn't any of our business. Lord Yenaro seems to be taking a great deal of interest in you. One can't help wondering if there might be some hidden connection. Sifting through that hired thug's hierarchy would be tedious and time-consuming for my department. And what would we find at the end?" Vorreedi's eye fell coolly on Miles. "Just how angry *were* you at getting your legs burned the other night, Lord Vorkosigan?"

"Not that angry!" Miles denied hastily. "Give me credit for a sense of proportion, at least, sir! No. It wasn't me who hired the goon." Though he had just as surely set up Yenaro for this, by attempting to play all those cute little head-games with his possible patrons, Kety, Prince Slyke, and the Rond. *You wanted a reaction, you got one.* "But . . . it's just a feeling, you understand. But I think pursuing this lead might be time and resources well spent."

"A feeling, eh?"

"You surely have trusted your intuition before, in your work, sir."

"Used, yes. Trusted, never. An ImpSec officer should be clear about the difference."

"I understand, sir."

They all rose to continue the tour of the exhibition, Miles carefully not glancing at the scorched spot on the pavement as they passed on. As they approached the west side of the dome, Miles searched the robed crowd for his contact-lady. There she was, sitting near a fountain, frowning. But he would never succeed in ditching Vorreedi now; the man was stuck like glue. He tried anyway. "Excuse me, sir. I have to speak to a lady."

"I'll come with you," said Vorreedi pleasantly.

Right. Miles sighed, hastily composing his message. The dignified ghem-lady looked up as he approached with his unwelcome companions. Miles realized he didn't know the woman's name.

"Pardon me, milady. I just wanted to let you know that I will not be able to accept your invitation to visit, uh, this afternoon. Please convey my deepest regrets to your mistress." Would she, and the haut Rian, interpret this as intended, as *Abort, abort abort!*? Miles could only pray so. "But if she can arrange instead a visit to the man's cousin, I think that would be most educational."

The woman's frown deepened. But she only said, "I will convey your words, Lord Vorkosigan."

Miles nodded farewell, mentally blessing her for avoiding the pitfall of any more complicated reply. When he looked back, she had already swept to her feet and was hurrying away.

CHAPTER ELEVEN

Miles had not entered the sacred confines of the Barrayaran embassy's ImpSec offices before, having stayed discreetly upstairs in the diplomatic corps' plusher territory. As he'd posited, it was on the second lowest basement level. A uniformed corporal ushered him past security scanners and into Colonel Vorreedi's office.

It was not as austere as Miles expected, being decorated all about with small examples of Cetagandan art objects, though the powered sculptures were all turned off this morning. Some might be mementos, but the rest suggested the so-called protocol officer was a collector of excellent taste, if limited means.

The man himself was seated at a desk cleared in utilitarian bareness. Vorreedi was dressed as usual in the underlayers and robes of a middle-ranking ghem-lord of painfully sober preferences, subdued blues and grays. Except for the lack of face paint, in a crowd of ghem Vorreedi would practically disappear, though behind a Barrayaran ImpSec comconsole desk the effect of the ensemble was a little startling.

Miles moistened his lips. "Good morning, sir. Ambassador Vorob'yev told me you wanted to see me."

"Yes, thank you, Lord Vorkosigan." Vorreedi's nod dismissed the corporal, who withdrew silently. The doors slid shut behind him with a heavy sealing sound. "Do sit down."

Miles slipped into the station chair across the desk from Vorreedi, and smiled in what he hoped seemed innocent good cheer. Vorreedi looked across at Miles with keen, undivided attention. Not good. Vorreedi was second in authority here only to Ambassador Vorob'yev, and like Vorob'yev, had been chosen as a top man for one of the most critical posts in the Barrayaran diplomatic corps. One might count on Vorreedi to be a very busy man, but never a stupid one. Miles wondered if Vorreedi's meditations this past night had been one half so busy as his own. Miles braced himself for an Illyanesque opening shot, such as *What the hell are you up to, Vorkosigan, trying to start a damned war single-handed?!*

Instead, Colonel Vorreedi favored him with a long, thoughtful stare, before observing mildly, "Lieutenant Lord Vorkosigan. You are an ImpSec courier officer, by assignment."

"Yes, sir. When I am on duty."

"An interesting breed of men. Utterly reliable and loyal. They go here, go there, deliver whatever is asked of them without question or comment. Or failure, short of intervention by death itself."

"It's not usually that dramatic. We spend a lot of time riding around in jumpships. One catches up on one's reading."

"Mm. And to a man, these glorified mailmen report to Commodore Boothe, head of ImpSec Communications, Komarr. With one exception." Vorreedi's gaze intensified. "*You* are listed as reporting directly to Simon Illyan himself. Who reports to Emperor Gregor. The only other person I know of offhand in a chain of command that short is the Chief of Staff of the

Imperial Service. It's an interesting anomaly. How do you explain it?"

"How do *I* explain it?" Miles echoed, temporizing. He thought briefly of replying, *I never explain anything*, except that was both 1) already evident and 2) clearly not the answer Vorreedi was looking for. "Why . . . every once in a while Emperor Gregor needs a personal errand run for himself or his household which is too trivial, or too inappropriate, to assign to working military personnel. Perhaps he wants, say, an ornamental breadfruit bush brought from the planet Pol to be planted in the garden of the Imperial Residence. They send me."

"That's a good explanation," Vorreedi agreed blandly. There was a short silence. "And do you have an equally good story for how you acquired this pleasant job?"

"Nepotism, obviously. Since I am clearly," Miles's smile thinned, "physically unfit for normal duties, this post was manufactured for me by my family connections."

"Hm." Vorreedi sat back, and rubbed his chin. "Now," he said distantly, "if you were a covert ops agent here on a mission from God," meaning Simon Illyan— same thing, from the ImpSec point of view, "you should have arrived with some sort of *Render all due assistance* order. Then a poor ImpSec local man might know where he stood with you."

If I don't get this man under control, he can and will nail my boots to the floor of the embassy, and Lord X will have no impediment at all to his baroque bid for chaos and empire. "Yes, sir," Miles took a breath, "and so would anyone else who saw it."

Vorreedi glanced up, startled. "Does ImpSec Command suspect a leak in my communications?"

"Not as far as I know. But as a lowly courier, I can't ask questions, can I?"

By the slight widening of his eyes, Vorreedi caught

the joke. A subtle man indeed. "From the moment you set foot on Eta Ceta, Lord Vorkosigan, I have not noticed you *stop* asking questions."

"A personal failing."

"And . . . do you have any supporting evidence for your explanation of yourself?"

"Certainly." Miles stared thoughtfully into the air, as if about to pull his words from the thinnest part. "Consider, sir. All other ImpSec courier officers have an implanted allergy to fast-penta. It renders them interrogation-proof to illicit questioners, at fatal cost. Due to my rank and relations, that was judged too dangerous a procedure to do to me. Therefore, I am qualified for only the lowest-security sort of missions. It's all nepotism."

"Very . . . convincing."

"It wouldn't be much good if it weren't, sir."

"True." Another long pause. "Is there anything else you'd like to tell me—Lieutenant?"

"When I return to Barrayar, I will be giving a complete report of my m— excursion to Simon Illyan. I'm afraid you'll have to apply to him. It is definitely not within my authority to try and guess what he will wish to tell you."

There, whew. He'd told no lies at all, technically, even by implication. *Yeah. Be sure and point that out when they play a transcript of this conversation at your future court-martial.* But if Vorreedi chose to construe that Miles was a covert ops agent working on the highest levels and in utmost secrecy, it was no less than perfectly true. The fact that his mission here was spontaneously self-appointed and not assigned from above was . . . another order of problem altogether.

"I . . . could add a philosophical observation."

"Please do, my lord."

"You don't hire a genius to solve the most intractable imaginable problem, and then hedge him around with a lot of rules, nor try to micro-manage him from two weeks' distance. You turn him loose. If all you need is somebody to follow orders, you can hire an idiot. In fact, an idiot would be better suited."

Vorreedi's fingers drummed lightly on his comconsole desk. Miles felt the man might have tackled an intractable problem or two himself, in his past. Vorreedi's brows rose. "And do you consider yourself a genius, Lord Vorkosigan?" he asked softly. Vorreedi's tone of voice made Miles's skin crawl, it reminded him so much of his father's when Count Vorkosigan was about to spring some major verbal trap.

"My intelligence evaluations are in my personnel file, sir."

"I've read it. That's why we're having this conversation." Vorreedi blinked, slowly, like a lizard. "No rules at all?"

"Well, one rule, maybe. Deliver success or pay with your ass."

"You have held your current post for almost three years, I see, Lieutenant Vorkosigan. . . .Your ass is still intact, is it?"

"Last time I checked, sir." *For the next five days, maybe.*

"This suggests astonishing authority and autonomy."

"No authority at all. Just responsibility."

"Oh, dear." Vorreedi pursed his lips very thoughtfully indeed. "You have my sympathy, Lord Vorkosigan."

"Thank you, sir. I need it." Into the all-too-meditative silence that followed Miles added, "Do we know if Lord Yenaro survived the night?"

"He disappeared, so we think he has. He was last seen leaving the Moon Garden Hall with a roll of carpet over his shoulder." Vorreedi cocked an inquiring eye at Miles. "I have no explanation for the carpet."

Miles ignored the broad hint, responding instead

with, "Are you so sure that disappearance equates with his survival? What about his stalker?"

"Hm." Vorreedi smiled. "Shortly after we left him he was picked up by the Cetagandan Civil Police, who still have him in close custody."

"They did this on their own?"

"Let's say they received an anonymous tip. It seemed the socially responsible thing to do. But I must say, the Civils responded to it with admirable efficiency. He appears to be of interest to them for some previous work."

"Did he have time to report in to his employers, before he was canned?"

"No."

So, Lord X was in an information vacuum this morning. He wouldn't like that one bit. The mis-fire of yesterday's plot must make him frantically frustrated. He wouldn't know what had gone wrong, or if Yenaro had realized his intended fate, though Yenaro's disappearance and subsequent non-communication would surely be a fat clue. Yenaro was now as loose a cannon as Miles and Ivan. Which of them would be first on Lord X's hit list after this? Would Yenaro go seeking protection to some authority, or would the rumor of treason frighten him off?

And what method could Lord X come up with for disposing of the Barrayaran envoys one-half so baroque and perfect as Yenaro had been? Yenaro was a masterpiece, as far as the art of assassination went, beautifully choreographed in three movements and a crescendo. Now all that elaborate effort was wasted. Lord X would be as livid at the spoiling of his lovely pattern as at the failure of his plot, Miles swore. And he was an anxious impatient artist who couldn't leave well enough alone, who had to add those clever little touches. The kind of person who, as a child given his first garden, would dig up the seeds to see if they'd sprouted yet. (Miles felt a tiny twinge of sympathy for Lord X.) Yes, indeed, Lord X, playing for great stakes and losing both time and his inhibitions, was now well and classically primed to make a major mistake.

Why am I not so sure that's such a great idea?

"More to add, Lord Vorkosigan?" said Vorreedi.

"Hm? No. Just, uh, thinking." *Besides, it would only upset you.*

"I would request, as the embassy officer ultimately responsible for your personal safety as an official envoy, that you and Lord Vorpatril end your social contacts with a man who is apparently involved in a lethal Cetagandan vendetta."

"Yenaro is of no further interest to me. I wish him no harm. My real priority is in identifying the man who supplied him with that fountain."

Vorreedi's brows rose in mild reproach. "You might have said so earlier."

"Hindsight," said Miles, "is always better."

"That's for damned sure," sighed Vorreedi, in a voice of experience. He scratched his nose, and sat back. "There is another reason I called you here this morning, Lord Vorkosigan. Ghem-Colonel Benin has requested a second interview with you."

"Has he? Same as before?" Miles kept his voice from squeaking.

"Not quite. He specifically requested to speak with both you and Lord Vorpatril. In fact, he's on his way now. But you can refuse the interview if you wish."

"No, that's . . . that's fine. In fact, I'd like to talk to Benin again. I, ah . . . shall I go fetch Ivan, then, sir?" Miles rose to his feet. Bad, bad idea to let the two suspects consult before the interrogation, but then, this wasn't Vorreedi's case. How fully had Miles convinced the man of his secret clout?

"Go ahead," said Vorreedi affably. "Though I must say . . ."

Miles paused.

"I do not see how Lord Vorpatril fits into this. He's no courier officer. And his records are as transparent as glass."

"A lot of people are baffled by Ivan, sir. But . . . sometimes, even a genius needs someone who can follow orders."

Miles tried not to scamper, hustling down the corridor to Ivan's quarters. The luxury of privacy their status had bought them was about to come to a screeching halt, he suspected. If Vorreedi didn't turn on the bugs in both their rooms after this, the man either had supernatural self-control or was brain dead. And the protocol officer was the voraciously curious type; it went with his job.

Ivan unlocked his door with a drawl of "Enter," at Miles's impatient knock. Miles found his cousin sitting up in bed, half-dressed in green trousers and cream shirt, leafing through a pile of hand-calligraphed colored papers with an abstracted and not particularly happy air.

"Ivan. Get up. Get dressed. We're about to have an interview with Colonel Vorreedi and ghem-Colonel Benin."

"Confession at last, thank God!" Ivan tossed the papers up in the air and fell backward on his bed with a *woof* of relief.

"No. Not exactly. But I need you to let me do most of the talking, and confirm whatever I assert."

"Oh, damn." Ivan frowned up at the ceiling. "What *now*?"

"Benin has to have been investigating Ba Lura's movements, the day before its death. I'm guessing he's traced the Ba to our little encounter at the pod dock. I don't want to screw up his investigation. In fact, I want it to succeed, at least as far as identifying the

Ba's murderer. So he needs as many real facts as possible."

"Real facts. As opposed to what other kind of facts?"

"We absolutely can't bring up any mention of the Great Key, or the haut Rian. I figure we can tell events exactly as they happened, just leave out that one tiny detail."

"You figure, do you? You must be using a different kind of math than the rest of the universe does. Do you realize how pissed Vorreedi and the Ambassador are going to be about our concealing that little incident?"

"I've got Vorreedi under control, temporarily. He thinks I'm on a mission from Simon Illyan."

"That means you aren't. I knew it!" Ivan groaned, and pulled a pillow over his face, and squashed it tight.

Miles pulled it out of his grasp. "I am now. Or I would be, if Illyan knew what I know. Bring that nerve disruptor. But don't pull it out unless I tell you to."

"I am not shooting your commanding officer for you."

"You're not shooting anybody. And anyway, Vorreedi's not my commander." That could be an important legal point, later. "I may want it for evidence. But not unless the subject comes up. We volunteer nothing."

"Never volunteer, yes, that's the ticket! You're catching on at last, coz!"

"Shut up. Get up." Miles threw Ivan's undress uniform jacket across his prostrate form. "This is important! But you have to stay absolutely cool. I may be completely off-base, and panicking prematurely."

"I don't think so. I think you're panicking post-maturely. In fact, if you were panicking any later it would be practically posthumously. I've been panicking for *days*."

Miles tossed Ivan his half-boots, with ruthless finality. Ivan shook his head, sat up, and began pulling them on.

"Do you remember," Ivan sighed, "that time in the back garden at Vorkosigan House, when you'd been reading all those military histories about the Cetagandan prison camps during the invasion, and you decided we had to dig an escape tunnel? Except it was you who did all the designing, and me and Elena who did all the digging?"

"We were about eight," said Miles defensively. "The medics were still working on my bones. I was still pretty friable then."

"—and the tunnel collapsed on me?" Ivan went on dreamily. "And I was under there for *hours*?"

"It wasn't hours. It was minutes. Sergeant Bothari had you out of there in practically no time."

"It seemed like hours to *me*. I can still taste the dirt. It got stuffed up my nose, too." Ivan rubbed his nose in memory. "Mother would still be having the fit, if Aunt Cordelia hadn't sat on her."

"We were stupid little *kids*. What has this got to do with anything?"

"Nothing, I suppose. I just woke up thinking about it, this morning." Ivan stood up, fastened his tunic, and pulled it straight. "I never believed I'd miss Sergeant Bothari, but I think I do now. Who's going to dig me out this time?"

Miles wanted to snap out a sharp rejoinder, but shivered instead. *I miss Bothari too.* He had almost forgotten how much, till Ivan's words hit the scar of his regret, that secret little pocket of anguish that never seemed to drain. Major mistakes . . . Dammit, a man walking a tight-wire didn't need someone shouting from the sidelines how far down the drop was, or what lousy balance he had. It wasn't like he didn't know; but what he most needed was to forget. Even a momentary loss of concentration—of self-confidence—of forward momentum, could be fatal. "Do me a favor, Ivan. Don't try to think. You'll hurt yourself. Just follow orders, huh?"

Ivan bared his teeth in a non-smile, and followed Miles out the door.

They met with ghem-Colonel Benin in the same little conference room as before, but this time, Vorreedi rode shotgun personally, dispensing with the guard. The two colonels were just finishing the amenities and sitting down as Miles and Ivan entered, by which sign Miles hoped they'd had less time to compare notes than he and Ivan'd had. Benin was dressed again in his formal red uniform and lurid face paint, freshly and perfectly applied. By the time they'd all finished going through the polite greetings once more, and everyone was reseated, Miles had his breathing and heartbeat under control. Ivan concealed his nerves in an expression of blank benevolence that made him look, in Miles's opinion, remarkably sappy.

"Lord Vorkosigan," ghem-Colonel Benin began. "I understand you work as a courier officer."

"When I'm on duty." Miles decided to repeat the party line for Benin's benefit. "It's an honorable task, that's not too physically demanding for me."

"And do you like your duties?"

Miles shrugged. "I like the travel. And, ah . . . it gets me out of the way, an advantage that cuts two ways. You know about Barrayar's backward attitude to mutations." Miles thought of Yenaro's longing for a post. "And it gives me an official position, makes me somebody."

"I can understand *that*," conceded Benin.

Yeah, I thought you would.

"But you're not on courier duty now?"

"Not this trip. We were to give our diplomatic duties our undivided attention, and, it was hoped, maybe acquire a little polish."

"And Lord Vorpatril here is assigned to Operations, is that right?"

"Desk work," Ivan sighed. "I keep hoping for ship duty."

Not really true, Miles reflected; Ivan adored being assigned to HQ at the capital, where he kept up his own apartment and a social life that was the envy of his brother-officers. Ivan just wished his mother *Lady* Vorpatril might be assigned ship duty, someplace far away.

"Hm." Benin's hands twitched, as if in memory of sorting stacks of plastic flimsies. He drew breath, and looked Miles straight in the eyes. "So, Lord Vorkosigan—the funeral rotunda was *not* the first time you saw the Ba Lura, was it?"

Benin was trying for the rattling unexpected straight shot, to unnerve his quarry. "Correct," Miles answered, with a smile.

Expecting denial, Benin already had his mouth open for the second strike, probably the presentation of some telling piece of evidence that would give the Barrayaran the lie. He had to close it again, and start over. "If . . . if you wished to keep it a secret, why did you as much as flat tell me to look where I would be sure to find you? And," his tone sharpened with baffled annoyance, "if you didn't want to keep it a secret, why didn't you tell me about it in the first place?"

"It provided an interesting test of your competence. I wanted to know if it would be worth my while to persuade you to share your results. Believe me, my first encounter with the Ba Lura is as much a mystery to me as I'm sure it is to you."

Even from beneath the gaudy face paint, the look Benin gave Miles reminded him forcibly of the look he got all too often from superiors. He even capitalized it in his mind, The Look. In a weird backhanded way, it made him feel quite comfortable with Benin. His smile became slightly cheerier.

"And . . . how *did* you encounter the Ba?" said Benin.

"What do you know so far?" Miles countered. Benin would, of course, keep something back, to cross-check Miles's story. That was quite all right, as Miles proposed to tell almost the whole truth, next.

"Ba Lura was at the transfer station the day you arrived. He left the station at least twice. Once, apparently, from a pod docking bay in which the security monitors were deactivated and unchecked for a period of forty minutes. The same bay and the same period in which you arrived, Lord Vorkosigan."

"Our first arrival, you mean."

" . . . Yes."

Vorreedi's eyes were widening and his lips were thinning. Miles ignored him, for now, though Ivan's gaze cautiously shifted to check him out.

"Deactivated? Torn out of the wall, I'd call it. Very well, ghem-Colonel. But tell me—was our encounter in the pod dock the first or second time the Ba appeared to leave the station?"

"Second," Benin said, watching him closely.

"Can you prove that?"

"Yes."

"Good. It may be *very important* later that you can prove that." Ha, Benin wasn't the only one who could cross-check the truth of this conversation. Benin, for whatever reason, was being straight with him so far. Turn and turnabout. "Well, this is what happened from our point of view—"

In a flat voice, and with plenty of corroborative physical details, Miles described their confusing clash with the Ba. The only item he changed was to report the Ba reaching for its trouser pocket before he'd yelled his warning. He brought the tale up to the moment of Ivan's heroic struggle and his own retrieval of the loose nerve disruptor, and bounced it over to Ivan to finish. Ivan gave him a dirty look, but, taking his tone from Miles, offered a brief factual description of the Ba's subsequent escape.

Since it lacked face paint, Miles could watch Vorreedi's face darken, out of the corner of his eye. The man was too cool and controlled to actually turn purple or anything, but Miles bet a blood pressure monitor would be beeping in plaintive alarm right now.

"And why did you not report this at our first meeting, Lord Vorkosigan?" Benin asked again, after a long, digestive pause.

"I might," said Vorreedi in a slightly suffused voice, "ask you the same question, Lieutenant." Benin shot Vorreedi a raised-brow look, almost putting his face paint in danger of smudging.

Lieutenant, not *my lord*; Miles took the point. "The pod pilot reported to his captain, who will have reported to his commander." To wit, Illyan; in fact, the report, slogging through normal channels, should be reaching Illyan's desk right about now. Three days more for an emergency query to arrive on Vorreedi's desk from home, six more days for a reply and return-reply. It would all be over before Illyan could do a damned thing, now. "However, on my authority as senior envoy, I suppressed the incident for diplomatic reasons. We were sent with specific instructions to maintain a low profile and behave with maximum courtesy. My government considered this solemn occasion an important opportunity to send a message that we would be glad to see more normal trade and other relations, and an easing of tensions along our mutual borders. I did not judge that it would do anything helpful for our mutual tensions to open our visit with charges of an unmotivated armed attack by an Imperial slave upon the Barrayaran special representatives."

The implied threat was obvious enough; despite Benin's face paint, Miles could tell that one had hit home. Even Vorreedi looked like he might be giving the pitch serious consideration.

"Can you . . . prove your assertions, Lord Vorkosigan?" asked Benin cautiously.

"We still have the captured nerve disruptor. Ivan?" Miles nodded to his cousin.

Gently, using only his fingertips, Ivan drew the weapon from his pocket and laid it gingerly on the table, and returned his hands demurely to his lap. He avoided Vorreedi's outraged eye. Vorreedi and Benin reached simultaneously for the nerve disruptor, and simultaneously stopped, frowning at each other.

"Excuse me," said Vorreedi. "I had not seen this before."

"Really?" said Benin. *How extraordinary*, his tone implied. "Go ahead." His hand dropped politely.

Vorreedi picked up the weapon and examined it closely, among other things checking to see that the safety lock was indeed engaged, before handing it equally politely to Benin.

"I'd be glad to return the weapon to you, ghem-Colonel," Miles went on, "in exchange for whatever information you are able to deduce from it. If it can be traced back to the Celestial Garden, that's not much help, but if it was something the Ba acquired en route, well . . . it might be revealing. This is a check that you can make more easily than I can." Miles paused, then added, "Who did the Ba visit from the station the first time?"

Benin glanced up from his close contemplation of the nerve disruptor. "A ship moored off-station."

"Can you be more specific?"

"No."

"Excuse me, let me re-phrase that. Could you be more specific if you chose to?"

Benin set the disruptor down, and leaned back, his expression of attention to Miles, if possible, intensifying.

He was silent for a long thoughtful moment before finally replying, "No, unfortunately. I could not."

Rats. The three haut-governors' ships moored off that transfer station were Ilsum Kety's, Slyke Giaja's and Este Rond's. This could have been the final line of his triangulation, but Benin didn't have it. Yet. "I'd be particularly interested in how traffic control, or what certainly passed for traffic control, came to direct us to the wrong, or at any rate the first, pod dock."

"Why do *you* think the Ba entered your pod?" Benin asked in turn.

"Given the intense confusion of the encounter, I certainly would consider the possibility of it having been an accident. If it *was* arranged, I think something must have gone very wrong."

No shit, said Ivan's silent morose look. Miles ignored him.

"Anyway, ghem-Colonel, I hope this helps to anchor your time-table," Miles continued in a tone of finality. Surely Benin would be itching to run and check out his new clue, the nerve disruptor.

Benin didn't budge. "So what did you and the haut Rian *really* discuss, Lord Vorkosigan?"

"For that, I'm afraid you will have to apply to the haut Rian. She is Cetagandan to the bone, and so all your department." *Alas.* "But I think her distress at the death of the Ba Lura was quite genuine."

Benin's eyes flicked up. "When did *you* see enough of her to gauge the depth of her distress?"

"Or so I deduced." And if he didn't end this *now* he was going to put his foot in it so deep they'd need a hand-tractor to pull it out again. He had to play Vorreedi with the utmost delicacy; this was not quite the case with Benin. "This is fascinating, ghem-Colonel, but I'm afraid I'm out of time for this morning. But if you ever find out where that nerve disruptor came from, and where the Ba went to, I would be more than glad to continue the conversation." He sat back, folded his arms, and smiled cordially.

What Vorreedi *should* have done was announce loudly that they had all the time in the world, and let Benin continue to be his stalking-horse—Miles would have, in his place—but Vorreedi himself was clearly itching to get Miles alone. Instead, the protocol officer rose, signaling the official end to the interview. Benin, on embassy grounds as a guest, on sufferance—not his normal mode, Miles was sure—acceded without comment, rising to take his farewells.

"I *will* be speaking with you again, Lord Vorkosigan," Benin promised darkly.

"I certainly hope so, sir. Ah—did you take my other piece of advice, too? About blocking interference?"

Benin paused, looking suddenly a little abstracted. "Yes, in fact."

"How did it go?"

"Better than I would have expected."

"Good."

Benin's parting semi-salute was ironic, but not, Miles felt, altogether hostile.

Vorreedi escorted his guest to the door, but turned him over to the hall guard and was back in the little room before Miles and Ivan could make good their escape.

Vorreedi pinned Miles by eye. Miles felt a momentary regret that his diplomatic immunity did not extend to the protocol officer as well. Would it occur to Vorreedi to separate the pair of them, and break Ivan? Ivan was practicing looking invisible, something he did very well.

Vorreedi stated dangerously, "I am not a mushroom, Lieutenant Vorkosigan."

To be kept in the dark and fed on horseshit, right. Miles sighed inwardly. "Sir, apply to my commander," meaning Illyan—Vorreedi's commander too, in point of fact—"be cleared, and I'm yours. Until then, my best judgment is to continue exactly as I have been."

"Trusting your instincts?" said Vorreedi dryly.

"It's not as if I had any clear conclusions to share yet."

"So . . . do your instincts suggest some connection between the late Ba Lura, and Lord Yenaro?"

Vorreedi had instincts too, oh, yes. Or he wouldn't be in *this* post. "Besides the fact that both have inter-acted with me? Nothing that I . . . trust. I'm after proof. Then I will . . . be somewhere."

"Where?"

Head down in the biggest privy you ever imagined, at the current rate. "I guess I'll know when I get there, sir."

"We too will speak again, Lord Vorkosigan. You can count on it." Vorreedi gave him a very abbreviated nod, and departed abruptly—probably to apprise Ambassa-dor Vorob'yev of the new complications in his life.

Into the ensuing silence, Miles said faintly, "That went well, all things considered."

Ivan's lip curled in scorn.

They kept silence on the trudge back to Ivan's room, where Ivan found a new stack of colored papers waiting on his desk. He sorted through them, pointedly ignor-ing Miles.

"I have to reach Rian somehow," Miles said at last. "I can't afford to wait. Things are getting too damned tight."

"I don't want anything more to do with any of this," said Ivan distantly.

"It's too late."

"Yes. I know." His hand paused. "Huh. Here's a new wrinkle. This one has both our names on it."

"Not from Lady Benello, is it? I'm afraid Vorreedi will count her off-limits now."

"No. It's not a name I recognize."

Miles pounced on the paper, and tore it open. "Lady d'Har. A garden party. What does she grow in *her* garden, I wonder? Could it be a double meaning—referencing the Celestial Garden? Hm. Awfully short notice. It could be my next contact. God, I hate being at haut Rian's mercy for every setup. Well, accept it anyway, just in case."

"It's not my first choice of how to spend the evening," said Ivan.

"Did I say anything about a choice? It's a chance, we've got to take it." He went on nastily, "Besides, if you keep leaving your genetic samples all over town, your progeny could end up being featured in next year's art show. As bushes."

Ivan shuddered. "You don't think they would—that's not why—uh, could they?"

"Sure. Why, when you're gone, they could re-create the operative body parts that interest them, to perform on command, to any scale—quite the souvenir. And you thought that *kitten* tree was obscene."

"There's more to it than *that*, coz," Ivan stated with injured dignity. His voice faded in doubt. " . . . you don't think they'd really do something like that, do you?"

"There's no more ruthless passion than that of a Cetagandan artist in search of new media." He added firmly, "We're going to a garden party. I'm sure it's my contact with Rian."

"Garden party," conceded Ivan with a sigh. He stared off blankly into space. After a minute he commented offhandedly, "Y'know, it's too bad she can't just get the gene bank back from his ship. Then he'd have the key but no lock. *That'd* fox him up but good, I bet."

Miles sat down in Ivan's desk chair, slowly. When he'd got his breath back, he whispered, "Ivan—that's *brilliant*. Why didn't I think of that before?"

Ivan considered this. "'Cause it's not a scenario that lets you play the lone hero in front of the haut Rian?"

They exchanged saturnine looks. For once, Miles's gaze shifted first. "I meant that as a rhetorical question," he said tightly. But he didn't say it very loudly.

CHAPTER TWELVE

Garden party was a misnomer, Miles decided. He
stared past Ambassador Vorob'yev and Ivan as the three
of them exited from an ear-popping ride up the lift tube
and into the apparently open air of the rooftop. A faint
golden sparkle in the air above marked the presence
of a lightweight force-screen, blocking unwanted wind,
rain, or dust. Dusk here, in the center of the capital,
was a silver sheen in the atmosphere, for the half-
kilometer high building overlooked the green rings of
parkway surrounding the Celestial Garden itself.

Curving banks of flowers and dwarf trees, fountains,
rivulets, walkways, and arched jade bridges turned the
roof into a descending labyrinth in the finest
Cetagandan style. Every turn of the walkways revealed
and framed a different view of the city stretching to
the horizon, though the best views were the ones that
looked to the Emperor's shimmering great phoenix egg
in the city's heart. The lift-tube foyer, opening onto it
all, was roofed with arching vines and paved in an
elaborate inlay of colored stones: lapis lazuli, malachite,
green and white jade, rose quartz, and other miner-
als Miles couldn't even name.

Looking around, it gradually dawned on Miles why

the protocol officer had them all wearing their House blacks, when Miles would have guessed undress greens to be adequate. It was not possible to be overdressed here. Ambassador Vorob'yev was admitted on sufferance as their escort, but even Vorreedi had to wait in the garage below, tonight. Ivan, looking around too, clutched their invitation a little tighter.

Their putative hostess, Lady d'Har, stood on the edge of the foyer. Apparently being inside her home counted the same as being inside a bubble, for she was welcoming her guests. Even at her advanced age, her haut-beauty stunned the eye. She wore robes in a dozen fine layers of blinding white, sweeping down and swirling around her feet. Thick silver hair flowed to the floor. Her husband, ghem-Admiral Har, whose bulky presence would normally have dominated any room, seemed to fade into the background beside her.

Ghem-Admiral Har commanded half the Cetagandan fleet, and his duty-delayed arrival for the final ceremonies of the Empress's funeral was the reason for tonight's welcome-home party. He wore his Imperial bloodred dress uniform, which he could have hung with enough medals to sink him should he chance to fall in a river. He'd chosen instead to one-up the competition with the neck-ribbon and medallion of the deceptively simple-sounding Order of Merit. Clearing away the other clutter made this honor impossible for the viewer to miss. Or match. It was given, rarely, at the sole discretion of the Emperor himself. There were few higher awards to be had in the Cetagandan Empire. The haut-lady by his side was one of them, though. Lord Har would have pinned her to his tunic too, if he could, Miles felt, for all he had won her some forty years past. The Har ghem-clan's face paint featured mainly orange and green; the patterns lacked definition, crossing with the man's deeply age-lined features, and clashing horribly with the red of the uniform.

Even Ambassador Vorob'yev was awed by ghem-Admiral Har, Miles judged by the extreme formality of his greetings. Har was polite but clearly puzzled; *Why are these outlanders in my garden?* But he deferred to Lady d'Har, who relieved Ivan of his nervously proffered invitation with a small, cool nod, and directed them, in a voice age-softened to a honeyed alto, to where the food and drinks were displayed.

They strolled on. After he recovered from the shock of Lady d'Har, Ivan's head swiveled, looking for the young ghem-women he knew, without success. "This place is wall-to-wall old crusts," he whispered to Miles in dismay. "When we walked in, the average age here dropped from ninety to eighty-nine."

"Eighty-nine and a half, I'd say," Miles whispered back.

Ambassador Vorob'yev put a finger to his lips, suppressing the commentary, but his eyes glinted in amused agreement.

Quite. This was the real thing; Yenaro and his crowd were shabby little outsiders indeed, by comparison, excluded by age, by rank, by wealth, by . . . everything. Scattered through the garden were half-a-dozen haut-lady bubbles, glowing like pale lanterns, something Miles had not yet seen outside the Celestial Garden itself. Lady d'Har kept social contact with her haut-relatives, or former relatives, it appeared. *Rian, here?* Miles prayed so.

"I wish I could have got Maz in," Vorob'yev sighed with regret. "How *did* you do this, Lord Ivan?"

"Not me," denied Ivan. He flipped a thumb at Miles. Vorob'yev's brows rose inquiringly.

Miles shrugged. "They told me to study the power-hierarchy. This is it, isn't it?" Actually, he was not so sure anymore.

Where did power lie, in this convoluted society? With the ghem-lords, he would have said once without hesitation, who controlled the weapons, the ultimate threat of violence. Or with the haut-lords, who controlled the ghem, through whatever oblique means. Certainly not with the secluded haut-women. Was their knowledge a kind of power, then? A very fragile sort of power. Wasn't *fragile power* an oxymoron? The Star Crèche existed because the Emperor protected it; the Emperor existed because the ghem-lords served him. Yet the haut-women had created the Emperor . . . created the haut itself . . . created the ghem, for that matter. Power to create . . . power to destroy . . . he blinked, dizzy, and munched on a canapé in the shape of a tiny swan, biting off its head first. The feathers were made with rice flour, judging from the taste, the center a spicy protein paste. Vat-grown swan meat?

The Barrayaran party collected drinks, and began a slow circuit of the rooftop garden's walks, comparing views. They also collected stares, from the elderly ghem and haut scattered about; but none came up to introduce themselves, or ask questions, or attempt to start a conversation. Vorob'yev himself was only scouting, so far, Miles thought, but the man would surely pursue the evening's opportunities for contact-making soon. How Miles was to divest himself of the ambassador when his own contact turned up, he was not sure. Assuming this was where his contact was to meet him, and it wasn't all just his hyperactive imagination, or—

Or the next assassination attempt. They'd rounded some greenery to see a woman in haut-white, but with no haut-bubble, standing alone and staring out over the city. Miles recognized her from the heavy chocolate-dark braid falling down her back to her ankles, even at this three-quarters-turned view. The haut Vio d'Chilian. Was ghem-General Chilian here? Was Kety himself?

Ivan's breath drew in. Right. Except for their elderly

hostess, this was the first time Ivan had seen a haut-woman outside her bubble, and Ivan lacked the . . . inoculation of the haut Rian. Miles found he could view the haut Vio this time with scarcely a tremor. Were the haut-women a disease that you could only catch once, like the legendary smallpox, and if you survived it you were immune thereafter, however scarred?

"Who *is* she?" whispered Ivan, enchanted.

"Ghem-General Chilian's haut-wife," Vorob'yev murmured into his ear. "The ghem-general could order your liver fried for breakfast. *I* would send it to him. The free ghem-ladies can entertain themselves as they please with you, but the married haut are strictly off-limits. Understood?"

"Yes, sir," said Ivan faintly.

The haut Vio was staring as if hypnotized at the great glowing dome of the Celestial Garden. Longing for her lost life, Miles wondered? She'd spent years exiled in the hinterlands at Sigma Ceta with her ghem husband. What was she feeling, now? Happy? Homesick?

Some movement or sound from the Barrayarans must have broken her reverie, for her head turned toward them. For a second, just a second, her astonishing cinnamon eyes seemed copper-metallic with a rage so boundless, Miles's stomach lurched. Then her expression snapped into a smooth hauteur, as blank as the bubble she lacked, and as armored; the open emotion was gone so fast Miles was not sure the other two men had even seen it. But the look was not for them; it had been on her face even as she'd turned, before she could have identified the Barrayarans, blackly dressed in the shadows.

Ivan opened his mouth; *Please, no,* Miles thought, but Ivan had to try. "Good evening, milady. Wonderful view, eh?"

She hesitated a long moment—Miles pictured her

fleeing—but then answered, in a low-pitched, perfectly modulated voice, "There is nothing like it in the universe."

Ivan, encouraged, brightened and moved forward. "Let me introduce myself. I'm Lord Ivan Vorpatril, of Barrayar. . . . And, uh, this is Ambassador Vorob'yev, and this is my cousin, Lord Miles Vorkosigan. Son of You-know-who, eh?"

Miles winced. Watching Ivan babble in sexual panic would normally be entertaining, if it wasn't so excruciatingly embarrassing. It reminded Miles painfully of— himself. *Did I look like that much of a fool, the first time I saw Rian?* He feared the answer was *yes.*

"Yes," said the haut Vio. "I know." Miles had seen people talk to their potted plants with more warmth and expression than the haut Vio turned on Ivan.

Give it up, Ivan, Miles urged silently. *This woman is married to the first officer of a guy who maybe tried to kill us yesterday, remember?* Unless Lord X *was* Prince Slyke after all—or the haut Rond, or . . . Miles ground his teeth.

But before Ivan could dig himself any deeper, a man in Cetagandan military uniform rounded the corner, his face paint crinkling with his frown. Ghem-General Chilian. Miles froze, his hand wrapping Ivan's forearm and biting deep in warning.

Chilian's gaze swept the Barrayarans, his nostrils flaring in suspicion. "Haut Vio," he addressed his wife. "Come with me, please."

"Yes, my lord," she said, her lashes sweeping down demurely, and she escaped around Ivan with a bare nod of farewell. Chilian brought himself to nod also, acknowledging the outlanders' existence; with an effort, Miles felt. The general glanced once back over his shoulder as he whisked his wife away. So what sin had ghem-General Chilian committed to win *her?*

"*Lucky* guy," sighed Ivan in envy.

"I'm not so sure," said Miles. Ambassador Vorob'yev just smiled grimly.

They walked on, Miles's brain whirling around this new encounter. Was it accidental? Was it the start of a new setup? Lord X used his human tools like long-handled forks, to keep the heat at a distance. Surely the ghem-general and his wife were too close to him, too obviously connected. Unless, of course, Lord X wasn't Kety after all . . .

A glow ahead brought Miles's gaze front and center. A haut-bubble was approaching them along the evergreen-bounded walk. Vorob'yev and Ivan stood aside to let it pass. Instead it stopped in front of Miles.

"Lord Vorkosigan." The woman's voice was melodious even through the filter, but it was not Rian's. "May I speak privately with you?"

"Of course," said Miles, before Vorob'yev could put in an objection. "Where?" Tension shot through him. Was tonight to be his final assault already, upon the new target of Governor Ilsum Kety's ship? Too premature, still too uncertain . . . "And for how long?"

"Not far. We will be about an hour."

Not nearly long enough for a trip to orbit; this was something else, then. "Very well. Gentlemen, will you excuse me?"

Vorob'yev looked about as unhappy as his habitual control would allow. "Lord Vorkosigan . . ." His hesitation was actually a good sign; Vorreedi and he must have had a long and extraordinary talk. "Do you wish a guard?"

"No."

"A comm link?"

"No."

"You *will* be careful?" Which was diplomatic for *Are you sure you know what the hell you're doing, boy?*

"Oh, yes, sir."

"What do we do if you're *not* back in an hour?" said Ivan.

"Wait." He nodded cordially, and followed the bubble down the garden path.

When they turned into a private nook, lit by low colored lanterns and screened by flowering bushes, the bubble rotated, and abruptly blinked out. Miles found himself facing another haut beauty in white, riding in her float-chair like a throne. This woman's hair was honey-blond, intricately woven and tucked up around her shoulders, vaguely reminiscent of a gilt chain-mail neck guard. He would have guessed her age as forty-standard, which meant she was probably twice that.

"The haut Rian Degtiar instructs me to bring you," she stated. She moved her robes from the left side of the chair, uncovering a thickly padded armrest. "We have not much time." Her gaze seemed to measure his height, or shortness. "You can, um . . . *perch* here, and ride."

"How . . . fascinating." If only she *were* Rian . . . But this would test certain theories he had about the mechanical capacities of haut-bubbles, oh yes. "Uh . . . identification, milady?" he added almost apologetically. The last person he suspected of experiencing such a ride had ended up with its throat cut, after all.

She nodded, as if expecting this, and turned her hand outward, displaying the ring of the Star Crèche.

That was probably about as good as they could do, under the circumstances. Cautiously, he approached, and eased himself aboard, grasping the back of the chair above her head for balance. Each was careful not to actually touch the other. Her long-fingered hand moved over the control panel embedded in the right armrest, and the force-field snapped on again. The pale white light reflected off the flowered bushes, bringing out their color, and cast a glow before them as they began to move down the path.

Their view was quite clear, scarcely impeded by an eggshell-thin, ghostly sphere of mist that marked the boundary of the force-field as seen from this side. Sound too was transmitted with high clarity, much better than the deliberately muffled reverse effect. He could hear voices, and the clink of glassware, from a balcony above. They passed Ambassador Vorob'yev and Ivan again, who stared curiously, uncertain, of course, if this was the same bubble they'd seen before. Miles squelched an absurd impulse to wave at them, going by.

They came not to the lift-tube foyer, as Miles had expected, but to the edge of the rooftop garden. Their silver-haired hostess was standing waiting. She nodded at the bubble, and coded open the force-screen, letting the bubble pass through onto a small private landing pad. The reflected glow off the pavement darkened, as the haut-woman blacked out her bubble. Miles stared upward at the shimmering night sky, looking for the lightflyer or aircar.

Instead, the bubble moved smoothly to the edge of the building and dropped straight over the side.

Miles clutched the seat-back convulsively, trying not to scream, fling his arms around his hostess-pilot's neck, or throw up all over her white dress. They were *free-falling*, and he *hated* heights . . . was this his intended death, his assassin sacrificing herself along with him? *Oh, God—!*

"I thought these things only went a meter in the air," he choked out, his voice, despite his best efforts, going high and squeaky.

"If you have enough initial altitude, you can maintain a controlled glide," she said calmly. Despite Miles's horrified first impression, they were not actually dropping like a rock. They were arcing outward, across the boulevards far below, and the light-sparked green rings of parks, toward the dome of the Celestial Garden.

Miles thought wildly of the witch Baba Yaga, from the Barrayaran folk tales, who flew in a magic mortar. This witch didn't qualify as old and ugly. But he was not, at this moment, totally convinced she didn't eat bad children.

In a few minutes, the bubble decelerated again to a smooth walking pace a few centimeters above the pavement outside one of the Celestial Garden's minor entrances. A movement of her finger brought back the white glow.

"Ah," she said, in a refreshed tone. "I haven't done that in *years*." She almost cracked a smile, for a moment nearly . . . human.

Miles was shocked when they passed through the Celestial dome's security procedures almost as if they weren't there, except for a swift exchange of electronic codes. No one stopped or searched the bubble. The sort of uniformed men who'd shaken down the galactic envoys with beady-eyed thoroughness stood back respectfully, with downcast gaze.

"Why don't they stop us?" Miles whispered, unable to overcome the psychological conviction that if he could see and hear them, they could see and hear him.

"Stop me?" repeated the haut-woman in puzzlement. "I am the haut Pel Navarr, Consort of Eta Ceta. I *live* here."

Their further progress was happily ground-hugging, if faster than the usual walking-pace, through the increasingly familiar precincts of the Celestial Garden to the low white building with the bio-filters on every window. The haut Pel's passage through its automated security procedures was almost as swift and perfunctory as through the dome entrance itself. They passed silently down a set of corridors, but turned in a different direction from the labs and offices at the building's heart, and went up one level.

Double doors parted to admit them to a large

circular room done in subdued and subduing tones of silvery gray. Unlike any other place he'd seen in the Celestial Garden, it was devoid of living decorations, neither plant nor animal nor any of those disturbing creations in-between. Hushed, concentrated, undistracting . . . It was a chamber in the Star Crèche; he supposed he could dub it the Star Chamber. Eight women in white awaited them, sitting silently in a circle. His stomach should not still be turning over, dammit, the free fall was done.

The haut Pel brought her float-chair to a halt in a waiting empty gap in the circle, grounded it, and switched off the force-bubble. Eight extraordinary pairs of eyes focused on Miles.

No one, he thought, *should be exposed to this many haut-women at once*. It was some kind of dangerous overdose. Their beauty was varied; three were as silver-haired as the ghem-admiral's wife, one was copper-tressed, one was dark-skinned and hawk-nosed, with masses of blue-black ringlets tumbling down around her like a cloak. Two were blonde, his guide with her golden weave and another with hair as pale as oat straw in the sun, and as straight to the floor. One dark-eyed woman had chocolate-brown hair like the haut Vio, but in soft curling clouds instead of bound. And then there was Rian. Their massed effect went beyond beauty; where to, he was not sure, but *terror* came close. He slipped off the arm of the float chair, and stood away from it, grateful for the propping effect of his stiff high boots.

"Here is the Barrayaran to testify," said the haut Rian.

Testify. He was here as a witness, then, not as the accused. A Key witness, so to speak. He stifled a slightly manic giggle. Somehow he did not think Rian would appreciate the pun.

He swallowed, and got his voice unlocked. "You have the advantage of me, ladies." Though he could make a good guess who they all were, at this point. His gaze swept the circle, and he blinked hard against the vertigo. "I have only met your Handmaiden." He nodded toward Rian. On a low table before her the Empress's entire formal regalia was laid out, including the Seal and the false Great Key.

Rian tilted her head in acknowledgment of the reasonableness of his request, and proceeded to go around the circle with a bewildering slug of haut names and titles—yes, here indeed sat the consorts of the eight satrap planets. With Rian the ninth, sitting in for the late Empress. The creative controllers of the haut-genome, of the would-be master race, were all met here in some extraordinary council.

The chamber was clearly set up for just this purpose; such meetings must also occur when the consorts journeyed home to escort the child-ships. Miles particularly focused on the consorts of Prince Slyke, Ilsum Kety, and the Rond. Kety's woman, the Consort of Sigma Ceta, was one of the silver-haired ones, closer to being contemporary with the late Empress than anyone else in the room. Rian introduced her as the haut Nadina. The oat-straw blonde served Prince Slyke of Xi Ceta, and the brown-curled woman was the Consort of Rho Ceta. Miles wondered anew at the significance of their titles, which named them all consorts of their planets, not of the men.

"Lord Vorkosigan," said the haut Rian. "I would like you to repeat for the consorts how you say you came into possession of the false Great Key, and all the subsequent events."

All? Miles did not blame her in the least for switching strategies from playing all cards close to her chest to calling in reinforcements. It was not before time, in his opinion. But he disliked being taken by surprise. It would have been nice if she'd at least *consulted* him, first. *Yeah? How?*

"I take it you understood my message to abort the infiltration of Prince Slyke's ship," he countered.

"Yes. I expect you will explain why, in due order."

"Excuse me, milady. I do not mean to insult . . . anyone here. But if one of the consorts is a traitoress, in collusion with her satrap governor, this will pipeline everything we know straight to him. How do you *know* you are entirely among friends?"

There was enough tension in the room to go with any number of treasons, certainly. Rian raised a hand, as if to stem it. "He is an outlander. He cannot understand." She gave him a slow nod. "There is treason, we believe, yes, but not on *this* level. Further down."

"Oh . . . ?"

"We have concluded that even with the bank and Key in his hands, the satrap governor could not run the haut-genome by himself. The haut of his satrap would not cooperate with such a sudden usurpation, the overturning of all custom. He must plan to appoint a new consort, one under his own control. We think she has already been selected."

"Ah . . . do you know who?"

"Not yet," Rian sighed. "Not yet. She is someone, I fear, who does not wholly understand the goal of haut. It is all of a piece. If we knew which governor, we could guess which haut-woman he has suborned; if we knew which woman . . . well."

Dammit, this triangulation *had* to break soon. Miles chewed on his lower lip, then said slowly, "Milady. Tell me—if you can—something about how your force-bubbles are keyed to their individual operators, and why everyone is so damned convinced they're dead-secure. The keypad on those control panels looks like a palm-lock, but it can't just be a palm-lock; you can get around palm-locks."

"I cannot give *you* the technical details, Lord Vorkosigan," said Rian.

"I don't expect you to. Just the general logic of it."

"Well . . . they are keyed genetically, of course. One brushes one's hand across the pad, leaving a few skin cells. These are sucked in and scanned."

"Does it scan your entire genome? Surely that would take a lot of time."

"No, of course not. It runs through a tree of a dozen or so critical markers that individually iden-tify a haut-woman. Starting with the presence of an X chromosome pair, and going down a branching list until confirmation is achieved."

"How much chance is there of duplicating the mark-ers in two or more individuals?"

"We do not clone ourselves, Lord Vorkosigan."

"I mean, just of the dozen factors, just enough to fool the machine."

"Vanishingly small."

"Even among closely related members of one's own constellation?"

She hesitated, exchanging a glance with Lady Pel, who raised her brows thoughtfully.

"There's a reason I ask," Miles went on. "When ghem-Colonel Benin interviewed me, he let slip that six haut-bubbles had entered the funeral rotunda during the time period the Ba Lura's body must have been placed at the foot of the bier, and that it presented him with a major puzzle. He didn't tell me which six, but I bet you could get him to disgorge the list. It's a brute-force triage of a major data dump, but—suppose you ran the markers of those six through your records, and checked for accidental duplicates among living haut-women. If the woman is serving the satrap governor, she might have served him in that murder, too. You might finger your traitoress without ever having to leave the Star Crèche."

Rian, momentarily alert, sat back with a weary sigh.

"Your reasoning is correct, Lord Vorkosigan. We could do that—if we had the Great Key."

"Oh," said Miles. "Yeah. That." He reverted from an eager parade-rest to a deflated at-ease. "For what it's worth, my strategic analysis and what little physical evidence I've wrung from ghem-Colonel Benin so far suggests either Prince Slyke or the haut Ilsum Kety. With the haut Rond a distant third. But as Rho Ceta and Mu Ceta would bear the brunt of it if open conflict with Barrayar was actually engineered, my own choice has settled pretty firmly between Slyke and Kety. Recent . . . events point to Kety." He glanced again around the circle. "Is there anything any of the consorts have seen or heard, or overheard, that would help pin him more certainly?"

A murmur of negatives; "Unfortunately, no," said Rian. "We have discussed that problem already this evening. Please begin."

On your head be it, milady. Miles took a deep breath, and launched into the full true account, minus most of his opinions, of his experiences on Eta Ceta from the moment the Ba Lura lurched into their personnel pod. He paused occasionally, to give Rian a chance to hint him away from anything she wanted to conceal. She appeared to want to conceal nothing, instead drawing him on with skillful questions and prompts to disgorge every detail.

Rian had seen, he slowly realized, that the secrecy problem cut two ways. Lord X could assassinate Miles, maybe Rian as well. But even the most megalomanic Cetagandan politician must find it excessively challenging to try to get away with disposing of all eight satrap consorts. His voice strengthened.

He felt his underlying assumptions slowly wringing inside-out. Rian seemed less and less like a damsel in distress all the time. In fact, he was beginning to wonder if he was trying to rescue the dragon. *Well, dragons need to be rescued too, sometimes. . . .* Nobody even blinked at his description of his near-assassination the day before. If anything, there was a subliminal murmur of appreciation for its elegance of form and style, and of faintly sympathetic disappointment at its foiling. The judges had no appreciation for the governor's originality in attempting to muscle in on their own territory, though. The Sigma and Xi Cetan consorts looked increasingly stony, exchanging a raised-brow glance or a nod of understanding now and then.

There was a long silence when he'd finished. *Time to present Plan B?* "I have a suggestion," Miles said boldly. "Recall all the duplicate gene banks from the satrap governors' ships. If they are all returned, you will have stripped him of his ability to carry out his larger plans. If he resists releasing it, you will have smoked him out."

"Bring them *back*," said the haut Pel in dismay. "Do you have any idea how much trouble we had getting them *up* there?"

"But he might take both bank and Key, and flee," objected the brown-curled Consort of Rho Ceta.

"No," said Miles. "That's the one thing he *can't* do. There are too many Imperially guarded wormhole jumps between him and home. Speaking militarily, open flight is impossible. He'd never make it. He cannot reveal a thing about any of this till he's safely in orbit around . . . Something Ceta. In a weird way, we have him cornered till the funeral is over." *Which will be all too soon, now.*

"That still leaves the problem of retrieving the real Key," said Rian.

"Once you have the bank back, you may be able to negotiate the Key's return, in exchange for, say, amnesty. Or you can claim he stole it—perfectly true—and set your own security to get it back for you. Once the other governors are freed of the incriminating evidence they're holding, you may be able to cut him out of the herd, so to speak, with their goodwill. In any case, it will open up a lot of tactical options."

"He may threaten to destroy it," worried the Consort of Sigma Ceta.

"You must know Ilsum Kety better than anyone else here, haut Nadina," said Miles. "Would he?"

"He is . . . an erratic young man," she said reluctantly. "I am not yet convinced that he is guilty. But I know nothing about him that makes your accusations impossible."

"And your governor, ma'am?" Miles nodded to the Consort of Xi Ceta.

"Prince Slyke is . . . a determined and brilliant man. The plot you describe is not beyond his capacities. I'm . . . not sure."

"Well . . . you *can* re-create the Great Key, eventually, can't you?" Push or shove, the Empress's great plan would be canned for a generation. A very desirable outcome, from Barrayar's point of view. Miles smiled agreeably.

A faint groan went around the room. "Recovering the Great Key undamaged is the highest priority," Rian said firmly.

"He still wants to frame Barrayar," said Miles. "It may have started as cold-blooded astro-political calculation, but I'm pretty sure it's a personal motivation by now."

"If I recall the banks," said Rian slowly, "we will entirely lose this opportunity to distribute them."

The Consort of Sigma Ceta, the silver-haired Nadina, sighed, "I had hoped to live to see the Celestial Lady's vision of new growth carried out. She was right, you know. I have seen the stagnation increasing in my lifetime."

"Other opportunities will come," said another silver-haired lady.

"It must be done more carefully next time," said the brown-curled Consort of Rho Ceta. "Our Lady trusted the governors too much."

"I'm not so sure she did," said Rian. "I was only attempting to go as far as distributing inactive copies for backup. The Ba Lura felt our Mistress's desires keenly, but did not understand her subtlety. It wasn't *my* idea to attempt to distribute the Key now, and I'm not convinced it was hers, either. I don't know if the Ba had a separate understanding with her, or just a separate misunderstanding. And now I never will." She bowed her head. "I apologize to the Council for my failure." Her tone of voice made Miles think of inward-turning knives.

"You did your best, dear," said the haut Nadina kindly. But she added more sternly, "However, you should not have attempted to handle it all alone."

"It was my charge."

"A little less emphasis on the *my*, and a little more emphasis on the *charge*, next time."

Miles tried not to squirm at the general applicability of this gentle correction.

A glum silence reigned, for a time.

"We may need to consider altering the genome to make the haut-lords more controllable," said the Rho Cetan consort.

"For renewed expansion, we need the opposite," objected the dark consort. "More aggression."

"The ghem-experiment, filtering favorable genetic combinations upward from the general population, surely suffices for *that*," said the haut Pel.

"Our Lady, in her wisdom, aimed at less uniformity, not more," conceded Rian.

"I believe we have long made a mistake in leaving the haut-males so entirely to their own devices," said the Rho Cetan consort stubbornly.

Said the dark one, "But how else should we select

among them, if there is no free competition to sort them out?"

Rian held up a restraining hand. "The time for this larger debate . . . must be soon. But not now. I myself have been convinced by these events that further refinement must come before further expansion. But that," she sighed, "is a new Empress's task. *Now* we must decide what state of affairs she will inherit. How many favor the recall of the gene banks?"

The ayes had it. Several were slow in coming, but in some occult way a unanimous vote was achieved through nothing more than an exchange of unreadable glances. Miles breathed relief.

Rian's shoulders slumped wearily. "Then I so order you all. Return them to the Star Crèche."

"As what?" asked the haut Pel in a practical tone.

Rian stared into the air a moment, and replied, "As collections of human genomic materials from your various satrapies, requested by the Lady before her death, and received by us in trust for the Star Crèche's experimental files."

"That will do nicely on this end," nodded the haut Pel. "And on the other end?"

"Tell your governors . . . we discovered a serious error in the copy, which must be corrected before the genome can be released to them."

"Very good."

The meeting broke up, the women activating their float-chairs, though not yet their private bubbles, and leaving in twos and threes in a murmur of intense discussion. Rian and the haut Pel waited until the room emptied, and Miles perforce waited with them.

"Do you still want me to try and retrieve the Key for you?" Miles asked Rian. "Barrayar remains vulnerable until we nail the satrap governor with solid proof, data a clever man can't diddle. And I especially don't like the toehold he seems to have in your own security."

"I don't know," said Rian. "The return of the gene banks cannot take less than a day. I'll . . . send someone for you, as we did tonight."

"We'll be down to two days left, then. Not much margin. I'd rather go sooner than later."

"It cannot be helped." She touched her hair, a nervous gesture despite its grace.

Watching her, he searched his heart. The impact of his first mad crush was surely fading, in this drought of response, to be replaced by . . . what? If she had slaked his thirst with the least little drop of affection, he would be hers body and soul right now. In a way he was glad she wasn't faking anything, depressing as it was to be treated like a ba servitor, his loyalty and obedience assumed. Maybe his proposed disguise as a ba had been suggested by his subconscious for more than practical reasons. Was his back-brain trying to tell him something?

"The haut Pel will return you to your point of origin," Rian said.

He bowed. "In my experience, milady, we can never get back to exactly where we started, no matter how hard we try."

She returned nothing to this but an odd look, as he rode out again on the haut Pel's float-chair.

Pel carried him through the Celestial Garden as before, in reverse. He wondered if she was as uncomfortable with their compressed proximity as he was. He made a stab at light conversation.

"Did the haut-ladies make all this plant and animal life in the garden? Competing, like the ghem bioestheties fair? I was particularly impressed by the singing frogs, I must say."

"Oh, no," said the haut Pel. "The lower life-forms are all ghem work. That's their highest reward, to have their art incorporated into the Imperial garden. The haut only work in human material."

He didn't recall seeing any monsters around. "Where?"

"We mostly field-test ideas in the ba servitors. It prevents the accidental release of any genomic materials through sexual routes."

"Oh."

"*Our* highest honor is for a favorable gene complex we have developed to be taken up into the haut-genome itself."

It was like some golden rule in reverse—never do unto yourself what you have not first tried on another. Miles smiled, rather nervously, and did not pursue the subject further. A groundcar driven by a ba servitor waited for the haut Pel's bubble at the side entrance to the Celestial Garden, and they were returned to Lady d'Har's penthouse by more normal routes.

Pel let him out of her bubble in another private nook, in an unobserved moment, and drifted away again. He pictured her reporting back to Rian—*Yes, milady, I released the Barrayaran back into the wild as you ordered. I hope he will be able to find food and a mate out there. . . .* He sat on a bench overlooking the Celestial Garden, and meditated upon that view until Ivan and Ambassador Vorob'yev found him.

They looked, respectively, scared and angry. "You're late," said Ivan. "Where the hell did you go?"

"I almost called out Colonel Vorreedi and the guards," added Ambassador Vorob'yev sternly.

"That would have been . . . futile," sighed Miles. "We can go now."

"Thank God," muttered Ivan.

Vorob'yev said nothing. Miles rose, wondering how soon the ambassador and Vorreedi were going to stop taking *Not yet* for an answer.

Not yet. Please, not yet.

CHAPTER THIRTEEN

There was nothing he would have liked more than a day off, Miles reflected, but not *today*. The worst was the knowledge that he'd done this to himself. Until the consorts completed their retrieval of the gene banks, all he could do was wait. And unless Rian sent a car to the embassy to pick him up, a move so overt as to be vigorously resisted by both sets of Imperial Security, it was impossible for Miles to make contact with her again until the Gate-song Ceremonies tomorrow morning at the Celestial Garden. He grumbled under his breath, and called up more data on his suite's comconsole, then stared at it unseeing.

He wasn't sure it was wise to give Lord X an extra day either, for all that this afternoon would contain a nasty shock for him when his consort came to take away his gene bank. That would eliminate his last chance of sitting tight, and gliding away with bank and Key, perhaps dumping his old centrally appointed and controlled consort out an airlock en route. The man must realize now that Rian would turn him in, even if it meant incriminating herself, before letting him get away. Assassinating the Handmaiden of the Star Crèche hadn't been part of the Original Plan, Miles was fairly

225

sure. Rian had been intended to be a blind puppet, accusing Miles and Barrayar of stealing her Key. Lord X had a weakness for blind puppets. But Rian was loyal to the haut, beyond her own self-interest. No right-minded plotter could assume she would stay paralyzed for long.

Lord X was a tyrant, not a revolutionary. He wanted to take over the system, not change it. The late Empress was the real revolutionary, with her attempt to divide the haut into eight competing sibling branches, and may the best superman win. The Ba Lura might have been closer to its mistress's mind than Rian allowed. *You can't give power away and keep it simultaneously.* Except posthumously.

So what would Lord X do now? What *could* he do now, but fight to the last, trying anything he could think of to avoid being brought down for this? It was that or slit his wrists, and Miles didn't think he was the wrist-slitting type. He would still be searching for some way to pin it all on Barrayar, preferably in the form of a dead Miles who couldn't give him the lie. There was even still a faint chance he could bring that off, given the Cetagandan lack of enthusiasm for outlanders in general and Barrayarans in particular. Yes, this was a good day to stay indoors.

So would the results have been any better if Miles had publicly turned over the decoy Key and the truth on the very first day? No . . . then the embassy and its envoys would be mired right now in false accusations and public scandal, and no way to prove their innocence. If Lord X had picked any other delegation but Barrayar's upon which to plant his false Key—say, the Marilacans, the Aslunders, or the Vervani—his plan might yet be running along like clockwork. Miles hoped sourly that Lord X was Very, Very Sorry that he'd targeted Barrayar. *And I'm going to make you even sorrier, you sod.*

Miles's lips thinned as he turned his attention back to his comconsole. The satrap governors' ships were all to the same general plan, and a general plan, alas, was all the Barrayaran embassy data bank had available without tapping in to the secret files. Miles shuffled the holovid display though the various levels and sections of the ship. *If I were a satrap governor planning revolt, where would I hide the Great Key? Under my pillow?* Probably not.

The governor had the Key, but not the Key's key, so to speak; Rian still possessed that ring. If Lord X could open the Great Key, he could do a data dump, possess himself of a duplicate of the information-contents, and maybe, in a pinch, return the original, divesting himself of material evidence of his treasonous plans. Or even destroy it, hah. But if the Key were easy to get open, he should have done this already, when his plans first began to go seriously wrong. So if he was still trying to access the Key, it ought to be located in some sort of cipher lab. So where on this vast ship was a suitable cipher lab . . . ?

The chime of his door interrupted Miles's harried perusal. Colonel Vorreedi's voice inquired, "Lord Vorkosigan? May I come in?"

Miles sighed. "Enter." He'd been afraid all this comconsole activity would attract Vorreedi's attention. The protocol officer had to be monitoring from downstairs.

Vorreedi trod in, and studied the holovid display over Miles's shoulder. "Interesting. What is it?"

"Just brushing up on Cetagandan warship specs. Continuing education, officer-style, and all that. The hope for promotion to ship duty never dies."

"Hm." Vorreedi straightened. "I thought you might like to hear the latest on your Lord Yenaro."

"I don't think I own him, but—nothing fatal, I hope," said Miles sincerely. Yenaro might be an important witness, later; upon mature reflection Miles was beginning to regret not offering him asylum at the embassy.

"Not yet. But an order has been issued for his arrest."

"By Cetagandan Security? For treason?"

"No. By the civil police. For theft."

"It's a false charge, I'd lay odds. Somebody's trying to use the system to smoke him out of hiding. Can you find out who laid the charge?"

"A ghem-lord by the name of Nevic. Does that mean anything to you?"

"No. He's got to be a puppet. The man who put Nevic up to it is the man we want. The same man who supplied Yenaro with the plans and money for his funfountain. But now you have two strings to pull."

"You imagine it to be the same man?"

"Imagination," said Miles, "has nothing to do with it. But I need proof, stand-up-in-court type proof."

Vorreedi's gaze was uncomfortably level. "Why did you guess the charge against Yenaro would be treason?"

"Oh, well . . . I wasn't thinking. Theft is much better, less flashy, if what his enemy wants is for the civil police to drag Yenaro out into the open where he can get a clear shot at him."

Vorreedi's brows crimped. "Lord Vorkosigan . . ." But he appeared to think better of whatever he'd been about to say. He just shook his head and departed.

Ivan wandered in later, flung himself onto Miles's sofa, put up his booted feet on the armrest, and sighed.

"You still here?" Miles shut down his comconsole, which was by now making him cross-eyed. "I thought you'd be out making hay, or rolling in it, or whatever. Our last two days here and all. Or did you run out of invitations?" Miles jerked his thumb ceilingward, *We may be bugged.*

Ivan's lip curled, *Screw it.* "Vorreedi has laid on more bodyguards. It kind of takes the spontaneity out of things." He stared into the air. "Besides, I worry about where I put my feet, now. Wasn't it some queen of Egypt who was delivered in a rolled-up carpet? Could happen again."

"Could indeed," Miles had to agree. "Almost certainly will, in fact."

"Great. Remind me not to stand next to you." Miles grimaced.

After a minute or two Ivan added, "I'm bored." Miles chased him from his room.

The ceremony of Singing Open The Great Gates did not entail the opening of any gates, though it did involve singing. A massed chorus of several hundred ghem, both male and female, robed in white-on-white, arranged themselves near the eastern entrance inside the Celestial Garden. They planned to pass in procession around the four cardinal directions and eventually, later in the afternoon, finish at the north gate. The chorus stood to sing along an undulating area of ground with surprising acoustic properties, and the galactic envoys and ghem and haut mourners stood to listen. Miles flexed his legs, inside his boots, and prepared to endure. The open venue left lots of space for haut-lady bubbles, and they were out in force—some hundreds, scattered about the glade. How many haut-women *did* live here?

Miles glanced around his little delegation—himself, Ivan, Vorob'yev, and Vorreedi all in House blacks, Mia Maz dressed as before, striking in black and white. Vorreedi looked more Barrayaran, more officer-like, and, Miles had to admit, a lot more sinister out of his deliberately dull Cetagandan civvies. Maz rested one hand on Vorob'yev's arm and stood on tiptoe as the music started.

Breathtaking, Miles realized, could be a quite literal term—his lips parted and the hairs on the backs of his arms stood on end as the incredible sounds washed

over him. Harmonies and dissonances followed one
another up and down the scale with such precision, the
listener could make out every word, when the voices
were not simply wordless vibrations that seemed to
crawl right up the spine, and ring in the back-brain in
a succession of pure emotions. Even Ivan stood trans-
fixed. Miles wanted to comment, to express his astonishment, but breaking into the absolute concentration
the music demanded seemed some sort of sacrilege.
After about a thirty-minute performance, the music
came to a temporary close, and the chorus prepared
to move gracefully off to its next station, followed more
clumsily by the delegates.

The two groups took different routes. Ba servitors
under the direction of a dignified ghem-lord majordomo shepherded the delegates to a buffet, to both
refresh and delay them while the chorus set up for its
next performance at the southern gate. Miles stared
anxiously after the haut-lady bubbles, which naturally
did not accompany the outlander envoys, but floated
off in their own mob in yet a third direction. He was
getting less distracted by the diversions of the Celestial Garden. Could one finally grow to take it entirely
for granted? The haut certainly seemed to.

"I think I'm getting used to this place," he confided
to Ivan, as he walked along between him and Vorob'yev
in the ragged parade of outlander guests. "Or . . . I
could."

"Mm," said Ambassador Vorob'yev. "But when these
pretty folks turned their pet ghem-lords loose to pick
up some cheap new real estate out past Komarr, five
million of *us* died. I hope that hasn't slipped your mind,
my lord."

"No," said Miles tightly. "Not ever. But . . . even you
are not old enough to remember the war personally,
sir. I'm really starting to wonder if we'll ever see an
effort like that from the Cetagandan Empire again."

"Optimist," murmured Ivan.

"Let me qualify that. My mother always says, behavior that is rewarded is repeated. And the reverse. I think . . . that if the ghem-lords fail to score any new territorial successes in our generation, it's going to be a long time till we see them try again. An expansionist period followed by an isolationist one isn't a new historical phenomenon, after all."

"Didn't know you'd taken up political science," said Ivan.

"Can you prove your point?" asked Vorob'yev. "In less than a generation?"

Miles shrugged. "Don't know. It's one of those subliminal gut-feel things. If you gave me a year and a department, I could probably produce a reasoned analysis, with graphs."

"I admit," said Ivan, "it's hard to imagine, say, Lord Yenaro conquering anybody."

"It's not that he couldn't. It's just that by the time he ever got a chance, he'd be too old to care. I don't know. After the next isolationist period, though, all bets are off. When the haut are done with ten more generations of tinkering with themselves, I don't know what they'll be." *And neither do they. That* was an odd realization. *You mean no one is in charge here?* "Universal conquest may seem like a crude dull game from their childhood after that. Or else," he added glumly, "they'll be unstoppable."

"Jolly thought," grumbled Ivan.

A delicate breakfast offering was set up in a nearby pavilion. On the other side of it, the float-cars with the white silk upholstery waited to convey refreshed funeral envoys the couple of kilometers across the Celestial Garden to the South Gate. Miles nabbed a hot drink, refused with concealed loathing the offer of a pastry tray—his stomach was knotting with nervous anticipation—and watched the movements of the ba servitors with hawk-like attention. *It has to break today. There's no more time. Come on, Rian!* And how the devil was he to take Rian's next report when he had Vorreedi glued to his hip? The man was noting his every eye-flicker, Miles swore.

The day wore on with a repeat of the cycle of music and food and transportation. A number of the delegates were looking glassily over-loaded with it all; even Ivan had stopped eating in self-defense at about stop three. When the contact did come, at the buffet after the fourth and last choral performance, Miles almost missed it. He was making idle chit-chat with Vorreedi, reminiscing about Keroslav District baking styles, and wondering how he was going to distract and ditch the man. Miles had reached the point of desperation of fantasizing slipping Ambassador Vorob'yev an emetic and siccing, so to speak, the protocol officer on his superior while Miles ducked out, when he saw out of the corner of his eye Ivan talking with a grave ba servitor. He did not recognize this ba; it was not Rian's favorite little creature, for it was young and had a brush of blond hair. Ivan's hands turned palm-out, and he shrugged, then he followed the servitor from the pavilion, looking puzzled. *Ivan? What the hell does she want Ivan for?*

"Excuse me, sir," Miles cut across Vorreedi's words, and around his side. By the time Vorreedi had turned after him, Miles had darted past another delegation and was halfway to the exit after Ivan. Vorreedi would follow, but Miles would just have to deal with that later.

Miles emerged, blinking, into the artificial afternoon light of the dome just in time to see the dark shadow and boot-gleam of Ivan's uniform disappear around some flowering shrubbery, beyond an open space featuring a fountain. He trotted after, his own boots scuffing unevenly on the colored stone walks threading the greenery. "Lord Vorkosigan?" Vorreedi called after him. Miles didn't turn around, but raised his hand in an acknowledging, but still rapidly receding, wave. Vorreedi was too polite to curse out loud, but Miles could fill in the blanks.

The man-high shrubbery, broken up by artistic groupings of trees, wasn't quite a maze, but nearly so. Miles's first choice of directions opened onto some sort of unpeopled water meadow, with the stream generated from the nearby fountain running like silver embroidery through its center. He ran back along his route, cursing his legs and his limp, and swung around the other end of the bushes.

In the center of a tree-shaded circle lined with benches, a haut-chair floated with its high back to Miles, its screen down. The blond servitor was gone already. Ivan leaned in toward the float-chair's occupant, his lips parted in fascination, his brows drawn down in suspicion. A white-robed arm lifted. A faint cloud of iridescent mist puffed into Ivan's surprised face. Ivan's eyes rolled back, and he collapsed forward across the seated occupant's knees. The force-screen snapped up, white and blank. Miles yelled and ran toward it.

The haut-ladies' float-chairs were hardly race cars, but they could move faster than Miles could run. In two turns through the shrubbery it was out of sight. When Miles cleared the last stand of flowers, he found himself facing one of the major carved-white-jade-paved walkways that curved through the Celestial Garden. Floating along it in both directions were half a dozen haut-bubbles, all now moving at the same dignified walking pace. Miles had no breath left to swear, but black thoughts boiled off his brain.

He spun on his heel, and ran straight into Colonel Vorreedi.

Vorreedi's hand descended on his shoulder and took a good solid grip on the uniform cloth. "Vorkosigan, what the hell is going on? And where is Vorpatril?"

"I'm . . . just about to go check on that right now, sir, if you'll permit me."

"Cetagandan Security had better know. I'll light up their lives if they've—"

"I . . . don't think Security can help us on this one, sir. I think I need to talk to a ba servitor. Immediately."

Vorreedi frowned, trying to process this. It obviously did not compute. Miles couldn't blame him. Until a week ago, he too had shared the universal assumption that Cetagandan Imperial Security was in charge here. *And so they are, in some ways. But not all ways.*

Speak of the devil. As Miles and Vorreedi turned to retrace their steps to the pavilion, a red-uniformed, zebra-faced guard appeared, striding rapidly toward them. Sheepdog, Miles judged, sent to round up straying galactic envoys. Fast, but not fast enough.

"My lords," the guard, a low-ranker, nodded very politely. "The pavilion is this way, if you please. The float-cars will take you to the South Gate."

Vorreedi appeared to come to a quick decision. "Thank you. But we seem to have mislaid a member of our party. Would you please find Lord Vorpatril for me?"

"Certainly." The guard touched a wrist com and reported the request in neutral tones, while still firmly herding Miles and Vorreedi pavilion-ward. Taking Ivan, for now, as merely a lost guest; that had to happen fairly often, since the garden was designed to entice the viewer on into its delights. *I give Cetagandan Security maybe ten minutes to figure out he's really disappeared, in the middle of the Celestial Garden. Then it all starts coming apart.*

The guard split off as they climbed the steps to the pavilion. Back inside, Miles approached the oldest bald servitor he saw. "Excuse me, Ba," he said respectfully. The ba glanced up, nonplussed at not being invisible. "I must communicate immediately with the haut Rian

Degtiar. It's an emergency." He opened his hands and stood back.

The ba appeared to digest this for a moment, then gave a half bow and motioned Miles to follow. Vorreedi came too. Around a corner in the semi-privacy of a service area, the ba pulled back its gray and white uniform sleeve and spoke into its wrist-comm, a quick gabble of words and code phrases. Its non-existent eyebrows rose in surprise at the return message. It took off its wrist-comm, handed it to Miles with a low bow, and retreated out of earshot. Miles wished Vorreedi, looming over his shoulder, would do the same, but he didn't.

"Lord Vorkosigan?" came Rian's voice from the comm—unfiltered, she must be speaking from inside her bubble.

"Milady. Did you just send one of your . . . people, to pick up my cousin Ivan?"

There was a short pause. "No."

"I witnessed this."

"Oh." Another, much longer pause. When her voice came back again, it had gone low and dangerous. "I know what is happening."

"I'm glad somebody does."

"I will send *my* servitor for you."

"And Ivan?"

"*We* will handle that." The comm cut abruptly. Miles almost shook it in frustration, but handed it back to the servitor instead, who took it, bowed again, and scooted away.

"Just what did you witness, Lord Vorkosigan?" Vorreedi demanded.

"Ivan . . . left with a lady."

"What, *again*? Here? *Now*? Does the boy have no sense of time or place? This isn't Emperor Gregor's Birthday Party, dammit."

"I believe I can retrieve him very discreetly, sir, if

you will allow me." Miles felt a faint twinge of guilt for slandering Ivan by implication, but the twinge was lost in his general, heart-hammering fear. Had that aerosol been a knockout drug, or a lethal poison?

Vorreedi took a long, long minute to think this one over, his eye cold on Miles. Vorreedi, Miles reminded himself, was Intelligence, not Counter-intelligence; curiosity, not paranoia, was his driving force. Miles shoved his hands into his trouser pockets and tried to look calm, unworried, merely annoyed. As the silence lengthened, he dared to add, "If you trust nothing else, sir, please trust my competence. That's all I ask."

"Discreet, eh?" said Vorreedi. "You've made some interesting friends here, Lord Vorkosigan. I'd like to hear a lot more about them."

"Soon, I hope, sir."

"Mm . . . very well. But be prompt."

"I'll do my best, sir," Miles lied. It had to be today. Once away from his guardian, he wasn't coming back till the job was done. *Or we are all undone.* He gave a semi-salute, and slipped away before Vorreedi could think better of it.

He went to the open side of the pavilion and stepped down into the artificial sunlight just as a float-car arrived that was not funerally decorated: a simple two-passenger cart with room for cargo behind. A familiar aged little bald ba was at the controls. The ba spotted Miles, and swung closer, and brought its vehicle to a halt. They were intercepted by a quick-moving red-clad guard.

"Sir. Galactic guests may not wander the Celestial Garden unaccompanied."

Miles opened his palm at the ba servitor.

"My Lady requests and requires this man's attendance. I must take him," said the ba.

The guard looked unhappy, but gave a short, reluctant nod. "My superior will speak to yours."

"I'm sure." The ba's lips twitched in what Miles swore was a smirk.

The guard grimaced, and stepped away, his hand reaching for his comm link. *Go, go!* thought Miles as he climbed aboard, but they were already moving. This time, the float-car took a shortcut, rising up over the garden and heading southwest in a straight line. They actually moved fast enough for the breeze to ruffle Miles's hair. In a few minutes, they descended toward the Star Crèche, gleaming pale through the trees.

A strange procession of white bubbles was bobbing toward what was obviously a delivery entrance at the back of the building. Five bubbles, one on each side and one above, were . . . *herding* a sixth, bumping it along toward the high, wide door and into whatever loading bay lay beyond. The bubbles buzzed like angry wasps whenever their force-fields touched. The ba brought its little float-car calmly down into the tail of this parade, and followed the bubbles inside. The door slid closed behind them and sealed with that solid clunk and cacophony of chirps that bespoke high security.

Except for being lined with colored polished stone in geometric inlays instead of gray concrete, the loading bay was utilitarian and normal in design. It was presently empty except for the haut Rian Degtiar, standing in full flowing white robes beside her own float-chair, waiting. Her pale face was tense.

The five herding bubbles settled to the floor and snapped off, revealing five of the consorts Miles had met in the council night before last. The sixth bubble remained stubbornly up, white and solid and impenetrable.

Miles swung out of his cart as it settled to the pavement, and limped hurriedly to Rian's side. "Is Ivan in there?" he demanded, pointing at the sixth bubble.

"We think so."

"What's happening?"

"Sh. Wait." She made a graceful, palm-down gesture; Miles gritted his teeth, jittering inside. Rian stepped forward, her chin rising.

"Surrender and cooperate," said Rian clearly to the bubble, "and mercy is possible. Defy us, and it is not."

The bubble remained defiantly up and blank. Stand-off. The bubble had nowhere to go, and could not attack. *But she has Ivan in there.*

"Very well," sighed Rian. She pulled a pen-like object from her sleeve, with a screaming-bird pattern engraved in red upon its side, adjusted some control, pointed it at the bubble, and pressed. The bubble winked out, and the float-chair fell to the floor with a reverberant thump, all power dead. A yelp floated from a cloud of white fabric and brown hair.

"I didn't know anyone could do that," whispered Miles.

"Only the Celestial Lady has the override," said Rian. She put the control back in her sleeve, and stepped forward again, and stopped.

The haut Vio d'Chilian had recovered her balance instantly. She now half-knelt, one arm under Ivan's black-uniformed arm, supporting his slumping form, the other hand holding a thin knife to his throat. It looked very sharp, as it pressed against his skin. Ivan's eyes were open, dilated, shifting; he was paralyzed, not unconscious, then. *And not dead. Thank God.* *Yet.*

The haut Vio d'Chilian, unless Miles missed his guess, would have no inhibitions whatsoever about cutting a helpless man's throat. He wished ghem-Colonel Benin were here to witness this.

"Move against me," said the haut Vio, "and your Barrayaran *servitor* dies." Miles supposed the emphasis was intended as a hautish insult. He was not quite sure it succeeded.

Miles paced anxiously to Rian's other side, making an arc around the haut Vio but venturing no closer. The haut Vio followed him with venomous eyes. Now directly behind her, the haut Pel gave Miles a nod; her float-chair rose silently into the air and slipped out a doorway to the Crèche. Going for help? For a weapon? Pel was the practical one . . . he had to buy time.

"Ivan!" Miles said indignantly. "*Ivan's* not the man you want!"

The haut Vio's brows drew down. "What?"

But of course. Lord X always used front men, and women, for his legwork, keeping his own hands clean. Miles had been galloping around doing the legwork; therefore, Lord X must have reasoned that Ivan was really in charge. "Agh!" Miles cried. "What did you think? That because he's taller, and, and cuter, he had to be running this show? It's the haut way, isn't it? You—you *morons! I'm* the brains of this outfit!" He paced the other way, spluttering. "I had you spotted from Day One, don't you know? But no! Nobody ever takes me seriously!" Ivan's eyes, the only part of him that apparently still worked, widened at this rant. "So you went and kidnapped the *wrong man.* You just blew your cover for the sake of grabbing the *expendable* one!" The haut Pel hadn't gone for help, he decided. She'd gone to the lav to fix her hair, and was going to take *forever* in there.

Well, he certainly had the undivided attention of everyone in the loading bay, murderess, victim, haut-cops and all. What next, handsprings? "It's been like this since we were little kids, y'know? Whenever the two of us were together, they'd always talk to *him* first, like I was some kind of idiot alien who needed an interpreter—" the haut Pel reappeared silently in the doorway, lifted her hand—Miles's voice rose to a shout, "Well, I'm sick of it, d'you hear?!"

The haut Vio's head twisted in realization just as the

haut Pel's stunner buzzed. Vio's hand spasmed on the knife as the stunner beam struck her. Miles pelted forward as a line of red appeared at the blade's edge, and he grabbed for Ivan as she slumped unconscious. The stun nimbus had caught Ivan too, and his eyes rolled back. Miles let the haut Vio hit the floor on her own, as hard as gravity took her. Ivan he lowered gently.

It was only a surface cut. Miles breathed again. He pulled out his pocket handkerchief and dabbed at the sticky trickle of blood, then pressed it against the wound.

He glanced up at the haut Rian, and the haut Pel, who floated over to examine her handiwork. "She knocked him over with some kind of drug-mist. Stun on top of that—is he in medical danger?"

"I think not," said Pel. She dismounted from her float-chair, knelt, and rummaged through the unconscious haut Vio's sleeves, and came up with an assortment of objects, which she laid out in a methodical row on the pavement. One was a tiny silvery pointed thing with a bulb on the end. The haut Pel waved it under her lovely nose, sniffing. "Ah. This is it. No, he's in no danger. It will wear off harmlessly. He'll be very sick when he wakes up, though."

"Maybe you could give him a dose of synergine?" Miles pleaded.

"We have that available."

"Good." He studied the haut Rian. *Only the Celestial Lady has the override.* But Rian had used it as one entitled, and no one had blinked, not even the haut Vio. *Have you grasped this yet, boy? Rian is the acting Empress of Cetaganda, until tomorrow, and every move she's made has been with full, real, Imperial authority. Handmaiden, ha.* Another one of those impenetrable, misleading haut titles that didn't say what it meant; you had to be in the know.

Assured of Ivan's eventual recovery, Miles scrambled

to his feet and demanded, "What's happening now? How did you find Ivan? Did you get all the gene banks back, or not? What did you—"

The haut Rian held up a restraining hand, to stem the flood of questions. She nodded to the dead bubble-chair. "This is the Consort of Sigma Ceta's float-chair, but as you see, the haut Nadina is not with it."

"Ilsum Kety! Yes? What *happened*? How'd he diddle the bubble? How'd you detect it? How long have you known?"

"Ilsum Kety, yes. We began to know last night, when the haut Nadina failed to return with her gene bank. All the others were back and safe by midnight. But Kety apparently only knew that his consort would be missed at this morning's ceremonies. So he sent the haut Vio to impersonate her. We suspected at once, and watched her."

"Why *Ivan*?"

"That, I do not know yet. Kety *cannot* make a consort disappear without great repercussions; I suspect he meant to use your cousin to divest himself of guilt somehow."

"Another frame, yes, that would fit his *modus operandi*. You realize, the haut Vio . . . must have murdered the Ba Lura. At Kety's direction."

"Yes." Rian's eyes, falling on the prostrate form of the brown-haired woman, were very cold. "She too is a traitor to the haut. That will make her the business of the Star Crèche's own justice."

Miles said uneasily, "She could be an important witness, to clear Barrayar and me of blame in the disappearance of the Great Key. Don't, um . . . do anything premature, till we know if that's needed, huh?"

"Oh, we have *many* questions for her, first."

"So . . . Kety still has his bank. And the Key. And a warning." *Damn.* Whose idiot idea had it been . . . ? Oh. Yes. *But you can't blame Ivan for this one. You thought recalling the gene banks was a great move. And Rian bought it too. Idiocy by committee, the finest kind.*

"And he has his consort, whom he knows he cannot let live. Assuming she still lives now. I did not think . . . I would be sending the haut Nadina to her death." The haut Rian stared at the far wall, avoiding both Miles's and Pel's eyes.

Neither did I. Miles swallowed sickness. "He can bury her in the chaos of his revolt, once it gets going. But he can't start his revolt yet." He paused. "But if, in order to arrange her death in some artistic way that incriminates Barrayar, he needs Ivan . . . I don't think she'll be dead yet. Saved, held prisoner on his ship, yes. Not dead yet." *Please, not dead yet.* "We know one other thing, too. The haut Nadina is successfully concealing information from him, or even actively misleading him. Or he wouldn't have tried what he just tried." Actually, that could also be construed as convincing evidence that the haut Nadina *was* dead. Miles bit his lip. "But now Kety's made enough overt moves to incriminate himself, for charges to stick to him and not to me, yes?"

Rian hesitated. "Maybe. He is clearly very clever."

Miles stared at the inert float-chair, sitting slightly canted, and looking quite ordinary without its magical electronic nimbus. "So are we. Those float-chairs. Somebody here must security-key them to their operators in the first place, right? Would I be making too silly a wild-ass guess if I suggested that person was the Celestial Lady?"

"That is correct, Lord Vorkosigan."

"So you have the override, and could encode this to anybody."

"Not to anybody. Only to any haut-woman."

"Ilsum Kety is expecting the return of this haut-bubble, after the ceremonies, with a haut-woman and a Barrayaran prisoner, yes?" He took a deep breath. "I think . . . we should not disappoint him."

CHAPTER FOURTEEN

"I found Ivan, sir." Miles smiled into the comconsole. The background beyond Ambassador Vorob'yev's head was blurred, but the sounds of the buffet winding down—subdued voices, the clink of plates—carried clearly over the comm. "He's getting a tour of the Star Crèche. We'll be here a while yet—can't insult our hostess and all that. But I should be able to extract him and catch up with you before the party's over. One of the ba will bring us back."

Vorob'yev looked anything but happy at this news. "Well. I suppose it will have to do. But Colonel Vorreedi does not care for these spontaneous additions to the planned itinerary, regardless of the cultural opportunity, and I must say I'm beginning to agree with him. Don't, ah . . . don't let Lord Vorpatril do anything inappropriate, eh? The haut are not the ghem, you know."

"Yes, sir. Ivan's doing just fine. Never better." Ivan was still out cold, back in the freight bay, but the returning color to his face had suggested the synergine was starting to work.

"Just how did he obtain this extraordinary privilege, anyway?" asked Vorob'yev.

"Oh, well, you know Ivan. Couldn't let me score a coup he couldn't match. I'll explain it all later. Must go now."

"I'll be fascinated to hear it," the ambassador murmured dryly. Miles cut the comm before his smile fractured and fell off his face.

"*Whew*. That buys us a little time. A very little time. We need to move."

"Yes," agreed his escort, the brown-haired Rho Cetan lady. She turned her float-chair and led him out of the side-office containing the comconsole; he had to trot to keep up.

They returned to the freight bay just as Rian and the haut Pel finished re-coding the haut Nadina's bubble-chair. Miles spared an anxious glance for Ivan, laid out on the tessellated pavement. He seemed to be breathing deeply and normally.

"I'm ready," Miles reported to Rian. "My people won't come looking for us for at least an hour. If Ivan wakes up . . . well, *you* should have no trouble keeping him under control." He licked lips gone dry. "If things go wrong . . . go to ghem-Colonel Benin. Or to your Emperor himself. No Imperial Security middlemen. Everything about this, especially the ways Governor Kety has been able to diddle what everyone fondly believed were diddle-proof systems, is screaming to me that he's suborned a connection high up, probably very high up, in your own security who's giving him serious aid and comfort. Being rescued by him could be a fatal experience, I suspect."

"I understand," said Rian gravely. "And I agree with your analysis. The Ba Lura would not have taken the Great Key to Kety for duplication in the first place if it had not been convinced that he was capable of carrying out the task." She straightened from the float-chair arm, and nodded to the haut Pel.

The haut Pel had filled her sleeves with most of the

little items she had taken from the haut Vio. She nodded back, straightened her robes, and gracefully settled herself aboard. The little items did not, alas, include energy weapons, the power packs of which would set off security scanners. *Not even a stunner*, Miles thought with morbid regret. *I'm going into orbital battle wearing dress blacks and riding boots, and I'm totally disarmed. Wonderful.* He took his place again at Pel's left side, perched on the cushioned armrest, trying not to feel like the ventriloquist's dummy that he glumly fancied he resembled. The bubble's force-screen enclosed them, and Rian stood back, and nodded. Pel, her right hand on the control panel, spun the bubble, and they floated quickly toward the exit, which dilated to let them pass; two other consorts exited simultaneously, and sped off in other directions.

Miles felt a brief pang in his heart that Pel and not Rian was his companion in arms. In his heart, but not in his head. It was essential not to place Rian, the most creditable witness of Kety's treason, in Kety's power. And . . . he liked Pel's style. She had already demonstrated her ability to think fast and clearly in an emergency. He still wasn't sure that drop over the side of the building night before last hadn't been for her amusement, rather than for secrecy. A haut-woman with a sense of humor, almost . . . too bad she was eighty years old, and a consort, and Cetagandan, and . . . *Give it up, will you? Ivan you aren't nor ever will be. But one way or another, Governor the haut Ilsum Kety's treason is not going to last the day.*

They joined Kety's party as it was making ready to depart at the south gate of the Celestial Garden. The haut Vio would have been sent to collect Ivan at the last possible moment, to be sure. Kety's train was large, as befit his governor's dignity: a couple of dozen ghem-guards, plus ghem-ladies, non-ba servitors in his personal livery, and rather to Miles's dismay, ghem-General

Chilian. *Was* Chilian in on his master's treason, or was he due to be dumped along with the haut Nadina on the way home, and replaced with Kety's own appointee? He had to be one or the other; the commander of Imperial troops on Sigma Ceta could hardly be expected to stay neutral in the upcoming coup.

Kety himself gestured the haut Vio's bubble into his own vehicle for the short ride to the Imperial shuttleport, the exclusive venue for all such high official arrivals to and departures from the Celestial Garden. Ghem-General Chilian took another car; Miles and the haut Pel found themselves alone with Kety in a vanlike space clearly designed for the lady-bubbles.

"You're late. Complications?" Kety inquired cryptically, settling back in his seat. He looked worried and stern, as befit an earnest mourner—or a man riding a particularly hungry and unreliable tiger.

Yeah, and I should have known he was Lord X when I first spotted that fake gray hair, Miles decided. This was one haut-lord who didn't want to wait for what life might bring him.

"Nothing I couldn't handle," reported Pel. The voice-filter, set to maximum blur, altered her tones into a fair imitation of the haut Vio's.

"I'm sure, my love. Keep your force-screen up till we're aboard."

"Yes."

Yep. Ghem-General Chilian definitely has an appointment with an unfriendly air lock, Miles decided. *Poor sucker.* The haut Vio, perhaps, meant to get back into the haut-genome one way or another. So was she Kety's mistress, or his master? Or were they a team? Two brains rather than one behind this plot could account for its speed, flexibility, and confusion all together.

The haut Pel touched a control, and turned to Miles. "When we get aboard, we must decide whether to look first for the haut Nadina or the Great Key."

Miles nearly choked. "Er . . ." He gestured toward Kety, sitting less than a meter from his knee.

"He cannot hear us," Pel reassured him. It seemed to be so, for Kety turned abstracted eyes to the passing view outside the luxurious lift-van's polarized canopy.

"The recovery of the Key," Pel went on, "is of the highest priority."

"Mm. But the haut Nadina, if she's still alive, is an important witness, for Barrayar's sake. And . . . she may have an idea where the Key is being kept. I think it's in a cipher lab, but it's a damned big ship, and there's a lot of places Kety may have tucked a cipher lab."

"Both it and Nadina will be close to his quarters," Pel said.

"He won't have her in the brig?"

"I doubt . . . Kety will have wished many of his soldiers or servitors to know that he holds his consort prisoner. No. She will most likely be secreted in a cabin."

"I wonder where Kety figures to stage whatever fatal crime he's planned involving Ivan and the haut Nadina? The consorts move on pretty constricted paths. He won't site it on his own ship, nor his own residence. And he probably doesn't dare repeat the performance inside the Celestial Garden, that would be just *too* much. Something downside, I fancy, and tonight."

Governor Kety glanced at their force bubble, and inquired, "Is he waking up yet?"

Pel touched her lips, then her controls. "Not yet."

"I want to question him, before. I must know how much they know."

"Time enough."

"Barely."

Pel killed her outgoing sound again.

"The haut Nadina first," Miles voted firmly.

"I . . . think you're right, Lord Vorkosigan," sighed Pel.

∾   ∾   ∾

Further dangerous conversation with Kety was blocked by the confusion of loading the shuttle to convey the portion of retinue that was going to orbit; Kety himself was busied on his comm link. They did not find themselves alone with the governor again until the whole mob had disgorged into the shuttle hatch corridor aboard Kety's State ship, and gone about their various duties or pleasures. Ghem-General Chilian did not even attempt to speak with his wife. Pel followed at Kety's gesture. From the fact that Kety had dismissed his guards, Miles reasoned that they were about to get down to business. Limiting witnesses limited the murders necessary to silence them, later, if things went wrong.

Kety led them to a broad, tastefully appointed corridor obviously dedicated to upper-class residence suites. Miles almost tapped the haut Pel on the shoulder. "Look. Down the hall. Do you see?"

A liveried man stood guard outside one cabin door. He braced to attention at the sight of his master. But Kety turned in to another cabin first. The guard relaxed slightly.

Pel craned her neck. "Might it be the haut Nadina?"

"Yes. Well . . . maybe. I don't think he'd dare use a regular trooper for the duty. Not if he doesn't control their command structure yet." Miles felt a strong pang of regret that he hadn't figured out the schism between Kety and his ghem-general earlier. Talk about exploitable opportunities . . .

The door slid closed behind them, and Miles's head snapped around to see what they were getting into now. The chamber was clean, bare of decoration or personal effects: an unused cabin, then.

"We can put him here," said Kety, nodding to a couch in the sitting-room portion of the chamber. "Can you keep him under control chemically, or must we have some guards?"

"Chemically," responded Pel, "but I need a few

things. Synergine. Fast-penta. And we'd better check him for induced fast-penta allergies first. Many important people are given them, I understand. I don't think you want him to die *here*."

"Clarium?"

Pel glanced at Miles, her eyes widening in question; she did not know that one. Clarium was a fairly standard military interrogation tranquilizer—Miles nodded.

"That would be a good idea," Pel hazarded.

"No chance of his waking up before I get back, is there?" asked Kety in concern.

"I'm afraid I dosed him rather strongly."

"Hm. Please be more discreet, my love. We don't want excessive chemical residues left upon autopsy. Though with luck, there will not be enough left to autopsy."

"I'm reluctant to count on luck."

"*Good*," said Kety, with a peculiar exasperation. "You're learning at last."

"I'll await you," said Pel coolly, by way of a broad hint. As if the haut Vio would have done anything else.

"Let me help you lay him out," Kety said. "It must be crowded in there."

"Not for me. I'm using him for a footrest. The floatchair is . . . most comfortable. Let me . . . enjoy the privilege of the haut a little longer, my love," Pel sighed. "It has been so long. . . ."

Kety's lips thinned in amusement. "Soon enough, you shall have more privileges than the Empress ever had. And all the outworlders at your feet you may desire." He gave the bubble a short nod, and departed, striding quickly. Where would a haut-governor with an interrogation chemistry shopping list go? Sickbay? Security? And how long would it take?

"Now," said Miles. "Back up the corridor. We have to get rid of the guard—did you bring any of that stuff that the haut Vio used on Ivan?"

Pel pulled the tiny bulb from her sleeve and held it up.

"How many doses are left?"

Pel squinted. "Two. Vio over-prepared." She sounded faintly disapproving, as if Vio had lost style-points by this redundancy.

"I'd have taken a hundred, just in case. All right. Use it sparingly—not at all if you don't have to."

Pel floated her bubble out of the cabin again, and turned up the corridor. Miles slid around behind the float-chair, crouching with his hands gripping the high back and his boots slipping slightly on base which held the power pack. *Hiding behind a woman's skirts?* It was frustrating as hell to have his transportation—and everything else—under the control of a Cetagandan, even if the rescue mission *was* his idea. *But needs must drive*. Pel came to a halt before the liveried guard.

"Servitor," she addressed him.

"Haut," he nodded respectfully to the blank white bubble. "I am on duty, and may not assist you."

"This will not take long." Pel flicked off her force-screen. Miles heard a faint hiss, and a choking noise. The float-chair rocked. He popped up to find Pel with the guard slumped very awkwardly across her lap.

"Damn," said Miles regretfully, "we should have done this to Kety back in the first cabin—oh, well. Let me at that door pad."

It was a standard palm-lock, but set to whom? Very few, maybe Kety and Vio only, but the guard must be empowered to handle emergencies. "Move him up a little," Miles instructed Pel, and pressed the uncon-scious man's palm to the read-pad. "Ah," he breathed in satisfaction, as the door slid aside without alarm or protest. He relieved the guard of his stunner, and tip-toed inside, the haut Pel floating after.

"*Oh*," huffed Pel in outrage. They had found the haut Nadina.

The old woman was sitting on a couch similar to the one in the previous cabin, wearing only her white bodysuit. The effects of a century or so of gravity were enough to sag even her haut body; taking away her voluminous outer wrappings seemed a deliberate indignity only barely short of stripping her naked. Her silver hair was clamped, half a meter from its end, in a device obviously borrowed from engineering and never designed for this purpose, but locked in turn to the floor. It was not physically cruel—the length of the rest of her hair still left her nearly two meters of turning room—but there was something deeply offensive about it. The haut Vio's idea, perhaps? Miles thought he knew how Ivan had felt, contemplating the kitten tree. It seemed a Wrong Thing to do to a little old lady (even one from a race as obnoxious as the haut) who reminded him of his Betan grandmother—well, not really, *Pel* actually seemed more like his Grandmother Naismith in personality, but—

Pel dumped the unconscious guard unceremoniously on the floor and rushed from her float-chair to her sister consort. "Nadina, are you injured?"

"Pel!" Anyone else would have fallen on her rescuer's neck in a hug; being haut, they confined themselves to a restrained, if apparently heartfelt, handclasp.

"Oh!" said Pel again, gazing furiously at the haut Nadina's situation. Her first action was to skin out of her own robes and donate about six underlayers to Nadina, who shrugged them on gratefully, and stood a little straighter. Miles completed a fast survey of the premises to be sure they were indeed alone, and returned to the women, who stood contemplating the hair-lock. Pel knelt and tugged at a few strands, which held fast.

"I've tried that," sighed the haut Nadina. "They won't come out even one hair at a time."

"Where is the key to its lock?"

"Vio had it."

Pel quickly emptied her sleeves of her mysterious arsenal; Nadina looked it over and shook her head.

"We'd better cut it," said Miles. "We have to go as quickly as possible."

Both women stared at him in shock. "Haut-women *never* cut their hair!" said Nadina.

"Um, excuse me, but this is an emergency. If we go at *once* to the ship's escape pods, I can pilot you both to safety before Kety awakes to his loss. Maybe even get away clean. Every second's delay costs us our very limited margin."

"No!" said Pel. "We must retrieve the Great Key first!"

He could not, unfortunately, send the two women off and promise to search for the Key on his own; he was the only qualified orbital pilot in the trio. They were going to have to stick together, blast it. One haut-lady was bad enough. Managing two was going to be worse than trying to herd cats. "Haut Nadina, do you know where Kety keeps the Great Key?"

"Yes. He took me to it last night. He thought I might be able to open it for him. He was very upset when I couldn't."

Miles glanced up sharply at her tone; there were no marks of violence on her face, at least. But her movements were stiff. Arthritis of age, or shock-stick trauma? He returned to the guard's unconscious body, and began searching it for useful items, code cards, weapons . . . ah. A folded vibra-knife. He palmed it out of sight, and returned to the ladies.

"I've heard of animals gnawing their legs off, to escape traps," he offered cautiously.

"Ugh!" said Pel. "Barrayarans."

"You don't understand," said Nadina earnestly.

He was afraid he did. They would stand here arguing

about Nadina's trapped haut-hair until Kety caught up with them. . . . "Look!" He pointed at the door.

Pel jerked to her feet, and Nadina cried, "What?"

Miles snapped open the vibra-knife, grabbed the mass of silver hair, and sliced through it as close to the clamp as he could. "There. Let's *go.*"

"Barbarian!" cried Nadina. But she wasn't going to go over the edge into hysterics; she shrieked her belated protest quite quietly, all things considered.

"A sacrifice for the good of the haut," Miles promised her. A tear stood in her eye; Pel . . . Pel looked as if she were secretly grateful the deed had been done by him and not her.

They all boarded the float-chair again, Nadina half across Pel's lap, Miles clinging on behind. Pel exited the chamber and raised her force-screen again. Float-chairs were supposed to be soundless, but the engine whined protest at this overload. It moved forward with a disconcerting lurch.

"Down this way. Turn right here," the haut Nadina directed. Halfway down the hall they passed an ordinary servitor, who stepped aside with a bow, and did not look back at them.

"Did Kety fast-penta you?" Miles asked Nadina. "How much does he know of what the Star Crèche suspects about him?"

"Fast-penta does not work on haut-women," Pel informed him over her shoulder.

"Oh? How about on haut-men?"

"Not *very* well," said Pel.

"Hm. Nevertheless."

"Down here." Nadina pointed to a lift tube. They descended a deck, and continued down another, narrower corridor. Nadina touched the silver hair piled in her lap, regarded the raggedly cut end with a deep frown, then let the handful fall with an unhappy, but rather final-sounding, snort. "This is all highly improper.

I trust you are enjoying your opportunity for sport, Pel. And that it will be brief."

Pel made a non-committal noise.

Somehow, this was not the heroic covert ops mission that Miles had envisioned in his mind—blundering around Kety's ship in tow of a pair of prim, aging haut-ladies—well, Pel's allegiance to the proprieties was highly suspect, but Nadina appeared to be trying to make up for it. He had to admit, the bubble beat the hell out of his trying to disguise his physical peculiarities in the garb of a ba servitor, especially given that the ba appeared to be uniformly healthy and straight. Enough other haut-women were aboard that the sight of a passing bubble was unremarkable to staff and crew. . . .

No. We've just been lucky, so far.

They came to a blank door. "This is it," said Nadina.

No give-away guard this time; this was the little room that wasn't there. "How do we get in?" asked Miles. "Knock?"

"I suppose so," said Pel. She dropped her force-screen just long enough to do so, then raised it again.

"I meant that as a *joke*," said Miles, horrified. Surely no one was in there—he'd pictured the Great Key kept alone in some safe or coded compartment—

The door opened. A pale man with dark rings under his eyes, dressed in Kety's livery, pointed a device at the bubble, read off the electronic signature that resulted, and said, "Yes, haut Vio?"

"I . . . have brought the haut Nadina to try again," said Pel. Nadina grimaced in disapproving editorial.

"I don't think we're going to need her," said the liveried man, "but you can talk to the General." He stood aside to let them pass within.

Miles, who had been calculating how to knock the man out with Pel's aerosol again, started his calculations over. There were three men in the—floating cipher lab, yes. An array of equipment, festooned with temporary cables, cluttered every available surface. An even more whey-faced tech wearing the black undress uniform of Cetagandan military security sat before a console with the air of a man who'd been there for days, as evidenced by the caffeinated drink containers littered around him in a ring, and a couple of bottles of commercial painkillers sitting atop a nearby counter. But it was the third man, leaning over his shoulder, who riveted Miles's attention.

It wasn't ghem-General Chilian, as his mind had first tried to assume. This officer was a younger man, taller, sharp-faced, who wore the bloodred dress uniform of the Celestial Garden's own Imperial Security. He was not wearing his proper zebra-striped face paint, though. His tunic was rumpled and hanging open. Not the Chief of Security—Miles's mind ratcheted down the list he had memorized, weeks ago, in mis-aimed preparation for this trip—ghem-General Naru, yes, that was the man, third in command in that very inner hierarchy. Kety's deduced seduced contact. Called in, apparently, to lend his expertise in cracking the codes that protected the Great Key.

"All right," said the whey-faced tech, "start over with branch seven thousand, three-hundred and six. Only seven hundred more to go, and we'll have it, I swear."

Pel gasped, and pointed. Piled in a disorderly heap on the table beyond the console was not one but eight copies of the Great Key. Or one Great Key and seven copies . . .

Could Kety be attempting to carry out the late Empress Lisbet's vision after all? All the rest of the chaos of the past two weeks some confused misunderstanding? No . . . no. This had to be some other scam. Maybe he planned to send his fellow governors home with bad copies, or give Cetagandan Imperial Security seven more decoys to chase, or . . . a multitude of possibilities, as long as they advanced Kety's own personal agenda and no one else's.

Firing his stunner would set off every alarm in the place, making it a weapon of last resort. Hell, his victims, if clever—and Miles suspected he faced three very clever men—might jump him just to make him fire it.

"What *else* do you have up your sleeve?" Miles whispered to Pel.

"Nadina," Pel gestured to the table, "which one is the Great Key?"

"I'm not sure," said Nadina, peering anxiously at the clutter.

"Grab them *all*. Check *later*," urged Miles.

"But they could all be false," dithered Pel. "We must know, or it could all be for nothing." She fished in her bodice, and pulled out a familiar ring on a chain, with a raised screaming-bird pattern. . . .

Miles choked. "For God's sake, you didn't bring that *here*? Keep it out of sight! After two weeks of trying to do what that ring does in a second, I guarantee those men wouldn't hesitate to kill you for it!"

Ghem-General Naru wheeled from his tech to face the pale glowing bubble. "Yes, Vio, what is it now?" His voice was bored, and dripping with open contempt.

Pel looked a little panicked; Miles could see her throat move, as she sub-vocalized some practice reply, then rejected it.

"We're not going to be able to keep this up for much longer," said Miles. "How about we attack, grab, and run?"

"How?" asked Nadina.

Pel held up her hand for silence from the on-board debating team, and essayed a temporizing reply to the general. "Your tone of voice is most improper, sir."

Naru grimaced. "Being back in your bubble makes you proud again, I see. Enjoy it while it lasts. We'll have

all of those damned bitches pried out of their little for-
tresses after this. Their days of being cloaked by the
Emperor's blindness and stupidity are numbered, I
assure you, *haut* Vio."

Well . . . Naru wasn't in on this plot for the sake
of the late Empress's vision of genetic destiny, that was
certain. Miles could see how the haut-women's traditional privacies could come to be a deep, itching
offense, to a dedicated, properly paranoid security man.
Was that the bribe Kety had offered Naru for his cooperation, the promise that the new regime would open
the closed doors of the Star Crèche, and shine light
into every secret place held by the haut-women? That
he would destroy the haut-women's strange and fragile
power-base, and put it all into the hands of the ghem-
generals, where it obviously (to Naru) belonged? So
was Kety stringing Naru along, or were they near-equal
co-plotters? Equals, Miles decided. *This is the most
dangerous man in the room, maybe even on the ship.*
He set the stunner for low beam, in a forlorn hope
of not setting off alarms on discharge.

"Pel," Miles said urgently, "get ghem-General Naru
with your last dose of sleepy-juice. I'll try to threaten
the others, get the drop on them, without actually firing. Tie them up, grab the Keys, and get out of here.
It may not be elegant, but it's fast, and we're *out of
time.*"

Pel nodded reluctantly, twitched her sleeves back,
and readied the little aerosol bulb. Nadina gripped the
chair-back: Miles prepared to spring away and take up
a firing stance.

Pel dropped her bubble and squirted the aerosol
toward Naru's startled face. Naru held his breath and
ducked away, barely grazed by the iridescent cloud of
drug. His breath puffed back out on a yell of warning.

Miles cursed, leapt, stumbled, and fired three times

in rapid succession. He dropped the two scrambling
techs; Naru nearly succeeded in rolling away again, but
at least the beam nimbus brought the ghem-general
to a twitching halt. Temporarily. Naru lumbered around
on the deck like a warthog mired in a bog, his voice
reduced to a garbled groan.

Nadina hurried to the table full of Keys, swept them
into her outermost robe, and brought them back to Pel.
Pel began trying the ring-key on each one. "Not that
one . . . not that . . ."

Miles glanced at the door, which remained closed,
would remain closed until an authorized hand pressed
its palm-lock. Who would be so authorized? Kety . . .
Naru, who was already in here . . . any others? *We're
about to find out.*

"Not . . ." Pel continued. "Oh, what if they're *all*
false? No . . ."

"Of course they are," Miles realized. "The real one
must be, must be—" He began tracing cables from the
cipher tech's comconsole. They led to a box, stuffed
in behind some other equipment, and in the box was—
another Great Key. But this one was braced in a comm
light-beam, carrying the signals that probed its codes.
"— *here.*" Miles yanked it from its place, and sprinted
back to Pel. "We've got the Key, we've got Nadina,
we've got the goods on Naru, we've got it all. Let's *go.*"

The door hissed open. Miles whirled and fired.

A stunner-armed man in Kety's livery stumbled backward. Thumps and shouts echoed from the corridor,
as what seemed a dozen more men stood quickly out
of the line of fire. "*Yes,*" cried Pel happily, as the cap
of the real Great Key came off in her hand, demon-
strating its provenance.

"Not now!" screeched Miles. "Put it back, Pel, put
your force-screen up, *now!*"

Miles ducked aboard the float-chair; its force-screen
snapped into place. A blast of massed stunner fire

roiled through the doorway. The stunner fire crackled harmlessly around the sparkling sphere, only making it glitter a bit more. But the haut Nadina had been left outside. She cried out and stumbled backward, painfully grazed by the stun-nimbus. Men charged through the door.

"You have the Key, Pel!" cried the haut Nadina. "Flee!"

An impractical suggestion, alas; as his men secured the room and the haut Nadina, Governor Kety strolled through the door and closed it behind him, palm-locking it.

"Well," he drawled, eyes alight with curiosity at the carnage before him. "Well." He might at least have had the courtesy to curse and stamp, Miles thought sourly. Instead he looked . . . quite thoroughly in control. "What have we here?"

A Kety-liveried trooper knelt by ghem-General Naru, and helped straighten him and hold him up by his shoulders. Naru, struggling to sit, rubbed a shaking hand over his doubtless numb and tingling face—Miles had experienced the full unpleasantness of being stunned himself, more than once in his past—and essayed a mumbling answer. On the second try he managed slurred but intelligible speech. "'S the Consorts Pel and Nadina. An' the Barray'arn. *Tol* you those damned bubbles were a secur'ty menace!" He slumped back into the trooper's arms. "'S' all right, though. We have 'em all now."

"When that voyeur is tried for his treasons," said the haut Pel poisonously, "I shall ask the Emperor to have his eyes put out, before he is executed."

Miles wondered anew at the sequence of events here last night; how *had* they extracted Nadina from her bubble? "I think you're getting a little ahead of us, milady," he sighed.

Kety walked around the haut Pel's bubble, studying

it. Cracking this egg was a pretty puzzle for him. Or
was it? He'd done it once before.

Escape was impossible; the bubble's movements were
physically blocked. Kety might besiege them, starve
them out, if he didn't mind waiting—no. Kety couldn't
wait. Miles grinned blackly, and said to Pel, "This float-
chair has communication link capacity, doesn't it? I'm
afraid it's time to call for help."

They had, by God, *almost* brought it off, almost made
the entire affair disappear without a trace. But now that
they'd identified and targeted Naru, the threat of secret
aid for Kety from inside Cetagandan Imperial Security was neutralized. The Cetagandans should be able
to unravel the rest of it for themselves. *If I can get the
word out.*

Governor Kety motioned the two men holding the
haut Nadina to drag her forward to what he apparently
guessed was in front of the bubble, except that he was
actually about forty degrees offsides. He relieved one
guardsman of his vibra-knife, stepped behind Nadina,
and lifted her thick silver hair. She squeaked in terror,
but relaxed again when he only laid the knife very
lightly against her throat.

"Drop your force-screen, Pel, and surrender. Immediately. I don't think I need to go into crude, tedious
threats, do I?"

"No," whispered Pel in agreement. That Kety would
slit the haut Nadina's throat now, and arrange the body
later, was unquestionable. He'd gone beyond the point
of no return some time ago.

"Dammit," grated Miles in anguish. "Now *he's* got
it all. Us, the Great Key . . ." *The Great Key.* Chock
full it was of . . . coded information. Information the
value of which lay entirely in its secrecy and unique-
ness. Everywhere else people waded through floods of
information, information to their eyebrows, a clogging
mass of data, signal and noise . . . all information was

transmittable and reproducible. Left to itself, it multiplied like bacteria as long as there was money or power to be had in it, till it choked on its own reduplication and the boredom of its human receivers.

"The float-chair, your comm link—it's all Star Crèche equipment. Can you download the Great Key from it?"

"Do *what*? Why . . ." said Pel, struggling with astonishment, "I suppose so, but the chair's comm link is not powerful enough to transmit all the way back to the Celestial Garden."

"Don't worry about that. Patch it through to the commercial navigation's emergency communication net. There'll be a booster right outside this ship on the orbital transfer station. I have the standard codes for it in my head, they're made simple on purpose. Maximum emergency overrides—the booster'll split the signal and dump it into the on-board computers of every ship, commercial or military, navigating right now through the Eta Ceta star system, and every station. Supposed to be a cry-for-help system for ships in deep trouble, you see. So Kety'll have the Great Key. So will a couple thousand other people, and where is his sly little plot then? We may not be able to win, but we can take his victory from him!"

The look on Pel's face, as she digested this outrageous suggestion, transformed from horror to a fey delight, but then to dismay. "That will take—many minutes. Kety will never let—no! I have the solution for that." Pel's eyes lit with understanding and rage. "What are those codes?"

Miles rattled them off; Pel's fingers flashed over her control panel. A dicey moment followed while Pel arranged the opened Great Key in the light-beam reader. Kety cried from outside the bubble, "Now, Pel!" His hand tightened on the knife. Nadina closed her eyes and stood in dignified stillness.

Pel tapped the comm link start code, dropped the

bubble's force-screen, and sprang out of her seat, dragging Miles with her. "All right!" she cried, stepping away from the bubble. "We're out."

Kety's hand relaxed. The bubble's screen snapped back up. The force of it almost pushed Miles off his feet; he stumbled into the unwelcoming arms of the haut-governor's guards.

"That," said Kety coldly, eyeing the bubble with the Great Key inside, "is annoying. But a temporary inconvenience. Take them." He jerked his head at his guards, and stepped away from Nadina. "You!" he said in surprise, finding Miles in their grip.

"Me." Miles's lips peeled back on a white flash of teeth that had nothing to do with a smile. "Me all along, in fact. From start to finish." *And you are finished. Of course, I may be too dead to enjoy the spectacle. . . .* Kety dared not let any of the three interlopers live. But it would take a little time yet to arrange their deaths with civilized artistry. How much time, how many chances to—

Kety caught himself just before his fist delivered a jaw-cracking blow to Miles's face. "No. You're the breakable one, isn't that right," he muttered half to himself. He stepped back, nodded to a guard. "A little shock-stick on him. On them all."

The guard unshipped his standard military issue shock-stick, glanced at the white-robed haut consorts, and hesitated. He shot a covertly beseeching look at Kety.

Miles could almost see Kety grind his teeth. "All right, just the Barrayaran!"

Looking very relieved, the guard swung his stick with a will and belted Miles three times, starting with his face and skittering down his body to belly and groin. The first touch made him yell, the second took his breath away, and the third dropped him to the floor, blazing agony radiating outward and drawing his arms and legs in. Calculation stopped, temporarily. Ghem-General Naru, just being helped to his feet, chuckled in a tone of one happy to see justice done.

"General," Kety nodded to Naru, then to the bubble, "how long to get that open?"

"Let me see." Naru knelt to the unconscious whey-faced tech, and relieved him of a small device, which he pointed at the bubble. "They've changed the codes. Half an hour, once you get my men waked up."

Kety grimaced. His wrist comm chimed. Kety's brows rose, and he spoke into it. "Yes, Captain?"

"Haut-governor," came the formal, uneasy voice of some subordinate. "We are experiencing a peculiar communication over emergency channels. An enormous data dump is being speed-loaded into our systems. Some kind of coded gibberish, but it has exceeded the memory capacity of the receiver and is spilling over into other systems like a virus. It's marked with an Imperial override. The initial signal appears to be originating from *our* ship. Is this . . . something you intend?"

Kety's brows drew down in puzzlement. Then his gaze rose to the white bubble, glowing in the center of the room. He swore, one sharp, heartfelt sibilant. "No. Ghem-General Naru! We have to get this force-screen down *now*!"

Kety spared a venomous glare for Pel and Miles that promised infinite retribution later, then he and Naru fell to frantic consultation. Heavy doses of synergine from the guards' med-kit failed to return the techs to immediate consciousness, though they stirred and groaned in a promising fashion. Kety and Naru were left to do it themselves. Judging by the wicked light in Pel's eyes, as she and the haut Nadina clung together, they were going to be way too late. The pain of the shock-stick blows were fading to pins and needles, but Miles remained curled up on the floor, the better not to draw further such attentions to himself.

Kety and Naru were so absorbed in their task and their irate arguments over the swiftest way to proceed, only Miles noticed when a spot on the door began to glow. Despite his pain, he smiled. A beat later, the whole door burst inward in a spray of melted plastic and metal. Another beat, to wait out anyone's hair-trigger reflexes.

Ghem-Colonel Benin, impeccably turned out in his bloodred dress uniform and freshly applied face paint, stepped firmly across the threshold. He was unarmed, but the red-clad squad behind him carried an arsenal sufficient to destroy any impediment in their path up to the size of a pocket dreadnought. Kety and Naru froze in mid-lurch; Kety's liveried retainers suddenly seemed to think better of drawing weapons, opening their hands palm-outward and standing very still. Colonel Vorreedi, equally impeccable in his House blacks, if not quite so cool in expression, stepped in behind Benin. In the corridor beyond, Miles could just glimpse Ivan looming behind the armed men, and shifting anxiously from foot to foot.

"Good evening, haut Kety, ghem-General Naru." Benin bowed with exquisite courtesy. "By the personal order of Emperor Fletchir Giaja, it is my duty to arrest you both upon the serious charge of treason to the Empire. And," contemplating Naru especially, Benin's smile went razor-sharp, "complicity in the murder of the Imperial Servitor the Ba Lura."

CHAPTER FIFTEEN

From Miles's eye-level, the deck sprouted a forest of red boots, as Benin's squad clumped in to disarm and arrest Kety's retainers, and march them out with their hands atop their heads. Kety and Naru were taken along with them, sandwiched silently between some hard-eyed men who didn't look as though they were interested in listening to explanations.

At a growl from Kety, the procession paused in front of the entering Barrayarans. Miles heard Kety's voice, icy-cold: "Congratulations, Lord Vorpatril. I hope you may be fortunate enough to survive your victory."

"Huh?" said Ivan.

Oh, let him go. It would be too exhausting to try and sort out Kety about his confused inversion of Miles's little chain-of-command. Maybe Benin would have it straight. At a sharp word from their sergeant the security squad prodded their prisoners back into motion and clattered on down the corridor.

Four shiny black boots made their way through the mob and halted before Miles's nose. Speaking of explanations . . . Miles twisted his head and looked up the odd foreshortened perspective at Colonel Vorreedi and Ivan. The deck was cool beneath his stinging cheek, and he didn't really want to move, even supposing he could.

Ivan bent over him, giving an upside-down view up his nostrils, and said in a strained tone, "Are you all right?"

"Sh-sh-shock-stick. Nothing b-broken."

"Right," said Ivan, and hauled him to his feet by his collar. Miles hung a moment, shivering and twitching like a fish on a hook, till he found his unsteady balance. By necessity, he leaned on Ivan, who supported him with an un-commenting hand under his elbow.

Colonel Vorreedi looked him up and down. "I'll let the ambassador do the protesting about that." Vorreedi's distant expression suggested he thought privately that the fellow with the shock-stick had stopped too soon. "Vorob'yev is going to need all the ammunition he can get. You have created the most extraordinary public incident of his career, I suspect."

"Oh, Colonel," sighed Miles. "I predict there's going to b-be nothing p-public 'bout *this* incident. Wait 'n see."

Ghem-Colonel Benin, across the room, was bowing and scraping to the hauts Pel and Nadina, and supplying them with float-chairs, albeit lacking force-screens, extra robes, and ghem-lady attendants. Arresting them in the style to which they were accustomed?

Miles glanced up at Vorreedi. "Has Ivan, um, *explained* everything, sir?"

"I trust so," said Vorreedi, in a voice drenched with menace.

Ivan nodded vigorously, but then hedged, "Um . . . all I could. Under the circumstances."

Meaning, lack of privacy from Cetagandan eavesdroppers, Miles presumed. *All, Ivan? Is my cover still intact?*

"I admit," Vorreedi went on, "I am still . . . . assimilating it."

"What h-happened after I left the Star Crèche?" Miles asked Ivan.

"I woke up and you were *gone*. I think that was the worst moment of my life, knowing you'd gone haring off on some crazy self-appointed mission with no backup."

"Oh, but *you* were my backup, Ivan," Miles murmured, earning himself a glare. "And a good one too, as you have just demonstrated, yes?"

"Yeah, your favorite kind—unconscious on the floor where I couldn't inject any kind of sense into the proceedings. You took off to get yourself killed, or worse, and everybody would have blamed me. The last thing Aunt Cordelia said to me before we left was, 'And *try* to keep him out of trouble, Ivan.'"

Miles could hear Countess Vorkosigan's weary, exasperated cadences quite precisely in Ivan's parody.

"Anyway, as soon as I figured out what the hell was going on, I got away from the haut-ladies—"

"*How?*"

"God, Miles, they're just like my mother, only eight times over. Ugh! Anyway, the haut Rian insisted I go through ghem-Colonel Benin, which I was willing to do—*he* at least seemed like he had his head screwed on straight—"

Perhaps attracted by the sound of his name, Benin strolled over to listen in on this.

"—and God be praised he paid attention to me. Seemed to make more sense out of my gabble than I did at the time."

Benin nodded. "I was of course following the very unusual activities around the Star Crèche today—"

Around, not *in*. Quite.

"My own investigations had already led me to suspect something was going on involving one or more of the haut-governors, so I had orbital squads on alert."

"Squads, ha," said Ivan. "There's three Imperial battle cruisers surrounding this ship right now."

Benin smiled slightly, and shrugged.

"Ghem-General Chilian is a dupe, I believe," Miles put in. "Though you will p-probably wish to question him about the activities of his wife, the haut Vio."

"He has already been detained," Benin assured him.

Detained, not arrested, all right. Benin seemed exactly on track so far. But had he realized yet that all the governors had been involved? Or was Kety elected sole sacrifice? *A Cetagandan internal matter,* Miles reminded himself. It was not his job to straighten out the entire Cetagandan government, tempting as it would be to try. His duty was confined to extracting Barrayar from the morass. He smiled at the glowing white bubble still protecting the real Great Key. The hauts Nadina and Pel were consulting with some of Benin's men; it appeared that rather than attempting to get the force-screen down here they were making arrangements to transport it and its precious contents whole and inviolate back to the Star Crèche.

Vorreedi gave Miles a grim look. "One thing that Lord Vorpatril has not yet explained to my satisfaction, Lieutenant Vorkosigan, is why you concealed the initial incident involving an object of such obvious importance—"

"Kety was trying to frame Barrayar, sir. Until I could achieve independent corroborative evidence that—"

Vorreedi went on inexorably, *"From your own side."*

"Ah." Miles briefly considered a relapse of shock-stick symptoms, rendering him unable to talk. No, alas. His own motives were obscure even to him, in retrospect. What *had* he started out wanting, before the twisting events had made sheer survival his paramount concern? Oh, yes, promotion. That was it.

Not this time, boy-o. Antique but evocative phrases

like *damage control* and *spin doctoring* free-floated through his consciousness.

"In fact, sir, I did not at first recognize the Great Key for what it was. But once the haut Rian contacted me, events slid very rapidly from apparently trivial to extremely delicate. By the time I realized the full depth and complexity of the haut-governor's plot, it was too late."

"Too late for what?" asked Vorreedi bluntly.

What with the shock-stick residue and all, Miles did not need to feign a sick smile. But it seemed Vorreedi had drifted back to the conviction that Miles was not working as a covert ops agent for Simon Illyan after all. *That's what you want everybody to think, remember?* Miles glanced aside at ghem-Colonel Benin, listening in fascination.

"You would have taken the investigation away from me, you know you would have, sir. Everyone in the wormhole nexus thinks I'm a cripple who's been given a cushy nepotistic sinecure as a courier. That I might be competent for more is something Lieutenant Lord Vorkosigan would never, in the ordinary course of events, ever be given a chance to publicly prove."

To the world at large, true. But Illyan knew all about the pivotal role Miles had played in the Hegen Hub, and elsewhere, as did Miles's father Prime Minister Count Vorkosigan, and Emperor Gregor, and everyone else whose opinion really counted, back on Barrayar. Even Ivan knew about that extraordinary covert ops coup. In fact, it seemed the only people who didn't know were . . . the enemy he'd beaten. The Cetagandans.

So did you do all this only to shine in the haut Rian's beautiful eyes? Or did you have a wider audience in view?

Ghem-Colonel Benin slowly deciphered this outpouring. "You wanted to be a hero?"

"So badly you didn't even care for which *side*?" Vorreedi added in some dismay.

"I *have* done the Cetagandan Empire a good turn, it's true." Miles essayed a shaky bow in Benin's direction. "But it was Barrayar I was thinking of. Governor Kety had some nasty plans for Barrayar. Those, at least, I've derailed."

"Oh, yeah?" said Ivan. "Where would they, and you, be right now if we hadn't shown up?"

"Oh," Miles smiled to himself, "I'd already won. Kety just didn't know it yet. The only thing still in doubt was my personal survival," he conceded.

"Why don't you sign up for Cetagandan Imperial Security, then, coz," suggested Ivan in exasperation. "Maybe ghem-Colonel Benin would promote you."

Ivan, damn him, knew Miles all too well. "Unlikely," Miles said bitterly. "I'm too short."

Ghem-Colonel Benin's eyebrow twitched.

"Actually," Miles pointed out, "if I was free-lancing for anyone, it was for the Star Crèche, not for the Empire. I have not served the Cetagandan Empire, so much as the haut. Ask *them*." He nodded toward Pel and Nadina, getting ready to exit the room with their ghem-lady escorts fussing over their comfort.

"Hm." Ghem-Colonel Benin seemed to deflate slightly.

Magic words, apparently. A haut-consort's skirts made a stronger fortification behind which to hide than Miles would have thought possible, a few weeks ago.

The haut Nadina's bubble was hoisted into the air by some men with hand-tractors, and maneuvered out of the room. Benin glanced after it, turned again to Miles, and opened his hand in front of his chest in a sketch of a bow. "In any case, Lieutenant Lord Vorkosigan, my Celestial master the Emperor haut Fletchir Giaja requests you attend upon him in my company. Now."

Miles could decipher an Imperial command when he heard one. He sighed, and bowed in return, in proper honor of Benin's august order. "Certainly. Ah . . ." He glanced aside at Ivan and the suddenly agitated Vorreedi. He wasn't exactly sure he wanted witnesses for this audience. He wasn't exactly sure he wanted to be alone, either.

"Your . . . friends may accompany you," Benin conceded. "With the understanding that they may not speak unless invited to do so."

Which inviting would be done, if at all, solely by Benin's Celestial Master. Vorreedi nodded in partial satisfaction. Ivan began to practice looking blank with all his might.

They all herded out, surrounded and escorted—but not arrested, of course, that would violate diplomatic protocol—by Benin's Imperial guards. Miles found himself, still supported by Ivan, waiting to exit the doorway beside the haut Nadina.

"Such a nice young man," Nadina commented in a well-modulated undertone to Miles, nodding at Benin, whom they could glimpse out in the corridor directing his troopers. "So neatly turned-out, and he understands the proprieties. We'll have to see what we can do for him, don't you agree, Pel?"

"Oh, quite," Pel said, and floated on through.

After a lengthy walk through the great State ship, Miles cycled through the air lock into the Cetagandan security shuttle in the company of Benin himself, who had not let him out of his sight. Benin looked cool and alert as ever, but there was an underlying . . . well, *smugness* leaking through his zebra-striped facade. It must have given Benin a moment of supreme Cetagandan satisfaction, arresting his commanding officer for treason. The one-up high point of his career. Miles would have bet Betan dollars to sand Naru was the man who'd assigned the dapper and decorous

Benin to close the case on the Ba Lura's death in the first place, setting him up to fail.

Miles ventured, "By the way, if I didn't say it before, congratulations on cracking your very tricky murder case, General Benin."

Benin blinked. "Colonel Benin," he corrected.

"That's what you think." Miles floated forward, and helped himself to the most comfortable window seat he could find.

"I don't believe I've seen this audience chamber before," Colonel Vorreedi whispered to Miles, his gaze flicking around to take in their surroundings. "It's not one ever used for public or diplomatic ceremonies."

Unusually, they had come not to a pavilion, but to a closed, low-lying building in the northern quadrant of the Celestial Garden. The three Barrayarans had spent an hour in an antechamber, cooling their heels while their internal tension rose. They were attended by half a dozen polite, solicitous ghem-guards, who saw to their physical comforts while courteously denying every request for outside communication. Benin had gone off somewhere with the hauts Pel and Nadina. In view of their Cetagandan company, Miles had not so much reported to Vorreedi as exchanged a few guarded remarks.

The new room reminded Miles a bit of the Star Chamber, simple, undistracting, deliberately serene, sound-baffled and cool in shades of blue. Voices had a curious deadened quality that hinted that the entire chamber was enclosed in a cone-of-silence. Patterns on the floor betrayed a large concealed comconsole table and station-chairs that could be raised for conferences, but for now, the supplicants stood.

Another guest was waiting, and Miles raised his brows in surprise. Lord Yenaro stood next to a red-clad ghem-guard. Yenaro looked pale, with dark greenish circles under his eyes, as if he had not slept for about two days. His dark robes, the same clothes Miles had last seen him wearing at the bioestheties exhibition, were rumpled and bedraggled. Yenaro's eyes widened in turn at the sight of Miles and Ivan. He turned his head away and tried not to notice the Barrayarans. Miles waved cheerfully, dragging a reluctantly polite return nod from Yenaro, and starting a very pained crease between his eyebrows.

And here came something to keep Miles's mind off his own lingering shock-stick pains right now. Or rather, someone.

Ghem-Colonel Benin entered first, and dismissed the Barrayarans' guards. He was followed by the hauts Pel, Nadina, and Rian in their float-chairs, shields down, who silently arranged themselves on one side of the room. Nadina had tucked the cut ends of her hair out of sight among her garments, the same robes Pel had shared and which Nadina had not stopped to change. They had all obviously been closeted for the past hour in a debriefing at the highest level, for last of all a familiar figure strode in, shedding more guards in the corridor outside.

Close-up, Emperor the haut Fletchir Giaja seemed even taller and leaner than when Miles had seen him at a distance at the elegy-reading ceremonies. And older, despite his dark hair. He was for the moment casually dressed, by Imperial standards, in a mere half a dozen layers of fine white robes over the usual masculine-loose but blinding-white bodysuit, befitting his status as chief mourner.

Emperors *per se* did not unnerve Miles, though Yenaro swayed on his feet as though he were about to faint, and even Benin moved with the most rigid formality. Emperor Gregor had been raised along with Miles practically as his foster-brother; somewhere in the back of Miles's mind the term *emperor* was coupled with such identifiers as *somebody to play hide-and-seek with.* In this context those hidden assumptions could be a psychosocial land mine. *Eight planets, and older than my father*, Miles reminded himself, trying to inculcate a proper deference to the illusion of power Imperial panoply sought to create. One chair at the head of the room rose from the floor to receive what Gregor would have sardonically dubbed The Imperial Ass. Miles bit his lip.

It was apparently going to be a most intimate audience, for Giaja beckoned Benin over and spoke to him in a low voice, and Benin subsequently dismissed even Yenaro's guard. That left the three Barrayarans, the two planetary consorts and Rian, Benin, the Emperor, and Yenaro. Nine, a traditional quorum for judgment.

Still, it was better than facing Illyan. Maybe the haut Fletchir Giaja was not disposed to razor-edged sarcasms. But anyone related to all those haut-women had to be dangerously bright. Miles swallowed against a babbling burst of explanations. *Wait for your straight lines, boy.*

Rian looked pale and grave. No clue there, Rian always looked pale and grave. A last pang of desire banked itself to a tiny, furtive ember in Miles's heart, secret and encysted like a tumor. But he could still be afraid for her. His chest was cold with that dread.

"Lord Vorkosigan," Fletchir Giaja's exquisite baritone broke the waiting silence.

Miles suppressed a quick glance around—it wasn't like there were any other Lords Vorkosigan present, after all—stepped forward, and came to a precise parade rest. "Sir."

"I am still . . . unclear, just what *your* place was in these recent events. And how you came by it."

"My place was to have been a sacrificial animal, and it was chosen for me by Governor Kety, sir. But I didn't play the part he tried to assign to me."

The Emperor frowned at this less-than-straight-forward reply. "Explain yourself."

Miles glanced at Rian. "Everything?"

She gave an almost imperceptible nod.

Miles closed his eyes in a brief, diffuse prayer to whatever sportive gods were listening, opened them again, and launched once more into the true description of his first encounter with the Ba Lura in the personnel pod, Great Key and all. At least it had the advantage of simultaneously getting in Miles's overdue confession to Vorreedi in a venue where the embassy's chief security officer was totally blocked from making any comment or reply. Amazing man, Vorreedi, he betrayed no emotion beyond one muscle jumping in his jaw.

"As soon as I saw the Ba Lura in the funeral rotunda with its throat cut," Miles went on, "I realized my then-unknown opponent had thrown me into the logically impossible position of having to prove a negative. There was no way, once I had been tricked into laying hands on the false key, to prove that Barrayar had not effected a substitution, except by the positive testimony of the one eyewitness then lying dead on the floor. Or by positively locating the real Great Key. Which I set out to do. And if the Ba Lura's death was not a suicide, but rather a murder elaborately set up to pass as a suicide, it was clear someone high in the Celestial Garden's security was cooperating with the Ba's killers, which made approaching Cetagandan Security for help quite dangerous at that point. But then somebody assigned ghem-Colonel Benin to the case, presumably with heavy hints that it would be well for his career to bring in a quick verdict confirming suicide. Somebody who seriously underestimated Benin's abilities," *and ambition*, "as a security officer. *Was* it ghem-General Naru, by the way?"

Benin nodded, a faint gleam in his eye.

"For . . . whatever reason, Naru decided ghem-Colonel Benin would make a suitable additional goat. It was beginning to be a pattern in their operations, as you must realize if you've collected testimony from Lord Yenaro here—?" Miles raised an inquiring eyebrow at Benin. "I see you found Lord Yenaro before Kety's agents did. I think I'm glad, in all."

"You should be," Benin returned blandly. "We picked him up—along with his very interesting carpet—last night. His account was critical in shaping my response to your cousin's, um, sudden onslaught of information and demands."

"I see." Miles shifted his weight, his parade rest growing rather bent. He rubbed his face, because it didn't seem like the time or place to rub his crotch.

"Does your medical condition require you to sit?" Benin inquired solicitously.

"I'll manage." Miles took a breath. "I tried, in our first interview, to direct ghem-Colonel Benin's attentions to the subtleties of his situation. Fortunately, ghem-Colonel Benin is a subtle man, and his loyalty to you," *or to the truth*, "outweighed whatever implied threats to his career Naru presented."

Benin and Miles exchanged guarded, appreciative nods.

"Kety tried to deliver me into the hands of the Star Crèche, accused by means of Ba Lura's false confession to the Handmaiden," Miles continued carefully. "But once again his pawns ad libbed against his script. I entirely commend the haut Rian for her cool and collected response to this emergency. The fact that she kept her head and did not panic allowed me to continue to try to clear Barrayar of blame. She is, um, a credit to the haut, you know." Miles regarded her anxiously for a cue. *Where are we?* But she remained as glassily attentive as if that now-absent force-bubble had become one with her skin. "The haut Rian acted throughout for the good of the haut, never once for her own personal aggrandizement or safety." Though one might argue, apparently, over where *the good of the haut* actually lay. "Your late August Mother chose her Handmaiden well, I'd say."

"That is hardly for you to judge, Barrayaran," drawled the haut Fletchir Giaja, whether in amusement, or dangerously, Miles's ear could not quite tell.

"Excuse me, but I didn't exactly volunteer for this mission. I was suckered into it. My *judgments* have brought us all here, one way or another."

Giaja looked faintly surprised, even a little nonplussed, as if he'd never before had one of his gentle hints thrown back in his face. Benin stiffened, and Vorreedi winced. Ivan suppressed a grin, the merest twitch, and continued his Invisible Man routine.

The emperor took another tack. "And how did you come to be involved with Lord Yenaro?"

"Um . . . from my point of view, you mean?" Presumably Benin had already presented him with Yenaro's own testimony; a cross-check was in order, to be sure. In carefully neutral phrasing, Miles described his and Ivan's three encounters with Yenaro's increasingly lethal practical jokes, with a lot of emphasis on Miles's clever (once proved) theories about Lord X. Vorreedi's face drained to an interesting greenish cast upon Miles's description of the go-round with the carpet. Miles added cautiously, "In my opinion, certainly proved by the incident with the asterzine bomb, Lord Yenaro was as much an intended victim as Ivan and myself. There is no treason in the man." Miles cut off a slice of smile. "He hasn't the nerve for it."

Yenaro twitched, but did not gainsay any of it. Yeah, slather on the suggestion of Imperial mercy due all 'round, maybe some would slop over on the one who needed it most.

At Benin's direction, Yenaro, in a colorless voice,

confirmed Miles's account. Benin called in a guard and had the ghem-lord taken out, leaving eight in this chamber of Imperial inquisition. Would they work their way down to one?

Giaja sat silent for a time, then spoke, in formally modulated cadences. "That suffices for my appraisal of the concerns of the Empire. We must now turn to the concerns of haut. Haut Rian, you may keep your Barrayaran creature. Ghem-Colonel Benin. Will you kindly wait in the antechamber with Colonel Vorreedi and Lord Vorpatril until I call you."

"Sire." Benin saluted his way out, shepherding the reluctant Barrayarans.

Obscurely alarmed, Miles put in, "But don't you want Ivan too, Celestial Lord? He witnessed almost everything with me."

"No," stated Giaja flatly.

That settled that. Well . . . until Miles and Ivan were out of the Celestial Garden, indeed, out of the Empire and halfway home, they wouldn't be any safer anyway. Miles subsided with a faint sigh; then his eyes widened at the abrupt change in the room's atmosphere.

Feminine gazes, formerly suitably downcast, rose in direct stares. Without awaiting permission, the three float-chairs arranged themselves in a circle around Fletchir Giaja, who himself sat back with a face suddenly more expressive; dryer, edgier, angrier. The glassy reserve of the haut vanished in a new intensity. Miles swayed on his feet.

Pel glanced aside at the motion. "Give him a chair, Fletchir," she said. "Kety's guard shock-sticked him in the best regulation form, you know."

In her place, yes.

"As you wish, Pel." The Emperor touched a control in his chair-arm; a station chair near Miles's feet rose from the floor. He fell more than sat in it, grateful and dizzy, on the edge of their circle.

"I hope you all see now," said the haut Fletchir Giaja more forcefully, "the wisdom of our ancestors in arranging that the haut and the Empire shall have only one interface. Me. Only one veto. Mine. Issues of the haut-genome *must* remain as insulated as possible from the political sphere, lest they fall into the hands of politicians who do not understand the goal of haut. That includes most of our gentle ghem-lords, as ghem-General Naru has perhaps proved to you, Nadina." A flash of subtle, savage irony there—Miles suddenly doubted his initial perception of gender issues on Eta Ceta. What if Fletchir Giaja was haut first, and male second, and the consorts too were haut first, female second. . . . Who was in charge here, when Fletchir Giaja knew himself as a product of his mother's high art?

"Indeed," said Nadina, with a grimace.

Rian sighed wearily. "What can you expect from a half-breed like Naru? But it is the haut Ilsum Kety who has shaken my confidence in the Celestial Lady's vision. She often said that genetic engineering could only sow, that winnowing and reaping must still be done in an arena of competition. But Kety was not ghem, but *haut*. The fact that he could try what he tried . . . makes me think we have more work to do before the winnowing and reaping part."

"Lisbet always did have an addiction for the most primitive metaphors," Nadina recalled with faint distaste.

"She was right about the diversity issue, though," Pel said.

"In principle," Giaja conceded. "But this generation is not the time. The haut population can expand many times over into space presently held by servitor classes, without need for further territorial aggrandizement. The Empire is enjoying a necessary period of assimilation."

"The Constellations have been deliberately limiting

their numerical expansion of late decades, to conserve their favored economic positions," observed Nadina disapprovingly.

"You know, Fletchir," Pel put in, "an alternate solution might be to require more constellation crosses by Imperial edict. A kind of genetic self-taxation. Novel, but Nadina is right. The Constellations have grown more miserly and luxurious with each passing decade."

"I thought the whole point of genetic engineering was to avoid the random waste of natural evolution, and replace it with the efficiency of reason," Miles piped up. All three haut-women turned to stare at him in astonishment, as if a potted plant had suddenly offered a critique of its fertilization routine. "Or . . . so it seems to me," Miles trailed off in a much smaller voice.

Fletchir Giaga smiled, faint, shrewd, and wintry. Belatedly, Miles began to wonder why he was being kept here, by Giaja's suggestion/command. He had a most unpleasant sensation of being in a conversation with an undertow of cross-currents which were streaming in three different directions at once. *If Giaja wants to send a message, I wish he'd use a comconsole.* Miles's whole body was throbbing in time with the pulsing of his headache, several hours past midnight of one of the longer days of his short life.

"I will return to the Council of Consorts with your veto," said Rian slowly, "as I must. But Fletchir, you must address the diversity issue more directly. If this generation is not the time, it is still certainly not too soon to begin planning. And the diversification issue. The single-copy method of security is too horrifyingly risky, as recent events also prove."

"Hm," Fletchir Giaja half-conceded. His eye fell sharply upon Miles. "Nevertheless—Pel—whatever possessed you to spill the contents of the Great Key across the entire Eta Ceta system? As a joke, it does not amuse."

Pel bit her lip; her eyes, uncharacteristically, lowered.

Miles said sturdily, "No joke, sir. As far as we knew, we were both going to die within a few minutes. The haut Rian stated that the highest priority was the recovery of the Great Key. The receivers got the Key but no lock; without the gene banks themselves it was valueless gibberish from their point of view. One way or another, we assured you would be able to recover it, in pieces maybe, even after our deaths, regardless of what Kety did subsequently."

"The Barrayaran speaks the truth," affirmed Pel.

"The best strategies run on rails like that," Miles pointed out. "Live or die, you make your goal." He shut up, as Fletchir Giaja's stare hinted that perhaps outlander barbarians had better not make comments that could be construed as a slur on his late mother's abilities, even when those abilities had been pitted against him.

You can't get anywhere with these people, or whatever they are. I want to go home, Miles thought tiredly. "What will happen to ghem-General Naru, anyway?"

"He will be executed," said the Emperor. To his credit, the bald statement clearly brought him no joy. "Security *must* be . . . secured."

Miles couldn't argue with that. "And the haut Kety? Will he be executed too?"

"He will retire, immediately, to a supervised estate, due to ill health. If he objects, he will be offered suicide."

"Er . . . forcibly, if necessary?"

"Kety is young. He will choose life, and other days and chances."

"The other governors?"

Giaja frowned annoyance at the consorts. "A little pragmatic blindness in that direction will close matters. But they will not find new appointments easy to come by."

"And," Miles glanced at the ladies, "the haut Vio? What about her? The others only tried to commit a crime. She actually succeeded."

Rian nodded. Her voice went very flat. "She too will be offered a choice. To replace the servitor she destroyed—de-sexed, depilated, and demoted to ba, her metabolism altered, her body thickened . . . but returned to a life inside the Celestial Garden, as she desired with a passion beyond reason. Or she may be permitted a painless suicide."

"Which . . . will she choose?"

"Suicide, I hope," said Nadina sincerely.

A multiple standard seemed at work in all this justice. Now that the thrill of the chase was over, Miles felt a nauseated revulsion at the shambles of the kill. *For this I laid my life on the line?*

"What about . . . the haut Rian? And me?"

Fletchir Giaja's eyes were cool and distant, light-years gone. "That . . . is a problem upon which I shall now retire and meditate."

The Emperor called Benin back in to escort Miles away, after a short murmured conference. But away to where? Home to the embassy, or head-first down the nearest oubliette? Did the Celestial Garden have oubliettes?

Home, it appeared, for Benin returned Miles to the company of Vorreedi and Ivan, and took them to the Western Gate, where a car from the Barrayaran embassy already waited. They paused, and the ghem-Colonel addressed Vorreedi.

"We cannot control what goes into your official reports. But my Celestial Master . . ." Benin paused to select a suitably delicate term, "*expects* that none of what you have seen or heard will appear as social gossip."

"That, I think I can promise," said Vorreedi sincerely.

Benin nodded satisfaction. "May I have your words upon your names in the matter, please."

He'd been doing his homework upon Barrayaran customs, it seemed. The three Barrayarans dutifully gave their personal oaths, and Benin released them into the dank night air. It was about two hours till dawn, Miles guessed.

The embassy aircar was blessedly shadowed. Miles settled into a corner, wishing he had Ivan's talent for invisibility, but wishing most of all that they could cut tomorrow's ceremonies and start home immediately. No. He'd come this far, might as well see it through to the bitter end.

Vorreedi had gone beyond emotion to silence. He spoke to Miles only once, in chill tones.

"What *did* you think you were doing, Vorkosigan?"

"I stopped the Cetagandan Empire from breaking up into eight aggressively expanding units. I derailed plans for a war by some of them with Barrayar. I survived an assassination attempt, and helped catch three high-ranking traitors. Admittedly, they weren't *our* traitors, but still. Oh. And I solved a murder. That's enough for one trip, I hope."

Vorreedi struggled with himself for a moment, then bit out helplessly, "*Are* you a special agent, or not?"

On a need-to-know list . . . Vorreedi didn't. Not really, not at this point. Miles sighed inwardly. "Well, if not . . . I *succeeded* like one, didn't I?"

Ivan winced. Vorreedi sat back with no further comment, but radiating exasperation. Miles smiled grimly, in the dark.

CHAPTER SIXTEEN

Miles woke from a late, uneasy doze to find Ivan cautiously shaking him by the shoulder.

He closed his eyes again, blocking out the dimness of his suite and his cousin. "Go *'way*." He tried to pull the covers back up over his head.

Ivan renewed his efforts, more vigorously. "Now I know it was a mission," he commented. "You're having your usual post-mission sulks."

"I am not *sulking*. I am *tired*."

"You look terrific, you know. Great blotch on the side of your face that goon left with his shock-stick. Goes all the way up to your eye. It'll show from a hundred meters. You should get up and look in the mirror."

"I hate people who are cheerful in the morning. What time is it? Why are you up? Why are you *here*?" Miles lost his clutch on his bedclothes as Ivan dragged them ruthlessly from his grip.

"Ghem-Colonel Benin is on his way here to pick you up. In an Imperial land-cruiser half a block long. The Cetagandans want you at the cremation ceremony an hour early."

"What? *Why*? He can't be arresting me from here,

diplomatic immunity. Assassination? Execution? Isn't it a little late for that?"

"Ambassador Vorob'yev also wants to know. He sent me to rustle you up as swiftly as possible." Ivan propelled Miles toward his bathroom. "Start depilating, I've brought your uniform and boots from the embassy laundry. Anyway, if the Cetagandans really wanted to assassinate you, they'd hardly do it here. They'd slip something subtle under your skin that wouldn't go off for six months, and then would drop you mysteriously and untraceably in your tracks."

"Reassuring thought." Miles rubbed the back of his neck, surreptitiously feeling for lumps. "I bet the Star Crèche has some great terminal diseases. But I pray I didn't offend *them.*"

Miles suffered Ivan to play valet, on fast-forward, with editorials. But he forgave his cousin all sins, past, present, and future, in exchange for the coffee bulb Ivan also shoved into his hand. He swallowed and stared at his face in the mirror, above his unfastened black tunic. The shock-stick contusion across his left cheek was indeed turning a spectacular polychrome, crowned by a blue-black circle under his eye. The other two hits were not as bad, as his clothing had offered some protection. He still would have preferred to spend the day in bed. In his cabin on the outbound ImpSec jumpship, heading home as fast as the laws of physics would allow.

They arrived at the embassy's lobby to find not Benin but Mia Maz waiting in her formal black and white funeral clothing. She had been keeping Ambassador Vorob'yev company when they'd dragged in last night— this morning, rather—and could not have had much more sleep than Miles. But she looked remarkably fresh, even chipper. She smiled at Miles and Ivan. Ivan smiled back.

Miles squinted. "Vorob'yev not here?"

"He's coming down as soon as he's finished dress-ing," Maz assured him.

"You . . . coming with me?" Miles asked hopefully. "Or . . . no, I suppose you have to be with your own delegation. This being the big finish and all."

"I'll be accompanying Ambassador Vorob'yev." Maz's smile escaped into a chipmunk grin, dimples every-where. "Permanently. He asked me to marry him last night. I think it was a measure of his general distrac-tion. In the spirit of the insanity of the moment, I said yes."

If you can't hire help . . . Well, that would solve Vorob'yev's quest for female expertise on the embassy's staff. Not to mention accounting for all that bombard-ment of chocolates and invitations. "Congratulations," Miles managed. Though perhaps it ought to be *Con-gratulations* to Vorob'yev and *Good luck* to Maz.

"It still feels quite strange," Maz confided. "I mean, *Lady Vorob'yev*. How did your mother cope, Lord Vorkosigan?"

"You mean, being an egalitarian Betan and all? No problem. She says egalitarians adjust to aristocracies just fine, as long as they get to be the aristocrats."

"I hope to meet her someday."

"You'll get along famously," Miles predicted with confidence.

Vorob'yev appeared, still fastening his black tunic, at almost the same moment as ghem-Colonel Benin was escorted inside by the embassy guards. Correction. Ghem-General Benin. Miles smiled under his breath at the glitter of new rank insignia on Benin's blood-red dress uniform. *I called that one right, did I not?*

"May I ask what this is all about, ghem-General?" Vorob'yev didn't miss the new order.

Benin half-bowed. "My Celestial Master requests the attendance of Lord Vorkosigan at this hour. Ah . . . we *will* return him to you."

"Your word upon it? It would be a major embarrassment for the embassy were he to be mislaid . . . again." Vorob'yev managed to be stern at Benin while simultaneously capturing Maz's hand upon his arm and covertly stroking it.

"My word upon it, Ambassador," Benin promised. At Vorob'yev's reluctant nod of permission, he led Miles out. Miles glanced back over his shoulder, lonely for Ivan, or Maz, or somebody on his side.

The groundcar wasn't half a block long, but it was a very fine vehicle indeed, and not military issue. Cetagandan soldiers saluted Benin punctiliously, and settled him and his guest in the rear compartment. When they pulled away from the embassy, it felt something like riding in a house.

"May *I* ask what all this is about, ghem-General?" Miles inquired in turn.

Benin's expression was almost . . . crocodilian. "I am instructed that explanations must wait until you arrive at the Celestial Garden. It will take only a few minutes of your time, nothing more. I first thought that you would like it, but upon mature reflection, I think you will hate it. Either way, you deserve it."

"Take care your growing reputation for subtlety doesn't go to your head, ghem-General," Miles growled. Benin merely smiled.

It was definitely an Imperial audience chamber, if a small one, not a conference chamber like the room last night. There was only one seat, and Fletchir Giaja was in it already. The white robes he wore this morning were bulky and elaborate to the point of half-immobilizing him, and he had two ba servitors waiting to help him with them when he rose again. He had his icon-look plastered back on his face again, his expression so reserved it resembled porcelain. Three white bubbles floated silently beyond his left hand. Another ba servitor brought a small flat case to Benin, who stood upon the Emperor's right.

"You may approach my Celestial Master, Lord Vorkosigan," Benin informed him.

Miles stepped forward, deciding not to kneel. He and the haut Fletchir Giaja were almost eye to eye as he stood.

Benin handed the case to the emperor, who opened it. "Do you know what this is, Lord Vorkosigan?" Giaja asked.

Miles eyed the medallion of the Order of Merit on its colored ribbon, glittering on a bed of velvet. "Yes, sir. It is a lead weight, suitable for sinking small enemies. Are you going to sew me into a silk sack with it, before you throw me overboard?"

Giaja glanced up at Benin, who responded with a *Didn't I tell you so?* shrug.

"Bend your neck, Lord Vorkosigan," Giaja instructed him firmly. "Unaccustomed as you may be to doing so."

Was not Rian in one of those bubbles? Miles stared briefly at his mirror-polished boots, as Giaja slipped the ribbon over his head. He stepped back half a pace, tried and failed to keep his hand from touching the cool metal. He would not salute. "I . . . refuse this honor, sir."

"No, you don't," Giaja said in an observant tone, watching him. "I am given to understand by my keenest observers that you have a passion for recognition. It is a . . ."

Weakness that can be exploited—

"—an understandable quality that puts me much in mind of our own ghem."

Well, it was better than being compared to the hauts' other semi-siblings, the ba. Who were not the palace eunuchs they seemed, but rather some sort of incredibly valuable in-house science projects—the late Ba Lura might be better than half-sibling to Giaja himself, for all Miles knew. Sixty-eight percent shared chromo-somal material, say. Quite. Miles decided he would have more respect for, not to mention caution of, the silent slippered ba after this. They were all in on this haut-business together, the putative servitors and their puta-tive masters. No wonder the emperor had taken Lura's murder so seriously.

"As far as recognition goes, sir, this is hardly some-thing that I will be able to show around at home. More like, hide it in the bottom of the deepest drawer I own."

"Good," said Fletchir Giaja in a level tone. "As long as you lay all the matters associated with it along-side."

Ah. That was the heart of it. A bribe for his silence. "There is very little about the past two weeks that I shall take pleasure in remembering, sir."

"Remember what you will, as long as you do not recount it."

"Not publicly. But I have a duty to report."

"Your classified military reports do not trouble me."

"I . . ." He glanced aside at Rian's white bubble, hov-ering near. "Agree."

Giaja's pale eyelids swept down in an accepting blink. Miles felt very strange. Was it a bribe to accept a prize for doing exactly what he'd been going to do, or not do, anyway?

Come to think of it . . . would his own Barrayarans think he had struck some sort of bargain? The real reason he'd been detained for that unwitnessed chit-chat with the Emperor last night began to glimmer up at last in his sleep-deprived brain. *Surely they can't imagine Giaja could suborn me in twenty minutes of conversation. Could they?*

"You will accompany me," Giaja went on, "on my left hand. It's time to go." He rose, assisted by the ba, who gathered up his robes.

Miles eyed the hovering bubbles in silent desperation. His last chance . . . "May I speak with you one more time, haut Rian?" he addressed them generally, uncertain which was the one he sought.

Giaja glanced over his shoulder, and opened his long-fingered hand in a permissive gesture, though he himself continued on at the decorous pace enforced by his costume. Two bubbles waited, one followed, and Benin stood guard just outside the open door. Not exactly a private moment. That was all right. There was very little Miles wanted to say out loud at this point anyway.

Miles glanced back and forth uncertainly at the pale glowing spheres. One blinked out, and there Rian sat, much as he had first seen her, stiff white robes cloaked by the inkfall of shining hair. She still took his breath away.

She floated closer, and raised one fine hand to touch his left cheek. It was the first time they had touched. But if she asked, *Does it hurt?*, he swore he'd bite her.

Rian was not a fool. "I have taken much from you," she spoke quietly, "and given nothing."

"It's the haut way, is it not?" Miles said bitterly.

"It is the only way I know."

The prisoner's dilemma . . .

From her sleeve, she removed a dark and shining coil, rather like a bracelet. A tiny hank of silken hair, very long, wound around and around until it seemed to have no end. She thrust it at him. "Here. It was all I could think of."

That's because it is all you have that you truly own, milady. All else is a gift of your constellation, or the Star Crèche, or the haut, or your emperor. You live in the interstices of a communal world, rich beyond the dreams of avarice, owning . . . nothing. Not even your own chromosomes.

Miles took the coil from her. It was cool and smooth in his hand. "What does this signify? To you?"

"I . . . truly do not know," she confessed.

Honest to the end. Does the woman even know how to lie? "Then I shall keep it. Milady. For memory. Buried very deep."

"Yes. Please."

"How will you remember me?" He had absolutely nothing on him that he could give away right now, he realized, except for whatever lint the embassy laundry had left in the bottoms of his pockets. "Or will it please you to forget?"

Her blue eyes glinted like sun on a glacier. "There is no danger of that. You will see." She moved gently away from him. Her force-screen took form around her slowly, and she faded like perfume. The two bubbles floated after the emperor to seek their places.

The dell was similar in design to the one where the haut had held the elegiac poetry recitations, only larger, a wide sloping bowl open to the artificial sky of the dome. Haut-lady bubbles and haut- and ghem-lords in white filled its sides. The thousand or so galactic delegates in all their muted garbs crowded its circumference. In the center, ringed by a respectfully unpeopled band of grass and flowers, sat another round force dome, a dozen meters or more in diameter. Dimly through its misted surface Miles could see a jumble of objects piled high around a pallet, upon which lay the slight, white-clad figure of the haut Lisbet Degtiar. Miles squinted, trying to see if he could make out the polished maplewood box of the Barrayaran delegation's gift, but Dorca's sword was buried somewhere out of sight. It hardly mattered.

But he was going to have a ringside seat, a nearly Imperial view of it all. The final parade, down an alley cleared to the center of the bowl, was arranged in inverse order of clout; the eight planetary consorts and the Handmaiden in their nine white bubbles, seven—

count 'em folks, seven—ghem-governors, then the emperor himself and his honor guard. Benin blended into ghem-General Naru's former place without a ripple. Miles limped along in Giaja's train, intensely self-conscious. He must present an astonishing sight, slight, short, sinister, his face looking like he'd lost a space-port bar fight the night before. The Cetagandan Order of Merit made a fine show against his House blacks, quite impossible to miss.

Miles supposed Giaja was using him to send some kind of signal to his haut-governors, and not a terri-bly friendly one. Since Giaja clearly had no plans to let out the details of the past two weeks' events, Miles could only conclude it was one of those *catch it if you can* things, intended to unnerve by doubt as much as knowledge, a highly delicate species of terrorism.

Yeah. Let 'em wonder. Well, not *them*—he passed the Barrayaran delegation near the front of the galactic mob. Vorob'yev stared at him stunned. Maz looked sur-prised but pleased, pointing at Miles's throat and saying something to her fiancé. Vorreedi looked wildly sus-picious. Ivan looked . . . blank. *Thank you for your vote of confidence, coz.*

Miles himself stared for a moment when he spot-ted Lord Yenaro in the back row of ghem-lords. Yenaro was dressed in the purple and white garb of a Celes-tial Garden ghem-lord-in-waiting of the tenth rank, sixth degree, the lowest order. The lowest of the highest, Miles corrected himself. *Looks like he got that assis-tant perfumer's job after all.* And so the haut Fletchir Giaja brought another loose cannon under control. Smooth.

They all took their assigned places at the center of the bowl. A procession of young ghem-girls laid a final offering of flowers all around the central force-bubble. A chorus sang. Miles found himself attempting to cal-culate the price in labor alone of the entire month's

ceremonies if one set the time of everyone involved
at some sort of minimum wage. The sum was . . .
celestial. He became increasingly aware that he hadn't
had breakfast, or nearly enough coffee. *I will not pass
out. I will not scratch my nose, or my ass. I will not—*

A white bubble drifted up in front of the emperor.
A short, familiar ba paced alongside it, carrying a com-
partmented tray. Rian's voice spoke from the bubble,
ceremonial words; the ba laid the tray before Giaja's
feet. Miles, at Giaja's left hand, stared down into the
compartments and smiled sourly. The Great Key, the
Great Seal, and all the rest of Lisbet's regalia, were
returned to their source. The ba and the bubble
retreated. Miles waited in mild boredom for Giaja to
call forth his new empress from somewhere in the mob
of hovering haut-bubbles.

The emperor motioned Rian and her ba to approach
again. More formal phrases, so convoluted Miles took
a full belated minute to unravel their meaning. The ba
bowed and picked up the tray again on its mistress's
behalf. Miles's boredom evaporated in a frisson of
shock, muffled by intense bemusement. For once, he
wished he were shorter, or had Ivan's talent for invisibility, or could magically teleport himself somewhere,
anywhere, out of here. A stir of interest, even astonishment, ran through the haut and ghem audience.
Members of the Degtiar constellation looked quite
pleased. Members of other constellations . . . looked
on politely.

The haut Rian Degtiar took possession of the Star
Crèche again as a new Empress of Cetaganda, fourth
Imperial Mother to be chosen by Fletchir Giaja, but
now first in seniority by virtue of her genomic responsibility. Her first genetic duty would be to cook up her
own Imperial prince son. God. Was she happy, inside
that bubble?

Her new . . . not husband, mate, the emperor—

might never touch her. Or they might become lovers. Giaja might wish to emphasize his possession of her, after all. Though to be fair, Rian must have known this was coming before the ceremony, and she hadn't looked like she objected. Miles swallowed, feeling ill, and horribly tired. Low blood sugar, no doubt.

Good luck to you, milady. Good luck . . . good-bye.

And Giaja's control extended itself, softly as fog. . . .

The Emperor raised his hand in signal, and the waiting Imperial engineers solemnly went into motion at their power station. Inside the great central force-bubble, a dark orange glow began, turning red, then yellow, then blue-white. Objects inside tilted, fell, then roiled up again, their forms disintegrating into molecular plasma. The Imperial engineers and Imperial Security had doubtless had a tense and sweaty night, arranging the Empress Lisbet's pyre with the utmost care. If that bubble burst now, the heat-effects would resemble a small fusion bomb.

It really didn't take very long, perhaps ten minutes altogether. A circle opened in the gray-clouded dome overhead, revealing blue sky. The effect was extremely weird, like a view into another dimension. A much smaller hole opened in the top of the force-bubble. White fire shot skyward as the bubble vented itself. Miles assumed the airspace over the center of the capital had been cleared of all traffic, though the stream diffused into faint smoke quickly enough.

Then the dome closed again, the artificial clouds scurrying away on an artificial breeze, the light growing brighter and cheerier. The force-bubble faded into nothingness, leaving only an empty circle of undamaged grass. Not even ash.

A waiting ba servitor brought the Emperor a colorful robe. Giaja traded off his outer layer of whites, and donned the new garment. The Emperor raised a finger, and his honor guards again surrounded him, and the Imperial parade reversed itself out of the bowl. When the last major figure cleared the rim, the mourners gave a collective sigh, and the silence and rigid pattern broke in a murmur of voices and rustle of departing motion.

A large open float-car was waiting at the top of the dell to take the emperor . . . away, to wherever Cetagandan emperors went when the party was over. Would Giaja have a good stiff drink and kick off his shoes? Probably not. The attendant ba arranged the Imperial robes, and sat to the controls.

Miles found himself left standing beside the car as it rose. Giaja glanced over at him, and favored him with a microscopic nod. "Good-bye, Lord Vorkosigan."

Miles bowed low. "Until we meet again."

"Not soon, I trust," Giaja murmured dryly, and floated off, trailed by a gaggle of force-bubbles now turned all the colors of the rainbow. None paused as if to look back.

Ghem-General Benin, at Miles's elbow, almost cracked an expression. Laughing? "Come, Lord Vorkosigan. I will escort you back to your delegation. Having given your ambassador my personal word to return you, I must personally—*redeem* it, as you Barrayarans say. A curious turn of phrase. Do you use it in the sense of a soul in a religion, or an object in a lottery?"

"Mm . . . more in a medical sense. As in the temporary donation of a vital organ." Hearts and promises, all redeemed here today.

"Ah."

They came upon Ambassador Vorob'yev and his party, looking around as galactic delegates boarded float-cars for a ride to one last fantastical meal. The cars' white silk seats had all been replaced, in the last hour, by assorted colored silks, signifying the end of official mourning. At no discernible signal, one came promptly to Benin. No waiting in line for them.

"If we left now," Miles noted to Ivan, "we could be in orbit in an hour."

"But—the ghem-ladies might be at the buffet," Ivan protested. "Women like food, y'know."

Miles was starving. "In that case, definitely leave straightaway," he said firmly.

Benin, perhaps mindful of his Celestial Master's last broad hint, supported this with a bland, "That sounds like a good choice, Lord Vorkosigan."

Vorob'yev pursed his lips; Ivan's shoulders slumped slightly.

Vorreedi nodded at Miles's throat, a glint of puzzled suspicion in his eyes. "What was *that* all about . . . Lieutenant?"

Miles fingered his silken collar with the Cetagandan Imperial Order of Merit attached. "My reward. And my punishment. It seems the haut Fletchir Giaja has a low taste for high irony."

Maz, who had obviously not yet been brought up to speed on the subtext of the situation, protested his lack of enthusiasm. "But it's an extraordinary honor, Lord Vorkosigan! There are Cetagandan ghem-officers who would gladly die for it!"

Vorob'yev explained coolly, "But rumors of it will hardly make him popular at home, love. Particularly circulating, as they must, without any real explanation attached. Even more particularly in light of the fact that Lord Vorkosigan's military assignment is in Barrayaran Imperial Security. From the Barrayaran point of view, it looks . . . well, it looks *very* strange."

Miles sighed. His headache was coming on again. "I know. Maybe I can get Illyan to classify it secret."

"About three thousand people just saw it!" Ivan said.

Miles stirred. "Well, that's your fault."

"Mine!"

"Yeah. If you'd brought me two or three coffee bulbs this morning, instead of only one, my brain might have been on-line, and I could've ducked faster and avoided this. Bloody slow reflexes. The implications are still dawning on me." For example: if he had *not* bowed his head to Giaja's silk collar in polite compliance, how dramatically would the chances have risen of his and Ivan's jumpship meeting some unfortunate accident while exiting the Cetagandan Empire?

Vorreedi's brows twitched. "Yes . . ." he said. "What *did* you and the Cetagandans talk about last night, after Lord Vorpatril and I were excluded?"

"Nothing. They never asked me anything more." Miles grinned blackly. "That's the beauty of it, of course. Let's see *you* prove a negative, Colonel. Just try. I want to watch."

After a long pause, Vorreedi slowly nodded. "I see."

"Thank you for that, sir," breathed Miles.

Benin escorted them all to the South Gate, and saw them out for the last time.

The planet of Eta Ceta was fading in the distance, though not fast enough to suit Miles. He switched off the monitor in his bunk aboard the ImpSec courier vessel, and lay back to nibble a bit more from his plain dry ration bar, and hope for sleep. He wore loose and wrinkled black fatigues, and no boots at all. He wriggled his toes in their unaccustomed freedom. If he played it right, he might be able to finesse his way through the entire two-week trip home barefoot. The Cetagandan Order of Merit, hung above his head, swayed slightly on its colored ribbon, gleaming in the soft light. He scowled meditatively at it.

A familiar double-knock sounded on his cabin door; for a moment he longed to feign sleep. Instead he sighed, and pushed himself up on his elbow. "Enter, Ivan."

Ivan had skinned out of his dress uniform and into fatigues as fast as possible also. And friction-slippers, hah. He had a sheaf of colored papers in his hand.

"Just thought I'd share these with you," Ivan said. "Vorreedi's clerk handed 'em to me just as we were leaving the embassy. Everything we're going to be missing tonight, and for the next week." He switched on Miles's disposal chute, in the wall. A yellow paper. "Lady Benello." He popped it in; it whooshed into oblivion. A green one. "Lady Arvin." Whoosh. An enticing turquoise one; Miles could smell the perfume from his bunk. "The inestimable Veda." Whoosh—

"I get the point, Ivan," Miles growled.

"And the food," Ivan sighed. "—*why* are you eating that disgusting rat bar? Even courier ship stores can do better than that!"

"I wanted something plain."

"Indigestion, eh? Your stomach acting up again? No blood leakage, I hope."

"Only in my brain. Look, why are you here?"

"I just wanted to share my virtuous divesting of my life of decadent Cetagandan luxury," Ivan said primly. "Sort of like shaving my head and becoming a monk. For the next two weeks, anyway." His eye fell on the Order of Merit, turning slowly on its ribbon. "Want me to put that down the disposer too? Here, I'll get rid of it for you—" He made to grab it.

Miles came up out of his bunk in a posture of defense like a wolverine out of its burrow. "Will you get out of here!"

"Ha! I *thought* that little bauble meant more to you than you were letting on to Vorreedi and Vorob'yev," Ivan crowed.

Miles stuffed the medal down out of sight, and out of reach, under his bedding. "I frigging earned it. Speaking of blood." Ivan grinned, and stopped circling

for a swoop on Miles's possessions, and settled down
into the tiny cabin's station chair.

"I've thought about it, you know," Miles went on.
"What it's going to be like, ten or fifteen years from
now, if I ever get out of covert ops and into a real line
command. I'll have had more practical experience than
any other Barrayaran soldier of my generation, and it's
all going to be totally invisible to my brother officers.
Classified. They'll all think I spent the last decade
riding in jumpships and eating candy. How am I going
to maintain authority over a bunch of overgrown
backcountry goons—like you? They'll eat me alive."

"Well," Ivan's eye glinted, "they'll try, to be sure. I
hope I'm around to watch."

Secretly, Miles hoped so too, but he would rather
have had his fingernails removed with pliers, in the old-
fashioned ImpSec interrogation style of a couple of generations ago, than say so out loud.

Ivan heaved a large sigh. "But I'm still going to miss
the ghem-ladies. And the food."

"There's ladies and food at home, Ivan."

"True." Ivan brightened slightly.

"S'funny." Miles lay back on his bunk, shoving his
pillow behind his shoulders to prop himself half-up. "If
Fletchir Giaja's late Celestial Father had sent the haut-
women to conquer Barrayar, instead of the ghem-lords,
I think Cetaganda would own the planet right now."

"The ghem-lords were nothing if not crude," Ivan
allowed. "But we were cruder." He stared at the ceiling.
"How many more generations, d'you think, before we
can no longer consider the haut-lords human?"

"I think the operative question is, how many generations till the haut-lords no longer regard *us* as
human." *Well, I'm used to that even at home. Sort of
a preview of things to come.* "I think . . . Cetaganda
will remain potentially dangerous to its neighbors as
long as the haut are in transition to . . . wherever

they're going. Empress Lisbet and her predecessors," *and her heiresses,* "are running this two-track evolutionary race—the haut fully controlled, the ghem used as a source of genetic wild cards and pool of variations. Like a seed company keeping strains of wild plants even when they only sell a monoculture, to permit development in the face of the unexpected. The greatest danger to everybody else would be for the haut to lose control of the ghem. When the ghem are allowed to run the show—well, Barrayar knows what it's like when half a million practicing social Darwinists with guns are let loose on one's home planet."

Ivan grimaced. "Really. As your esteemed late grandfather used to tell us, in gory detail."

"But if . . . the ghem fail to be consistently militarily successful in the next generation or so—our generation—if their little expansionist adventures continue to be embarrassing and costly, like the Vervain invasion debacle, maybe the haut will turn to other areas of development than the military in their quest for superiority. Maybe even peaceful ones. Perhaps ones we can scarcely imagine."

"Good luck," snorted Ivan.

"Luck is something you make for yourself, if you want it." *And I want it more, oh yes.* Keeping one eye out for sudden moves from his cousin, Miles re-hung his medallion.

"You going to wear that? I dare you."

"No. Not unless I have a need to be really obnoxious sometime."

"But you're going to keep it."

"Oh, yes."

Ivan stared off into space, or rather, at the cabin wall, and into space beyond by implication. "The wormhole nexus is a big place, and constantly getting bigger. Even the haut would have trouble filling it all, I think."

"I hope so. Monocultures are dull and vulnerable. Lisbet knew that."

Ivan chuckled. "Aren't you a little short to be thinking of re-designing the universe?"

"Ivan." Miles let his voice grow unexpectedly chill. "Why should the haut Fletchir Giaja decide he needed to be polite to me? Do you *really* think this is just for my father's sake?" He ticked the medallion and set it spinning, and locked eyes with his cousin. "It's not a trivial trinket. Think again about all the things this means. Bribery, sabotage, and real respect, all in one strange packet . . . we're not done with each other yet, Giaja and I."

Ivan dropped his gaze first. "You're a frigging crazy man, you know that?" After an uncomfortable minute of silence, he hoisted himself from Miles's station-chair, and wandered away, muttering about finding some real food on this boat.

Miles settled back with slitted eyes, and watched the shining circle spin like planets.

MILES VORKOSIGAN/NAISMITH:
HIS UNIVERSE AND TIMES

Chronology	Events	Chronicle
Approx. 200 years before Miles's birth	Quaddies are created by genetic engineering.	*Falling Free*
During Beta-Barrayaran War	Cordelia Naismith meets Lord Aral Vorkosigan while on opposite sides of a war. Despite difficulties, they fall in love and are married.	*Shards of Honor*
The Vordarian Pretendership	While Cordelia is pregnant, an attempt to assassinate Aral by poison gas fails, but Cordelia is affected; Miles Vorkosigan is born with bones that will always be brittle and other medical problems. His growth will be stunted.	*Barrayar*
Miles is 17	Miles fails to pass physical test to get into the Service Academy. On a trip, necessities force him to improvise the Free Dendarii Mercenaries into existence; he has unintended but unavoidable adventures for four months. Leaves the Dendarii in Ky Tung's competent hands and takes Elli Quinn to Beta for rebuilding of her damaged face; returns to Barrayar to thwart plot against his	*The Warrior's Apprentice*

Chronology	Events	Chronicle
	father. Emperor pulls strings to get Miles into the Academy.	
Miles is 20	Ensign Miles graduates and immediately has to take on one of the duties of the Barrayaran nobility and act as detective and judge in a murder case. Shortly afterward, his first military assignment ends with his arrest. Miles has to rejoin the Dendarii to rescue the young Barrayaran emperor. Emperor accepts Dendarii as his personal secret service force.	"The Mountains of Mourning" in *Borders of Infinity* *The Vor Game*
Miles is 22	Miles and his cousin Ivan attend a Cetagandan state funeral and are caught up in Cetagandan internal politics.	*Cetaganda*
	Miles sends Commander Elli Quinn, who's been given a new face on Beta, on a solo mission to Kline Station.	*Ethan of Athos*
Miles is 23	Now a Barrayaran Lieutenant, Miles goes with the Dendarii to smuggle a scientist out of Jackson's Whole. Miles's fragile leg bones have been replaced by synthetics.	"Labyrinth" in *Borders of Infinity*

Chronology	Events	Chronicle
Miles is 24	Miles plots from within a Cetagandan prison camp on Dagoola IV to free the prisoners. The Dendarii fleet is pursued by the Cetagandans and finally reaches Earth for repairs. Miles has to juggle both his identities at once, raise money for repairs, and defeat a plot to replace him with a double. Ky Tung stays on Earth. Commander Elli Quinn is now Miles's right-hand officer. Miles and the Dendarii depart for Sector IV on a rescue mission.	"The Borders of Infinity" in *Borders of Infinity* *Brothers in Arms*
Miles is 25	Hospitalized after previous mission, Miles's broken arms are replaced by synthetic bones. With Simon Illyan, Miles undoes yet another plot against his father while flat on his back.	*Borders of Infinity*
Miles is 28	Miles meets his clone brother Mark again, this time on Jackson's Whole.	*Mirror Dance*
Miles is 29		*Memory* (forthcoming)